PRAISE FOR JENNIFER PROBST

"For a sexy, fun-filled, warmhearted read, look no further than Jennifer Probst!"

—Jill Shalvis, *New York Times* bestselling author

"Jennifer Probst is an absolute auto-buy author for me."

—J. Kenner, *New York Times* bestselling author

"Jennifer Probst knows how to bring the swoons and the sexy."

—Amy E. Reichert, author of *The Coincidence of Coconut Cake*

"As always, Jennifer Probst never fails to deliver romance that sizzles and has a way of tugging those emotional heartstrings."

—*Four Chicks Flipping Pages*

"Jennifer Probst's books remind me of delicious chocolate cake. Bursting with flavor, decadently rich . . . very satisfying."

—*Love Affair with an e-Reader*

the
start
of
something
good

OTHER BOOKS BY JENNIFER PROBST

Nonfiction

*Write Naked: A Bestseller's Secrets to Writing Romance &
Navigating the Path to Success*

The Billionaire Builders Series

Everywhere and Every Way
Any Time, Any Place
Somehow, Some Way
All or Nothing at All

The Searching for . . . Series

Searching for Someday
Searching for Perfect
Searching for Beautiful
Searching for Always
Searching for You
Searching for Mine
Searching for Disaster

The Billionaire Marriage Series

The Marriage Bargain
The Marriage Trap
The Marriage Mistake
The Marriage Merger
The Book of Spells

The Steele Brothers Series

Catch Me
Play Me
Dare Me
Beg Me
Reveal Me

Sex on the Beach Series

Beyond Me
Chasing Me

The Hot in the Hamptons Series

Summer Sins

Stand-Alone Novels

Dante's Fire
Executive Seduction
All the Way
The Holiday Hoax
The Grinch of Starlight Bend

the
start
of
something
good

JENNIFER
PROBST

Montlake
Romance

Published by Montlake Romance, Seattle

www.apub.com

Amazon, the Amazon logo, and Montlake Romance are trademarks of Amazon.com, Inc., or its affiliates.

ISBN-13: 9781503901858
ISBN-10: 1503901858

Cover design by Shasti O'Leary Soudant

Printed in the United States of America

For you, Dad.
I loved how you told everyone you met that your
daughter was a famous writer and tried to get them
to buy my books. I loved how you taught me to bet
on horses like a pro and play a mean game of poker,
and how you challenged me at every turn during our
Scrabble tournaments. The world is just not
the same without you in it.
I miss you every day.

Chapter One

"But why had he always felt so strongly the magnetic pull of home, why had he thought so much about it and remembered it with such blazing accuracy, if it did not matter, and if this little town, and the immortal hills around it, was not the only home he had on earth? He did not know. All that he knew was that the years flow by like water, and that one day men come home again."

—Thomas Wolfe, *You Can't Go Home Again*

His feet knew the road ahead like a long-lost memory, but this time, Ethan Bishop had to pause halfway to rest. The nagging ache throbbed behind his knee like a deeply ingrained splinter, slowly trying to drive him mad, but he packaged the pain into a box and shoved it down deep, along with the hot flare of shame.

He was the lucky one.

The mantra had been repeated regularly for the last sixty-two days yet still felt like words recited in a play to someone he was pretending to be. No matter. Eventually, he may believe them.

He shifted his weight and stared at the sprawling blue-and-white farmhouse hidden behind the storybook white fence and framed by the majestic Shawangunk Mountains. His heart stopped, stuttered, then began beating again. Gardiner may be a small town in upstate New

York, but its beauty and quirky charm made it a favorite for visitors. He'd forgotten how long he'd been away from home. A rush of memories washed over him like a tide of warm water, reminding him of that laughing, free-spirited young kid tearing his way around the farm with big dreams that his small upstate town could never hold. After years of hard work and chasing those elusive ambitions, he thought he'd finally succeeded.

He'd been so wrong.

Gritting his teeth, he resumed walking, taking in the extensive updates with approval. His sisters had invested a large chunk of money to not only renovate the actual house but also freshen up the visual curb appeal of the bed-and-breakfast. The new ROBIN'S NEST B & B sign welcomed visitors from the gate in blinding white and robin's-egg blue, matching the shutters and bold-blue door. As he approached the wraparound porch, he noticed the creative touches Ophelia must have spearheaded—the clay pots of colored mums, the tea cart filled with pitchers of sweet tea and sugar cookies, the wind chimes tinkling in the soft summer breeze. The rockers and footstools were charmingly mismatched in various wicker, and large coffee-table books with glossy pictures were casually thrown about.

Yes, they'd finally claimed their heritage just as he'd run from it. Mom would have been proud.

The familiar bark rose to his ears, and he turned in astonishment, dropping his bag. The black Lab tore across the lawn—ears pinned back, mouth turned up in a joyous doggy grin—and barreled into his arms.

"Wheezy!" The dog stuck a wet nose in his crotch, and a laugh exploded in the air. It took him a while to realize it had come from him, the sound rusty from disuse. Ethan ran his fingers over now whitish fur that wriggled in delight, the dog's belly rounded with the extra weight of middle age. "I missed you, boy. God, how old are you now, buddy? Fourteen? Fifteen?"

"Sixteen. And in better shape than all of us. Welcome home, Ethan."

He craned his neck around. Ophelia stood on the porch, her lips curved in a soft smile. She was dressed in an ankle-length floral skirt, sandals, and a yellow, gauzy tank top, showing off her willowy form. Her strawberry-blonde hair was pulled back from her face in a ponytail. She'd always reminded him of a fairy, with her pointed chin, too-large eyes, and petite build. Of course, his sister had an inner strength and thirst for life like no other he'd ever known, hidden beneath a Tinker Bell surface. Once, he'd imagined she'd be bigger than the singer Adele, with her giant voice that mesmerized anyone in her vicinity, but it seemed she'd decided to settle for running the family bed-and-breakfast.

"Tink. You look good."

She groaned, taking the few steps down to close the distance. "Don't call me that! It was torturous enough when we were kids—I refuse to accept it as an adult."

He grabbed her, enjoying her laugh as he spun her around and Wheezy barked. "I can still make you fly," he said, pressing a kiss to the top of her head. "And older brothers have a responsibility to annoy their younger siblings."

"Fine. Have I told you I put your room next to Mr. and Mrs. Alders? They're in their seventies and celebrating their anniversary." Her blue eyes danced. "Very loudly. Every night."

He shuddered. "You fight dirty, Tink. No way am I staying in a house full of strangers. I told you I'm setting up in the bungalow."

"I was hoping I'd change your mind," she said lightly. "The bungalow doesn't have a full working kitchen. The place is run-down and needs a bunch of updates. No one's been in there for years."

"Doesn't bother me as long as there's a bed or a couch."

"It's isolated. Plus, it's a long walk to the main house."

He narrowed his gaze, getting closer to the truth. She shifted her weight and fussed with her skirt. "You worried about something else?"

At least she didn't lie to him. "I'm worried about leaving you alone."

The words fell between them and lay there like broken glass. His gut clenched with familiar shame, but he ignored it, making sure to keep his voice firm. "I came back so I could be alone for a bit. Need to get my shit together. Can't think of a better job than fixing up the bungalow and spending some time helping you out."

She seemed to mull over his words to figure out if he was lying. Then, she nodded. "Okay. Does it hurt?"

"Not much. Just need to continue some PT."

"Counseling?"

The corner of his lip lifted. Ever since the incident, not many people asked direct questions that may embarrass them or him. His muscles relaxed a bit, glad his sister wouldn't treat him any differently. "Did my mandated time. If I feel like I need more, I'll find someone."

"Good enough for me. But be careful about telling Harper you have free time. She'll have you working with the horses nonstop so she can rescue more."

"Still saving the world one animal at a time?"

"She's the Angelina Jolie of rescues and pissing off more people than I can count."

"Where is she?"

"At the auction. She'll be home for dinner. In the meantime, why don't you get settled in, and I can show you around. We've done a lot of improvements." She eyed the duffel bag at his feet. "Is that all you have?"

"I learned to travel light. Do we have to eat with your guests?"

She grinned. "Not tonight. But we have quite a crew for the week. I think you're going to like them."

"I'm not up for much social interaction, Tink. Especially with strangers. Better to keep my distance."

Her face softened. "Understood. But now's a good time to begin easing your way back in. You've always charmed everyone in your path."

Her eyes sparkled with mischief. "And, as Mom used to say, 'a happy guest is a returning guest.' Part of your job here is to make the guests happy. Better start getting used to it."

He groaned, but she only shot him a wink and disappeared back into the house. Yeah, his sister never candy-coated anything.

Ethan stood in the hot sun, thinking about the life he'd run far away from for something bigger and better. He'd finally come full circle—back in the place he started, trying to heal all the broken pieces life had thrown at him. So fucking ironic.

As if Wheezy knew exactly what he was thinking, the dog regarded him with serious, soulful eyes.

Then he lifted his leg and peed on Ethan's bag.

Welcome home.

Chapter Two

Mia Thrush grabbed her skinny vanilla latte from the Starbucks counter and squeezed herself into a corner table. She spoke into the wireless earpiece. "Bernard, I told you I don't bluff. If you don't endorse Jonathan Lake as mayor, good luck getting reelected. The public will never believe you want to lock up the bad guys, and my PR team will personally make that fact known."

She didn't interrupt the blistering array of profanity on the other end. Why did judges have the worst tempers of all?

Mia pried the plastic lid off her organic Greek yogurt with five blueberries. She popped one perfect spoonful into her mouth, then chewed slowly to savor the firm tartness of the fruit. She wasn't allowed to eat again for another four hours, so she had to relish breakfast. She'd shed those last pesky ten pounds with sheer grit and torturous intent, even if it made her grumpy.

The judge paused to take a breath, and she cut in. "Lake is already the front-runner in the polls. Do you want to get on board the winning train or be left at the station? He's got one of the best records in the DA's office. This isn't personal. Be smart."

The popular family circuit judge had a ridiculous prior beef with her client, and it was affecting his final endorsement, which was crucial in tying up a segment of voters. The occasional petty social media rants made her nervous. Mia intended to shut the negative publicity down before it escalated. She sweetened the deal, sensing victory close.

"I know Jonathan will be grateful for your support. Very grateful."

Politics were all about veiled promises with no proof, but Mia also knew Jonathan was different from the others. The man didn't hold grudges and would be truly grateful to the judge. Another reason Mia worked day and night to make sure he won this election.

His reluctant surrender rang in her ears. On impulse, she spooned up two blueberries at once in pure celebration. "A wise choice, sir. Jonathan will be proud to announce your support and how well the both of you will work together in the future. Thank you."

She tapped the button and ended the call. Adrenaline bubbled in her veins like a frothy glass of champagne. God, she loved her job. Besides being a constant challenge, it never bored her, and she got to fight for the good guys. And since Jonathan had signed on to her publicity firm, her client list and profits had begun to skyrocket.

She bit into her last blueberry, already mourning the end of her meager meal. Maybe she could throw an extra olive into her salad later. A small one. She had to look up the calories. That Gucci dress she had her eye on was completely unforgiving.

Holding back a sigh, she threw out her empty yogurt container, grabbed her coffee, and strode back out into the streets. The June morning was muggy, and the stale Manhattan air clung to her skin and clogged her lungs. Her nude Prada heels clicked steadily over the pavement while she pushed her way through the crowds milling around busy street corners crammed with food trucks, her mind furiously working on the next step of her plan.

She needed to focus on building more social-friendly media posts. Lake's work as district attorney was heavy on reducing crime, but he lacked the well-rounded family dynamics of his competitor. Because he was a widower, the public was more sympathetic, but eventually they'd want to see his softer side, especially with his daughter. At least summer was close. Chloe would be home for two months from college, and Mia could plan some family time to remind the public Jonathan Lake believed in core values. Nothing was better than the city watching his teen daughter stand by his side. Mia was already planning a bunch of events that piggybacked on his stellar record of convictions. At this point in the campaign, barring a sex scandal, she was poised to get Lake elected.

Her private phone beeped in her ear. She hit the button without pause. Only four people had her secure line: her assistant, her parents, and her personal trainer. The latter had bullied her into giving up the number after she'd missed an appointment, which he'd made her pay for dearly. Puking between sets had not been her idea of fun. But damned if she'd ever missed an appointment again.

She prayed it was anyone other than her mother. "Yes?"

"We have a problem."

Her assistant's voice held the musical lilt of a southern accent tempered with a hard-nosed New York attitude. Mia tamped down a frustrated growl. She wanted one perfect day. Just one, where there were no scandals, or lit embers to extinguish, and everyone was ecstatically happy. Of course, Gabby would immediately tell her that would put both of them out of a job. "I already took care of the judge."

"Good. Now we have another issue to deal with."

Her heart thundered. "Please don't tell me it has to do with a prostitute. Oh, please. Please, please—"

"It's not a prostitute."

"Then we can handle it."

"It's Lake's daughter. I can't tell you over the phone. How close are you to the office?"

"Give me ten."

Mia made it in seven using her famous technique of bob and weave. Kind of like driving recklessly without the car or highway. Navigating a packed city street took skill, precision, and no small amount of courage, especially in four-inch heels. She pushed through the frosted glass doors with the bold-red sign, STRATEGY SOLUTIONS PR, and headed straight to Gabby's desk. Waving a greeting to her receptionist and part-time file clerk, she flicked a gaze quickly over the office, making sure everything looked perfect. Moving her office from an old warehouse stinking of stale cigarettes to a fancy street off Broadway enforced she was in a whole new league. She was the first to realize appearances were everything, and her office screamed creativity with the sense of security new clients needed.

Decorated in bold red and steel gray, the furniture was sleek and modern but gentled with gorgeous silver-beaded pillows, brightly colored landscape paintings on the walls, and a knockout crystal chandelier that brought all the elements together. The large green ferns banking the window added necessary warmth. Mia knew exactly what she wanted her company to reflect, and she'd finally reached her goal. The hefty rent was completely worth it.

Her team was small so she could always be in control. Most clients enjoyed the personal touch rather than the big pricey firms where only large conglomerates got the needed attention.

As usual, Gabby was perched on her chair, barely visible behind the piles of papers, folders, and boxes. Her short, bright-red curls were the only beacon to help Mia find her in the chaos that made up Gabby's desk. Mia had learned long ago, though, not to mess with her mojo. Once, the cleaning lady had tried to organize her pens and sticky notes, and Gabby spent the whole day moaning about her inability to focus.

Mia had solved it by dumping out the pens and scattering the notes all over so her assistant could get back to work.

Mia dropped into the opposite chair, leaning forward to rest her elbows on her knees. "Okay, tell me everything."

"Lake's campaign manager called. Seems Chloe got in trouble up at school. She vandalized her professor's car."

"What? Why would she do something like that? Was she drunk?"

"This was the same professor who gave her academic probation for cheating on his exam."

Irritation scratched at her nerve endings. So many kids couldn't even afford school. She hated when opportunities were squandered in the drive for either attention or rebellion. Of course, she'd never met Lake's daughter and didn't like to judge. She swallowed back her angry retort, already searching for ways to fix it. "When did this happen?"

"A few weeks ago."

Her eyes widened. "You're kidding me. Wait, why didn't I know about this?"

"Lake was sure he could make it go away without involving you. After all, he's the DA and running for mayor. He figured fixing the car and a healthy donation to the school would solve the issue."

She hated the resentment that curled in her belly. She'd agreed to run his PR because she genuinely believed in Lake's ideals and felt he had a good heart, with a passion to serve the city. But she disapproved of trying to buy his daughter out of trouble. Still, he wasn't the usual greedy politician. She'd conducted a ton of research before deciding to take him on as a client, and he'd never once rang her bullshit meter. Her father always told her she had the ability to spot a lie immediately, and it would be a gift that served her well.

And it had. Her gift guided her to accept only clients whose ideals and nature were similar to her own.

"Okay, so I'm guessing the school didn't agree with Lake's reparation plan?"

Gabby sighed. "It backfired. The professor was so outraged, he pressed charges, and Chloe had to go to court."

"You're telling me Lake wasn't able to get in contact with the local court and arrange something?"

"He assumed it wouldn't be a problem. But this judge didn't care who Chloe's father was or what strings could be pulled. Guess he planned to teach Chloe a lesson, and no one was going to stop him."

Mia groaned. "Why am I terrified to hear how this story ends?"

"They assigned her to community service for the summer."

She sprang from the chair and began pacing, trying to fit the pieces together. "Okay. We can work with this. She wasn't expelled, which is huge, and we can arrange for her to fulfill the hours at the DA's office or any of the not-for-profit organizations we deal with. I need to contact Bob to see if we can keep the details private and off the radar from the press."

"I'm not done. The sentencing already occurred. She's required to do her service at a local horse-rescue farm in the town. I guess it's also a popular bed-and-breakfast for tourists."

"She has to stay there all summer?"

"Yep."

"Why on earth would they pick a horse farm for her service?"

Gabby shrugged. "Guess the place needs volunteers."

"Okay. We can handle this. I'll take the angle that Chloe wants to stay at school this summer and keep her off the radar. I just need Bob to help bury the sentencing deep enough that no one gets to it."

Gabby regarded her with a sympathetic expression. "Lake has a different viewpoint on this. He's afraid Chloe will get in more trouble without someone to watch out for her this summer."

"He has a point. Who is he sending out to stay with her?"

That's when she noticed Gabby's expression hadn't changed. The realization came slowly, tumbling over her like a horror movie unfolding screen by screen. Her mind fought it, already coming up with a thousand denials and excuses ready to spring from her lips. Unfortunately, all that came out was one word.

"No."

"Lake's going to be here at noon to talk to you about it."

A humorless laugh burst out. "No. No way, Gabby. I'm no babysitter; I'm a woman with my own company and apartment and a, a . . . life! I despise small country towns with their ridiculous rules and judgments. Plus, teenagers scare the crap out of me. Why do you think I don't want any children? Because they grow up to be teens!"

Gabby sighed. "I know. Look, you'll need to stand your ground when he comes. I'm sure there's another alternative, but I also know how persuasive Lake can be. That's why he's such a beast in the courtroom. He makes you believe his solutions are critical to solving the problem." She gave a mock shiver. "The man is scary good. And hot as hell." Gabby cocked her head curiously. "You spend a lot of time with him, and he's just your type. Intelligent. Passionate. A bit of a control freak. Alpha male to the max. Don't you have just the tiniest crush on him?"

Mia paused, considering her friend's words. Jonathan Lake had a dynamic presence that served him well on camera. With his thick, dark hair; ocean-blue eyes; and energized persona combined with lethal charm, he reminded her of JFK Jr., poised to take on the world. Her heart ached every time she thought about the tragic loss that took JFK and Jackie's son way too soon. But the moment Jonathan reached out to shake her hand, she knew there would never be a relationship between them. Yes, he was attractive, and yes, he checkmarked all her boxes, but there was no chemistry. No zing. No charge. Just a flat frequency that warned of nothingness.

Thank God. Being involved with a client was a big no-no, and that would've been a sticky obstacle to overcome.

"Nope. I'm happy to report there is zero attraction between us, and that's why we work so well together."

"After all those deadbeats hurt you, I figured you'd be done with that chemistry test. Ever think you need some computer nerd or overall nice guy? You can start as friends and grow to respect and eventually love each other?"

Mia rolled her eyes. "Too many Hallmark movies, Gabby. I steamroll over nice guys—they can't keep up. And without an innate attraction, I'm just not interested. I've decided celibacy is my best option at this point. At least until the election is over."

"Then I know what to get you for a birthday present."

"What?"

Gabby grinned with mischief. "A hell of a lot of batteries."

Mia laughed. "You're such a good friend."

"I know." She reached out and plucked a red folder from the teetering stack. "Here's everything I found on Chloe Lake, along with the charges and sentencing. You need a plan before he gets here, or you'll be stuck upstate for the summer. Do you even own riding boots or a pair of jeans?"

She shuddered at the thought. She loved everything about this messy, dirty, gorgeous city and had sworn long ago to never leave. Not when she could score designer shoes, tampons, and a grilled chicken salad with yogurt-dill dressing on the same exact block. "Of course I own jeans. Just not ones for actually doing things in. And do my new Coach boots count?"

"Not when you can't wear them in the rain. Plus, they have fur, with a three-inch wedge heel."

"Then we both better get to work on an alternative plan. 'Cause I'm not going to ruin my summer, and I refuse to let Jonathan Lake order me around. I'm his PR rep, not his personal assistant. Let Bob head upstate to get her out of this mess."

They looked at each other and burst into laughter. Lake's campaign manager, Bob, was a former marine who ran a ruthless schedule and never showed a hint of emotion. With a massive, muscled build; shaven head; and cold, dark eyes, he'd eat Chloe for breakfast. But he was a hell of a manager and the ultimate pit bull protector of Lake.

"Just be firm," Gabby advised. "How about we hire a cleaner?"

"Are we now involved in the mob?"

"Sorry, been watching too many political dramas. How about we find someone else to watch her? Someone who can make sure she finishes her community service without getting into any more trouble?"

"Good. Let's get a list together and screen some candidates so we're ready at noon."

"Got it." She paused, then frowned. "Umm, should I start with Care.com?"

"No! We know people. Don't we? Start with Bob. Maybe he has some friends on the softer side."

"Sure. I'll get on it right away." Gabby went back to her scary desk, and Mia headed into her office. She dove into her endless email pile, sorting through potential new clients and allowing herself to feel the tiny pulse of pride flowing through her veins. She'd built her company by sheer grit, hard work, and a little luck. Her dream of being successful at thirty was finally coming true, and Lake's election would put her over the top. She had almost six months to push through before Election Day, and she intended to do anything to win.

Then she'd finally achieve justice for her father.

At exactly noon, there was a quick tap on her door. Jonathan Lake stepped into her office, automatically shrinking the space around him. His aura practically vibrated with energy. Clad in a navy-blue suit with a sharp red tie, he emanated a successful businessman without the show of money. Another perfect balance for the election. He was rich but not too rich, and his clothes bespoke serving the people, not his ego.

Without a word, he put down his briefcase and took the chair opposite her desk. They stared at one another for a while in silence, both preparing for the conversation.

"You received all the details of our current dilemma?" he finally asked. His voice was clipped and no-nonsense, but Mia caught the tired lines bracketing his eyes and the weary slump of his shoulders.

"I did. I'm sorry, Jonathan. I didn't realize Chloe was in trouble," she said gently.

He winced. "I thought after the cheating incident, we wouldn't have any other problems. Dammit, she's a good kid! I don't know what's gotten into her lately."

"She's nineteen. I remember I thought I was immortal and knew everything."

A grim smile twisted his lips. "Yeah. She hasn't had the most normal life, either. But this could be critical. If word gets out my daughter vandalized property, I'm done. I'm supposed to stand for family values. They'll crucify me."

"Maybe not. Has Bob tried to bury it?"

"I think we're good for now. But there's no way my daughter is going to spend the summer alone where she can get into more trouble. The press will have a field day. Something has to be done."

"I'm already on it. I have Gabby gathering up a list of options to find someone to be with your daughter twenty-four seven. Have you thought about a bodyguard?"

"Absolutely not. It has to be someone I trust. Definitely a female. Preferably a person who knows what we have at stake and who can be in constant contact with me. A person who's smart yet kind enough to be with my daughter."

Oh, he was good. She narrowed her gaze as he ticked off his wish list and his voice filled with emotion and concern. Too bad she had his number.

"I'm not doing it, Jonathan," she said firmly. "It's simply not possible."

"Why?"

She blew out a breath at his demand. "I have a business to run. An apartment to look after."

"Do you have cats? Dogs?"

She frowned. "No."

"I'll get you a house sitter, vetted by me. I'll get you a temp and set you up with anything you need to do work from another location."

"No. I also hate traveling and despise the country. I'm allergic to horses."

He snapped that electric blue gaze to her face. "You're lying."

"Fine. But I hate horses and the smell and small towns and anything vintage. I hate bed-and-breakfast places where strangers eavesdrop on your conversation and butt into your business. I'm also terrible with kids."

"You hate them?"

"No! But I can't relate to them. I feel awkward and stupid, and I'd be the worst person in the world to help your daughter. She'd hate me. She'd be miserable and beg you to take me off her hands. Better to get the right person for her in the beginning. Someone more matronly."

He grinned. "She's going to love you."

Her temper swirled. She leaned her elbows on the desk and spoke in a deliberately cold voice. "No, Jonathan, I'm not doing it. You can't bully me or bribe me or buy me. I'm your PR person, not your assistant or girlfriend or campaign manager. Get Bob to do it."

"Chloe can't relate to him. She's met him a few times, and they just stare at each other in wary silence. I think he scares her."

"Don't you have one of those kind, silver-haired secretaries who'll be over the moon to take a long vacation from the DA's office?"

He snorted. "Hell no. My assistants are scarier than Bob."

She slammed a palm on the desk. "I'm scary! I'll terrify her. I mean it. We are not discussing this option anymore. There is no way in hell I'm spending the summer watching your daughter at some horse farm. Are we clear?"

She steeled herself for his killer charm or skillful debates. Instead, he stared at her with a defeated look in his eyes. "I don't know what to do, Mia," he said. Truth rang out in his words. "Chloe needs someone to trust. Someone to protect her from all the stuff that can happen to a kid involved in politics. If she makes another wrong decision, my entire election could be at stake. And there's no way I can concentrate on winning an election when I'm worried about my daughter."

He lifted his hands and leaned over. "You're my last hope. I'm asking you, not as an employee but as a friend. Please help me."

Her bullshit meter remained eerily silent. There was nothing but the simple plea of a father who needed help and had no one else to trust. She remembered what it felt like to watch her family dragged through the mud of the media: the consistent nervousness of being in the spotlight, the fear of failures being discovered and exploited in the latest gossip column for all to laugh at.

The memories tugged at her. When Henry Thrush announced his desire to run for Congress, her mother had embraced every aspect of political life. She became the perfect wife, standing by his side, guiding Mia in the careful steps a political candidate's family needed to take to win. They were so proud—and though her father was an underdog, his impassioned speeches showed a truth within his words his opposition just didn't have. The polls got closer, and Mia was ready to watch her father head to DC.

Until the scandal.

An interview popped up where a woman claimed to have slept with her father on a regular basis. She had no proof. No photos or gifts or receipts to show the world, but it hadn't mattered. The scent of ruin was in the air, and the public became greedy for more.

Overnight, Mia watched her family get torn apart and their marriage suddenly questioned. The woman told of hotel trysts and deviant sexual images. Suddenly, her classmates tortured and teased her, mercilessly mocking her family. Her father's opponent whipped up crowds to outrage, tearing his campaign to pieces, until the election was over before it had even been run. Her mother left, not believing her father's vehement claims of innocence. Mia became the casualty of political war, and she learned that the truth sometimes didn't matter, and it didn't set you free.

Because the truth could be manipulated.

After the election, it was proven the woman had lied, paid off by nameless strangers the new congressman swore he didn't know. The story broke and peaked in twenty-four hours before being buried in the middle of the occasional paper or magazine. Her mother ended up returning, both of them desperate to salvage the torn shreds of their once-strong marriage.

Mia knew they tried. She knew they loved each other. There had just been so much to get past that had changed them both. After a year, they ended up parting ways. Her mom remarried and moved out to California. Henry Thrush settled in a small town, practiced law, and never entered the political arena or public eye again.

But, oh, how she burned for justice.

She wanted to show the good that could be done by being on the correct side of the public-relations campaign. She vowed to avenge her father by backing her own candidate to office and making sure he or she won.

Jonathan Lake was her shot at winning. At finally putting those memories aside and starting new. Lake was the face of her father—a man who was good and wanted to enter the political field for what he could bring and change and be. Not for power or sex or money.

He needed to win the election at all costs. How could she forgive herself if a disaster occurred with his daughter because she'd refused his request?

At least she understood what the girl was going through.

Jonathan's voice ripped her out of her reverie. "Mia? Will you help me?"

Mia closed her eyes in defeat.

Crap.

She was so screwed.

Chapter Three

"Ethan, I need your help."

He turned. His sister, Harper, stood behind him, studying the newly sanded wall that had once been stained by water leaks. Her short, dark-brown hair framed her face and screamed no-nonsense, and her skin had already turned a warm, brown color from the sun. Those sea-green eyes were just as direct and startling as he remembered. Why did she get the Black Irish gene while he and Ophelia were stuck as gingers? She was tall like their father, hovering near six feet. The students had bullied her at school, calling her an ugly Amazon, and the girls formed a hate club, spending their days gleefully torturing her. He watched his once-joyous little sister slowly lose her zest for life, folding into herself until her only friends were the horses at the stables. His family had all tried to help, but everything they did backfired, pushing her further into her own world, where she was safe.

Now she was a powerhouse, leaving that once shy, isolated girl behind. But Ethan knew the past left permanent scars most couldn't see.

She wore her usual outfit of old jeans, high riding boots, and a faded baby-blue T-shirt. Ethan bet she had one T-shirt and one pair of jeans for every day of the week. His sister was as low maintenance with her wardrobe as she was high maintenance with her causes.

"Hey, Harp. What's up?"

"The place looks great. You've really turned the bungalow into a home these past few weeks."

"Most of it was an easy fix. Now that I got the roof patched, the walls can get a new paint job."

"It doesn't smell anymore."

He laughed. "Just some good old-fashioned elbow grease. Just like—"

"Mom used to say," she finished, a rare smile curving her lips. Ethan poked at the wound, but time had finally lessened the sting of his mother's absence. From his sister's face, it looked like she felt the same way. His mother's Irish blood had given them all a fierce loyalty to family, stoicism to get through hard times, and a deep love of land. He knew his mother had been hurt when he announced he needed to leave, but his sisters had risen to leadership and seemed to be happy about where their paths had led. He'd never thanked them, though. Never told them how he appreciated their support, allowing him the freedom to do something else without the guilt.

The accident dragged too many hard truths to the surface.

He was back to face them all.

In tune to his thought, his knee throbbed, and he shifted his weight to take some of the pressure off. Harper studied his face, her bright eyes assessing his condition in true sisterly style. "How's the leg?" she asked.

"Better. What'd you need?" he asked, trying to direct her attention back to her original request.

She gestured to the now-shaggy facial hair that had little structure. "You ever gonna shave that beard?"

He ran a hand over his chin and shrugged. "Don't know. It's nice not to worry about what I look like."

"You look scary, dude. Like one of those crazy *Duck Dynasty* guys."

He grinned. "They're kind of cool."

She kept staring. "It's been three weeks, and Ophelia said you rarely come to the main house. You're bunked up back here alone like some crazy hermit."

"Lots of work to do on the bungalow. Not in the mood for chatting with strangers. You avoid it all the time."

She gave a suffering sigh. "I make my appearances when I have to. Play the good hostess. But that's Ophelia's territory. Plus, I go into town and talk to actual people other than Wheezy and Hei Hei."

The Lab heard his name, picking up his head to give Harper a drooly, happy grin, then dropping his chin back onto the floor and snorting.

"Wheezy's great company. I missed him. That chicken is another story."

On cue, they both looked out the window at the black Polish chicken with a bunch of crazy feathers sticking out of his head. He clucked and clawed at the ground and seemed to have the run of the place.

"He was another rescue. When I found him this winter, his poor feathers were almost frozen because they never let him inside. He's blossomed since he's been here."

"And did you have to name him after another Disney movie?" He groaned. "I feel like I'm living at Disney World."

"Nothing wrong with Disney. Mom always taught us all problems can be solved or figured out by watching those movies. Stop trying to change the subject."

"What subject?" he asked innocently.

"We're worried, okay?"

He stiffened, hating the concern in her eyes and knowing why it was there. His voice softened. "I'm doing fine, Harp. Seriously. Just need some alone time to process shit."

"It wasn't your fault."

He jerked. His gut clenched. "Yep."

Frustration shot off her figure. "Forget it—I know you don't want to talk. But you'll have to get over your solitary status for a little bit and help me out. I just found out I inherited a young girl who got mandated community service. She's here for the summer to work."

"Thought they assigned kids to clean up parks or pick up garbage on the highways?"

"Punishment has evolved. She's a college student who got in trouble. Guess who heard her case?"

"Who?"

"Judge Bennett."

He winced, shaking his head. "He's still on the bench? He's older than Wheezy."

"I know. He's still serving and living in that big old empty house in town, raining terror on college students. He's big on making an example of bad behavior."

"Why us?"

Harp lifted a brow. "Mom, of course. He used to send the troubled kids over to the horse farm to work off their community service. Mom got volunteers, and he got the joy of justice. Of course, I told him after Mom passed we didn't need any extra volunteers, but he still throws us one occasionally. Guess he decided we'd be the lucky recipients of her horse expertise."

"Oh, she knows about horses?"

Harper shot him a glare. "No. That's my problem. This can be a nightmare, Ethan. Imagine a hormonal-ridden, snarky teen who knows nothing about running a horse-rescue farm or a bed-and-breakfast. I'm slammed and working overtime. I can't deal with teaching her crap. You have to do it."

He stared at her. "You're kidding."

"No. You're in charge of her. Show her the ropes. Teach her how to take care of the horses—I don't care. Give her jobs that will help, but keep her out of my hair."

"Fuck no. Give her to Ophelia. She'd love getting an assistant at the inn."

"Already talked to her. She runs a tight ship and just hired an extra cleaner she can't lay off. Said she'll throw her an occasional odd job, but she doesn't want her underfoot."

Ethan muttered a curse. "Why can't we reassign her somewhere she's actually needed?"

"Judge Bennett wanted her to have a place to stay since the dorms shut down for the summer. I guess her parents won't allow her to have a place of her own and intend to keep her at the inn under a watchful eye. She must be a troublemaker. Another reason you need to be in charge. She'll listen to you. You won't put up with any bullshit."

"Neither would you! Harp, I don't think this is possible. I still have to finish up the bungalow, and then I have other stuff to do."

She placed her hands on her hips. "Like what? Yes, you've helped me at the stables, but you still refuse to train the new horses or come with me to the auction. You avoid the inn. You rarely go into town and haven't left this place since you arrived. Am I missing something?"

Ah, shit. He should've known Harper wouldn't leave him alone, and now he'd be stuck with a spoiled kid who didn't even want to be here. "What if I find her another place? Maybe I can ask around."

"I couldn't care less. Why don't you appeal to Judge Bennett? He's down at Bea's Diner every morning for breakfast."

"Fine. I'll talk to him and see what we can work out."

"Great. In the meantime, I'll tell her she reports to you. They'll be here this afternoon."

Harper turned and headed toward the door.

"Wait—today? Who else is with her?" he demanded.

"I think her aunt since the last name is different. Mia. Girl is Chloe. They'll be checking in, but you should at least introduce yourself. John could use another hand down at the stables, too."

"You're just full of happy advice, aren't you?"

She shot him a false, cheeky grin. "That's me. I just shit out happiness and rainbows."

Then she was gone.

He smothered a groan, too aggravated to give in to her sense of humor. He walked into the small area he'd made into a half-functional kitchen and refilled his coffee mug, tempted to spike it with his favorite Irish whiskey. But that would be too easy. He'd learned to take his medicine without the spoonful of sugar, and he wasn't about to go back now. Sipping the hot brew from a chipped red mug that screamed I'M HORSING AROUND!, he brooded about this latest mess on his hands. He'd come home for some damn peace and quiet—not to babysit. Hell, that was the reason he avoided the auction and training the new horses.

He couldn't help anyone right now, human or animal. Best to avoid it all.

Tomorrow, he'd head to the diner and convince the judge to get the girl reassigned. Then he could get back to a peaceful, quiet existence for the rest of the summer while he figured out his future.

He slugged down the rest of the coffee and put the mug in the sink. "Come on, Wheezy, let's take a stroll."

The Lab's bones creaked as he got up, but his tail did a mad dance of glee as he followed him down the back path. Hei Hei regarded both of them with fowl-like arrogance, then dismissed them with a shake of feathers. The thick woods muffled sounds and sun, wrapping him in a temporary peace he didn't take for granted. He needed no markers to follow the dirt trail that sloped downward, twisted around various-size rocks, and suddenly ended at a tangle of brush.

Wheezy howled in excitement, knowing what came next, and bounded around the scary thorn bushes, following the secret trail hidden in plain sight.

Ethan followed the Lab's lead and stepped out of the woods.

And gazed upon what he imagined heaven looked like.

The stables lay ahead of him in organized chaos. Endless acres of open green hills rolled ahead of him, dotted with white fences, the colors of various horses and hay piles like map markings. His gaze tracked the stretch of land that morphed into over fifty acres of trails and woods, then reached farther to finally stop in glory at the mighty thrust of the Shawangunk Mountains—commonly termed the Gunks—highlighted under an azure sky.

Ethan stared at the earthly colors and textures revealed in perfect glory. Shivers of memory raced down his spine, bringing him back to the years spent in this exact place, perched on his favorite rock, pondering his life. This was where his dreams and plans were laid out. Where hurts and heartbreaks were healed. Where the joy of childhood freedom and endless possibilities lay within the reach of trees and rock and mountain, with no one to judge him other than the horses and birds and creatures great and small.

For a few precious seconds, the ragged hole in his soul took a breath and sighed.

He moved forward, ready to greet what was ahead.

The sudden scream of bullets shot through the air, shattering the idyllic view, tearing away the peace. He staggered and went down fast, hands over his head, heart thundering like a pack of Thoroughbreds. Dirt and rocks scraped against his chest, and his breath strangled in his lungs.

"Don't let me die."

"I won't. I swear to God I won't let you die."

His vision blurred. He fought hard for consciousness. For sanity. For—

The low whimper and touch of fur and wetness pressed against the side of his head. Still trying to gulp precious air to stay alive, it took him a while to register the wild lap of a tongue covering every part of his body. His sight cleared, and he slowly raised his head.

Wheezy met his gaze with delight, his brown eyes full of greeting and joy. He panted, covering his face with doggy kisses, and Ethan unfolded himself from the ground. The same sound ricocheted through the air, but this time, he recognized it as a nail gun, spotting a guy in the distance fixing up a fallen piece of wood from the barn.

Fuck.

He'd hoped his freak-outs were behind him, but it seemed they still lay in wait for the right time to jump out. Just like the monsters under the bed that had kept him up at night, courtesy of his love of Stephen King. He was unsuitable for the outside world. Better to keep his shit to himself and deal with it.

At least horses didn't care how broken he was on the inside. At least he could make himself useful for a little while.

He stood up and brushed the dirt from his clothes. Ignoring the throb in his knee from his ground hit, Ethan walked into the stables.

Chapter Four

Mia drove past rolling green hills and fields dotted with knotted apple trees, ice-cream stands, and white picket fences holding herds of cows. The scent of fertilizer and earth drifted through the vents, even though her windows were tightly closed and the air conditioner set at a comfortable sixty-eight degrees. The sky was a beautiful pale blue, stuffed with round, puffy clouds. At one point, she'd caught a rainbow spilling from earth's ceiling to cast myriad bright colors in a perfect arch stretched in the distance, urging her forward into a land of happiness.

It was official.

She'd arrived in hell.

Muttering under her breath, she consulted her Waze app briefly before making the turn on Route 32. She was officially en route to meet a teenage girl who probably already resented her. Seemed Chloe's final act of rebellion was refusing to let Mia pick her up. Her friends were dropping her off at three p.m. to start her servitude, and Mia wanted to arrive early to get settled.

A touch of depression pressed down on her. She turned Adam Levine up higher on the radio, but even his delicious voice wasn't helping. Maybe she'd eat the last half of her KIND bar? Her stomach growled on cue, but after calculating the calories, especially with her dinner unknown, it'd be best to keep it for emergencies.

What would she do if the town had no vegan or vegetarian options? Or gluten free?

What would happen if the B & B only served carbohydrates like gravy and biscuits and grits?

But maybe that was the South. At this point, it didn't matter. If it wasn't the city, everything else was subpar and dangerous. She refused to be a size fatter at the end of summer because she was stuck in a town overrun by potatoes and cheese.

Or was that Wisconsin?

Ah, hell, it didn't matter. She better be close, though. She'd been driving for almost three hours in a crappy rented Kia, and she needed to stretch. She glanced at her Waze app again, hoping to see that blinking red dot announcing her arrival, when the screen suddenly went blank.

No signal.

Smothering a curse, she glared at the mountains blocking her signal and punched some buttons, trying to get it back up. After a few minutes, she realized she was left both directionless and without Levine's voice to soothe her nerves. Even the rental-car company was cursing her today. They'd given away her gorgeous convertible in a mishap and stuck her with a Kia with no GPS.

Okay, people did this all the time before the internet. Not that she could read a map. The last time she'd glanced at Waze, she had noted the place was off a funny-sounding road. Of course, if they'd done any type of decent marketing, there would've been signs long ago leading her right to it.

Guess they didn't believe in advertising.

After more driving through uniform country roads and passing the same damn hills and cows, she spotted a crooked sign that read **Goosey Drive**.

That sounds right! Yes, that was the funny-sounding name. She was on the right path.

Puffing up with pride over her memory skills, she followed the road, noticing a single unpaved lane winding toward the left. It was heavily wooded but definitely a road. As she got closer, she saw a tiny sign that said INN HORSE TRAIL.

Yes. The inn is part of a rescue farm, so this must be it.

The Kia bumped along potholes, mud, and scattered brush blocking the lane. Her temper grew as she drove. How was a guest able to find this place? Why on earth wasn't it paved and well marked? Had she been dropped into one of those horrid *Wrong Turn* movies to find herself being chased by deformed country bumpkins?

Finally, the car jerked to a halt at the end of the path. She stared openmouthed at the tiny bungalow in front of her.

Holy shit.

This was the place she was staying at?

Horror unfolded. It wasn't even Victorian. It had no sprawling front porch that served tea and cookies. It was just a mud-brown house with standard-issue windows, a basic concrete stoop, and a plain-beige door. No cheery potted geraniums or herbal gardens or quirky antiques like she'd imagined a B & B to have. Instead, there was a bunch of chickens roaming around, squawking and pecking at the unpaved ground. No real parking lot. Just a battered black truck parked in front. Was she the only guest?

And if so, now she knew why.

She was going to have a panic attack.

Clutching the door handle in a merciless grip, she dragged in deep breaths and tried to calm herself. Maybe the inside was amazing. Maybe it was a lesson so she'd learn the motto "Don't be fooled by the surface, because great things lie beneath." Or in this case, inside.

She gritted her teeth and got out of the car, giving the chickens a wary glance. Her Prada shoes were open toed. Could chickens draw blood if they pecked at her toes? She stilled, watching them carefully, but they didn't seem interested in a stranger, so she began to walk toward the house. Her heels sank into the mud, aggravating her even more. Why wasn't anyone here to take her luggage or greet her?

Worst. B & B. Ever.

"Hello?" she called out. "Anyone around?"

The answer was not what she expected.

From behind the dirty, red coop thing, a massive chicken monster appeared in response to her call. She froze, mouth opening in horror, staring at the thing that seemed like a scary crossover of animal-genetic madness.

He had a giant head covered in crazy white feathers, sticking out from every angle like in one of those memes on her Facebook newsfeed. Beady eyes focused on her with sheer fowl suspicion. Fat, red jowls hung down beside his massive beak. His body was a mottled, inky black that ended with tremendous clawed feet.

"Umm, nice chicken?"

A pissed-off sound emitted from the creature's beak, and he began lurching forward in a drunken walk of doom. She backed up, hands out, terrified she would die of a chicken attack in the backwoods, where no one would find her.

"Stay away from me!" she warned. "I mean it. I'll make you the main course of my Thanksgiving, you freak!"

The thing clucked harder, beginning to flap his wings in crazed motions, his long, curly clawed toes moving faster toward her, beak open, ready for the kill.

She screamed.

"Hei Hei!" The masculine voice snapped through the air in command. The chicken monster stopped midcharge, cranking its feathery head toward the house. "Leave her alone."

The chicken let out a murderous shriek.

"Wanna be left out this winter so your feathers freeze? I mean it, Hei Hei, I won't save you like Harper. Go back and finish your lunch."

Feathers shook. With one last glance at her that promised retribution, the chicken monster disappeared back behind the house. The man who saved her propped his hands on his hips and didn't budge. "Sorry, he's a bit temperamental. Can I help you?"

The long howl of a dog made her jump back. What now? Was this place a zoo? A black Lab came racing out with one intention: to take her down. She squared her shoulders, stood her ground, and prayed he or she was friendly.

He or she was. The dog bounded around her without jumping up, seeming thrilled to have some company. She reached down and pet the dog. At least one animal made sense out here. She'd always loved dogs. Not cats. Not chickens. Not horses or squirrels or chipmunks or snakes. Just dogs.

The man whistled. "Wheezy, come here. She's had enough of the animal-crew welcome." The dog obeyed, trotting back to his or her master and settling down near his feet. "Let's try this again. Can I help you?"

Her words seemed to drift away. She stared at him in total fascination, her mind short circuiting the endless possibilities of this man.

She'd just met a semihot Grizzly Adams.

The man was tall. Super tall—at least six four. Feet braced apart, hands on hips, he towered with an impressive presence, clad in worn, tight jeans and a basic black T-shirt that stretched over his muscular build. Russet-colored hair curled wildly over his brow and brushed the nape of his neck. A striking beard hugged his jaw and was longer than the usual goatee, bordering on wild. His features were an odd slashing of crude bone structure that kept him from ever looking pretty or soft. But his eyes. She'd never seen anything like them.

A pale ice blue, with a piercing intensity that froze her in place. The startling contrast of light and dark was mesmerizing. She wasn't usually a fan of gingers or beards, but his entire presence as a whole gave her a funny lurch in her tummy.

There were no laugh lines to spot. No humor or warmth in his eyes. This man had seen things, done things, and wasn't about to share them with anyone.

"Miss? Are you lost?"

She shook off her odd thoughts and reconnected with the land of the living. Also, her temper. This entire day had been craptastic. "I'm here to check in. I don't know what type of place you run here, but the roads are atrocious, and being greeted by a psychopath chicken won't get you a five-star rating on Yelp."

His brow arched. "Check-in's not till three p.m."

She pressed her lips together and prayed for patience. "I know that. I'm early. That doesn't excuse your setup. Now, if you can take my luggage from the car, get me some water with lemon, and show me to my room, I'd be grateful."

"I don't work here."

Her temper frayed. "Then can you get me someone who does before I lose my shit?"

Those eyes narrowed. "You're from the city, aren't you?"

"Yes. I'm exhausted, and hot, and cranky, so I'd appreciate some help."

"This isn't the B & B. You must've taken a wrong turn."

Relief shot through her, followed by annoyance. "Well, I'm relieved, since this place looks like a nightmare, but I did follow the sign. Why isn't anything marked properly here?"

"It is. It clearly states *Inn Horse Trail.*"

She rolled her eyes. "Fine. So this is where the horse people sleep?"

He just stared at her, his gaze flicking from her head to her toes in complete dismissal. "Nah, they just sleep in the barns. The hay is super soft. They even have an outhouse."

She ignored his comment, knowing he was making fun of her. Yes, she was acting bitchy, but she hadn't eaten the last half of her KIND bar, and her stomach was ravenous. She was damn hangry. "I don't have time to exchange clever banter with you. Just show me where the inn is, and I'll be on my way."

"Go out the way you came from. Take a left. Go farther down about half a mile, and you'll see the right sign."

She forced a fake smile, already disliking him as much as the chicken. "Thanks so much for your *help*."

He cocked his head. His drawl was as sarcastic as her comment. "No problem, princess."

With one last withering look, she got into the car and bumped her way back to the road, leaving the horrible man and cabin and chicken behind her. Oh, she'd dealt with plenty of his kind in her years of PR. Men who thought women who enjoyed nice things were entitled and silly. Men who had such big egos, they couldn't comprehend a successful woman clearly stating what she wanted and how she wanted it. She shuddered. He probably mansplained to his girlfriend.

No, thank you.

At least she'd never have to see him again.

She finally made it to the correct turn and parked in the spacious lot of the Robin's Nest B & B. Lord, even the name gave her a cavity. But she had to admit the spread was beautifully set up, lending a fairytale-and-rustic charm. From the gorgeous pop of the robin's-egg blue shutters and door, to the huge wraparound porch outfitted with wicker rockers and tables, the place was classic B & B. A pink garden gnome peeked from his spot on the front lawn, and the sound of merry wind chimes tinkled in the breeze. Tulips, geraniums, and roses mixed together and filled the spaces between lush green lawn and old, giant trees. This time, when she climbed the front steps, no animal attacked her. A two-tiered antique cart was already set out with chunky chocolate-chip cookies and a pitcher of tea. She practically had to bite her fingers to stop them from snatching one of the sugary sweets, but she allowed herself one cup of tea. The cold brew slid down her throat, immediately quenching her thirst. She gave a sigh of pleasure. "Now that's much better," she murmured to herself.

She was about to open the door when a willowy strawberry blonde spotted her through the screen. "Oh my, I didn't hear you pull up. Are you Mia Thrush?"

Her tension began to ease from her shoulder. "Yes. Chloe's arriving a bit later, so I thought I'd get here a little early. Is that a problem?"

The woman stepped outside, waving her graceful fingers in the air. "Of course not! Check-in's at three p.m. but we never turn away a guest. Since its midweek, we're empty at the moment, but we'll have a full house come Friday. My name is Ophelia, and I run the Robin's Nest. Why don't I grab your luggage and get you settled so you can relax a bit. Did you have a long drive?"

"Over three hours. Then I got lost, so I'm a bit stressed out. I'm surprised there were no clearly marked signs."

"You poor thing. And yes, these country roads aren't known for their signage. Just sit down and drink your tea. It's a hot day."

Ophelia floated down the stairs and left before Mia could utter another word. In record time, she carted her two overstuffed Luis Vuitton suitcases like they weighed nothing and placed them at Mia's feet with a smile. "I can give you a tour later, but if you'll fill out some forms, you can settle in. Follow me."

The scent of vanilla and chocolate filled the air as she entered. Her breath caught. It was truly beautiful. Maybe not like the Plaza or Waldorf, but there was a thoughtfulness to the decor and how the space was used that Mia appreciated. The oak floors set off the pale-yellow walls, and the high ceiling held a gorgeous golden waterfall chandelier. Tapestry rugs were set around the space in rich oriental colors. A brick fireplace took up one wall, where cozy chairs and sofas were positioned in a half circle. Antique lamps and pine furniture added to the custom decor.

Ophelia walked over to an old-fashioned writing desk that held a computer and a wooden organizer with bunches of neatly filed papers. Her fingers flew over the keyboard. "Mia Thrush and Chloe Lake. Both staying till August. And I see Chloe will be helping out on the horse farm."

Mia drew in a breath. "That's correct. I'll be her guardian for the summer."

A slight frown creased the woman's brow. "You're not her mother, then?"

"No. Her mother passed away, I'm afraid."

"Oh, I'm so sorry." Genuine sympathy glinted in her powder-blue eyes.

"Thank you. I'm her . . . aunt." The sentence choked out of her mouth. "Well, I'm such a close family friend, I've been dubbed as her honorary aunt." She hoped she carried that off, and Ophelia nodded and smiled. "Her father was unable to be here due to work obligations, so I'll be taking care of things. Do you know how many hours she has to work daily?"

"My brother, Ethan, will be in charge of the work schedule. He'll be coming by later to meet you both."

"I appreciate it."

"We'll do our best to make you happy during your stay. Breakfast is served daily in the main dining room, but guests like to take it out on the porch. You can use the back deck or even sit in the gardens—wherever you feel comfortable. Do you have any allergies? Food limitations?"

"I'd prefer meals with no carbs or processed sugar."

Ophelia nodded. "I'll be sure to put out fresh fruit, yogurt, and eggs."

"Egg whites?"

"Of course. Cookies and tea are served at one p.m. on the porch. Coffee and water are always available. Since you're one of our long-term residents, I've placed you in a room with a small refrigerator."

"I prefer green tea, if it's not a problem. Is there a place I can get a skinny vanilla latte and a kale shake?"

"Yes, there's a grocery store in town, along with some fruit-and-vegetable markets, so anything you need should be easy to get to. We have some wonderful cafés that serve blended organic coffee. Since summer is our high time, we serve snacks and wine at six. We have a few local delivery places—I've placed all the menus in this folder for you. Information on everything at the inn and attached farm, including horseback-riding lessons, is in there. Do you have any questions?"

"I'll be working every day on my laptop. I'm hoping Wi-Fi won't be a problem?"

"We've had no issues, so you should be fine."

Some of the tension eased. Ophelia seemed competent and ready to meet her needs. "Great, thank you."

"I'll show you your room." Ophelia grabbed the suitcases, lifted both hands, and began the walk up the staircase. "I put you on the second floor. We don't have an elevator, so I hope that's not a problem."

"That's fine."

Ophelia inserted an old-fashioned key into the lock of the Cardinal Room and swung open the door. The high four-poster bed had a sheer lace curtain, fluffy pillows, and a quilt with embroidered cream-and-cornflower-blue flowers. A trunk with hand-painted roses sat at the foot of the bed. Daisies were scattered in vases, and the furniture was a light oak, adding to the airiness of the room. It was spacious, with a stone fireplace, large windows, and small desk for working.

"I love it," Mia said simply, peeking her head into the en suite bath. A claw-footed tub was the main star, with the color components of clean white and soft blue carried through with the towels, rugs, and tile. A lighted makeup mirror and stool sat in the right corner.

"Good, I'm glad. Housekeeping comes daily, but you can always put the 'Privacy' sign on the knob by ten a.m. Let me know if you need anything. I'll buzz you when Chloe gets here."

"Thanks, Ophelia."

The door shut, and the room was shrouded in silence. Mia sat on the edge of the bed. Exhaustion seeped into her muscles. With a groan, she lay back on the overstuffed pillow and closed her eyes. There was so much to do. Unpack and get organized. Call into the office. Catch up on emails and work for her other clients. Go shopping for low-calorie food before she ate the cookies. And make a good first impression on Lake's daughter. Maybe even get Chloe to like her. At least a little bit.

She needed a minute. Maybe two. If she rested, her mind would become strong again, and her tigress instinct would resurge.

Just a few minutes.

The knock pierced through the fog. Mia shot up out of bed, looking around wildly until she remembered where she was. Glancing at the clock on the bedside table, she realized over an hour had passed.

Now that's what she called a power nap.

Pushing her hair out of her eyes, she walked across the room and opened the door.

"Hey."

The greeting came from black-painted lips. Mia blinked, taking in Lake's daughter and wondering if she could find another job so she could get the hell out of Dodge. This wasn't the girl she'd expected to meet. What happened?

The multiple pictures on Lake's phone and desk showed a girl with long, dark hair and intense blue eyes, with a fresh-faced look of youth. She'd been dressed in the all-American way of teens—jeans and a T-shirt.

This girl still had long, straight hair, but it was now colored bright purple. A diamond glinted from her nose piercing, and a ring winked from her eyebrow. Her features reminded Mia of Jonathan—defined cheekbones, strong jawline, and high-arched brows. She had the same deep blue eyes, except hers were masked by so many coats of mascara, Mia was amazed she could see. Her outfit consisted of ragged denim shorts that barely covered her privates, a skimpy black Ed Hardy tank that screamed LOVE HURTS, and black combat boots. A tat of a skull was inked on her left arm. She was stunning and badass and terrifying all in one. Mia had never experienced the true rebel teen years, choosing to follow the good-girl path, get into good colleges, and be the perfect model daughter.

Mia swallowed. "Hey, Chloe, I'm Mia Thrush. I'm sorry—Ophelia was supposed to call me when you arrived."

The girl shrugged. "I told her I'd come up. My room is next to yours, so you can jail me properly."

"Umm, right. Do you like it?"

Another shrug. "Not really, but it doesn't matter. There's so many flowers on my bed, I'm afraid they'll strangle me in my sleep."

She laughed. "Yeah, there's definitely a Victorian-type theme going on. Come on in. We can chat a bit."

Chloe strode over on long, lean legs, the denim exposing part of her ass. Lake would have a heart attack if he saw her walking around in those clothes. Is that why she did it? When had she changed her style?

Mia grabbed two bottles of water that had been placed in the room and handed one to her. Nerves danced in her stomach. It was ridiculous to be intimated by a young girl, yet here she was, trying not to stutter. She dragged in a breath and tried to act confident and like a damn grown-up.

"Your dad filled me in on everything. You know I help him run his social media campaign, and it's a critical time for the election process. We're hoping to keep your community service out of the news, and we've done the job so far, but we need your help. I'm here to make things easier on you and help you this summer."

Chloe snorted. "You're here 'cause dear old Dad is too busy, and he hired you as my watchdog. I know the drill. Believe me, I've been living it for way too long." Her voice held a bitter edge. She began picking at her black nails, brows creased in a frown. The resemblance to Jonathan was uncanny. Mia's heart softened a bit as she stared at his daughter. Losing a mother at her age was devastating, and losing her father to an election process was a double hit.

"We're both stuck here for the summer together," Mia pointed out. "We both have jobs to do. Personally, I'm up for being open and getting to know one another before you decide if I suck."

The girl kept picking at her thumb, refusing to look up. Mia felt as if they were on the verge of a tentative agreement that was crucial. "You want to try to be friends?" Chloe asked.

"Yes, I'd like that."

"So if something happens, and I ask you not to tell my dad, you'd respect my wishes? Try to help me?"

"No." Chloe lifted her head and stared back in surprise. "I tell your dad everything. He's your parent, not me, and I respect your relationship. Look, Chloe, I won't be a pawn in the game with you and your dad. I know things are tough right now, and I'm not going to even try to understand what it's like to lose your mom and get dragged into the political arena because of your dad. But I don't play sides. I'm here because your dad needs you to finish your community service and not get into any more trouble this summer. Whatever happens, I tell him the truth. And if I'm worried, I'll call him."

The girl narrowed her gaze, suspicion glinting deep. "You're involved with my dad, aren't you?"

Mia gasped. "No! I swear to you, I am not involved with your father in any way, shape, or form. He's my client, and I respect him. And though you probably don't want to hear it, I know he loves you. I know he loved your mom. I know he's a wreck about not being here with you for the summer, and he refused to have anyone else come out here because I've earned his trust. And I won't lie to you. About anything. I swear."

She waited for the verdict. Waited for Chloe to say something snarky and stamp out and begin the whole vicious cycle that would set off the summer.

Instead, the girl nodded. "Okay. That's fair."

Mia tried not to let her mouth drop open in surprise. "Good. Now, we're meeting your boss in a few, and then I say we grab some dinner. I've told everyone I'm your honorary aunt—a family friend who earned the title. I think it makes things easier to explain our summer stay."

The girl went back to her shrugs. "Sure."

"Cool."

Mia tried not to grin like a silly fool. She knew it was only round one in a very long match, but she'd also learned a valuable lesson from her father that served her well:

Celebrate every small victory in life. You never know when they'd come around again.

Chapter Five

"Chloe? I'm Ethan Bishop. I'll be overseeing your work at the horse farm."

He stood outside the bed-and-breakfast by the front porch. The girl gave him a firm handshake back and met his gaze head-on. His muscles relaxed slightly. Sure, her clothes and appearance were scary, but he'd seen plenty of teen rebels. What he couldn't stand were mouthy brats who believed they were too good for old-fashioned hard work. Discipline was one of his core beliefs, along with respect. For now, he'd try not to judge her, even though cheating and vandalism bugged him.

"Nice to meet you," she said politely.

"Your mom or dad here?"

She jerked. Immediately, her face changed, becoming distant. She gazed at the ground. "No. A friend of my dad's is with me—but I call her my aunt. She should be down in a minute; she's running late."

He made a mental note to never mention her family dynamics again. Definitely a raw spot. "I happen to like punctuality, so we'll get along fine. It's your aunt who's already in trouble." That got him a ghost of a smile from her black lips. "Know anything about horses? Or farms?"

"No, sorry."

Hopefully, he'd get her a more suitable service job once he spoke with Judge Bennett in the morning. For now, he'd keep the tour low key. "Okay, why don't I take you down to the barns so you can see the setup?"

The door banged open. Irritated, he looked up. The woman rushed out, looking like she was about to embark on a *Vogue* fashion shoot rather than walk in the fields. Her feet were clad in ridiculous sparkled platform sneakers that contradicted the entire point of sneakers. Her pants were cream, in some kind of linen material, and her sleeveless top looked like silk. She'd be covered in dirt and sweat in minutes. Irritation flashed, but then he got a good look at her face, and horror slowly washed over him in waves.

No. Not her. Anyone but her.

"I'm sorry, I had a minicrisis, but it's all set. Hi, I'm Mia Thr—*you*!"

Seems she was just as horrified. Those pretty golden eyes widened, and her hand pressed against her mouth like she'd encountered a beastly creature. His lips tightened. He pegged her type immediately. Her honey-colored hair framed her face in a shaggy, chic cut with angular bangs that screamed expensive Manhattan stylist. From the flash of her manicured nails, to the gilded gold bracelet, to her pale, flawless skin protected by endless sunscreen, she emanated class, snobbery, and money. Her body was way too thin, probably from starving to get into the famed size six women tortured themselves to achieve. He had no patience left for a silly, spoiled city princess who looked down on anyone who earned a living by sweat. Oh, he'd been with those types before. Knew how to live in their world, flourish, and conquer. As the bodyguard of a famous actress in Hollywood, Ethan had been caught up in the whirlwind of gala events, paparazzi, and glamour. Where appearances and social media and the right designer dress could make or break a career. Hell, once he'd even embraced all the aspects of the shallow lifestyle and been one of the few welcomed into the tight circle. He'd gotten engaged, believing he could flit in and out between the real world and the one of make-believe. But he'd been wrong. And now he was done with those from his past and had no desire to return.

"Yes, me. Ethan Bishop, to be exact. I see you found your way to civilization," he said, the words clipped.

She threw her shoulders back as if trying to stand as tall as possible, which wasn't much due to her petite frame. Her voice dripped icicles. "Yes, and no killer chickens barred my path. Ophelia also has something called *manners*. They're quite lovely."

He regarded her with distaste. "Ophelia is nice to everyone. I'm more selective. I was just telling Chloe how much I appreciate punctuality."

Her teeth gnashed. Animosity radiated from her figure. "I had something important to clear up first."

"Next time you have a fashion crisis, I'd choose footwear that's more practical for walking through horse dung. Chloe, your boots work fine. But next time, wear jeans. There's ticks and it's better to have your legs covered."

Chloe glanced back and forth at them in confusion. "Umm, have you guys met before?"

"Briefly. She made a wrong turn, in more ways than one. Follow me."

He ignored Mia's gasp, turned, and started walking, not bothering to see if they'd follow. Chloe kept pace. Mia was probably trying to keep her balance with the uneven ground and her silly shoes, but that wasn't his problem. He concentrated on Chloe, since she was the one he'd be working with. "You have to fulfill a certain amount of hours per day, but as long as you put in the work, I'm flexible. I'll show you a couple of tasks, and we'll see where you're suited best. The farm has two functions: we offer riding lessons and boarding, and we also rescue and sell horses. There are two separate barns, but everyone works together, so you'll meet all the volunteers and employees in both sections."

He heard a small yelp and stopped short. "You okay back there?"

"Fine. Just a rock," Mia spit out.

He tried not to smile at her smothered curse and kept talking. "You'll be doing a lot of cleaning tasks at first, but as you get more comfortable, we'll give you some more interesting stuff to do."

"Will I be able to ride the horses?"

"Not during work hours, but if you're interested, I'm sure we can set up some lessons."

"Sweet."

"Here we are." The massive red barns came into view, with all the chaotic activity that had once formed the seams of his life. Chickens roamed freely, and various horses were penned in gates amid hay and water buckets while people swarmed around, focused on their tasks. Wheezy chased his playmate, barking and nipping at Bolt's tail. Another one of Harper's rescues, the spotted white-and-black pup adored Wheezy and consistently trotted after him in canine hero worship. Battered trucks parked in a line among tractors, horse trailers, and endless mechanical equipment that all held a purpose. He led them around a horse getting hosed down and into the cool darkness of the barn—a place he had spent most of his childhood. The dank scents, along with the memories, rose up to greet him.

Noses poked out of stalls, smelling guests, and Ethan walked down the line, giving a greeting to each of the animals. "I think the best thing to do is give you a guide on what's in the barn and what everything's used for. Then you can give some carrots to the horses to get familiar with them."

"Is this really safe?" Mia asked. "She has no experience. I don't want her getting hurt or being pushed to do something she's not comfortable with."

"I don't intend to promise comfort. But I can promise I'll never put her in harm's way or make her do something dangerous."

She nodded, seeming to ponder his words, and he turned his back on her again. "Chloe, come with me." He took her into the stall filled with saddles, bridles, and other horse equipment, where they spent some time going over the various pieces and how they worked with the horses. She paid close attention, asking intelligent questions, and by the end of the hour, he felt a bit better about his new apprentice. Hell, he'd even consider keeping her on if it wasn't for her pain-in-the-ass companion. No way was he getting stuck with her high-drama ways all summer. Chloe had mentioned she wasn't her biological aunt, which probably meant the woman was dating Chloe's father and didn't relish being the new stepmother. Mia even refused to go near the horses, choosing to wrinkle her nose from the smell and stand quietly to the side.

"John!" He motioned over one of the assistants. "This is Chloe. She'll be helping us out this summer. Can you give her a quick tour of the other barn? Also, show her the office—she may be able to help do invoices and stuff for Harper."

"Sure thing." His brown face wreathed in a welcome smile, showing off a gold tooth. He was stout, round, and so muscular, he could easily lift and haul equipment with barely a sweat. He'd been working at the farm for years and was Harper's main right hand. "Hey, I like your lipstick!"

"Thanks."

Ethan shook his head as John chattered and led the girl away. Pulling in a breath, he faced Mia. "Can you tell me the dynamics so I know what's going on? She said you were her aunt but not by blood. Her dad's not here. Where's her mom?"

Evidently by her glowering stare, he was being rude again. "Why is that your business?"

"Why is it a trade secret? I'll be working with her daily, and I'd like to get my bearings. She's getting community service for a reason, and sometimes kids act out when there's crap going on at home. I just want to know what I'm dealing with."

She stared at him for a while, and those golden eyes flashed with hidden temper. Yeah, she definitely didn't like him, either. He couldn't think of a time when a woman wasn't interested. He'd never been egotistical about it—just happy female companionship was easy for him. Mia could be a fun challenge if he'd been up for it or if she was someone with potential. Was it the beard she hated? Or his bad temper? Maybe Harper was right. He'd let his appearance and social skills plummet since he'd arrived home.

"Fine. Chloe's father is running for office. He can't leave his job for the summer, so he sent me here to look out for her. Her mom passed away two years ago."

Sympathy cut through him. He'd practically fallen apart after his mother's death, and he'd been a full-fledged adult. "Tough. Lake, right? Oh, he's running for mayor."

She pursed her lips like she'd tasted something rotten. "I'd appreciate it if you didn't run off and gossip to your friends about this. Chloe needs to stay under the radar, for her sake and her father's. If the press got a hold of the story, you'd put her in a difficult situation."

"I'll try not to spout off at my next bingo get-together. I just want to know about Chloe. You and Lake are hooked up, then?"

"That is none of your business. I'm here to watch Chloe and do my job and hopefully stay away from you."

He grinned. Kind of fun to get her riled up. "Trust me, princess. You couldn't do one task around here without crying over breaking a nail. I'll stay out of your hair if you stay out of mine."

Her eyes sparked whiskey fire. "Oh, I get it. You think because I dress nice and don't get all mushy over horses and don't like the smell of a barn that I'm beneath you. You think I'm a silly, clueless, conceited, stupid female who doesn't have a clue about the real world. How am I doing so far?"

"I never thought 'stupid.'"

She practically spit in outrage. "I deal with sharks and barracudas on a regular basis. I was born and bred in New York City and learned more street lessons than you could in a lifetime. I've built a successful PR business from the ground up in one of the most competitive industries in the world. So don't talk down to me, horse man, just because I like a good designer brand. Got it?"

Surprise flashed through him. Well, damned if her temper wasn't the best part of her. It was certainly entertaining, and more honest than the rest of her. Too bad she was in such a sleazy profession. Publicity was as bad as politics. There were no morals, no rules, and no ethics in the PR business. It was based on who spun lies better and who won, not how the game was played.

God knows he'd experienced that firsthand.

"Yeah, I got it. But let's lay out a few ground rules for you, too." He cocked a hip and regarded her with a lazy dismissal he knew would piss her off. "Chloe is my responsibility while she works for me, and I don't appreciate any interference. I'll make sure she's safe, respected, and taken care of, but I don't need any high-maintenance distractions for any of us around here. Especially drama. We all have jobs to do, so if you don't want to get dirt on your fancy clothes or bugs in your pretty hair, or if you don't enjoy the smell of sweat and horse manure, I'd suggest you stay at the inn, where things are more . . . civilized. You can do your computer work and sip tea on the porch during the day. I'll deliver Chloe back around five, and you can eat a nice dinner together and do some evening shopping. But I think we can both agree keeping Chloe busy and tired will keep her out of trouble. Correct?"

Steam rose from her. She took a step forward, her nostrils flaring, eyes burning, reminding Ethan of a not-yet-broken filly who still believed she was in charge and vowed to prove it. Damned if a strange crackle of attraction didn't zip right through him before he reminded himself this woman was a nightmare of epic proportions and exactly the type he vowed to avoid. Unfortunately, he'd always been a sucker for a challenge, especially a feisty, passionate filly.

But he'd stick to the horses.

"You"—she breathed in fury, pointing her finger in the air—"are an arrogant, egotistical, ill-mannered boor! The only reason you surround yourself with horses is because you suck at people skills. As for Chloe, I'm the one in charge of her this summer, and I'll be the one who decides if she's taken care of and respected. I don't trust you to do either. I'll be keeping a close eye on you and ready to kick your ass if you step out of line. And those are my ground rules, horse man."

She pivoted on her wedged heel and stalked out of the barn.

She didn't trust him? Was she kidding? The woman couldn't find her way to a summer inn without depending on a computer app or neon signs. She disliked animals. She wore designer clothes to a farm, like she was ready to be photographed any moment. And she was definitely banging the father. Why else would she volunteer to accompany his daughter?

Oh, he had to get the judge to transfer Chloe. No way could he put up with that woman all summer.

The scream bounced off the rafters and startled the horses.

He raced out and found her pressed against the side of the barn. Hei Hei was blocking her path, his wings shaking in excitement, pecking madly at nothing on the ground in his usual display of emotion when he sensed a person didn't like him. His tendency to charge at random and his crazy feathers had earned him a reputation at the farm. He was harmless, but Ethan decided not to tell Mia that important fact.

Not yet.

"Get him away from me," she choked out. "I'll sue you if he pecks me, Ethan, I swear it!"

"Just stay still," he warned. "Don't move a muscle, and he won't charge."

A shrill shriek escaped her lips.

He couldn't help it. He burst into laughter.

"Wow, what a kick-ass chicken!" Chloe ran up, staring at the crazed fowl in excitement. "Mia, are you okay?"

"Chloe! Stay away from him, honey; he's dangerous."

Ethan whistled. "Hei Hei, no. Go pick on someone your own size." The chicken regarded Mia, then turned toward Chloe, rushing toward her. "He won't hurt you, Chloe. He likes to play."

Chloe knelt down, and the chicken raced around her in mad circles, clucking madly, happily imitating Wheezy, whom he thought he was. Chloe laughed in delight, putting out her hand, and the chicken pushed against her in ecstasy. "You named him Hei Hei," she said. "Just like in *Moana*!"

"Yeah, my sisters, Ophelia and Harper, are Disney nuts. Most of the animals have been named straight from Disney movies. If you like them, the B & B has a killer DVD collection."

"That's lit. You watched *Moana*, right, Mia?" Chloe asked.

Mia gingerly left the wall of the barn, glaring at both Ethan and the chicken. "I've never watched a Disney movie," she retorted. "And after meeting that psycho chicken, I don't think I'm going to."

Ethan stared at her in astonishment. Chloe gasped.

"You've never watched Disney?" Chloe practically shrieked. "What type of life have you led? How is that possible?"

Mia shrugged. "My parents were more the *All the President's Men* type. I grew up watching the History channel for fun."

"Maybe if you had a better relationship with animated animals, you'd be less afraid of real ones," he pointed out.

He didn't think it was possible, but her glare grew even darker. "Just keep your chicken away from me. Is the tour over?"

"Yep. Chloe, I have some business tomorrow, so I'll meet you at ten a.m. here in the barn."

"Okay."

"Mia, I'll see you—"

"Hopefully never," she grumbled. "Thanks. It's been enlightening."

Chloe looked at him in confusion, shrugged, and followed Mia back up the path. He watched them go while Hei Hei mourned for his new friend. The back of her silk shirt was smeared with dirt, and there was a tiny tear where a nail had dug in.

Shaking his head, Ethan headed into the barn, pushing Mia out of his mind.

Mia sipped her lemon water and allowed herself another drizzle of vinaigrette on her greens for an added treat. The café was simple and small but boasted healthy options and allowed them some privacy, since it was practically empty. She'd noticed some type of market place on Main Street that looked interesting, but the signage had been terrible, and she'd passed it before she realized what it was. Not that it mattered. Chloe was equally unimpressed with any of her suggestions, even though SUNY New Paltz was a few miles from town, and she knew her surroundings well.

Mia figured she'd be on her own a lot.

As long as Ethan stayed far away from her. Oh, she'd caught his glee when the chicken had attacked her. And of course, his assumption she was sleeping with Chloe's father was evident. She'd been so mad, she refused to deny the charges. Let him think what he wanted.

"How do you feel about working with the horses?" she asked.

Chloe picked at her panini with a chipped black nail and ate the homemade chips instead. Mia tried not to look at them. Crispy and thin, sprinkled with sea salt, they cried out to her, but she kept the image of that Gucci dress in her mind. She would not let all her work go to hell this summer for a few chips. She had control. "Better than picking up garbage," she muttered. "Ethan seemed nice, though. How come you don't like him?"

She tried to find an answer that encompassed the endless list of reasons. "He thinks he knows it all," she said. "If he does anything to upset you, just tell me. I'll take care of it."

"Whatever."

She fell back into silence.

Great. Mia tried again. "Do you like New Paltz? I was surprised you wanted to study upstate. What made you pick the school?"

"Dad wouldn't let me go out of state. Figured this was far enough away to have a life of my own."

"What are you studying in school?"

Her voice was full of suffering, as if the conversation was killing her. "Psych."

"Sounds interesting."

No response.

Mia mentally strangled Jonathan Lake. The girl hadn't said more than a handful of words to her since they'd sat down. "I know your father was shocked when he heard about the cheating and vandalism. Said it wasn't like you at all. What made you do it?"

Her direct question seemed to startle the girl, but Mia had learned early in life that sometimes the best way to connect was to ask the hard stuff. No use pretending it didn't happen. Chloe's blue eyes flickered with anger before fading just as fast. "I was crapping out in bio. Kept asking the professor for extra-credit assignments or help, but he gave me nothing. I didn't want my whole GPA to tank in the first semester."

Mia lifted a brow. "How'd that work out for you?"

The shrugging was back. "It didn't. Thanks for the reminder."

Mia let out a breath. Even though she frowned upon the girl's actions, a surge of sympathy hit her. "I'm not trying to give you a lecture, Chloe. I just know that academic probation must've been a hard thing to accept. Why would you take it up a notch by vandalizing his car? Didn't you realize it was a criminal act?"

Chloe's teeth bit down on her black lower lip. Her hands fisted around her napkin, showing off an elaborate silver thumb ring. "I fucked up, okay? I'll do my time, but what I don't need is you pretending to be some mother figure who's suddenly gonna change me into this perfect politician's daughter. I get enough of that from my dad. Look, let's just do our thing. I'll stay out of trouble so Dad can be mayor, and we don't have to see each other after the summer."

Mia's bullshit meter was buzzing loudly. Why? Something seemed off, even with all the angry rebellion coming her way. "Well, I'll respect your decision, but I'd truly like to get to know you better. Not because your dad is forcing me, but because it would be nice to have a friend out here."

"Whatever. Look, my friends want to go out later, so I need to get back."

Mia tilted her head and narrowed her gaze. "You start early tomorrow. Maybe you should skip hitting the town tonight until you get into a routine?"

Stubbornness emanated from the girl in waves. "I'll be there on time. Unless you really do want to jail me in the floral room and watch me die slowly of boredom."

Mia swallowed a frustrated growl. Is this what she was in for? Sarcasm and drama? She reminded herself one more time that she was an adult. She could do this. Kind of. "Fine, I'll get you back. I'd like to meet your friends, though."

Her eyes widened in horror. "No! That's just way too weird for me. I'm nineteen, not twelve."

Mia shifted her weight in the chair. Maybe she'd call Jonathan later and ask if she needed to check out her friends. She had no idea what was cool or not. "Fine. Let's go."

She may not have made a lot of progress, but she was determined to eventually crack through some of Chloe's shell. Maybe she could help.

After all, there was nothing else to focus on this summer.

Chapter Six

Ethan opened the door and stood in the entrance of Bea's Diner. The ghosts of his past danced in his vision as his gaze took in the familiar surroundings. How long had it been since he'd stepped foot into town?

Too long, Harper would retort. News had leaked he'd returned home, but he'd refused to go into town for the last month, and his sisters had been covering his ass so no guests showed up at his bungalow door. But even he realized he couldn't keep pretending he wasn't part of the town to avoid questions.

The place hadn't changed. Still the standard diner model, with red booths, black-and-white checkered floors, and a large breakfast counter with high-topped spinning stools. The antique jukebox still stood in the corner, belting out classic hits from the nineties and the occasional disco pop. He'd spent his youth in the right back booth with his crew of friends, eating bacon burgers with cheese fries and spinning elaborate dreams of what they'd accomplish: His best friend, Kyle, vowed to be a famous writer on par with King. His cousin, Hunter, swore he'd take Manhattan by storm and be richer than Bloomberg. Ophelia intended to sing onstage and change people with music. And him? He'd wanted to save people and get into Special Forces. Be the fucking hero of the world.

So that others may live.

His gut clenched. The room began a slow, sickly spin that was all too familiar. The breath strangled in his lungs, and he grabbed for calm, closing his eyes, trying desperately to focus on an empty room with no noise, no sound, no memory. Not here. Not now, when he was facing people for the first time. One breath. Two. Three. Slow and steady. Four . . .

"Ethan Bishop!"

His name came from a distance, but somehow he managed to connect back with the present, and the panic attack slowly receded to lie in wait for another time. He blinked, focusing on the woman wearing a high beehive of gray hair, blue eye shadow, and hot-pink lipstick. Her outfit matched her lips, from the frilly, pink apron wrapped around hot-pink leggings and matching T-shirt that was way too tight for her age, to the pink Converse high-top sneakers. He was immediately attacked in a warm hug, and the scent of lilacs still clung to her skin.

"Bea, good to see you."

After the hug, she belted him hard in the arm, brown eyes filled with indignation. "Where the hell you been hiding? I spoke to your sisters, asking when you'll be in for your usual, and all I get is a bunch of excuses. You too good for us now? You get your burgers at the fancy-schmancy Five Guys now instead of us?"

He laughed. Bea was both the owner and the best waitress in town. "Never. Just needed to settle in. Fixing up the bungalow and helping out a bit."

"When are you going to shave that atrocity? I can't see your face."

His lips twitched. "I will, eventually."

"How's your leg? You seem to be walking fine. No cane?"

"No, the PT has helped. Surgeries were successful. I'm good."

"Then I expect to see you more. Brian's been asking about you at the comic book store—you know how damn grouchy he is—and Fran's driving me nuts since she opened up that natural-foods market in town. She says it's failing and not competing with Whole Foods in the town

56

over. You need to see Tattoo Ted—his cousin had leg surgery, and he wanted to talk to you—and Lacey said she wants you to come to dinner to meet her coworker, who's single, pretty, and dying to meet you. Heard you got a new worker at the horse farm."

"Yep, that's why I'm here. I need to talk to Judge Bennett."

"Right at his usual table, sweetie. I'll bring you over coffee. Still like the ham-and-cheese omelet?"

"Yes, please."

"You got it."

The scents of coffee and bacon filled the air. He stopped to say a few casual words to the locals throwing him greetings and a barrage of questions before finally reaching the booth. "Judge Bennett?"

The older man was reading the paper and didn't look up. Ethan waited patiently, knowing the drill. The man's bald head gleamed to a high polish, and he wore his usual black suit, freshly pressed, with one red carnation in the lapel. He went to Sally's Floral Shop every morning before heading to court. Ethan once asked him why he bothered to wear a fresh flower when it was covered by his robe. The judge replied *he* knew it was there, and the routine reminded him to make a fresh effort each day to offer his best, so it didn't matter that no one else knew. Now Ethan realized the wisdom of the words that hadn't made any sense when he was younger.

"Ethan Bishop." His name snapped out with perfect precision. "Please join me."

He slid into the seat. Bea dropped a mug of coffee and creamer in front of him. "It's good to see you," he said politely. "How are you?"

The judge snorted. His dark eyes gleamed behind his sparkling black-framed glasses. "I have arthritis and a lack of tolerance for acidity. Doctor said to stay away from all food and drink that causes a flare-up, so I'm stuck shopping at Fran's new organic café. It's too expensive, though. She's not doing too well with her rate of consumership."

"I heard. Sir, I was hoping I could discuss something important with you."

"Chloe Lake."

"Yes. I appreciate you thinking of Robin's Nest, but I don't think it's the right fit. She has no experience with horses or farms, and I think she'd be a better fit serving her sentence at Tantillos Farm. They're always looking for extra help in the summer at the warehouse. She can check people out, help with the ice-cream stand, and I know they'd appreciate it."

Judge Bennett forked up his egg on a piece of toast and neatly popped it in his mouth. Bea floated over, set down Ethan's omelet with ketchup, winked, and disappeared. "Do you know her father is running for mayor?"

"Yes, I do. Her aunt is here for the summer since Lake was unable to be here. Did you ever think of allowing her to serve her sentence in Manhattan? It would be easier for the family that way."

"Professor Altman was approached by Lake to make the charges go away. As if just the mention of money, power, or politics is enough to forgive a crime. Chloe needs to be taught actions have consequences. I worked with your mother for years, and every time I sent her a troubled youth, he or she emerged differently. It was a mutually beneficial relationship. I miss that."

Ethan's heart panged as he stared at the elderly man who'd served his town with pride and believed old-fashioned work could cure ails. The judge had always been good to his family and respected his mother. "I miss her, too," he said a bit gruffly.

"I deliberately assigned Chloe there because she needs an experience contradictory to her city culture. Animals help heal wounds if allowed." Judge Bennett's gaze suddenly lifted and drilled into his. Ethan swallowed. "You should know that best out of all of us, Ethan."

He ignored the words loaded with meaning and focused on the real problem. "I'm sorry we can't take on volunteers like we used to, but Harper is slammed. The farm has grown, and there's no people to train her."

"You can. Never seen anyone so skilled with a broken horse or a person in trouble. Always had a gift."

Pain exploded in his gut. Ethan no longer had that skill, but arguing would be useless. The judge sipped his coffee, flipped the page, and fired another bomb at him. "Why haven't you been in town? It's been a month since you got back."

Ethan shifted in his seat. The judge never avoided sticky subjects—just dove right in without apology. "Been busy."

"Bullcrap. You've been avoiding us because it's easier. Easier to ignore us and pretend nothing ever happened. That you didn't go away and get hurt and come back changed. But you're also not allowing us to claim you as ours, and even though it's been years, you belong to this town, Ethan Bishop. The faster you realize it, the better things will be."

Shock rippled through Ethan. The words hit home, but the judge didn't even bother to look up. Just kept reading his paper and continued speaking.

"Do you remember when you damaged the stone wall at the college during an evening of debauchery with your friends?"

Ethan bit back a groan. "How could I forget? You made Kyle and me scrub the stone wall with small specialty brushes. It took us over four hours to get it clean."

"You never damaged another item in this town, though, did you?"
He sighed. "No."

"Chloe Lake needs to feel needed. There's something she's hiding about the crime, too. Maybe you can get it out of her."

"I'm not a child therapist. I'm just here to oversee her work so she can return to school and I can get back to my life."

The judge nodded. "A worthy goal. Just not very honest."

Ethan refused to touch the comment. It stung too much. "You won't change your mind?"

"No. You need to contact Lacey Black. She'd like to invite you to dinner so she can introduce you to someone."

"Yeah, I heard. I'm not interested in being set up with anyone right now."

"Understood. But it would be nice if you called her anyway."

The man turned back to his paper, and the table fell silent. Ethan finished his omelet, all hopes of shedding himself of Mia Thrush vanishing as quickly as a man the morning after a one-night stand.

Hopefully, he scared her enough yesterday. Hopefully, she'd be happy enough locked up at the inn and content to stay away from his rude, boorish behavior.

Hopefully.

Mia pushed her laptop away and stared out the window. This was her third day at the inn. So far, she'd logged in countless hours of work in her air-conditioned room and, with the aid of Gabby, had all her current clients under control. There were no crises, scandals, or dramatic interludes to fix. She checked in with Jonathan daily and was able to report Chloe was doing well. She disappeared at nine a.m. to go to the stables, worked all day, and arrived back at the inn around four. She retired to her room until about six, and then Mia took her to eat somewhere in town. They made strained conversation, then returned to their separate rooms. Mia worked some more in between bouts of television, went to bed, and started all over.

She was bored out of her frikkin' mind.

Everything was too quiet. Too peaceful. Too . . . perfect. It was like being trapped in a robotic Stepford-land where nothing could be real. The colors were bright, the air was sweet, and even the sounds of birds chirping and horses softly neighing added to the mystical element of falseness. Ophelia was always cheerful, giving her helpful information and running the inn with ruthless organization. Mia had stayed far away from the guests, choosing to eat breakfast in her room instead of the packed porch, and only ventured out when everyone had scattered for the day to engage in various activities.

She hated it here.

Groaning, she covered her face with her hands and wondered what she should do. She'd go stark-raving insane if she had to spend eight more weeks doing this. Her business was usually full of chaos and activity, but summer was definitely a downtime, and it seemed her clients had retired to laze away on vacation and not cause any issues. No one had leaked the news about Chloe. Other than a few appearances, the summer was clear for Lake, and most of the craziness wouldn't begin before fall. Add her awful insomnia problem, and she'd go mental. Her dad had diagnosed her as high strung, but it was only the past few years that her failure to sleep had reached epic proportions. At least in Manhattan, she always had a place to go. She'd walk by the bagel place at four a.m. just to smell the scent of carbs. Hit the all-night gym for a good workout. There were endless possibilities to help her not think about how she never slept. But here?

Nothing but silence. Who was the idiot who said silence was golden? It certainly didn't help her sleep. And she had no place to go but the front porch.

What if she was stuck doing nothing all summer trapped in la la land?

She had to get out of here.

Decision made, she freshened up her makeup, donned her favorite camel-colored Ugg sandals, and headed into town. She'd explore a bit and pick up some groceries. She'd been living on fruit, Greek yogurt, and tuna, portioning out her meals. She'd managed to drop another pound and a half, which was a huge success, even though she was hungry and regularly cranky.

At least she'd be able to order that new Gucci dress now.

She climbed into her Kia and headed into town, turning right and deciding to do a drive-by before parking and exploring on foot. The standard Main Street was small but had a quirky, artsy type atmosphere she appreciated. Indie bookstores, yoga-and-art studios, cafés, and various restaurants adjoined the uneven sidewalks. There were at least three college bars, one boasting a nightclub, and a tattoo parlor that looked deserted. She wondered how many people got tats after getting drunk. It was a good location but looked kind of seedy.

She'd always wanted one, but it seemed too reckless. Too permanent. Too *bad girl*.

Now, she was too old.

Tamping down a regretful sigh, she parked the car and took her time investigating the town. She bought a skinny vanilla latte in the organic coffee shop and had to admit it was better than any Starbucks she'd ever had. There was a diner, movie theater, and a few standard stores, including a supermarket, hardware, and pharmacy. The boutiques were filled with cotton blends, vintage designs, and yoga wear. Cute, but nothing she'd buy.

The real problem was the sweets.

Mia had never seen so many shops dedicated to sugar. There was the bakery that tempted her with scents of fresh bread and pastries. Then there was the chocolate shop, filled to the brim with truffles, chocolate-covered pretzels, chocolate-dipped gourmet apples and strawberries, and dozens of other items meant to drive women with PMS mad with lust.

But Mia surmised the worst of the worst were the ice-cream shops. Every person walking down the streets seemed to be holding an ice-cream cone. Her body shuddered with longing, and her stomach growled in protest. What was wrong with this town? How could they offer vegan specialties and organic coffee on the same block as candy, ice cream, and cookies?

By the time she'd finished exploring, she was in a bad mood. Maybe she'd stop at one of the cafés and surprise Chloe with lunch. She was due a few more calories before dinner, right? Even Gucci would allow a little bit more.

She pushed her way into the Market Food Pantry and browsed the aisles, more and more impressed with what New Paltz had accomplished in the food industry. It rivaled Whole Foods in many ways, from the packed deli and fruit-and-produce aisles, to the assortment of homemade soups and salads for lunch hours. She filled her basket to take home to the inn and wondered why the store was empty. It was prime time, and no one seemed to be here.

Did everyone eat ice cream for lunch here instead? Did people magically not gain any weight in this town?

She picked out a vegetable soup with miso broth, a kale salad, and organic balsamic vinaigrette dressing. When she came to the prepared food aisle, she gasped.

It was perfection.

Fresh salads with grilled Japanese eggplants, mashed sweet potatoes, perfectly rare tuna with wasabi and peppercorns, chilled jumbo shrimp with homemade horseradish cocktail sauce, quinoa with cranberry and walnuts—the list was endless. Each was beautifully labeled, calories counted, and available in various sizes.

"Welcome to the Market," a cheerful voice greeted. "We have free samples for you to enjoy. Is there anything specific I can help you with today?"

The woman had tight, curly brown hair, as if it had been permed too many times and had finally surrendered. She wore jeans, a hunter-green shirt with the Market logo, and no jewelry. Her dark eyes looked weary, but her smile was genuine. Mia noticed that her name tag pegged her as MANAGER.

"Your store is amazing," she said genuinely. "So much better than Whole Foods."

And then it happened.

The woman's lip began to tremble. Her chin quivered. In horror, Mia watched the manager struggle for about half a minute until she surrendered fully to the emotional experience.

She burst into tears.

Mia swallowed hard and took a step back. Her New Yorker instincts told her to run and let this woman handle herself, but her heart softened at the outpouring of real emotion she rarely saw in her daily routine. Emotion was the first thing to go in the PR business. Mia lost her ability to cry or grieve a long time ago. This woman still had a chance.

"I'm so sorry, are you okay?" she asked gently.

The woman grabbed a tissue from her pocket and wiped her eyes. She wasn't a pretty crier, either. Her nose swelled and turned red, and her eyes dripped messy tears, not the dainty trickle, like in the movies. "No, I'm sorry!" she wailed. "I just don't understand! I did all the research, poured every last dollar into this endeavor, yet people won't shop here. They're still traveling half an hour to go shop at the other places! What have I done wrong?"

Mia bit her lip. "Umm, when did you open?"

The woman gave a big, messy sniff. "Over a month ago. We had traffic the first few days, then nothing. It's like we don't exist. They'll go to the café and the farmers' market and the diner, but no one comes here. Are you from out of town?"

"Yes, I am."

The woman cried harder. "That's what I thought! I'll never make this business run on the occasional out-of-towners. I can't figure it out. I haven't slept with anyone or made Sylvia Daniels mad at me or picked a fight with Darla from bingo. I've done nothing!"

Mia looked frantically around for help, but there was no one there. "Umm, maybe it's just going to take some time to catch on. With good referrals and a solid landing page on Yelp, maybe you can pull in more traffic from the surrounding areas."

The woman mopped her face with a tissue. "Maybe. I'm sorry, this isn't your problem. What's Yelp?"

Mia blinked. "Yelp. On the internet. It's a reviewer service where people rate stores, hotels, shops, etc. You should be on it."

"Okay, I'll look it up tonight."

Mia shook her head, wondering what owner in her right mind didn't know about Yelp. This town was definitely strange. "Great. I'm sure things will pick up. I think it's a lovely store."

The woman beamed. "Thank you. I'm Fran. What's your name? Where are you staying? What are you doing in town?"

"Mia. I'm over at the Robin's Nest B & B in Gardiner for vacation with my niece." The lie rolled off her tongue gracefully. "Taking some time away from the city."

"How wonderful! Ophelia will take good care of you. And now that Ethan's back, I bet the horseback-riding lessons will pick up again. He's a true horse whisperer, and we're thrilled to have him back."

Back? Hmm, maybe this was an opportunity to get the dirt. "Yes, I bet. He was away a long time, right? About—"

"Eight years. Came home for his mama's funeral, then left shortly after that. 'Course he always had big dreams. Never wanted to run the inn or farm like his sisters. How's his leg doing?"

She tilted her head. *Interesting.* She'd suspected he walked a bit differently, as if favoring one leg over the other, but she'd been too distracted by his other annoying qualities. "Better." Mia buried her guilt and pushed on. "Shame what happened, huh?"

Fran's face lost all traces of animation. Her brown eyes filled with a dark emotion and . . . sympathy? Pity? For annoying horse man? Even her voice changed to a seriousness that made goose bumps prickle on her skin. "It's a tragedy. After everything Ethan's gone through, he didn't deserve this. I hope he can find some peace at home. Now, let me stop my babbling and check you out. Anything else?"

She went on pure impulse and decided to surprise Chloe with lunch. And Ethan. Maybe she should make an effort. Move past their difficult first meeting. She'd be the better person. "Actually, can you pack up a platter of turkey wraps, hummus with veggies, and the sweet potato mash? I'll need silverware and napkins, too."

"Of course! Oh, I hope you like it. Please come back and let me know."

"I will."

Mia left the Market with a lighter step. It was nice to talk to another person in town and get a bit more on the mysterious Ethan. Had he been in a bad car accident? It was the only scenario that made sense. Had he been at another farm and decided to come back home? No, that wouldn't make sense. Maybe he had gotten another job and decided to leave after he hurt his leg.

The idea of such an arrogant, powerful man hiding a physical weakness bothered her. Imagining him in pain made her stomach feel funny. Even though he pissed her off, she didn't like the idea of him hurting or dealing with the aftereffects of a bad experience. She'd had a client once who'd been in the hospital for weeks after a car wreck, and he had terrible nightmares for months.

Why was that familiar deep clanging in her gut warning her of a mistruth? Like she was missing something big. Something more than a car crash.

She had to dig further and find out. For now, she'd bring lunch as a peace offering and see if they could be civil.

Mia drove back to the inn, reapplied a healthy amount of sunscreen to her face and a spritz of bug spray, and took the path toward the horse barn. She walked slow so she wouldn't trip, taking a deep breath of fresh air. Her lungs tried to rebel, but she forced more in. Maybe this wasn't so bad. All that smoke and smog and city sweat had to have a long-term effect on her health. By the end of summer, it'd be like returning from fat camp.

The woods broke away to reveal the red barns against the magnificence of green hills and mighty mountains. Horses grazed over the land, and the hum of chatter drifted in the breeze. She walked into the barn, following the human voices, and found Chloe and John in the barn.

They were both squeezed into a stall with a gigantic black horse. John was giving directions as Chloe rubbed a brush over the horse in circular motions. The horse's head lifted at Mia's interruption, and he or she snorted, studying her briefly before turning away in pure dismissal. Guess Wheezy was the only one who liked her around here. Who would've thought animals could be so high maintenance? Mia moved closer and cleared her throat.

They both turned toward her. "Hi, Mia," Chloe called out. "John's showing me how to groom the horses."

Her black-lipped smile seemed genuine. Mia smiled back, happy the girl appeared to like her servitude and wasn't miserable. She had even begun wearing full pants instead of Daisy Duke shorts. "I don't mean to interrupt, but I brought lunch for everyone. Are you allowed to take a break?"

John grabbed a rag, wiping his fingers. "I think we can manage a break," he said with a grin. "Ethan's out in the back; I'll let him know. Chloe, why don't you grab Sam from the fields and have him join us, too."

"Got it." She gave the horse a pat on the rear, put the brush down, and stepped out of the stall. Her purple hair was knotted and damp with sweat. Her shirt and jeans were covered in dirt, and her makeup had smudged over her face from the heat.

But she looked . . . happy.

Mia's curiosity peaked. She'd bet that after a few days, the girl would be miserable doing manual labor, but it seemed she was embracing the change.

"I'll be right back," John said. "Hey, Mia, why don't you feed Clarabelle a carrot while we're gone? She deserves a treat."

Her eyes widened. "Umm, I don't know."

His brown eyes twinkled. "There's nothing to it. Just offer her the carrot, and she'll take it. Not scary at all."

Clarabelle turned her massive head and waited. Did she understand the word *carrot*? Didn't seem like a big deal. It might be a good idea to get a bit more comfortable around the horses. John and Chloe disappeared, leaving her alone in the barn. Ignoring her rapidly pounding heart, Mia reached down and took a carrot from the bag.

Clarabelle moved closer to the slots in the stall, pushing her nose out, sniffing wildly. She could do this. It was just a carrot. Dragging in a breath, she offered the carrot out, holding the very end so she wouldn't have to get near any lips or teeth or tongue.

Clarabelle opened her mouth, grabbed the carrot, and took a bite. Her teeth crunched through the treat, and Mia practically laughed with the thrill of victory. She'd done it! Clarabelle reached for it again, but this time, she tugged hard, as if trying to swallow the whole thing. Mia's fingers grabbed for purchase around the slippery vegetable, and the carrot fell to the ground.

Clarabelle regarded her with pure irritation.

Mia stared back. "Umm, aren't you going to pick it up from the ground and finish it?"

Clarabelle gave a disgusted snort and pawed the ground.

Mia peered through the slots. The carrot had fallen close to the door. Did horses refuse to eat fallen vegetables? She looked around, but the barn was devoid of humans. Maybe she could just open the door, grab the carrot, and give it back to her?

Irritated by her fear of a silly horse, she set the lunch bags down on the bench and grabbed the latch to the gate. Pulling upward, the door swung a few inches open, and she reached down for the carrot.

Clarabelle nipped at her hair.

With a shriek, Mia fell back, and the door swung completely open. "Hey, no touching!" she scolded. "I'm trying to get you the stupid carrot!"

Clarabelle ignored her and began walking forward.

"What are you doing? Go back. Go back now."

With a swish of her tail, Clarabelle clomped calmly out of her stall and right past her, heading for the open acres behind the barn.

Uh-oh.

Mia blinked, watching the horse disappear around the corner, and knew she'd done something very, very wrong.

"Heard you brought us lunch."

The voice was a twist of sand and silk. Ethan walked into the barn with Chloe at his side. He looked half rugged cowboy, half Grizzly Adams. That massive ginger beard hugged a pair of sensual lips, but it was the only soft spot about him. Every muscled inch looked lean and mean, evident under the snug blue T-shirt and worn jeans that lovingly cupped his powerful thighs. His gaze matched his hard features as he studied her, like he was assessing her intentions of bringing lunch. Did he think she was going to poison him or something?

"Yes. Thought I'd be nice and treat you, since I came from town."

"I'll set it up on the picnic table," he said. "Do we need plates or silverware?"

"No, it's all in the bag. I think I should tell you something."

"You can tell me while we eat; I'm starving." He regarded her with grudging appreciation. "This was really nice of you."

"No problem. Umm, Ethan, there was a bit of an incident."

"Let's go, Chloe. You finished brushing all the horses, right?"

"Yes, Clarabelle was the last one and—" Chloe stared at the empty barn. "Wait, where is she?"

Ethan paused midstride. "Did John take her?"

"No, I'm here, boss," John said behind him. "She's in her stall."

"No, she's not."

"Yes, she is. Mia was going to feed her carrots."

Mia bit her lip as three pairs of eyes turned toward her. *Ah, crap.* "And I did. But I kind of dropped the carrot, so I had to open the door to get it, and then she kind of—well, she kind of walked off."

Ethan's jaw clenched. "What? Where did she go?"

Mia pointed toward the back fields. "Out there."

Ethan muttered something under his breath and stomped past her. "Why didn't you call someone?"

"It happened so fast. I'm sure she's not far." They raced to the edge of the barn and surveyed the fields. "Maybe she's eating hay. Or visiting a friend."

Ethan cut her a withering glance. "No, she's a runner, and these fields aren't fenced in. They lead to the horseback-riding trails."

"Is that bad?"

"It's over fifty acres of property, and she could be anywhere. You do the math." He turned and motioned toward John. "Let's head out and see if she's on the south side. Grab Sam, too. Chloe, go eat and wait for me to get back."

"Ethan, I'm—"

Suddenly, he leaned in. She stared, fascinated by the heat in his stinging blue eyes, the clench of his jaw, the flare of his nostrils. The scent of sweat and musk and horses swirled around her in an almost animalistic energy. Feet rooted to the floor, she could only wait for him to speak.

"I knew you'd be trouble. Five minutes and you've already cost me valuable time and lost my horse. Don't you have any respect at all for the work we do around here?"

Her mouth fell open. "I just wanted to get the carrot!"

"And I told you to do one thing: stay out of my barn. This isn't a petting zoo or a place you can amuse yourself when you're bored. Do us all a favor next time and get a manicure instead."

Her head began to swivel in pure rage. "Are you kidding me?"

"Trust me, princess. I'm not kidding anyone. From now on, there's one rule around here, and it's sacred, so I'll repeat it." His gaze pinned hers, full of masculine temper and a primitive energy that whipped around him. "Stay out of my barn."

He marched past her, barking out orders, and within minutes, he'd mounted a pretty black horse and took off down the trail without a backward glance.

How dare he? It had been a genuine mistake, and she'd even tried to apologize. But this man couldn't care less about good intentions or peace offerings. He'd truly shown his black soul, and she refused to spend another minute in his company ever again.

She'd die before she spoke another word to him.

D-I-E.

"He's protective over the horses," Chloe finally said, breaking the awkward silence. "I could've made the same mistake. It's not your fault."

Mia nodded, grateful for the support. It was the first nice thing the girl had offered her. "Thanks. But if he ever speaks like that to you, tell me. I'll kill him myself."

The girl shrugged. "He's super nice to me. But you guys have been fighting since you met. Maybe you should just stay out of each other's way?"

Mia sighed. "I've come to the same conclusion. Come on, let's go eat some lunch."

They ate. Instead of her usual silence, Chloe opened up and chattered about what she was learning about horses and the rescue efforts at the barn. Mia realized if she kept the topics away from Chloe's father, her friends, her future, or her past, she was in the safe zone.

Mia made a mental note to focus on horses.

Ethan still wasn't back after lunch, so she left the men their share, cleaned up the garbage, and headed back to the inn. Maybe she'd take a nap. Or play Candy Crush. Or check up on all her clients' social media pages to make sure she wasn't missing anything. At a time she was ready and willing to dive into the glorious mess of work, no one needed her.

She'd make sure she did one thing, though.

She intended to tell Ethan Bishop exactly what she thought of his unacceptable behavior. She'd made an honest mistake, and that was no way to talk to a paying guest. If she were a tattletale, she'd march right up to Ophelia and complain. What if she wrote them a bad review? That would teach him.

Still fuming, Mia counted down the hours until she could pounce.

Chapter Seven

Ethan got Clarabelle situated back in her stall and grabbed a water bottle. He guzzled half and poured the rest over his head. It was a scorcher today, and he was a walking sweat bomb. He craved a cold shower and even colder beer. In his bungalow. Alone.

Harper stuck her head in the barn. "Dinner tonight at the inn. Seven thirty. Heard you had a runaway."

He glowered. "Not tonight, but thanks. And our runaway was caused by the duchess of the manor, who probably found some way to twist the incident so I'm at fault."

"Hmm, a woman who doesn't like you? That's kind of historic. Are your boxers in a twist?"

He glared. "Hardly. She's not my type anyway."

She snorted. "Convenient. How's the parolee doing?"

"Not bad," he said grudgingly. "She listens. Her aunt is the bigger pain in the ass."

"Oh yeah, you like her." Her hooted laughter aggravated Ethan like he was twelve again. "And you're coming to dinner. Ophelia's cooking and I don't want to be the one stuck with the dishes this time. You've been making excuses for too long."

He groaned and rubbed his head. "I just want a beer and to not have to talk to anyone."

"You can have two beers, and we won't force you to talk. Just grunt. It goes with your new look."

"The beard again? Fine, I'll shave it. It's getting too hot anyway."

"Thank God. I'll tell Ophelia you're looking forward to it." His sister disappeared, leaving him in an even fouler mood. His knee throbbed like a bitch from pushing himself. He made a note to schedule an extra PT session this week. Since he'd been back in the barn, his leg was being used in a new way, and his body was still adjusting. Maybe he'd go crazy and take an Advil with a beer. Even at the worst of the agony after the operation, he refused meds. Better to get used to the level of pain that was natural in his body and learn to live with it. Too many poor schmucks got addicted to that feeling of pain-free happiness from a bottle. He'd termed it the *fake zone*. He may be grumpy, but at least he was real.

It was the last thing he had left to cling to.

He took his time walking back to the bungalow, babying the leg a bit, and thought over the past few days with his new charge. It was weird, but he was beginning to enjoy her company. Chloe was willing to learn and didn't complain, even when he asked her to shovel manure from the main path. Of course, it was still only three days. Maybe the novelty would wear off, and she'd get bored. Still, she seemed genuinely sweet and helpful around the farm, almost as if she enjoyed helping out and being part of a team. She hadn't copped an attitude, and she seemed excited about learning how to ride. Maybe she'd just hit a bad patch in college and acted out on impulse. Ethan had seen plenty of grown men who screwed up when pushed but then made it right. He respected that type of character. Maybe Chloe had it, too.

Wheezy bounded out of the woods and fell into step with him. The trees bent forward in protection against the sting of the sun. A squirrel scrambled across the path, holding a large nut. The wind stirred the sweet summer air. An inner peace slowly unfolded, fleeting as a bird's cry, but for a few precious moments, he savored the silence both inside and out.

Until he saw Mia Thrush waiting on his step.

A cloud of purpose practically floated around her. Still clad in those high-heeled sandals, a pair of white capris, and some lacy-type shirt, she looked like she should be yachting. She wore stacks of silver bracelets on her wrist, and diamond studs winked from her ears. Her arms were clasped in front of her chest while she tapped her foot with pure impatience, as if he were running late for their appointment. She caught sight of him, and those golden tigress eyes widened, taking in his disheveled appearance. Wheezy wasted no time in trotting over to give her some adoring kisses. Seemed dogs were the only animals she was safe to be around. She patted Wheezy with genuine affection, not seeming to care if he ruined her freshly pressed slacks. Ethan stopped a few feet away and narrowed his gaze. "What are you doing here?"

She steeled her shoulders, emphasizing the thrust of her pert breasts and her tiny waist, then had the gall to give him the stink eye. "I'm here for an apology."

A bark of laughter escaped his lips. *Damn, she had spunk.* "Let me get this straight. You come into my barn without permission, let a horse out of its stall, watch her disappear, and now *you* want an apology from *me?*"

"Yes."

"Princess, I have plenty of things to say to you, but none of them include an apology."

"I brought you lunch as a peace offering. I was trying to meet you halfway since we're neighbors. I was trying to be nice!"

"I never got to eat my lunch because it took me hours to find Clarabelle. I had to scour those damn woods and waste my entire afternoon because you dropped a carrot. Thank God she wasn't hurt and I was able to get her back safely."

This was the second time she began nibbling her lip—a definite tell when she felt guilty about something. "I tried to explain and apologize, but you got all boorish and started yelling to get out of your barn."

"I never yell. I told you very quietly to leave the barn."

"In a threatening tone."

He shook his head. "I bet you're an excellent PR person."

She looked surprised at the change of subject. "Thank you, I feel like I am. I do work hard."

"You're very good at twisting everything around like a pretzel. Bending the truth to suit your needs. No wonder Lake hired you."

Those Bambi eyes simmered with temper. "You think you're hot shit, with your beard and your sexy body and your fake cowboy drawl, but you're just mean! You pretend to be this broody loner type because you had an accident and hurt your leg. Big frikkin' deal. That doesn't give you a right to be cranky to everyone you meet."

His mouth practically dropped open. "What do you know about my leg?" he asked in a warning voice.

She didn't seem intimidated at all. In fact, she had the nerve to toss her mane of honey hair and come closer. "Car accident, right? I spoke to someone in town. Seems the consensus is you got hurt, left your previous job, and came home. You proceeded to lock yourself in some sad little bungalow and now refuse to come out. How am I doing so far?"

His head spun. Red mist shrouded his vision. Oh, she needed to learn some manners, and he was just the type to teach her. "You know nothing about what happened to me," he said softly. "Your entire career revolves around manipulating the truth. Let me ask you this, princess: Have you ever gotten real before? Do you even know what it is?"

She bared her teeth and gave a throaty growl. The sound was almost sexual and registered below his waist. Thank fuck he was too pissed off to care. "I can get real, anytime, anyplace, horse man. I'm not afraid to answer any question with the truth, and your cheap shots about my career are just that. Cheap. You know nothing about the people I try to protect or what I stand for."

"Any question, huh?"

They were close now. The scent of her perfume surrounded him—some type of exotic orange spice. Her lashes were thick and dark. Her lips were pursed with a furious focus, painted the color of pale apple cider. She had a dab of white sunscreen on her nose she'd forgotten to rub in and some type of shimmery gold shadow under her arched brows. She was infuriating and silly, and for one brief, horrifying moment, Ethan wanted to kiss her.

"Yes, any question," she snarled back.

Too bad the woman would break under one good passionate kiss, or else he'd be tempted to play a mean game of chicken to see who would retreat first.

Too bad she was already sleeping with Lake.

Instead, he leaned in and gave a slow, mocking smile. "You really think I'm sexy, huh?"

She jerked back, eyes wide with horror. "You are pure evil," she whispered.

Ethan chuckled. "Your secret is safe with me, princess. Anytime you wanna get real, give me a ring."

A shriek emitted from her lips. She stomped around him in those towering heels. "I will never, ever bring you lunch again!"

Suddenly, Hei Hei came racing around the corner, screeching in response to the noise. He stopped short when he spotted Mia, his crazy head feathers bobbing in mad glee, then tore off in pursuit. Ethan opened his mouth to stop the suicidal chicken, but she faced down her nemesis, bending over to get in the chicken's face, jabbing a finger wildly in the air.

"And you! I will not allow you to intimidate me, either, so unless you want to end up on the barbeque, back off!"

Hei Hei stopped short and stared at her with mute fascination.

With one last glare, Mia stalked off down the path.

Ethan looked at Hei Hei. "I think we really pissed her off," he offered. "Maybe you should give her some space before you try to make friends again."

With one last wild cluck, the chicken took off after her like a scorned lover on the path to redemption.

Ethan shook his head. "I warned him," he muttered. Then he headed inside to shower and change for dinner, wondering what strange spell Mia Thrush had cast that made him want to kiss her even for a moment.

Chapter Eight

"Mia, I'd like you and Chloe to join me for dinner tonight."

Still seething from her encounter, Mia blinked, as if coming out of a trance. She stood in the hallway before the staircase. "Dinner?"

Ophelia smiled. "Yes, since you're staying the whole summer, it would be nice to get to know one another better. I'd also like to give you a homemade meal. It can't be easy to eat out every night. All the other guests are out on their own, so it will be low key."

Mia hesitated. She wasn't up for a bunch of polite chitchat, but Ophelia seemed genuinely excited about the invitation. And Mia did like the woman's company. Maybe it would be good for her and Chloe to have a normal evening over a meal. She'd been isolating herself too much. "I'd love to."

"Wonderful! I'll meet you in the back dining room in an hour."

Mia went upstairs, informed Chloe of their plans, and began to freshen up. She needed to get Ethan out of her head and move on. She'd stay far away from that horse barn of his and keep contact to a minimum. The image of him towering over her flashed in her mind. Something strange had passed between them for a few seconds—a weird sexual attraction that was as horrifying as it was surprising. Probably the heat of her anger and a rush of adrenaline. A groan escaped her lips. Why, oh why had she slipped and said he had a sexy body? So. Embarrassing. And maybe his body was slamming, but his personality sucked, and that beard was out of control. Plus he was a ginger! She was not attracted to redheads at all. Even though he kind of reminded her of Michael Fassbender with that intriguing Irish flavor.

It was time to admit the real problem.

It had been way too long since she'd had a man in her life. She was used to polite, civilized men in custom suits that smelled of expensive bottled musk and made promises they'd never keep. She knew about smooth smiles and pretty words that hid true intentions. She lived in that world and memorized every hidden nook and cranny. She'd fallen in love or lust twice and realized the moment they'd lied when they told her she was the only one. Her gift to sniff out deceit and falsities served her well in the cutthroat world of politics, but it had eradicated her trust in her own heart. Twice, she'd been cheated on and had been unable to steep herself in denial. Twice, she'd thrown the bastards out the front door.

Unfortunately, the memory of their betrayal stayed and did a job on her confidence. Deep inside, she wondered if there was something wrong with her. Why would both men cheat so easily? In both of her relationships, they'd never even been challenged with hard times. Was she a woman who didn't inspire a man to stick around?

She despised such weak beliefs about herself, but they still came like clockwork in the dead of night, keeping her from sleep, driving her crazy.

It was easier to concentrate on her job, go out with friends, and have fun in the city's playground. There was always something to do to keep her body and mind active.

Here? Not so much.

Which must be why she experienced that flicker of heat with a man she didn't like.

Dear God, she hadn't even brought her vibrator.

Irritated from her spinning thoughts, she knocked on Chloe's door, and they headed downstairs to the dining area. It was situated across from the main room, where guests ate breakfast, and was decorated in a more intimate, casual feel. The table was carved pine, with thick, sturdy chairs, and painted in a warm Tuscan gold. Vases full of fresh flowers were situated around the room. A gorgeous wine rack in scrolled iron climbed up the corner of the wall, holding an impressive number of bottles. Framed pictures hung on the walls and filled the sideboard countertops. One wall was taken up with an elaborate photo collage that said FAMILY. Mia wandered over and studied the pictures: A beautiful woman with long, red hair laughed into the camera, hugging two girls and a boy. A magnificent horse was in the background, looking into the camera as if annoyed he wasn't asked to formally join the shoot.

Ophelia came in and dropped a large steaming bowl onto the hot plate. "That's my mom," she said, pointing at the laughing woman. "Me, Harper, and Ethan."

"You look so happy," Mia said. She remembered Fran's comment about the funeral. "When did your mom pass?"

"A few years ago. Cancer."

Like Chloe's mom. "I'm sorry," she said.

"Better to see her out of pain. But you're right, we were pretty happy. Growing up on a farm is an amazing experience as a kid."

"Who's the horse?" Chloe asked curiously.

"Patricia's Prince," Ophelia said. "My mom's horse. It was our first real rescue situation that began the whole idea of a farm."

A dark-haired, long-legged woman strolled in and jumped into the conversation. "Mom was at this farm, and she caught sight of a horse chained outside, bucking and kicking. When she asked about him, the owner said he was trouble and would be put on the next truck to the slaughterhouse. The horse was scrawny, mean, and refused to get close to anyone. Mom freaked out and asked to buy him. The guy laughed and made fun of her, but took the money."

Ophelia took up the thread, her face animated. "So Mom manages to get the horse home—we had only one barn back then—and begins to spend all this time outside his stall, talking to him. Eventually, he stopped going nuts when she came over and let her lead him outside to the paddock. Every two hours, she'd approach the horse and try to get him to take an apple from her hand. Each time, he'd throw a tantrum and run away."

Chloe widened her eyes. "What happened?"

Ophelia continued. "One day, she walked over and extended the treat. The horse regarded her for a long time, Mom said they stared at each other forever, and then he slowly went up and began eating the apple. Mom stroked his head and said, 'Now, no more silliness. You're safe here, and I'll never make you be someone you're not.' After that, he'd do anything for her. Even went on to the racing circuit for a while and brought in some serious cash. Mom decided we should build more barns and create a safe place to help more horses. She had one motto."

"What?" Mia asked curiously.

The masculine voice cut through the room. "'Every soul—both animal and human—deserves a worthy life.'"

A short silence settled in the room. Mia's heart squeezed at the beautiful words. "Sounds like your mother was the worthiest of all."

Her gaze crashed with pale-blue eyes. A mixture of emotions swirled in their depths, then quickly vanished to polite distance. She cleared her throat and took a step back. Dammit, now she was stuck conversing with her mortal enemy over the dinner table. If she'd known Ethan would be here, she would've declined the invite. She was almost tempted to make an excuse and leave. Almost.

But she refused to let the jerk win.

She'd just ignore him.

Ethan walked over to Ophelia and gave her an affectionate kiss on the top of her head. "Thanks for cooking, Tink."

"Ugh, I said not to call me that."

"Sorry." He grinned and tugged at her hair, confirming he definitely wasn't sorry. Ophelia swatted his arm away, but she was smiling. Mia was struck by their easy, intimate relationship. He seemed so much more open around his sister. Even sort of . . . nice.

The dark-haired woman stuck out her hand. She was dressed casually in a powder-blue T-shirt, jeans, and work boots. Her face held strong, sharp lines similar to her brother's, and her blue eyes were a few shades darker. She had a no-nonsense demeanor. "I'm Harper; I don't think we've met. I handle the rescue portion of the farm and the riding."

"Mia Thrush. Nice to meet you."

Harper turned to Chloe. "Heard you're impressing Ethan. Keep up the good work. We're happy to have you."

"Thanks. I like learning about the horses." Mia noticed the teen's shoulders straightened, as if she took pride in Harper's compliment.

"Ethan said you wanted to learn to ride. How about we squeeze in a lesson next week?"

"Sweet!"

Mia turned to Ophelia. "Can I help with dinner?"

She waved a graceful hand in the air. Her pretty yellow apron contrasted with her strawberry-gold hair and gave her an almost ethereal presence. "It's all done. Ethan, can you crack open a bottle of wine. Red or white, Mia?"

"I like both."

Ethan grabbed a pinot noir and walked over to the sideboard. Ophelia set out a pitcher of sweet tea and filled a glass for Chloe. The table was filled with various dishes that made Mia's stomach jump up and down in anticipation. The salad and hummus for lunch hadn't gone as far as she liked. But this? This was insanity.

A platter of moist turkey with a boat of rich gravy sat before her. She took in the biscuits that looked moist and flaky and a bowl of crisp green beans with almonds. The tempting rich scents rose up to her nostrils and begged her to succumb.

Everyone sat down and began passing around the platters. Mia scooped a few precious spoonfuls onto her plate, mournfully gazing at the biscuits practically calling out to her. No carbs. Anything but the carbs. One biscuit could be deadly and lead to another.

"So, Chloe, what are you studying in school?" Ophelia asked, slathering butter on a biscuit and pouring a trickle of gravy over it. Mia cut her turkey into tiny pieces to make them last longer.

"Psychology."

"Do you like it?"

The teen shrugged. "I'm stuck taking a bunch of other classes before I can take the real core courses."

Harper laughed. "Boy, do I remember that. Art history, algebra, biology, theater, sociology, all the things you'll never need to know for a real job." Chloe smiled back. "But I have to admit I liked being pushed a bit. Learning things keep you from being boring and lame."

"True," Ophelia agreed. "I despised Shakespeare until I took a class in college. The professor was able to relate the writing in relevant ways, and suddenly, a light bulb clicked on for me. After that, I had a new appreciation for more literature."

Chloe hesitated. "Well, I wish sometimes I could just focus on stuff like that, but I'm usually too worried about my grades."

"Scholarship?" Ethan asked.

"No, I just—I just need *A*s." A touch of frustration radiated from her figure. She dragged her fork across her plate. "Most of the stuff I'm good at, but I had to take this biology course to fit into my schedule, and it was harder than I thought. The drop date passed, so I got stuck. Then the professor didn't offer me any opportunities for extra credit or help."

Mia regarded the girl thoughtfully. Ah, that was the class where she cheated on the exam. She seemed quite focused on *A*s. Was she under extreme pressure to perform and panicked? Did Jonathan expect perfect grades? She made a mental note to dig further later.

Ethan nodded. "I get it. My nemesis was English. No professor was ever able to change my opinion on Shakespeare. I think Shakespeare sucks, and my grades proved it."

Mia smothered a smile. "I despise Jane Austen novels," she admitted.

Ophelia gasped. "Impossible. I don't think I've ever met a woman who wasn't in love with Austen. Even Harper swooned over *Pride and Prejudice*."

"I don't swoon over anything," Harper said. "But Austen is a great writer."

Mia wrinkled her nose. "Sorry, she's way too subtle for me. It's exhausting."

Ethan's deep laugh brought both surprise and a rush of warmth that flowed through her veins. Most of the time he looked like he wanted to strangle her. It was odd to think he may actually have a sense of humor.

Harper sighed. "Well, college isn't easy, and I'm sure you're sick of everyone always telling you to enjoy the best times of your life. First, it's high school, then college, then dating, then motherhood. There's always an opinion on when you should be happy. Then you feel guilty and ungrateful for not being happy. Sometimes it just is what it is, and that should be okay."

Chloe stared at Harper as if her brain had finally clicked on an important answer. "Yeah. That's how I feel a lot. Like everyone has these expectations for me to be a certain way."

"Once you start just accepting what it is you really want, things get a bit easier."

"Deep thoughts, Harp. We're all impressed."

"Screw you, Ethan."

Everyone laughed. Plates were passed around for second helpings. Mia took a few more greens and savored the saltiness of the almonds, the clean snap against her teeth, the sweetness of the bean.

"Tell us about your job, Mia," Ophelia prompted.

"I own a public relations firm, Strategy Solutions. Basically I help clients with their careers by handling social media accounts, news stories, events, and anything else that crops up. I have sports celebrities, a singer, and politicians as clients." She glanced at Chloe, keeping quiet about her father and hoping Ethan would respect the girl's privacy. Not that she didn't trust Harper and Ophelia. It was just easier to keep the relationship under wraps in case any news was leaked to the guests, even in an innocent manner. She'd learned firsthand how fast gossip could spread and ruin anyone in its path just to sell a few magazines and feed the ravenous public appetite for drama.

"Sounds exciting," Harper said. "What made you get into that field?"

She focused on her plate, trying not to stiffen up. "I believe everyone needs some help reaching their goals. In the age of the internet, with alternative facts and social media trolls, sometimes a PR representative can make a huge difference."

"Even if they have to lie?"

Ethan's direct question held an undercurrent of judgment. She kept her voice cool and impersonal. "I don't lie." She challenged him with her gaze. "In fact, I have a gift. I can spot a lie from anyone."

Ophelia's eyes widened. "No way."

Ethan snorted. "Impossible."

"Try me."

"I will!" Ophelia grabbed another biscuit. How was the woman so thin? "How about I tell you three things, and you tell me which is the lie?"

"Perfect. Go ahead."

Ophelia closed her eyes halfway. "Got it. I always wanted to be a singer. My hero is Walt Disney. My favorite color is blue."

Ethan rubbed his scalp and groaned. "That's the worst list I ever heard. Give her something hard."

"That was hard!"

Chloe made a sound suspiciously close to a giggle. "The last one is a lie," Mia said.

Ophelia sighed with defeat. "You're right. It's yellow."

"I'll give her a whirl," Harper cut in. "I graduated at the top of my class in high school. I once broke a leg falling off a horse. I attended a Britney Spears concert and sang at the top of my lungs."

Mia studied Harper's face, then slowly smiled. "First one is a lie."

Harper whistled. "You're right. Pretty good."

"Do Ethan next," Ophelia said. "Prove to Mr. Smarty Pants you can spot his lies."

Those baby blues gleamed with challenge. Her tummy tightened in an odd tingly sort of way as he propped his elbows on the table and smiled real slow. "Ready?" he drawled.

Ignoring her ridiculously galloping heart, she nodded. "Go ahead."

"I got suspended for kissing Penny Ryder in the third grade. I had a few beers with the actor Scott Eastwood. I mangled up my leg in a car accident."

Everyone seemed to hold a collective breath.

Mia let her gaze travel over his face, lingering on the slight crease of his brow, the clench of his jaw, the almost rebellious pout of his lips. He stared back in a watchful stillness, pushing her to dig deeper, dive further, and find . . .

Her voice was a whisper of sound. "That last one is a lie."

Ophelia and Harper gave a whoop. Chloe laughed.

Ethan jerked, as if woken from a strange trance. Surprise flickered over the hard lines of his face before quickly being masked. But it was too late. She'd spotted the shred of vulnerability and now she knew.

He had secrets he kept buried from everyone.

Even himself.

The room tilted as the realization broke over her and changed everything. No wonder she'd sensed wrong when she assumed it was a car crash. What had really happened to him? Why were there so many shadows banked so ruthlessly in his eyes? And why did she want to find out so badly? Her fingers shook slightly as she laid down her fork.

"I don't want you to do me," Chloe stated, making everyone laugh again and break the pulsating tension.

"Who wants one last serving before dessert?" Ophelia asked.

Mia glanced at the last biscuit on the platter and put out her hand. *Dessert?* "No, thanks. Everything was delicious."

Ethan rolled his eyes in pure mockery, back to his usual self. "Sure it was."

She shot him a withering look. "What is that supposed to mean? The food was delicious."

"You hardly ate anything. Five green beans and three bites of turkey isn't a meal."

Her voice chilled. "I ate a lot today. I was stuffed."

A delighted grin broke over his face. He leaned back in his chair. "Lie. What did you eat?"

She shifted her weight in the chair, the earlier peace forgotten. Oh, how she disliked this man with intensity. Why couldn't he mind his own business? Why couldn't he just be polite? "Plenty of healthy things. Fruit. Yogurt. Hummus. Carrot sticks. Okay?"

"I knew it. You're one of those women who doesn't eat. That's why you're so high strung!"

"Ethan!" Ophelia admonished. "That's not nice."

Mia gasped. "How dare you? What I do or don't eat is none of your business."

"Probably not, but starving must make you kind of miserable. Nothing wrong with enjoying good food. Bet you eat processed frozen diet meals and products that advertise no fat."

"I don't!" She only ate the frozen meals when she was forced to.

He scratched his chin and regarded her. Then chuckled. "Lie. Hmm, maybe I'm good at this game, too."

Ophelia glared at her brother. "There's a lot of reasons people don't eat. Mia, I'm so sorry. Just ignore him. Lord knows he can eat whatever he wants without gaining a pound, so he assumes we can all gorge on desserts."

Harper snorted. "Yeah, that was messed up, dude. You should just respect her decisions. No wonder she doesn't like you."

In that moment, Mia saw the looks on their faces and almost groaned. Of course, they believed she had an eating disorder, which was a sensitive subject. Her friend in high school had suffered from bulimia, and it had been tough watching her struggle. It took a lot of therapy for her to get healthy.

Ethan seemed to realize his error, pulling back in slight horror. "Sorry. Forget I said anything."

"I don't have an eating disorder," she said quietly. "Not that it's any of your business," she added, cutting a glance at Ethan. "But note to self for the future: don't share your opinions on a woman's food choices."

"Noted," he said gruffly.

Chloe tittered. "Mia, Ethan made a point, though. I never see you eat."

"If you must know, I'm trying to squeeze into a very expensive Gucci dress for an important event. I need to be careful."

"Maybe you should just buy another dress and treat yourself to some real food while you're here," Ethan threw out. "You're a size six already, for God's sake. Nothing wrong with food made with real cheese and milk and sugar. At least it has no additives and fake products that have no nutrients."

"I did read on the internet how whole milk, real butter, and even ice cream is good for you in moderation," Chloe offered.

"Did you try the biscuit?" Ethan asked. "Ophelia makes them homemade. When was the last time you had carbs?"

Even the word made her knees shake with longing. Irritation skated across her nerve endings. Damn him. Why did he always have to stir stuff up? "A while," she said with a grunt.

He grabbed the last biscuit, split it in half, and smeared a touch of butter over the inside. Real butter. Not the pretend kind. A tiny puff of steam rose from the dough. Suddenly, her mouth was full of drool. "Here. Just eat half and enjoy it."

She gazed at the weapon of mass destruction. "If I eat the damn biscuit, will you leave me alone?"

"Yes. For now."

"Fine." She grabbed it and took a bite. Then tried desperately to hide the orgasmic feeling of pure pleasure seizing her body. "Are you happy?"

"Yes. You're too skinny."

"I think you look beautiful," Ophelia defended. "I'm surprised at you, Ethan. You came straight from an industry that puts a lot of stock in a small-size designer dress. Why are you picking on her?"

"What do you mean?" Mia asked, mouth full of heavenly goodness. Oh God, it was so good, she was sweating. "What industry?"

"Ethan was a bodyguard in Hollywood. He protected movie stars and stuff. He knows firsthand how crazed we get about our weight and what the industry calls out as fat or skinny in today's world."

As another juicy bone from his past fell out of the closet, Mia found herself greedy for more. Ethan had lived a very different life than she'd originally thought. Maybe there were more layers underneath to reveal.

"Is that where you got to hang out with Scott Eastwood?" Chloe asked.

Now he was the one who looked uncomfortable. *Good. Payback is a bitch.* He seemed to gather himself together before answering. "Yep. Attended a whole bunch of those glitzy parties, where the media picked apart how they all looked, throwing the term *fat* around without caring what damage it did. I'm tired of watching women do that to themselves when every damn man you line up will tell you the truth: we like our women big, curvy, small, petite, tall, short, and every way in between. Wanna know what makes a woman really hot? If she's real and healthy and happy. Not the size dress she fits into."

Mia was struck speechless, the last of the biscuit crumbs still lingering on her lips. She'd dated men before who gave her pretty words on how she didn't have to diet, but they were the first ones to raise their brow when the waiter offered dessert. They were the ones who pointedly gazed at a curvy female and shook their head slightly, as if sympathetic for her plight. In her heart, she never believed them, and she had been right.

But she believed Ethan Bishop.

It radiated from his very aura, rang from his words still echoing in the air. In that moment, she believed he'd appreciate a woman in all aspects, especially naked, out of her designer dress, vulnerable to his gaze.

He'd make her feel like a queen.

Her cheeks flushed at the thought. *Dear Lord, what was happening to her?* She intensely disliked him!

"That's lit," Chloe said. "I know some girls at school who torture themselves by starving to get thinner."

"Agreed," Harper echoed, sharing a smile with the teen.

"On that note, I'm going to fetch the apple pie," Ophelia said. "But no pressure, Mia. It is homemade organic crust, fresh apples, cinnamon, sugar, and a few secret spices. Just to tempt you."

Chloe's phone buzzed and she glanced at the screen. "I need to take this," she mumbled, getting up from her chair. "Be back in a few."

Harper rose. "I'll put on some coffee." She disappeared into the kitchen.

Ah, crap.

Refusing to be intimidated, Mia crossed her arms in front of her chest and looked him dead in the eye. "How'd you really hurt your leg?"

"You're not going to eat that pie, are you?"

She pursed her lips. Considered. "Why do you want me to eat it?"

"'Cause it'll put you in a better mood."

She couldn't help it. A smile threatened. As much as he was a pain in the ass, he kept her consistently engaged with his banter. "You won't be around me much," she pointed out. "I'm barred from your barn."

"I dare you to eat the pie. A decent slice. Even the crust part."

She leaned over the table, resting the tips of her fingers together. "And if I don't take your ridiculous dare?"

He shrugged. "You miss out on pie and I know you don't have grit."

Her brows shot up. "Grit? Are we trapped in some old John Wayne movie, horse man?"

"Eat the pie, and I'll tell you what happened to my leg."

She pretended to consider. "I also want free access to the barn whenever I want. And no more yelling at me. You be civil at all times."

He gnashed his teeth together. "Hell no."

"Then I don't need the pie."

A grumpy frown creased his brow. He muttered a curse. "You can visit my barn, but if you do something stupid again, I get to yell."

She let out a long-suffering sigh. He was way too easy. She'd devour him whole in a business negotiation. Now she got to go where she wanted, had learned the truth, and would have a delicious piece of pie. "Fine. You win."

Ophelia and Harper came back and set the pie on the table.

Her mouth practically gaped open.

The crust was so high on top, it practically rose to a whole foot. Apples oozed out of the corners of the crust, and the color was a toasty brown. She bit her tongue to keep from moaning out loud. No, she wouldn't give him the satisfaction. He'd have to torture her first. "Looks good," she said casually.

Ethan grinned knowingly.

Plates were doled out. Chloe came back, adding a scoop of ice cream to hers and chattering with Harper about the rescue horses and what was involved. Ophelia excused herself to take care of a guest.

And Mia ate her pie.

It wasn't easy. She gathered all her forces to swallow each delicious bite without shaking in pleasure. Under the table, she squeezed her thighs together with merciless brutality and fought for focus. The rich flavors danced on her tongue with sheer abandon, coursing through her body like wildfire.

And the bastard watched her through every heavenly, torturous bite. Studied her face, delved into her eyes, devoured each flitter of expression that leaked out. It was one of the most intimate exchanges she'd ever experienced with a man. Every bite forked between her lips made her knees quiver and prickles of heat skip over her skin. Her panties dampened. Finally, when the last bit of crust had been consumed, she slowly put her fork down on her plate with slightly trembling fingers.

Gathering the last of her strength, she lifted her chin and stared at him with haughty demand. "Done."

His voice lowered to a husky pitch. "Was it good?"

She licked her lips. Those blue eyes focused on the action with pure greed. Her heart skipped in a mad beat, and the air suddenly buzzed like a wild live electrical wire that got dropped under water. She could barely drag in oxygen. "It was okay."

Oh, his smile was smug and sexy and wicked. Her nipples tightened and pushed against the thin silk of her top. Longing spilled through her for . . . something. What was happening?

"Lie," he whispered.

Her fingers itched to touch his hair. The ginger strands were thick, tousled, and glowed almost gold in the lamplight. She focused on the task at hand. "Now tell me how you hurt your leg."

His face changed. The connection broke like a cord ripped away, writhing and twisting on the floor. He stood up from the chair and headed toward the door. "Thanks for dinner, Ophelia. Chloe, see you tomorrow." He gave her a curt nod, like they never experienced that mind-blowing chemistry over the dinner table or made a bet that seethed with undercurrents of meaning.

She shot to her feet. "Hey, you owe me the truth. That was the bet."

He turned toward her. A smile tugged at those luscious lips. What would his face be like without that beard? Would his skin be rough or smooth? What were the true shape of his lips and jaw?

"I said I'd tell you. I didn't say when."

Her eyes widened. "You cheated!"

"You didn't specify the details of the terms. I would've thought better of you, princess. You work in PR."

And with a mocking wink, he walked out of the inn, whistling.

The bastard was whistling.

He was so going to get his.

Chapter Nine

The loud whirr of the copter was like a lullaby, his only focus as he guided Aresh Hammati forward. After parachuting in last night, he'd been able to secure and escort him from the meeting place to the pickup zone. The valuable informant had been key in gaining terrorist information for the United States, but he'd been outed. Ethan needed to get the man out of Iraq before he was killed.

There wasn't much time left.

"They're coming!" Aresh screamed. "We're going to die."

"Not today," he grit back. "We're here."

Keeping Aresh pinned to his side, Ethan pushed through the exhaustion as his boots pounded over the terrain, where scorched desert earth met burned-out trees, concentrating on the wildly bouncing copter as it lowered down. The door slid open, and Buckeye motioned him forward, gun trained on the emerging enemy.

No time to land. It would be a STABO extraction, and time was tight. Fuck.

Ethan reached the rope and checked the equipment. The whip of adrenaline tightened his body, but his mind remained crystal clear. He'd done it before, and though the environment and circumstance always changed, his reaction didn't. He could perform an extraction in the dark of night, on land or ocean, because he turned to automatic with a burning focus that ripped every other thought from his mind.

Save a life.

He got Aresh secured at the same time thick smoke rolled from the trees and the burst of gunfire exploded in the air. His gut clenched, and his neck prickled with warning. Too close. They were too close.

Ethan gave Buckeye the signal. Aresh grabbed him, his face sweaty and mad with fear. "Don't let me die," he begged wildly. "Promise."

"You're not going to die. I promise. Hang on, you're going up."

Hope flared in his deep dark eyes. A flicker of trust. A belief Ethan wouldn't let him down and would keep his damn promise, the vow that he lived and died for out here every minute of every day. With quick, deft motions, Ethan clipped himself in. The bird lifted, rising from the ground along with Aresh. Slowly, the cord began shortening. Inch by inch, they were brought closer to the door of the copter. Buckeye and Tyler waited to pull them in.

They'd make it.

The line of trees broke open, and men swarmed out, screaming and racing toward the rising copter. Gritting his teeth, Ethan held on, swinging in the air. They spun wildly, the wind ripping at the safety line, and then the sound of endless gunfire popped into the sky.

In slow motion, the scene unraveled in brutal familiarity that he couldn't escape.

The spray of bullets tearing into flesh and bone, burning up his leg until it hung uselessly under him. More pain knifed into his right shoulder. He trained his gaze on Aresh above him as he hovered close to safety, then watched the man jerk as bullets tore through him.

"No! Fuck, no, hold on," Ethan screamed.

They were carried away. Ethan saw Buckeye above him, yanking him from his restraints, the familiar gaze of knowledge he couldn't hide. Of death. Of injury. Of change.

Tyler was yelling something. Fighting consciousness, he rolled and reached for Aresh, praying he'd made it. They were both alive. They'd both made it. They both . . .

The man's head lolled to the side. Loosened muscles sagged lifelessly against him. His dead, dark eyes stared back into Ethan's, mocking him.

"Don't let me die. Don't let me die."

"I won't. I swear to God I won't let you die."

No.

His vision blurred. Nausea churned his gut. The world faded around him.

No, no, no, no . . .

Ethan shot up out of bed, his cry still lingering in the air. Sweat coated his body. He rolled off the mattress, feeling the panic attack grip him, and he sank to his knees, a whimper exploding from his lips.

Not again.

The raw fear and uncontrollable dread pumped through his veins and blurred his thoughts. He fought for breath, trying to slow it down as his heart madly thumped out of rhythm and seemed to explode in his chest.

He didn't know how long it took for the attack to surge and then slowly recede. When his body began to recover, Ethan stumbled to the bathroom, stepping into the shower to clean off the sweat and lingering dirt of the dream. He toweled off and threw on a pair of denim shorts and black tank, knowing sleep was done for the rest of the night. At this point, he was grateful for a few solid, uninterrupted hours and counted himself lucky.

After all, he was the lucky one.

He'd survived the bullets.

Aresh Hammati hadn't.

And he'd broken his promise.

Ethan rubbed his hands over his scalp. Aresh had been an important informant to protect. And once again, Ethan kept going over and over the scenario, wondering if he'd just been a little faster, trimmed a few precious minutes, would Aresh still be alive?

He knew it was useless to replay the event. He'd told that to his therapist, accepting the natural process of grief and guilt after a traumatic event. Always wondering why he'd been spared and another hadn't. He still talked on the phone and joked with Buckeye, but his friend was back in the shit, and Ethan was now home. His body would never recover enough to get back in the game, and it was as if a piece of his core had died with Aresh Hammati. So he left behind his second life in the military and his third life as bodyguard to Hollywood royalty.

He'd come back to his first life in search of some peace.

His knee ached, so he did some of his stretches to loosen the crumbled nerves and muscle. When he glanced at the clock, it was two a.m. Might as well take a walk and get some air to clear his head.

He grabbed a pocket flashlight, stuffed his feet into shoes, and headed out into the darkness.

The moonlight spilled in blotchy patches. The screech of crickets melded with the hoot of owls in a beautiful night melody. Fireflies glided by with miniswarms of gnats, and the trees kept still in the windless evening.

Ethan walked for a while, finally heading toward the inn. Maybe he'd sit in one of the wicker rockers on the porch and watch the eventual sunrise. He followed the path, passing his favorite Japanese cherry blossom trees that gave off a ripe floral scent, and stopped short.

A figure sat on the steps, caught in shadow. She leaned forward, resting her chin in her hands, staring into the night, lost in her thoughts. Her profile was all soft edges and graceful femininity, her petite frame clad in pink shorts and a scoop-necked, pink lacy shirt. Her bare feet were crossed at the ankles. Her glittery toenail polish popped in the darkness.

Ethan paused, torn between wanting to back up before she saw him and a longing to join her. Their encounters were a strange blend of hostility, humor, and attraction. She was the exact type of woman he'd never involve himself with, but there was something that kept pulling him toward her. Maybe it was the way she refused to back down or how she seemed to be able to make him laugh even when he was mad. Hell, when she ate that damn apple pie, his dick had practically strangled in his jeans. Those golden tigress eyes held him captive, challenging him to drag her across the table, devour her mouth, and make her hungry for more than food. She liked wicked games. The whole time she ate and tried not to let out sounds of pleasure drove him to the sweetest fantasy of all.

Making her scream in bed under his hands, his tongue, his teeth.

Fuck it.

"Couldn't sleep?"

She jerked around, searching for the voice. He moved forward, and the motion light clicked on, making them both blink in the sudden brightness. He braced his foot on the first step, leaning his arm on the column of the railing. For a few seconds, he wondered if she'd ignore him and return to her safe bed. But slowly, her body relaxed and she regarded him thoughtfully.

"I rarely sleep. I have insomnia."

He lifted a brow. "Nightmares?"

"No. My brain doesn't seem to shut down properly. After a few hours, I open my eyes and that's it. I start thinking of the stuff I need to do or the stuff I've done or the stuff that I should change. Part of my high-maintenance personality, I guess."

His lip twitched. "Makes sense."

"What about you?"

"Same."

"Lie." He stared at her for a long time. How could she intrigue and irritate him at the same time? And how the hell did she know his truth? He'd had buddies for years who never realized when he was bluffing or bullshitting them. Ethan opened his mouth, but she waved a hand in the air, cutting him off. "Sorry, forget it. I don't want to fight."

The light clicked off. She turned back to studying the inky blackness of the woods, the majestic shadow lines of mountains thrusting toward sky. His center of gravity shifted, confusing him, but he followed his gut and sat down next to her on the steps.

A comfortable silence settled between them. They sat together for a while, not speaking, their breath and the night creatures the only sounds in the dark. He wondered what she was thinking about, what secrets she buried in the light of day, what was most important to her. The questions whirled in his mind. It had been a very long time since any woman engaged his curiosity.

"Mia?"

"Yeah?"

"What worries you the most at night?"

Her shoulders tensed. She glanced at him with suspicion. "You'd only use it for blackmail."

He grinned. "How about calling an official truce?"

"Why?"

This time, he gave her the truth. "Because I'm tired, too."

She caught his meaning, evident in the widening of her extraordinary eyes and her slow nod. "Okay." She paused and dragged in a breath. "I worry that I'll never be enough."

Her answer puzzled him. Already, she struck him as a powerful, dynamic woman who blazed a path of success in her wake. He bet the men in her life were the same—the type of man he used to be back in Hollywood, with his custom suits and smooth charm and powerful network of friends. Hell, he'd believed he found real love in that world, only to realize that, too, had been a mirage he helped create. Had it ever been real, or had he needed it to be in order to fit his image of what he'd always wanted? More. More than this farm, or the inn, or this small town he'd grown up in.

Maybe Mia had someone in her life already that drove her from the bed to stare out into the night. A man who missed her while she was away.

Jonathan Lake.

And why did the thought make a pang of regret bolt through him?

"For who? Yourself? Your family? Your lover?"

She pushed her hair back, considering. "All of it. I'm driven at work to succeed and make something in my past right again. When I started my business, I struggled just to feed myself and keep afloat. I got lucky with a client who ended up becoming big under my tutelage, and I began growing by word of mouth. Eventually, I moved into the political arena—which was my ultimate goal—and moved my office from the back of a warehouse to a well-known Manhattan address."

"Seems impressive."

"Should be, right?" Her shrug said otherwise. "Yet I still wonder if it was just dumb luck that got me here. Like I'm waiting for people to find out I'm really a fraud and not as impressive as my reputation."

"Sounds like impostor syndrome."

"What's that?"

"A condition where you explain away your success instead of owning it and feeling accomplished. A good majority of women suffer from it." He'd learned about it in college and tried to diagnose his sisters. Harper had practically clocked him, and Ophelia counseled him on minding his own damn business.

"That's me! That's what I have! How do I get rid of it?"

Her razor-sharp focus to fix herself in an evening made him smile. Would she bring all that delicious intensity to the bedroom? Would she be an enthusiastic, assertive partner who told him exactly what she liked and didn't? He'd always loved a bit of a bossy woman. And why did he want to find out? He reined in his disturbing thoughts. No need to complicate the evening by letting his little head rule and ruin their tentative truce. Plus, she was taken. He didn't play around with commitment. "It takes time. Every time you have a success, you have to remind yourself it wasn't luck or coincidence or someone else. You have to own it and be proud. You embark on a brand-new mental habit."

She sighed and waved a hand in the air. "Forget it, I'm too old to retrain my brain now."

"I've done it, and I'm thirty-five."

"I'm thirty and I'll just deal with my insomnia."

He laughed. "Okay, so you worry about your job. What else?" He paused delicately. "Problems with Lake?"

"You mean the election?"

"I mean as your lover."

She frowned, then looked a little guilty. "Jonathan and I aren't involved. Besides my own morals about dating a client, there's nothing between us but business. I respect him, admire him, but I'm sure as hell not sleeping with him."

The pure relief that flooded his body should've worried him, but he didn't analyze it. "Another lover?"

"Nope. I'm single. I don't have good luck with men, so I'm taking a long break."

Oh, he needed more information on that statement. "Broken heart?"

"Broken trust. I've been cheated on twice. And each damn time, the guy denied it right to my face, which pissed me off even more."

He wondered who'd be stupid enough to cheat on her. Most of the time, men cheated because they were bored. Mia could probably spend an entire lifetime throwing out surprises and challenges to keep a man engaged. "I'm sorry, that sucks. Were they long relationships?"

"First one was a year. Second was about six months. Of course, that made me wonder if I just wasn't cut out for love on a permanent scale. Maybe I'm just too wrapped up in my career. Maybe I'm boring."

He laughed out loud, and she swung around to give him a murderous glare. "I thought we were on a truce here," she grit out. "No need to mock me."

"I'm sorry, I laughed because you are the most unboring person I've ever met. Trust me, that's not your problem."

"Oh yeah? Then what is?"

"You dated two complete assholes."

She practically gaped at him. "You just said something nice to me. And you weren't even lying."

He rolled his eyes. "Contrary to your opinion, I'm not in the habit of lying. Or cheating. Or hurting people I love."

"Just being generally hard-assed?"

"Maybe." They stared at one another. Emotion charged the air. He ached to reach out and touch her hair, trail his finger down her cheek to see if her skin was as silky as it appeared. Tonight, she didn't smell of orange blossoms, but clean and pure, like cucumber soap. Her lips parted slightly, as if waiting for something. He was used to the occasional kick of sexual tension, but this almost tender feeling was completely different. What the hell was going on?

As if she'd gauged his thoughts, she tore her gaze away and wrapped her arms around her knees. "Well, now you know I'm not as fabulous as I pretend. But I'm happy. I have a good life. And maybe one day I'll stop looking for . . ."

She broke off. He waited but she didn't finish her sentence. His heart paused in his chest. "For what?"

He didn't think she'd answer and decided not to ask again. The whisper came from her very soul, half-ragged with truth and want. "More."

The empty place inside reared up, seeking company, twisting in demand for his own secrets to be shared with this woman, on this night, in the dark.

"I got shot."

She looked up. Looked deep. He waited for her to ask a barrage of questions or look shocked, but she just kept staring at him with wide amber eyes, waiting for him to finish.

"I'm Special Forces. *Was.* I worked as a pararescue trooper. It's a part of the air force where I basically flew in with my team for specific missions and helped with medical aid or rescue. Joined when I graduated from college and went through two years of hell at superman school. Loved every damned minute of it. Always dreamed of doing something big and helping others in a different way. Loved being souped-up on adrenaline and the lure of saving someone that no one else could."

He shook his head, thinking of when he was younger and putting himself through one of the toughest schools in the world. He'd learned about all his hidden demons—his weaknesses and strengths. How relying on a team was the difference between life and death. He'd been broken, stripped down, and annihilated, then built back up to a man he was proud to be. Even with the missions, in his mind he'd been immortal. Superman. Maybe that had been the most dangerous part of all.

"When I wasn't away, I worked as a bodyguard. It was a perfect job to do in between gigs because I could come and go as I pleased, and I had a list of celebrities who wanted the Special Forces guy on their team. I had the best of both worlds."

He paused but she just kept quiet, those Bambi-like eyes giving him what he needed to continue. "I got called away to rescue an important informant. I thought we had enough time to get him to the copter—I was sure it was going to be okay. I swore to him I wouldn't let him die." The scene replayed in his mind, thickening his throat. "I was wrong. Enemy fire broke out before I could get him to safety. He died. I promised to save him and then watched the flare of hope in his eyes twist to death, and every fucking night I see those same eyes in my dreams."

The words bled from his soul, but already he felt cleaner. He'd learned bad shit was like a wound—if you didn't occasionally lance it open and expose it to the light, it slowly got infected from rotting alone in the dark.

"What about you?" she asked softly.

"My team saved me in time. My leg and shoulder got shot up. I was lucky. Besides getting to live, I came close to losing the leg, but they said it was a miracle. The surgery worked, I glided through PT, and all I have to show is a bit of pain and a limp."

A much better deal than Aresh Hammati.

He waited for her apologies and sympathy. He knew the drill well—people didn't know how to handle stories from war. They saw it in the newspapers or on television, clucked their tongue, and moved on to their evening meal or an argument with their spouse over who left the toothpaste cap off. It was almost as if he were split between two worlds—the world of his brothers, who lived to fight and defend, and the world that wanted to forget.

He didn't blame anyone. Hell, he'd deliberately joined the military for exactly that reason: to give citizens the luxury of forgetting. Hollywood had been good for that. He could return from missions and lose himself in the glamour and falsities that offered denial. But after Aresh Hammati, he couldn't seem to get back to that mind-set. He'd felt displaced, with nowhere to go but home.

"I guess we both have syndromes that keep us up at night," she finally said.

Ethan frowned. "What are you talking about?"

"I have impostor syndrome. You have god syndrome."

"What the hell is 'god syndrome'?"

Her face was serious as she spoke. "You graduated from superman school. You trained with the elite. You saved lives for a job. After a while, you must get a god complex, like you have control over everything. That if someone dies on your watch, it's your fault."

"It is. I take the motto serious. 'So others may live.'"

She nodded. "Sounds like you tried to do that with this last mission, too. But God decided to show you something important. You don't get to choose. You can do your very best—your superhuman best—but you can't save everyone. No one can. And now you're learning to live with that. You just have to go through to get to the other side."

The truth of her words struck him arrow straight, pierced his heart, and let sweet, pure air back inside. For a few precious seconds, the ragged void in his soul took a breath and sighed, once again full.

Because of her.

In all the time with his therapist, he'd circled around the realization, but Mia had given it to him straight. She sat a few inches from him, chin tilted up so she could meet his gaze. Shattered, head reeling, he looked deeply into her eyes, ready for her to utter her soft apologetic sayings or squeeze his hand or tell him he'd definitely get to the other side and everything would be okay.

Instead, she gave him a lopsided half smile. "At least I know now why you're such an arrogant ass."

And at that moment, he fell hard for Mia Thrush in a completely unexpected way.

Without thought, he reached over, cupped her cheeks, and lowered his head.

Then he kissed her.

Her lips parted in surprise, and he took full advantage. As if trying to unravel a mystery, he sipped at her lips, learning her taste and texture, nibbling softly, until a low, strangled moan broke from her chest, and he swallowed it whole and took the kiss deeper.

Honeyed sweetness with a little twist of spice. Her nails bit into his shoulders, and she tilted her head to allow him full access. In seconds, she melted against his chest, the rub of her tight nipples whipping hunger through his body. He let out a growl, holding her still while he explored every delicious, slick crevice, reveling in the thrust of her tongue against his as she battled him right back. Heat exploded between them. His dick throbbed, and within seconds, he was in a frenzy to get her naked, get her open, get her to come . . .

"Ethan." She breathed against his lips, her arms sliding around his shoulders to thrust into his hair and pull.

"Yeah?" He sucked on her lower lip, then bit gently. She shuddered in his embrace.

"What are we doing?"

"Don't know. Feels good. Do you want me to stop?"

"No." Her smile only made him hotter, especially when she ripped her mouth from his, dragging her tongue down his neck and sinking her teeth into his flesh. Ah, fuck, she was a little tigress who enjoyed play. He pulled her onto his lap, his hands cupping her ass, and she wrapped her arms tight around him. Those sexy hips began to rock against his hardness, kissing him back with an openness and genuine hunger he couldn't get enough of. She was burning up all around him, dragging him into a tunnel where he couldn't think about anything but how bad he wanted to ravish and please and torment.

Suddenly, the light flooded the porch, blinding in intensity. She jumped out of his arms, her butt landing hard on the porch step, and turned around in horror to see who had caught them.

No one was there.

Ethan gripped the railing and tried to get his head to stop spinning. *Holy shit.* That wasn't a kiss. That was a damn explosion of epic proportions.

That was big fucking trouble.

"Motion light," he managed to say. "Probably an animal tripped it."

Her expression told him the mood had definitely been broken. Her skin paled, and she raised a trembling hand to press against her now-swollen lips. "What did we do?"

Irritation ruffled his nerve endings. Did she have to look so horrified? He lifted a brow. "We kissed."

"But I called you an ass. Why did you kiss me?"

Raw hunger snapped into temper. "Why'd you kiss me back?"

"I didn't." He cocked his head and studied her. "Okay, fine, I did, but I was surprised. I don't think it's a good idea."

His ego took the hit like a man, but it stung. "Neither do I."

Her hand dropped, and she blew out a breath. "Then why on earth did you kiss me?"

Because in that moment, he'd felt completely connected to her.

Because he'd felt alive again.

Because he'd felt seen for the first time.

He offered her a half shrug. "Felt like a good idea at the time. Didn't know a simple kiss would freak you out so much, princess. It's not like we need to embark on a shotgun wedding."

Her glare made him feel better. This woman he could deal with. This bristly, judgy pain in the ass was easy to banter and amuse himself with. The one who molded himself perfectly to his body, uttered the perfect phrase to a heartfelt confession, and kissed him back with a burning heat and need?

Not so much.

"You are so rude," she muttered, standing up and brushing off her pajama pants. At this angle, her nipples were still hard against her pale-pink shirt. He decided to prove he could be a gentleman when he wanted to be by not pointing out that fact. "Next time you get hit by an impulse, smother it. Or you'll be sporting a black eye, horse man."

Ethan figured the truce was now officially over.

So much better this way.

He stretched lazily and stroked his beard. Her taste lingered on his lips. "Is that before you climb onto my lap or after the breathy moan of my name?"

Her golden eyes turned glassy with rage. Her sparkly nails flashed as she clenched her fists. "You are deplorable," she whispered.

Then she whipped around on her bare heel and slammed the screen door behind her.

Damned if she didn't surprise him. Damned if she wasn't one of the sexiest, most vibrant women he'd laid eyes on.

Damned if he'd do anything else about it.

As he strode back to his bungalow, adrenaline still buzzing in his veins, Ethan made one important decision.

It was definitely time to shave his beard.

Chapter Ten

Mia groaned when she spotted the time. She'd ended up falling asleep before dawn, and now she was way past her usual time of grabbing coffee and breakfast. She'd perfected the habit of appearing obnoxiously early to pick up her items, then disappearing into her room to avoid sitting on the porch and making conversation with guests.

She brushed her teeth, finger-combed her hair, and threw on shorts and flat sandals. Tiptoeing down two flights, she heard chatter drifting from the screened porch, but the dining room was empty. She quickly gathered her mug of coffee, some berries, and a dollop of Greek yogurt, then turned and headed toward the stairs.

"I haven't seen you around!" a loud voice boomed in her ear.

Ah, crap.

Forcing a smile, she faced an elderly woman staring at her with mad glee. She had tightly permed gray hair, thick-wired glasses, and obviously fake perfect white teeth. There was some type of blue plastic bird placed on her head, but Mia couldn't figure out if it was some form of barrette or hat. Either way, she didn't want to know. "Hello, I'm Mia. Nice to meet you."

"Ethel. Aren't you a pretty little thing? A little scrawny, though. Why don't you have an omelet or French toast instead of that bird food?"

Mia blinked. "Umm, no, thanks, I'm good. I was just going up to my room to—"

"Absolutely not, we've been looking for you all week. Come out. I have a nice rocker next to me, and we can chat. Fred! I met the last guest. Her name is Mia!"

Fred? Like Fred and Ethel from the old *I Love Lucy* show? Oh, this was going to be bad. She channeled her PR training for firm rejections. "Maybe another morning; I really have to get upstairs."

Ethel ignored her, grabbing her by the wrist like she were a wayward toddler and leading her outside to the porch. Barring ripping her hand away and yelling for help, Mia was stuck. Forcing a fake smile to her lips, she nodded to a chorus of *good morning*s and was gently pushed into a rocker. Her mug was placed on the small wicker table beside her. Blinking against the sunlight, Mia realized there were six people staring at her like she'd dropped out of the sky and had promised them a tutorial on invading Earth.

It also looked like a senior convention.

They all kind of looked the same. Curly gray hair, wrinkled skin, and an assortment of glasses. A few had canes propped up beside their chairs, and even in the humid morning heat, they all wore full-length pants and firmly tied old-people shoes. The men wore black. The women wore white.

Did their tour bus to Atlantic City get detoured?

Fred—he looked like Ethel's husband—patted Mia's arm, as if welcoming her into the group. "Ophelia said you were here, but no one could figure out where you've been hiding," he half scolded. "You've never once shown up for tea and cookies!"

Another lady cackled, lifting a glass full of something. It took Mia a few moments to realize it was her teeth. "We waited every morning to see if you'd leave your room. I'm Priscilla. This is my husband, Pete."

A tiny birdlike woman with a whispery voice leaned forward. "We tried to stay up late to introduce ourselves, but we usually fall asleep by seven p.m. Damn pills. I'm Dolly, by the way, and this is my husband, Ed."

Mia realized Ed was studying her with sheer suspicion. "I'm an FBI agent. Retired now, of course. Are you hiding from someone out here, ma'am? You seem very . . . cagey."

She swallowed back her fear and decided to face this head-on. She'd need to set the rules now and make them all see how she valued privacy. "No, I'm just an ordinary citizen, I'm afraid. I'm very busy with work, so I have little time to socialize. I hope you've been having a wonderful time at the inn, though."

They ignored her politeness and plowed on. "Ah, one of those high-powered jobs that suck the life out of you, right?" Fred said knowingly. "I learned early in my life that time is precious. These young people are working their way right into their graves, thinking money and success are important. They're not. You know what is?"

She glanced around as six sets of eyes peered over their lenses and waited for her response. "Health?" she guessed, grabbing her coffee like a lifeline.

"Time!" Priscilla crowed. "Fun! Family and friends and adventures. That's what we're all doing here. We're all going horseback riding and antiquing and skydiving."

Mia choked on the hot brew. "What?"

"That's right," Ethel said. "We're jumping out of planes at the parachute place a few miles away. The Ranch."

"Will they allow you to do that at your, umm, I mean—"

"At our age? Hell yes, or I'd sue for age discrimination," Pete bellowed. His button-down, pink-striped formal shirt stretched over his wide belly. His head gleamed shiny with sweat. "I'm a lawyer."

Priscilla patted her husband's knee soothingly. "And a great lawyer you are, my love."

"You made more money than me. I'm sorry you had to give up your career for me and the kids."

Mia cocked her head. "What was your career?"

Priscilla sighed in longing. "I was an actress on a soap for a while, but I made more money being a stripper. Of course, once the children came I had to retire, so I did commercials instead." Pete looked at her lasciviously. Priscilla winked.

Mia looked around to see if anyone else was shocked at the stripper comment, but there was little reaction. Holy crap, these people were crazy! "So what's your job, Mia?" Ethel asked. "Here, try this blueberry scone. It's homemade. Ophelia's baked goods should be patented. You look like you're wasting away."

"No, thank you."

Her request was ignored, and the scone was added to her plate. Mia had never known her grandparents. Now she knew what being trapped on a porch with six of them would be like.

"Let me guess," Priscilla jumped in. "You're in advertising?"

"PR. I have my own publicity firm in Manhattan," she said. Mia decided the only way to get out was to eat the scone, answer their questions, and tire them out. "I'm here just for the summer, but I work from my laptop."

"Who are you here with? Husband? Lover? Friend?" Ed asked.

Dolly slapped him. "Stop interrogating her. Maybe she's a lesbian, and that's okay with all of us."

"I'm with my niece. She's volunteering to do some work at the horse farm, and I thought I'd join her and get more work done. Less interruptions here." Her words sounded good, but Ed leaned in, his gray brows lowered in a fierce frown. Sweat beaded on her skin. Could he tell she was lying?

"Interesting," he finally muttered, nodding as if he'd figured out her game. "Very, very, interesting."

"What?" Dolly asked.

"Some things are better off left in the secrets of the soul," he stated.

Everyone nodded their heads in respect.

Mia shoved the scone in her mouth and shot up. Oh dear God, what was that taste? Real butter? The sweet tang of fresh blueberries danced with flavors she barely recognized. Her knees grew weak, and she had to fight for clarity. Is that what butter tasted like? Her body shivered with pleasure. "Well, thank you. Umm, thank you so much for welcoming me, but I need to go back to my room. I have to work. For a long time. A real long time."

"We'll see you later for tea, dear," Ethel said.

"Oh, I may be out or working."

"We'll knock on your door now that we're friends!" Priscilla beamed with pleasure. "We're going to play poker, so bring your money."

"Unless it's strip poker," Pete said, giving his wife another wink. His wife giggled.

Mia stumbled back toward the screen door. This was too much for her. Especially after her soul-stirring, panty-melting, mind-exploding kiss with the man she despised. "I'll be there! See you later!"

She raced back up the stairs, closing and locking the door behind her. She couldn't go out there again. She'd have to let Ophelia know to put out her breakfast at four a.m. and come up with a code to let her know when the porch was clear. Skydiving? Stripping? Poker?

No. Just . . . no. It was safer to spend the summer in her room like her original plan. No more dinners and moonlight kissing and apple pies and the Golden Girls Gone Wild club. Things were beginning to get out of control.

But, oh God, that kiss.

His beard wasn't rough, as she'd originally thought. It tickled and scraped the sensitive skin around her chin and had a bit of a silky feel when it glided down her neck. Though the lips hidden behind his beard should be illegal. Soft and firm and full. Completely in control, plunging her mouth, his tongue demanding in just the perfect mix of alpha yet almost humble in the way he'd gathered her taste and swallowed her moan and held her so tight. And his body? Oh, it was deadly. Lean and mean and deliciously hard everywhere. There was such controlled, leashed strength in his touch and energy. No man had ever been able to get her so wet with one simple kiss. It usually took a lot of foreplay and patience for Mia to get revved and ready to go.

But Ethan Bishop had slammed her motor into racing mode in a few seconds.

You want more, her inner slut whispered.

Too bad. That man would never be her summer fling. He was too infuriating and arrogant and rude. It was too sticky, especially with Chloe working with him. The sex would be too intense—not the type of casual affair she'd be able to have fun with and leave at the end of the summer without looking back.

The image of his face floated in her vision. Those pale-blue eyes usually so controlled, suddenly flaring with a ravaged pain that punched dead and center and left her raw. The way his features tightened as he told the story, refusing to acknowledge his own injury or that he deserved to be whole. He'd given her his complete truth and stripped himself naked for those precious moments in the moonlight.

It had meant everything to her.

She couldn't lie. If he hadn't reached over and kissed her, she would've done it herself. There were too many emotions chopping through her body, and she craved closer contact, ached to be in his arms and soothe his hurt.

But he didn't have to know that.

Mia dragged in a breath. She needed to keep those vulnerable feelings hidden, or he'd be able to control the whole game. He'd be able to tempt her, seduce her, and, eventually, break her. He had some type of power she couldn't understand, but she'd been taught to recognize danger, and all her animal instincts were on high alert.

Time to focus.

She spent the day with her rear firmly in the chair, computer on her lap, and headphones in her ears, making calls to all her clients. A popular mommy blogger reached out, frantic over a viral scandal that claimed she encouraged her children to not be "losers" and to do everything in their power to win. Of course, the internet spun it, and now she was trapped in a social media frenzy accusing her of being a bad mom, fielding calls from *Good Morning America* and *Today* show to set the record straight.

Whipped up from the crappy injustice of judgment, Mia secured the client and spent an hour on Skype with the female powerhouse, promising that after she was done, she'd be America's darling again. By the end of the call, Mia was back to being in control and her usual badass self. This was why she relished her job. It wasn't about covering up scandals or lying to the public—it was about spinning the real truth in a way that helped.

She got up from the chair and stretched. She'd planned to skip lunch after the scone incident, but her stomach growled in sheer rage. Maybe she'd take a drive into town and go back to the Market. They had plenty of low-calorie options, and she could get some exercise in.

She made sure to sneak outside and listen before deciding it was safe to exit. With the porch clear, the crazy group probably gone horseback riding or falling out of planes, she rushed out to her car.

Then shrieked.

Hei Hei was blocking her path. The moment he saw her, he launched into a series of chicken screeches and shot over to her. She stumbled back a few steps, but it was too late. He was bobbing his head in mad glee and rubbing his feathers all over her bare legs.

Yuck.

"Don't do that," she warned. "You're not a dog."

Wheezy must have heard, because he trotted over from the bushes and united with the chicken in a show of affection. Bolt followed his faithful companion and joined the crew. With one leg being rubbed by Hei Hei and the other being licked by Wheezy and Bolt, she felt trapped in some type of crazed animal movie.

"Okay, guys, I have to go." With one last lick and adoring glance, Wheezy and Bolt obeyed, going back to their spot and lying down in the sun.

Hei Hei glared. Then pecked at her toes.

"No! That's bad! Leave me alone."

With a warning glance, she hurried to her car and headed to town.

She sipped her water while she poked in and out of some shops. Surprised at the stunning quality of goods, she ended up buying a sheer silvery scarf and a pair of fun chandelier earrings with turquoise beads. They may not be designer, but Mia loved the uniqueness and knowing they were handcrafted. It was difficult for local artists to make a living now with cheap factory products dangled on every corner. She made a mental note to buy up a bunch of stuff and use them for Christmas gifts this year.

She made her way into the Market, noticing again the lack of customers. The scent of some type of vanilla coffee hung in the air. The prepared-foods aisle offered a fresh tomato-and-mozzarella salad and a spinach-gouda quiche that looked divine. In food heaven, she picked up some extras for her refrigerator and to share with Chloe.

A shadow fell across her.

"It hasn't gotten better," Fran stated, as if they were best friends and she'd just been waiting for her to stop in. "I put up specials on the blackboard, but no one came in. Every day, I'm losing more money. I invested my retirement into this idea, and now I'll be homeless with my cats, eating garbage."

Damn. Why couldn't she just stop in and get food without drama? "You should never invest everything you have in a business with today's unbalanced marketplace," she said kindly.

Fran's lower lip trembled.

"But this can still work!" Mia rushed on, praying the poor woman wouldn't break down again. "Did you look at Yelp like I told you?"

"I don't understand it. I'm not computer savvy, and I don't know anyone who is to help. I thought everyone would just come in once we opened. I didn't know I needed to do marketing!"

Mia rubbed her forehead and made a decision. This woman cared about her business, and local shops were dying too fast. It had been a long time since she used her skills to help people other than celebrities or politicians. "Look, I have some time. Do you want to sit down and go through some social media sites that can help?"

The woman lit up. "Would you? How about a cup of coffee on the house? It's freshly made with vanilla beans and a touch of coconut."

"Deal." Mia dropped her Michael Kors bag on the table and fished out her phone. She opened up a variety of apps and typed in the Market's address. Not possible. She looked up. "Fran, what's your website address?"

Fran laughed. "Oh, I don't have a website. That's silly. Everyone knows where I am."

"How about a Facebook page?"

Fran frowned. "That's just for young kids to post photos on."

Mia smothered a groan. This was going to end up taking longer than she thought. "Let's start with the basics. I'm going to set you up with a website right now. I can do this on my phone, but it'd be easier with a laptop. Do you have one?"

"That, I do have!"

Fran brought her the computer, and Mia settled in. She'd do a basic website, Facebook page, and Yelp, and then move on. Of course, she'd have to show Fran how to navigate and post her specials of the day. And maybe she should sponsor that craft festival she'd seen advertised for more prominence.

Her mind raced, and she got to work.

Chapter Eleven

Ethan decided to stop by the inn.

He was curious. Since that kiss, he hadn't seen her. He figured she'd swing by the barn today to prove she had the right to visit and annoy him, but she never showed. Not that he wanted to see her. He was just curious what she was up to. Chloe said she seemed busy with work and stopped in town, but she didn't give him further information. The teen had been doing well on the farm and was getting the hang of it. She was also great with the horses and had a gentle touch that was hard to teach. The only thing that seemed off was when her phone would ring and she'd look at it with half dread, then walk away to talk in private. Could be a boyfriend, but something was bothering him about her behavior. So far, though, there'd been no trouble. She seemed like a good kid.

Ophelia was bugging him to get up on the roof to secure one of the loose gutters. Now seemed like a good time to get it done and check on Mia to see what trouble she was up to.

Unfortunately, he'd picked the wrong time to do a stopover.

He paused close to the front porch, where six senior citizens were engaged in a rowdy game of cards. Tea and cookies were out, and they were yelling loudly at each other while music blasted in the background. Sounded like Rihanna. With . . . Eminem?

Must be the group he was scheduled to take horseback riding on Friday. Ethan paused, ready to turn back before they spotted him, but it was already too late.

"Hey, are you Ophelia's brother, Ethan?" The elderly woman had a bird sprouting out of her head as she walked closer to greet him.

He bit back a groan and forced a polite smile. "Yep, that's me. I'll be seeing you later on in the week for your lessons."

"We want to gallop. Fast."

His lips twitched. "I'll do my best. Don't mean to interrupt your game. Have fun and I'll talk to you later."

"No, stay! I'm Ethel. We need another player for poker. You have money?"

"Yeah, but I'm just here to secure one of the gutters. I'm sure Ophelia will want to play."

Another woman joined her, offering him a lascivious grin with no teeth. Was her gaze roaming over his body, or was he just imagining it? "Ophelia had to run into town for errands. We'll wait for you, handsome. I'm Priscilla. Mia's coming down to join us, and we like playing with eight, if possible."

"Mia? She's joining you in the game?"

"Yes, you know her?"

Oh, this was too good. Mia playing with a group of seniors? He had to see this for himself. "Sure. In that case, I'll play a round or two."

They clapped their hands. "We'll wait if you want to take off your shirt and get on the ladder to fix the gutter first," Priscilla said.

Take off his shirt? He'd heard of dirty old men, but this was a first. Ethel shook her head. "Priscilla, you're going to scare him. Come on, Ethan, we have everything set up. You can do the gutter after a few rounds."

Ethan climbed up the steps and found Ophelia had set up a large table for them to play on. A pitcher of iced tea and a platter of cookies were laid out. One glass held Priscilla's teeth, and spare pairs of glasses were littered across the table. Red and blue chips were stacked in piles. They made quick introductions of the couples, chatting casually as Ed cashed him in, shooting Ethan suspicious looks.

"Military?" He grunted, handing him a pile of chips.

"Yeah. How'd you know?"

"I was, too. You got the look." A flare of understanding passed between them. He poured himself a glass of iced tea and looked up as the screen door banged.

Mia held the desperate look of a woman praying for a savior. He bit back a grin at her obvious dread of playing poker at three p.m. on a weekday afternoon with strangers, but a grudging respect trickled through him. She could have said no or not answered the door or been rude. It said something that she allowed Ethel to direct her around because she was afraid to hurt her feelings. Most women he knew never would've given Ethel the time of day, no matter how pushy she was.

"You?" Those whiskey-colored eyes widened in part shock, part horror. "What are you doing here?"

He leaned back in his chair and crossed his ankles. "Good to see you, Mia. Been a long time." She glowered at the hidden meaning. "Just playing a little poker."

"She brought her money," Dolly whispered happily. "Deal her in, Ed."

"Mia, do you need some lessons?" Ethan asked innocently. "Poker is such a rough game. Do you even know how to play?"

Her gaze narrowed with a touch of meanness. Damn, she was hot. "Of course I know how to play. I can spot a bluff a planet away."

Priscilla cackled. "Good, I like a bloodthirsty game. We had to drop a few players along the way because they didn't have what it takes."

Ed slid over Mia's chips. "A few hard rules: Dealer's choice. We ante up. We don't play with wimpy wild cards. We don't borrow money from each other. We don't welch on bets. Got it?"

Ethan pressed his lips together and nodded. "Got it."

Mia nodded. "Got it."

"Have a cookie, dear," Ethel said, sliding over one of Ophelia's creations. Overlarge, gooey, and full of chocolate chips, they were guaranteed to wipe out any bad mood.

Sheer terror carved out the lines of Mia's face. "N-n-no thank you." Ethan noticed her fingers trembled, and her nose flared slightly as if trying to suck up the scent of the chocolate. Son of a bitch—when was the woman going to allow herself some damn simple pleasures?

He grabbed one, broke it in half, and handed her a piece. "Eat the cookie, Mia," he commanded.

She folded her arms in front of her chest and smiled. Sweetly. "No, thank you."

"You'll like it."

"Maybe later."

They stared at one another in a ridiculous challenge until Fred called out, "Ante up!"

Priscilla clapped, reached over, and stuck in her teeth. Ed began dealing. "Game is five-card stud."

Their gazes broke apart, but it wasn't over. Not by a long shot.

Ethan had played a lot of poker in his life. On missions, a deck of cards helped him alleviate the boredom and bond with his teammates. He'd learned the hard way—by losing a shitload of money—the proper way to bluff, when to fold, and when to take his shot. He quickly analyzed the table and figured out some things after the second round.

Ed was too black and white and didn't like risk. Priscilla and Ethel bet for fun. Fred was too laid back.

The real card sharks were Dolly, Pete, and Mia.

They were fearless, smart, and changed their game play enough to keep him off balance. But slowly, using all the tactics he'd learned, he flushed out Dolly until she dropped. He pegged Pete as his main competitor, but the man began getting distracted, looking away from his cards and getting a strange glassy-eyed stare that looked way too familiar.

Ethan glanced over at Priscilla.

The woman was leaning over the table, giving her husband a generous peek at her breasts.

Ethan jerked back, almost spilling his tea, and wished for bleach to remove the vision permanently.

"What's the matter?" Mia asked.

Ethan groaned. "Pete? Why don't you excuse yourself from the table?"

Priscilla giggled.

Pete stood up. "I fold," he announced. He grabbed his wife's hand and dragged her inside. "We're tired. We need a nap."

The door slammed.

Mia's mouth dropped open as the full implication seemed to finally hit her.

"There they go again," Ethel said. "Always banging."

Mia choked.

"Guess it's just you two," Fred said.

Ethan assessed his final competitor and threw in a blue chip. "I raise you five."

She never blinked or changed her expression. Her glittery nail polish flashed. "Call."

"What do you have?" he asked.

She laid out her cards in a perfect fan. "Three kings."

Son of a bitch. No way she was holding those when she'd asked for a card. "Nice job. Two pair."

She reached out and raked in the chips without delay, not even showing a shred of excitement over her victory. Oh, she was good.

But he was better. And he had a plan.

"Why don't we make things more interesting for the final deal?" he threw out. "How about a bet?"

She shot him a suspicious look. "What type of bet?"

"If I win, you go with me to the cupcake festival."

Dolly tittered. "He wants a date with her," she whispered to Ethel. Ethel sighed. "So romantic."

"What?" Mia screeched. "Why on earth would you want to go to a cupcake festival with me?"

He pasted on his best hurt expression. "What are you talking about? You know I've had a crush on you for a while. I'd love to take you to the festival."

Fred laughed. "Oh, he's good. Real good. Why don't you give him a chance, Mia?"

Trying hard not to laugh at her stunned face, Ethan knew the moment she realized the whole thing was a setup. Steam rose from her head. Ethel and Dolly were urging her to take pity on him, practically sighing over the romantic idea of trying to win a date. He was having so much fun, he almost didn't notice the gleam of revenge in those golden eyes.

Almost.

"Aww, that's so adorable, Ethan," she simpered for the audience. She even batted those lashes at him. "I accept. But if I win, I want something from you."

"What is it?"

Her smile was deadly. "Ethel was telling me they were dying to see the play *Mama Mia* at the Westchester Dinner Theater Saturday night, but they need someone to drive them. No one is comfortable driving at night, and it's over an hour away. Since I know how much you adore musicals, I think it would be wonderful if you accompanied them!"

Holy shit. She was pure evilness. The woman even managed to bat her eyelashes in innocence.

Ethel squealed. "What a wonderful bet! Thank you, Mia, that was so sweet of you!"

"You're welcome. Well, Ethan, do we have a deal?"

He needed to up the stakes. He leaned over and nailed her with his gaze. "Fine. But there's one clause included for our cupcake-festival date."

She blinked. Good—at least she was wary. "What?"

"You have to eat the cupcakes. As many as I say."

Her face paled. He caught the twist of lust for sugar and fear of getting out of control. That's when he knew he had to watch her eat a cupcake. It would be an orgasmic experience.

For both of them.

She gnashed her teeth together but managed to nod. "Fine."

"Done. I deal. Five-card stud. Ante up."

In an almost sulky silence, she threw her chips in, but he knew he had to watch her carefully. This round was absolutely crucial. There was no fucking way he was escorting a group of seniors to see *Mama Mia*. His man card would be permanently yanked.

The next two hands ended up being crap. He folded first round, she folded the next. On the third round, his nerves tingled pleasantly at the sight of two regal ladies. A glance over told him she was also interested.

She threw down one card.

He threw down two.

Tension rose in the air. He studied her face, noting the tiny tic of her right brow. Yes, she had a decent hand. The question would be if he had one better.

Since this was the final all-in round, there was no need for foreplay.

Three queens.

Sweat broke out on his skin. The towering pile of chips in the center wasn't the real prize, and they both knew it. But damned if she didn't look cool and composed. This was going to be close.

"Time to show. What do you have?"

The touch of a smile curved her lush, pink lips, distracting him for a second. It was worse now that he knew how she tasted. How could she practically ooze sugary sweetness when she never allowed herself to eat any?

"Two pair. Aces," she said.

It was a good hand, but not good enough. He savored the pure relief of not only escaping a musical but also being able to watch her eat cupcakes.

"Nice. But I have three queens."

The audience burst into applause. Ed slapped him on the back and grunted in approval. Dolly patted Mia's hand in sympathy.

"At least you'll get a date out of it," Dolly whispered loudly. "He's a nice man."

Ethan tried not to be offended at the strangled look on Mia's face. The woman could demolish a man's ego way too easily. He stood up from the chair and stretched. "Been a pleasure playing with you all. Gonna fix up that gutter, and I'll see everyone on Friday for the lessons," he said. "Wanna walk me out, Mia?"

Suddenly, Priscilla and Pete burst from the front door. "Who won?" Priscilla demanded. Pete had a goofy grin on his face. Both of their faces were sweaty, and there was a glow around them.

Holy shit, they were getting more action than he was.

Ethel sighed. "Ethan won and he's taking Mia out on a date to the cupcake festival. Pris, your blouse is on backward."

Priscilla looked down and giggled. "Oops."

Mia jumped up. "I'll walk you out!"

Ethan led her to the side of the house, where a large weeping willow tree hid them from the sting of the sun. Ophelia's bountiful vegetable garden offered an array of vivid colors and scents, carefully protected by a picket fence to keep out intruders. He opened the ladder he'd previously set out and fished around in his toolbox.

"That was dirty pool," she shot out, hands crossed in front of her chest. He tried not to notice the perfect swell of her breasts against the creamy silk of her tank top. His palm itched, remembering the sweet curve of their weight, the hard tips of her nipples pressed against his chest. He smothered a groan and focused on grabbing the right tools.

"Because I want to take you to the cupcake festival? You're right. I'm a horrific villain."

She practically seethed, which only added to his desire to grab her and work out all that energy in a totally different way. "You were mocking me. You don't even like me. You just want me to eat cupcakes!"

"I like you just fine," he muttered. Dear God, why did his skin suddenly feel hot? He turned away and climbed the ladder, wondering what was happening to him. He'd been known for his smooth charm in Hollywood and had women trailing his every move. Now, he sounded like an awkward teen. *Did* he like her? "When you had that apple pie, you changed. You relaxed. You looked happy. And you weren't so . . ."

"What?" Her voice dripped with suspicion.

"Uptight."

She let out a breath. Then went on a tirade close to the way Donald Duck got in a snit, so he took the opportunity to bang the nails in, and the noise smothered her rant. He checked the fit and tuned back in.

"—rude, and it's none of your business what I eat or don't, and the way you try to bully me—"

"Look, princess, that *Mama Mia* trick was as low as you can go. So don't talk to me about setups."

"Ethel did say she needed a driver. I was just trying to be nice."

"Sure. Besides, I think you deliberately wanted to lose."

Her mouth fell open, and they were back to the races. "What are you talking about?"

He climbed down the ladder, replaced his tools and shut the box, then smirked. "You could've folded again. Instead, you stayed in with an average hand. Maybe you wanted a date with me but were too embarrassed to pursue it. This way, you get to pretend it was forced on you."

Her skin flushed, and her golden eyes flamed. "You're delusional," she breathed. "I despise spending time with you."

"Ah, you protest a bit too much. Listen, it doesn't bother me. I like being pursued. It's kinda cute."

She was so mad, words seemed to escape her. Delight flowed through him. Actual sparks flew around her figure. It was the same type of chemistry that shot out when they'd kissed. If he took her to bed, would they both combust?

"This is war, horse man," she finally wrested out. "Make no doubt about it." She marched away, head held high in the air, fists clenched at her sides.

"See you Saturday!" he called out. "Oh, and wear something pretty." Ethan shook his head. The woman was definitely livening up his summer.

Chapter Twelve

Oh, he was so arrogant.

Mia fumed as she made her way back into her room. The porch was clear—her new friends off to wreak havoc on the town, probably—and she couldn't get that damn kiss out of her head.

A date. *Like hell.* She didn't want to date Ethan Bishop. He was a pain in the ass. Sure, he was Special Forces and put others' lives in front of his own. Sure, he'd been a bodyguard and seemed to have a deep protective instinct that gave her a sinking mushy pit in her stomach. Sure, he was hot, even with the Grizzly Adams beard.

But he was not her type. In August, she'd get out of this perfect country hellhole and back to the city, where she ruled and things made sense, and she picked whom she did and didn't want to go to bed with on her own terms.

Maybe she'd spend some time with Chloe. Her father called every few days for a check-in, but Mia sensed his daughter felt like he was just crossing off an item on his to-do list. She'd worked longer days at the stable than needed, so Ethan had given her the day off.

Mia knocked on her door. It took a few moments for her to open it. "Hey. How's it going?"

Chloe shrugged. Her purple hair was braided around her face. Her eyebrow ring flashed in the light. She wore tiny denim shorts and three layered multicolored tank tops with spaghetti straps. Her toenails were painted black. "Fine."

"Want to go into town with me? Figured you'd be bored. We could do some shopping."

Chloe flicked a judging gaze over Mia's conservative, polished outfit and smirked. Politely. "No, thanks. My friends called, and they're on their way over to pick me up."

Mia shifted in discomfort. This was the part she hated. She'd promised Jonathan to keep his daughter out of trouble, but she was in college for God's sake. She had to have a life, and this inn was beginning to be a type of prison, like Chloe originally termed it. "Okay. Make sure you check your cell in case I text for something."

Chloe rolled her eyes but nodded. "Sure."

Her tone dripped sarcasm, but Mia was grateful for any type of assent. "Your dad said he was going to try to come up next weekend for a visit."

Immediately, her face changed. Those gorgeous blue eyes hardened, and Mia's heart broke at the obvious resentment. "Tell him 'no, thanks.' What if the paparazzi track him down and find out his criminal daughter has been hidden from the world? Goodbye, NYC Mayor."

"You're more important to him than being mayor, Chloe," she said.

"Sure you're not sleeping with him? You're defending him like you are."

Mia narrowed her gaze. "I'm sure. He's my client, and I believe he's a good man. I also know he's nuts about you and didn't know how to handle it when you got in trouble. He's a guy. They're not very good at emotions."

That remark got her a slight smile.

She was halfway to the door when inspiration struck. "Hey, there's a cupcake festival on Saturday. Ethan mentioned it. Want to go?"

The girl shrugged. "I guess. Nothing else to do around here."

"Great."

She headed to her room. *Take that, Ethan.* It couldn't be an official date with Chloe there. She needed to prove she wasn't interested in spending any extra time with the man. The Golden Girls crew needed no other ammunition to try to match them up, or they'd drive her nuts the next two weeks.

The sound of rowdy laughter and curse words drifted up to her open window. She peeked her head out to see what was going on.

A battered black muscle car was parked outside. Three kids hooted Chloe's name, leaning against the side of the car, flicking cigarette ashes on the pavement. The two guys were tatted up, with baggy shorts hanging past their knees and large, round piercings in their ears. Definitely older. The lone girl sported bright-pink hair in a shaggy cut and wore barely-there denim shorts, wedged sandals, and a low-cut black shirt.

Mia frowned. These were Chloe's friends? Her gut told her to go downstairs and secure an introduction. She was here to watch out for Chloe, and though it was uncomfortable to play guardian, she owed that to Jonathan.

She skipped down the stairs quickly, heading toward the car at the same time Chloe reached her friends. Mia pasted on a bright smile as she approached.

"Hi, guys. I'm Mia, Chloe's . . . aunt. How are you?"

Chloe's eyes widened in horror. Her blue eyes flickered with a tinge of panic before she quickly ducked her head, muttering something under her breath. Why was she so afraid of introducing her friends? Was it a teen-embarrassment thing? Or something more?

The first guy looked bored, while the second one gave her a leer. Up close, they looked kind of alike, with short, spiky hair and brown eyes. Were they brothers? "Hey," one of them greeted. "You're the one guarding Chloe's ass, huh?"

Mia blinked. "An interesting way to phrase it, I guess. What's your name?"

"I'm Anthony, and this is Ben."

"Nice to meet you."

Ben didn't bother to answer her. God, how she hated rudeness. "You ready to go or what, Chloe?" he demanded in a sulky tone.

Mia ignored him and faced the pink-haired girl. "And you are?"

The girl scowled. "Theresa."

"Nice to meet you. Where you guys headed?"

"Out," Theresa said. "Unless she has to sign something in order to leave this hellhole."

Chloe grabbed Theresa and dragged her inside the car. "We're going for a hike at Minnewaska. Right, guys?"

"Yeah, right," Anthony said with a grin. "Good to meet you."

"Without water bottles?" Mia challenged. She caught Chloe's face flushing and knew something else was going on. Holy crap, was she really going to allow Lake's daughter to head out with this band of juvenile delinquents?

"We'll stop for some at the store," Chloe threw out in desperation, climbing into the back seat. "Don't wait up."

"Chloe, I don't know about this—"

She knew the words were a mistake the moment they were uttered. Chloe practically snarled back at her. "I do. You can't keep me locked up with a bunch of old people all summer. I'm outta here. See ya later."

Ben gave her a high five from the driver's seat and pulled out with a roar of his tires.

Mia bit her lip and fought the panic curling at her nerves. Dammit, she should've read some parenting books on how to handle teens. Seems like rule one was the moment you challenged them, they became monsters.

But she was nineteen years old and on her own. As long as she didn't get into trouble, how could she force her to stay?

She didn't like Chloe's friends. Not that she liked to judge based on appearances, but her gut screamed something was off. They were trouble. Chloe was a good kid. Mia had seen the way she acted on the farm with the horses. She was relaxed, and open. The girl actually laughed! But with this group, she looked uncomfortable, as if she was being forced to be with them.

Holding back a groan, Mia decided to try to talk to Chloe when she returned. Then she'd call Jonathan tonight and make sure he came up this weekend. Hopefully, he could have a heart-to-heart with his daughter and straighten things out.

Mia grabbed her purse and headed into town. It was time to go shopping for some crappy clothes.

Look pretty, indeed.

Chapter Thirteen

Ethan tried hard not to laugh when he spotted Mia sitting on the front porch waiting for him.

He'd been prepared for her to put a spin on this "date" he'd set up, but he had to admit she'd managed to surprise him. Chloe sat next to her, purple hair gleaming in the sunlight, her grungy high-topped combat boots propped up on the edge of the wicker table. Mia'd been savvy enough to bring a chaperone.

Nicely played.

But the best part? Her appearance. It was obvious she'd taken pains to clearly show him she was not interested in impressing him. Instead, she'd achieved the complete opposite.

She looked fucking adorable.

Her hair was caught in two tight braids at the sides of her head. The plain pink pocketed T-shirt had a V neck and was two sizes too big. Her jean shorts stopped at her knees and were cuffed at the edges. She wore brightly colored Hawaiian-type flip-flops he knew she'd picked up at the local dollar store in town. The knowledge she'd actually gone out to specifically shop for this date told him everything he needed to know.

She wanted him.

He just needed to consider what to do about it.

"Chloe, I'm glad you're joining us today. I was hoping Mia would invite you."

The teen jumped out of her chair. "Thanks, can't say no to cupcakes. Hey, you shaved your beard! It looks rad."

His hand came up to rub his newly shaven skin. "Yeah, it was time. We'll take the truck—wanna start it up for me?"

"Sure."

He tossed her the keys, and she skipped down the stairs. Mia still hadn't said a word, so he glanced over, already prepared for a smart-assed quip regarding his lack of a beard.

Then froze.

She was staring at him with raw, naked lust.

In moments, his dick hardened, and his gut clenched like he'd been punched. Those tigress eyes roved over his face, drinking in his appearance with a hunger she couldn't seem to hide. Sexual chemistry twisted and sizzled between them. He ground his teeth together and fought the urge to walk over, haul her into his arms, and kiss her. An aching silence stretched between them, pulsing with unsaid want.

"Your beard," she whispered. She cleared her throat, as if to try once again to speak. "It's gone."

"Yeah. You like it?"

She didn't answer. Her tongue flicked out and ran over her lower lip. His gaze pierced hers, refusing to let go. "You look . . . different."

Satisfaction slammed through him. She liked it. His male ego gave an approving roar. He wondered what it would feel like to stand naked in front of her and bask in all that feminine pleasure. "So do you."

A frown creased her brow. "You don't like the new duds, huh?"

A smile touched his lips. "I fucking love it. You look sexy. Touchable."

Her mouth fell open. "I look horrific!"

"That's the problem with women. They have no idea what a man really wants. Let's go fatten you up, princess."

Her mouth firmed with displeasure at his response, but she stalked off the porch and right past him like the high queen she was. "I only want to stay an hour," she said primly. "There was no time requirement for this outing."

"My truck. My schedule."

"You're so rude."

He tamped down a chuckle, opening the door and allowing her to slide in. He pulled out and hit the Bluetooth button. "What type of music do you like, Chloe?" he asked.

"Probably nothing you have," she said with a sigh.

He laughed. "Try me. I'm cooler than you think."

"I'm into alternative. I like Airborne Toxic Event, Arctic Monkeys, and Cage the Elephant."

"Those are the real names?" Mia asked in astonishment.

Ethan pressed a few buttons and cranked the volume. "Got you covered. Cage the Elephant is one of my faves."

"Dude, I'm lit."

"I'm pumped," Ethan said.

"I'm confused," Mia said, but she was laughing and shaking her head.

They introduced Mia to the joys of alternative music and drove past the sign that proclaimed CUPCAKE FESTIVAL and straight into the heart of Gardiner. Small, quaint Main Street was pumping with activity, so he parked in the field they'd designated for the endless cars the town rarely hosted. Vendor booths lined the road, set off by the regular shops selling art, handcrafted clothes, unique gifts, and endless food. A giant bouncy house welcomed excited children, and there was a long line for face painting. Pop music streamed from giant speakers set up. The library sold bags of used books, and antique stores pushed their wares on neighbors' lawns. People pushed baby strollers, walked dogs, and feasted on cupcakes as they enjoyed a summer weekend, relishing the simple pleasures of life.

Ethan braced himself for his nerves to hit. He couldn't seem to handle big crowds, especially accompanied by loud noises, but instead a sense of peace washed over him. For so many years, he'd chased bigger dreams and moments that would give him the satisfaction of making a difference. He'd accomplished many of them. He knew that in his heart, even though the nightmares plagued him and guilt was still his companion. But something about being home made him feel like this could be the place he really belonged now. He missed his team like a physical ache, so used to the male bonding that was part of the fabric of his days. But every day he stayed at the farm, he settled a bit more into a routine he relished rather than dreaded. Maybe it had taken all this time to be ready to come home.

His steps were light as he led Chloe and Mia down the street, pointing out various wares. "They have Cookie Monster cupcakes!" Chloe shrieked, pointing at a line interspersed with teens and toddlers. "He's my fave."

Ethan pushed some bills into her hand. "It's my treat today. Go break the seal."

"Thanks. I'll catch up with you later."

She bounded off with more enthusiasm than he'd seen, confirming the schizophrenic tendencies of teenagers. Mia shook her head. "Really? If that was all it took to make her happy, I would've stocked up for the rest of the summer."

"I'm more of a Count fan, but Cookie's cool."

"Don't be ridiculous. Elmo rules."

He couldn't help tugging on her braid, which got him a good glare that only made her sexier. Without her makeup, he glimpsed the smattering of freckles she usually covered and the blush-pink color of her natural lips. If she were his, he'd lock her up and keep her naked and stripped of all civilities.

Those golden eyes widened. "What are you thinking about? You look . . . dangerous."

He dropped his voice. "I dare you to ask me."

She snorted. "Keep dreaming. I want to check out the books."

He laughed, loving the way she kept him off balance. Damn, she was fun to flirt with. "Lead the way."

In the next hour, he discovered she loved historical and political books. When he shot her some trivia questions, she impressed him with her memory for dates and events. Intrigued, he pushed further. "Twenty-third president of the US?" he challenged.

"Benjamin Harrison."

"Impressive. How many presidents died in office?"

She ticked them off on her hands. "William Henry Harrison. Zachary Taylor. Abe Lincoln. James Garfield. William McKinley. Warren G. Harding. Franklin D. Roosevelt. And John F. Kennedy. Eight."

"Do you have a degree in history?" he asked curiously.

"My back-up career was a history professor, but I didn't want to go on for my PhD, and it wasn't exciting enough. My entire childhood revolved around my father's lectures on American history. The History channel was like my Cartoon Network."

He almost caught his breath at the sudden slam of attraction. He loved a good intellectual. Sure, he knew she was good at banter, but this just gave him a hard-on. "You're a closet nerd." It came out almost as an accusation.

"Don't let it get around and ruin my rep. What's in your pile?"

"I used to read a lot of military fiction and thrillers. Tom Clancy, Steve Berry, Lee Child, David Baldacci. Haven't been able to concentrate in a while, though. Figured I'd try this one."

"*Seabiscuit.* Laura Hillenbrand. She's a fabulous author; I haven't read that one yet."

"I'll lend it to you. What's that one?" He tapped the last book in her stack.

She slid it out to show him the colorful beach cover. "Melissa Foster. One of my favorite romance authors. Sometimes you just need a good love story, right?"

He grinned. "Hell yeah. Come on, enough delaying. It's cupcake time."

She rolled her eyes but allowed him to pay for her books with a gracious *thank you*. They took their time meandering through the booths. He watched her carefully as she read each of the signs boasting flavors such as red velvet, peanut butter and jelly, s'mores, and carrot. She pretended it wasn't a big deal, but when she caught sight of the coconut chocolate delight, he knew he had her.

"Anything good?" he drawled, already knowing her answer.

"Not really. Maybe I'm just not in the mood for cupcakes today."

Oh, she was a master. Her face remained neutral, but her golden eyes flared with lust. She had a thing for food porn. Who would've known it could be so deliciously sexy? "Well, I'm going to get one here," he announced, getting in line.

"Here?" she squeaked. Sheer panic seeped into her voice. "Umm, how about we try a Cookie Monster one?"

"No, thanks. I have my eye on a specific one right here."

As he moved up closer, she shifted in place, pulling at her shirt, growing more uncomfortable with every moment. Finally, a cheery woman with a hairnet and bright-red lipstick leaned forward. "Whatcha want, love?"

"I'll have two of those, please."

"You got it." She placed them in a plastic container, took the money, and handed it over. "Enjoy."

Mia stiffened. A cloud of silence settled over her as he led her to an unoccupied bench. She stared at the cupcakes, teeth nibbling on her lower lip in distress, and he reached out and tugged her down to sit beside him.

"How did you know?" she whispered.

"I can spot a lie, too. I guess we both have something in common after all. I love coconut." He spread out a napkin onto her lap and lifted the cupcake. It was a perfect size chocolate cake covered in shredded coconut with light, frothy cream and one chocolate swirl placed on the top. He handed it over, and her fingers trembled as she delicately held the sweet. Her face held so much longing, his heart squeezed. Why had she denied herself such simple pleasures for so long? If he accomplished one damn thing this summer, it would be to show this woman that an occasional indulgence was a gift in life and should never be wasted. "Mia?"

"Yes?"

"Eat your cupcake."

She did. He watched every precious, gut-wrenching, sensual moment of the experience and wondered if he'd ever be the same.

She was beautiful.

Her entire being softened as she ate. Her eyes glowed with pleasure, and she savored every tiny bite, her tongue licking over her lips to catch the last bit of icing. A low moan escaped her mouth. Her body shook slightly. And when that cupcake had been completely devoured, she let out a soft, sated sigh that slammed straight to his cock and made him want to weep in surrender.

He wanted Mia Thrush in his bed.

Almost sleepy, she looked up and met his gaze. "That was so good."

A smudge of chocolate lay in the corner of her mouth. He reached over slowly, wiping it off with his thumb. Nailing her with his stare, he deliberately put his thumb into his mouth and sucked.

Sexual attraction exploded between them. The sights and sounds faded around them, meaningless in the perfect connection of those precious seconds.

"Mia?"

"Yeah?" Her voice was a breathless whisper. A yearning. A question. It took all his willpower to keep from kissing her right here, so he could taste the sweetness of her lips and tongue mixed with chocolate and coconut. Instead, he locked down all his muscles and prayed no one could see his strangling erection.

"Will you do something for me today?"

"Depends."

He smiled. "For the rest of the afternoon, will you let me feed you?"

She blinked. It was a request, not a demand. It wasn't about a bet or a ruse or anything but the joy of watching her appreciate a small-town festival and its amazing food. He waited for a temper tantrum or sarcastic joke or a roll of her eyes.

"Okay."

Something shifted. Breathed. Changed. He didn't know what it was, but he also knew it would never be the same between them.

"Thank you."

They smiled at each other on a park bench in the middle of a cup-cake festival.

For the rest of the afternoon, he gifted her with morsels of food carefully selected from local vendors: A crisp Gala apple, freshly picked and drizzled with honey from Wrights Farm. A scoop of churned homemade black-cherry ice cream. A bite of shortbread topped with fresh strawberries and cream. A sip of chilled Whitecliff Vineyard Awosting White wine.

With each bite, she laughed more freely, linking her arm with his in an intimate gesture he enjoyed. For a few hours, they basked in the sun like young kids on a date, indulging in all the treats laid out for them to savor. Chloe joined them in their pursuit of the perfect bite, and they all finally found it when they tasted their final cupcake.

Banana cream pie with toasted coconut.

Even Chloe agreed, and she deemed herself a chocoholic.

Finally, exhausted and stuffed, they began to make their way back to the car. Her entire persona buzzed with contentment. If she were his woman, he'd feed her every damn day to relish the sated look on her face. In a few short hours, she had completely bloomed.

"Mia!"

Fran came running over, face wreathed in a happy smile. Guilt hit. Dammit, he'd promised Judge Bennett to stop in and see her. He'd heard her new business was struggling, and she'd been hoping he could suggest ways to help her bring in some profit. He opened his mouth to apologize, then realized she'd called out to Mia, not him.

She knew Mia?

"Hi, Fran!" The women hugged. "How are you?"

"Great! I got approved to sell food at the craft festival and just got on the list for the strawberry festival!"

"Smart move. Make sure you post it on the new page I set up. Oh, I stopped into Anderson's Hardware store and told them you'd give them a discount if they ordered lunch from you this week."

"He called me and let me know—thanks so much."

"No problem. Oh, this is Chloe, my niece. She's staying at Ophelia's for the summer with me."

"Hi, sweetie. Nice to meet you. Harper said you were doing a wonderful job with the horses. You must be such a help."

If Fran knew the girl had been sentenced to probation, she never let on. Chloe smiled. "Thanks, I really like it. I've eaten some of your food when Mia brings it home, and it's amazing."

"I'm so glad you like it."

Ethan watched the exchange with growing confusion. What was going on? "Umm, hi, Fran."

"Oh, sorry. Hi, Ethan." She gave him a quick hug. "Where have you been hiding?"

He shifted his weight. "Sorry, I've been busy lately. I'll stop by this week."

Fran waved a hand in the air. "Well, you're welcome anytime, but Mia has literally saved me. Besides getting me on social media, I now have a Yelp site with great reviews, and more people are visiting every day. She's a genius. I keep trying to pay her, but she won't take a cent."

"It barely takes up any time in my day. My pleasure," Mia replied.

"Well, Brian told me you met with him yesterday and started a whole new marketing campaign to get younger kids in the comic book store. I knew he was relying on the college crowd too heavily, but he refused to listen to anyone."

"I told him the same thing. He's stubborn, but I finally convinced him to participate in some kids' expo events and give out free comics. I'm working on his marketing plan."

Ethan cleared his throat. Brian despised outsiders, or anyone who told him how to run his business. He was gruff, short, and he rarely smiled. His customer service skills were shit. Now he was letting Mia help him? "Brian approached you for help?" he asked.

"Yes. He heard about Fran and asked for my opinion. I gave it to him, and he hated every one of my suggestions and stomped off."

"Was he mean to you?" he demanded. He'd kick Brian's ass himself if the man had said anything bad to Mia.

She laughed. "Oh, no, he's just a teddy bear underneath all that gruff. He called me later to apologize and asked if I could help him out. He's real sweet."

There were many words that described Brian, and *sweet* wasn't one of them. All this time, he had no idea she'd been going into town regularly, let alone interacting with everyone.

"Well, you're a gem," Fran said. "Bea from the diner also wanted to speak with you—have you eaten there yet? Popular hangout. Wait a minute—she's supposed to be here today; let me text her and tell her to come over."

"No, I have to go!" Chloe suddenly burst out. They turned to look at her. Ethan noticed her skin had gone pale, and she was gazing around with an almost panicked look in her eye. "Can we go now, please? I made plans with my friends tonight, and it's getting late."

Ethan frowned. Something else was going on. What had spooked her?

"Sorry, Fran, next time. We've been here for hours," Mia said.

"Of course. Thanks again and I'll see you later."

They said their goodbyes and headed toward the truck. Chloe seemed to calm down the moment she was inside, and they drove back to the inn, listening to the Arctic Monkeys while Mia begged for a music intervention. Poor thing liked Adam Levine. It was just wrong.

He parked the truck and said goodbye to Chloe, who ran off with her phone clutched tight in her hand. "Have you met her friends yet?" he asked casually.

"Yes, but Chloe freaked, and Jonathan said just to keep an eye out for them. I have to be careful not to push. Figured I need to let her breathe."

"Smart. Just wondering. Do you know if she has a boyfriend?"

"I asked her once over lunch, and she said no. I believed her. Why?"

"Nothing. Just a gut instinct she's worried about something."

"Her father is coming up next weekend, so I'll talk to him about it."

"Good idea." They stopped in front of the inn. "Want to walk me to my bungalow?"

That got a laugh from her. He enjoyed the throaty, full-on sound pumped with joy. "Are you trying to end this date on an official note?"

"Maybe."

"You already walked me to my door," she pointed out.

"In a traditional world, yes. But you, Mia Thrush, don't have a traditional bone in your body. And I'd like to spend a bit more time with you."

His words seemed to take her off guard. She stepped back in retreat, searching his face for her own answers. He wondered if she'd back off and hide behind the wall of sarcasm and banter they'd constructed, but she surprised him by nodding. "Lead the way."

They walked in comfortable silence. Fat bumblebees jumped from flower to flower, buzzing in ecstasy from too much pollen. The sun beat strong on their shoulders, but the faint breeze took away some of the sting, stirring the trees so they whispered in the woods. Their feet followed the winding path in unison.

"What was it like growing up here?" she asked.

"Peaceful. My parents worked hard to build up the bed-and-breakfast, but we ended up losing my dad too early to a heart attack. After that, Mom became obsessed with making the inn a success and later added the horse rescue. My sisters and I bitched a lot that we didn't have it as easy as other kids. She expected us to get up early, do chores, help run the business. She was tough. But loving. And fair."

"She sounds pretty amazing."

He smiled, a warm rush of memories comforting him. "Yeah. She was. Of course, I had bigger plans for my life and didn't want to get stuck in a small town taking care of guests and horses. Neither did Ophelia."

Her brow quirked. "You're kidding? I would've figured Harper would be the one to get itchy feet. Ophelia seems so perfect for this life."

He shook his head. "Hell no. She was the wild child. Sneaking out at night to cause trouble. Wanted to go to Hollywood and sing—her voice is extraordinary. She ran away from home for a while, but when she came back, she'd changed. Settled down some. She never told me what happened, but by then I was off pursuing my own dreams. Harper was the one obsessed with horses and making the farm a success."

Mia gave a small sigh. "I always wanted a sibling. It was lonely growing up an only child. Maybe that's why I got so involved with my dad and his career. I was really close to my parents and never went through any of those rebellious periods where I wanted to leave. They always made me feel safe."

"Nothing wrong with that. Are they still living happily somewhere in retirement?"

"Not together. Not anymore." Her face clouded. The flare of pain in those golden eyes made an odd ache squeeze his heart. He didn't like seeing her unhappy. That familiar protectiveness roared up inside, pushing him to stop walking and turn toward her.

"Divorced?" She nodded. He imagined how hard it was watching parents split, but there was something more underneath the surface. "Bad?"

She hesitated. Peered into his face as if to test how much she trusted him when they had just become tentative friends. Then she took the leap. "They split up over a lie. My father was running for senate years ago. A nasty rumor spread about him cheating on my mother in a sex scandal. The papers blew up, and he was tried and convicted before he had a chance. My mother didn't believe him, so she left. He lost his prospective seat and his wife."

"But he didn't do it?"

She slowly shook her head. Ghosts danced over her features. "We found out the truth after the election, but the press buried it and no one cared. By then, it was too late. They'd hurt each other too much, and the trust was gone. My father was brokenhearted. Mom remarried, but my father withdrew to a small town, practices law, and still lives alone." She blew out a breath, and the grief turned to anger. "I'm still so mad. Mad at the lies spun to hurt and frame. Mad at my mother for not fighting for her marriage. Mad at my father for giving up on his life. I swore I'd achieve justice by helping people who deserve to win a political seat. People who are good and have the right intentions. That's why I'm helping Lake's daughter. I don't want something like this to ruin his chances."

"If you can get him elected, you can right some of the past."

She jerked, looking up at him with startled eyes. At that moment, she was so beautiful, his heart stuttered out of rhythm, then stampeded in a mad rush to make up for the pause. Blood squeezed in his veins. The sheer grit and determination staring back at him punched him hard in the gut. She was a fighter, but she fought for good, for justice, for her beliefs. There was nothing that turned him on more than a woman who took loyalty and protectiveness to such a level.

And, suddenly, Mia Thrush became a lot more than a sexy woman who amused him.

The air thickened between them, scented with earth and sunshine and sweetness. His thumb tipped her chin up. His gaze locked with hers, relishing the tiny hitch in her breath and her dilated pupils. Relishing that she was as confused and turned on as he was.

"I'm sorry, sweetheart. Because I know you would've fought to your last breath to save something or someone you loved."

Seconds passed. The silence drenched them and pulsed with possibility.

She blinked, confused. "Ethan?"

He'd taken what he wanted the last time. This time, he needed the words. "I need to kiss you, Mia. Right now, I feel like I'll fucking die if I don't kiss you."

She didn't hesitate. Standing on tiptoes, her hands reached up and grabbed his shoulders. "Yes," she breathed against his lips, "kiss me now."

He did. His mouth covered hers, and his tongue dove inside her mouth to feast. He groaned and savored the taste of sugar and spice, of chocolate and coconut, of raw demand and sweet surrender. She fisted her hands in his hair, holding him tight, arching against him while her tongue tangled and battled his in a war they both won. Nipping at her delectable, lush bottom lip, he cupped her ass and hauled her higher up against him. The hard ridge of his cock begged for release against his jeans as she wriggled her hips to get closer. He needed her naked, spread-eagled on his bed. He needed her wet and aching and begging for him to fill her. He needed so much . . . more.

She rubbed her cheek against the smooth skin of his jaw and purred like a sexy kitten. "Feels so good," she murmured.

"Miss the beard?"

"Hell no." She nibbled at the corner of his mouth, then kissed him again, long and deep. "You were hiding a cleft chin. What guy does that?"

"One who wasn't ready for anything."

"And now?"

The challenge burned hot and bright between them. There wasn't a shy bone in her body, and he loved her sheer grit and honesty. This was someone who wouldn't run away from messiness. She'd just give it the stink eye and confront it head-on.

"And now I can't think of anything but dragging you into my cabin and doing some very dirty things to you."

"How dirty?"

"Filthy," he growled, his fingers digging into the lush curve of her ass. His knees almost weakened in need. "Depraved. Maybe highly illegal."

"Oh God, that's hot."

She hitched herself up higher, and they fell into another drugging, crazed kiss. He began stumbling backward, desperate to get inside, and then—

"Hello! Ethan? Are you here?"

Mia stiffened in his arms. The familiar voice hit his ears, and reality unfolded like a bad B-horror flick. Impossible. She wouldn't come to his private home, would she?

Yes, she would.

Ethel and Priscilla stood a few feet behind, staring at them with a mixture of delight and pride. "Oh my! Here you both are, this is wonderful. And from that kiss, I see the date went well?"

Priscilla giggled. "Personally, I think Mia waited way too long to test ride this one."

Mia practically fell out of his arms and clawed at her eyes. Probably trying to get that nasty image out of her head, like he was. Why was this happening to him? Had he done something to deserve this type of karma? Talk about wrecking a perfect moment.

He cleared his throat and tried to speak normally. "What do you ladies need today?"

"Sorry to interrupt, but we have wonderful news!" Ethel screeched. "Remember that *Mama Mia* play we needed a driver for?"

Warning tingles shot down his spine. A black cloud of dread battled away the sun. *Shit, shit, shit, shit . . .*

"Sure."

Ethel beamed. "We got a party bus, so there's no need to worry."

"With a stripper pole," Priscilla added.

"But that's not the best part," Ethel said.

He glanced over at Mia and knew. Knew the next few words were going to be very, very bad.

"We got both of you tickets to see the play with us!" Ethel announced. "We'll all be on the party bus together, have dinner, and see the play."

"Now this can be your official second date!" Priscilla screeched in delight.

Mia's mouth fell open. Ethan bit back a scathing curse word. The two women stared at them, waiting for a joyous reaction, and suddenly, the situation struck him full force, and he laughed.

He laughed hard and deep and loud, and then Mia was laughing with him and so were the older women, and he realized he was truly screwed.

Just not in the way he'd imagined a few moments ago.

Chapter Fourteen

Mia approached the barn, picking her way around the piles of mud and hay with a practiced eye. The scent of horse and dung assaulted her nostrils, but she was getting used to it. Her occasional visits kept Ethan on his toes and allowed her to still keep an eye on Chloe. They'd bonded a bit after the cupcake festival, but the girl was still stuck 24-7 to her phone, and conversation still lagged. With Jonathan coming to see her this weekend, Mia figured she'd bring a decent bribe to get her talking a bit more.

Ophelia's cookies may do it.

The teen had her back turned toward her. Her purple hair was snagged in a ponytail and damp with sweat. Dirt smeared her black tank. She rubbed some sort of brush over a pretty gray horse, talking in a warm, open tone Mia didn't even know the girl was capable of. The horse seemed to sense her presence first and gave a low whinny.

"Hi."

Chloe turned, a smile on her face as she met her gaze. "Hi, Mia. What's up?"

Mia raised her hand, holding out the still warm chocolate-chip cookie wrapped in a napkin. "I brought you a snack. The cookies are usually gone by the time you get home, so I snagged one for you."

"Thanks! Can you put it on the table for me while I finish up?"

"Sure." Mia set it down, then watched the girl continue her brushing, moving her hand around in slow, circular motions. "How are things going here?"

"Pretty good. Flower just got a good workout, so I'm brushing her down. Then I have to check on Big Red. His leg got screwed up, so he can't do the trails for a while, and he gets cranky when he's bored."

Mia blinked. "What do you do, then, with him to keep him occupied? Show him your Instagram feed?"

Chloe laughed. Was it her imagination, or was the girl finally beginning to soften? Something about her work with the horses revealed her nurturing, gentle heart. Her appearance had also changed. No more skintight clothes or heavy makeup. Oh, the piercings and black lipstick still showed up, but Mia could actually see her real face, which glowed a golden brown from the sun. She was even more beautiful and looked like a female version of her father.

"No, of course not," Chloe said. "I talk to him, pet him, brush him. He needs to feel important, or he gets depressed."

Mia raised a brow, walking closer to the stall. "I guess I never realized how sensitive horses can be. I figured they just ate, slept, and trotted around a bit, not caring too much about who takes care of them."

Chloe shook her head. "Ethan taught me how horses really bond with their caretakers or owners. If they're ignored for too long, they become lackluster and lose interest in things. And Harper told me a horse's heart is a gift. When they give you their trust, you need to take the relationship seriously."

Wow. That was the deepest dialogue she'd had with the teen since they arrived. "Did you have animals growing up?" Mia asked curiously.

"I had a dog named Lucky when I was little." Her face lit up with the memory. "We did everything together. She was a spotted brown mutt Dad rescued from the pound. I remember my mom used to tell me Lucky would wait for me to get home from school, guarding the door for hours, refusing to budge."

"How beautiful to have someone love you so much," Mia said softly.

"Yeah. She died a few years before my mom. I was heartbroken. Didn't come out of my room for a long time."

"I'm sorry, Chloe."

The girl shrugged. "Dad kept telling me he'd get me another dog, but I didn't want one. Didn't think anyone could replace Lucky, and then it became easier not getting attached again, especially after Mom passed."

The raw truth punched through Mia's gut. Loss was such an awful thing to deal with. Chloe was still fighting her way through to the other side. "Makes sense to me. Your heart can only take so much pain before you feel a need to protect yourself."

Their gazes locked. Understanding passed between them, an acknowledgment of something bigger, and Chloe nodded. "Yeah. Funny, though, being around the horses reminds me how happy Lucky made me. It feels . . . good."

Mia smiled. "Then maybe this isn't as crappy a summer as you thought it'd be."

The girl laughed then, and Mia wondered why the sound filled up all the spaces inside of her, making her happy as well. "Maybe you're right."

Flower butted her head against Chloe's arm, as if she wanted in on the lovefest. Chloe put down the brush and rubbed her ears, the connection between them pulsing live and true and real. Mia had forgotten how wonderful it was to be important to another—the give and take of touch and dialogue and affection, the beauty of truly being *seen*. It had been way too long since her defenses came down and she'd given herself the real opportunity to bond with someone who'd actually give a damn.

Maybe that someone was Ethan.

"Mia?"

"Yeah?"

"Wanna split the cookie with me?"

The gesture was small but symbolic. Mia didn't hesitate.

"Sounds like a plan." The smile they shared was natural and true, the connection between them fragile but finally beginning to blossom. Moving on instinct, she closed the distance and gave the girl a brief hug, hoping Chloe wouldn't push her away.

She didn't. After a brief pause, she hugged her back firmly. Mia swallowed past the lump in her throat, enjoying the rare contact. When they broke apart, something had changed between them.

"I'll get the cookie and some water," Mia said. "Don't forget to wash your hands."

"I won't."

"And you probably need to use more sunscreen; your skin is too fair. I got this organic oil for bugs and bought you a bottle in case you get bit. The outdoors can be treacherous."

This time, Chloe didn't roll her eyes. She just smiled and, with a pat to Flower's butt, exited the stall. They ate the cookie, chattering some more, and Mia hoped it was the beginning of something good.

The next day, Mia came down the stairs to grab some of Ophelia's cucumber-mint water, and stopped. The most beautiful voice echoed through the rooms, richly textured and hauntingly emotional. She paused, following the sound, and found Ophelia in the dining room where she served, folding napkins with economical grace, looking like she was lost in thought.

Ophelia jumped a bit when she caught sight of her. "Oh, Mia. I'm sorry, I didn't see you."

"No, my fault, I heard singing. Your voice is extraordinary."

A faint blush rose to the woman's cheeks. "Thank you. I forget I'm doing it sometimes."

Mia ventured a few steps farther in, sensing an odd sadness radiating from her. "It must get hard, surrounded by people all the time. No real privacy."

"I get more time alone in the winter, but I actually enjoy the guests. I love hearing their stories. It's exciting to know where they've been or what they plan to do. A few months ago, I met a man who'd climbed Everest at sixty years old and just met the love of his life. He was getting married for the first time. This past Valentine's Day, I had a lovely couple who stayed here for the weekend. She'd been told she would never conceive, and when she returned home from her vacation here, she found out she was pregnant." Her eyes misted with dreaminess. "She called me to tell me the news. Even though I only get a glimpse, I feel like I've been invited into their lives for a specific amount of time, and it's a gift."

Fascinated, Mia tilted her head. At first, she'd thought Ophelia was simple. She was the perfect hostess, organized, and always easygoing. But the more Mia chatted with her, she realized how many layers the woman hid underneath her graceful facade.

The words popped out of her mouth without thought. "What about your story? Do you ever wish you could leave here and experience something different?"

A shadow fell over her face, but it evaporated like fog being swallowed up by the woods. "I did once, a long time ago. But things happened, and I realized I was better off here. Carrying on my mother's legacy."

Mia's heart panged. "It was a boy, wasn't it?"

Ophelia laughed, the sound tinkling like wind chimes. "It's always a boy."

They shared a smile, and the bond between them deepened. It was nice to have another woman to talk to, and Ophelia was trustworthy. Her truthfulness practically shimmered around her. "I'm going to head into town; do you need anything?" Mia asked.

"No, but why don't you and Chloe join us for dinner again tonight?"

"We'd love that. Chloe's dad will be up here this weekend—you have him down for a reservation, right?"

"Yes, he's all set. Let me know if you need anything."

"Thanks, Ophelia." She filled up her water bottle and headed out to the porch. It was funny, she'd expected to be going stark-raving mad by now, but she'd begun to settle in a bit. The inn wasn't as bad as she'd originally thought. Even Gabby said she didn't seem to be as high-strung over the phone. Maybe it really was the fresh air out here. Almost like a detox.

A loud squawking interrupted her thoughts. Hei Hei bum-rushed her at high speed and crashed into her bare shins, screeching with chicken delight. She jumped back, trying to gain precious space.

"Why are you stalking me?" she yelled. "I don't like you, remember? And stop rubbing your feathers over me, it freaks me out."

The chicken bobbed his crazy head feathers in the air and circled her legs, continuing to rub against her in some type of fowl affection. *Ugh.* Lately she couldn't get rid of him. He followed her everywhere, trailing her steps and stalking the inn for when she'd reappear outside.

"I mean it, you need to go find another chicken to hang out with. This isn't a healthy relationship."

"He's bonded with you."

The gravelly, masculine voice stroked her ears. Her thighs squeezed in reaction, as if he'd just stroked her core. Why did her body get all needy and weak around this man? And why did their connection seem to be getting stronger, as if every word and look were leading her further down the path of something that both terrified and excited her?

"I didn't ask for a chicken mate," she shot back, a bit cranky at the way his body moved so gracefully, even with his damaged leg. His T-shirt clung to his body, damp with sweat, emphasizing massive biceps and lean muscles her fingers ached to stroke. The cleft in his jaw was deadly, and those full lips seemed carved out of a Michelangelo statue in sensual perfection. Oh, how she wished he'd kept his beard.

"Yet, you cast a spell on poor Hei Hei, so now he belongs to you."

The words seethed with underlying meaning and sexual tension. These games were getting dangerous. Ever since that fateful weekend of cupcake eating and humming "Dancing Queen" together, things had heated up. Who could've imagined they'd bond by chaperoning senior citizens on a party bus? She was still disappointed in Ethel for sneaking in those Jell-O shots and getting tipsy at the play. Mia had expected so much more from her.

But it was the kiss that haunted her. Because if they hadn't been interrupted, Mia was pretty sure she wouldn't have protested if he dragged her off to his bed. In fact, she'd probably have been the one doing the dragging.

She'd never experienced such a powerful connection with a man on both a mental and physical scale. In his presence, her body slammed into high alert . . . but even worse?

She relished their conversations. Sarcasm had now turned to flirty banter with seething undertones of foreplay. When she'd caught him humming some of the ABBA songs under his breath, it had taken everything she had not to crawl onto his lap and ravish him. As if catching her thoughts, at that exact moment, he'd turned to her with a wicked smirk. And done the worst thing possible to seal her fate.

He'd held her hand. Just reached over and entangled her fingers within his warm, strong grip. For the rest of the play, all her attention focused on the absent stroke of his thumb on her palm, the shivered shooting through her body as he caressed her crazily pounding pulse point. The bastard was seducing her at a *Mama Mia* play after feeding her luscious cupcakes and kissing her like the last woman on Earth.

How was she supposed to fight it?

Mia tried to rally and shot out her response. "Hei Hei will have to learn early that some things are not meant to be."

His bottom lip lifted in a half smile that was sexy as hell. He shifted closer, until just a foot of space lay between them. Her heart thundered, but she made sure her expression remained casual and neutral. She absolutely refused to pant over him like a mare in heat. Even though those rock-hard thighs encased in worn denim were completely mouth-watering. "He's hopeful. And determined." The chicken seemed to sense he was being talked about and butted his beak against her leg again. Ethan cocked out his hip and regarded her with a heated gaze. "He can be awfully persuasive."

"We are so not talking about Hei Hei."

Suddenly, he was looming over her. The primal scents of man, earth, and sweat rose to her nostrils, teasing a small moan from her chest. She swallowed it back just in time. Pure satisfaction carved out the lines of his features. He reached out and trailed one rough index finger down her cheek. "Then what are we talking about, princess?" he drawled.

"Sex," she spit out. Why was the inside of her body burning up? "We're talking about sex, horse man. And you know it."

"Sex, huh?" That finger traced the outline of her mouth, skating over the flesh in light, teasing strokes. Her body swayed forward, caught in a spell. "Then let's talk about sex." He raked his stinging-blue gaze over her face, as if memorizing every curve and line, pausing to dive deep to see what lay beneath. "You're shaking, and I haven't even really touched you," he whispered. "You're making me crazy."

A strangled laugh escaped her lips. "I'm not the one burning hot and cold. We'd be disastrous together."

"Not in the bedroom."

She fought a shudder. "I leave in a few weeks, back to my life. I don't do well with meaningless affairs."

In full daylight, he closed the space between them, sliding his hands from her shoulders down her arms to entangle her fingers within his. It was an intimate, sensuous gesture, firing off images of him doing that fully naked, exploring every part of her body, pleasuring her with his tongue and teeth and lips. "I don't do meaningless affairs, either," he growled, pressing his mouth against her ear, nipping at her sensitive lobe. Her body melted like hot caramel, helpless under his touch. *Damn.* He was becoming a master at turning from the rude, irritating man she disliked to this master of seduction. "But we have the rest of the summer to get to know one another. Enjoy each other. Do you know how many ways I've fantasized about making you come, Mia?"

Oh. My. God. She shuddered. His tongue licked the shell of her ear, hot and wet. Shivers bumped on her skin. "No," she squeaked out.

"There's too many to explain. I'd rather show you." Her knees gave out, and he caught her, a wicked laugh rumbling from his chest. "My sweet little tigress. Are you listening to my proposal?"

She blinked, wondering when her brain cells had decided to check out on a permanent vacation. "Proposal?"

"Yes. I want you for the rest of my summer. Naked. In my bed. I want to take you out and enjoy the last few weeks you're here. You've gotten under my skin, Mia. Do you understand what I'm saying?"

"You want a lot of sex?"

His chuckle warmed her. He tugged her closer and pressed kisses down her cheeks, soft and tender, making her feel so cherished, she didn't know what to do with all of the crazy rioting emotions flooding through her. "Yes, but more. Much more."

Her hands curled into his broad chest, savoring this brief, perfect moment before her mind clicked into overdrive. "This could be dangerous. We need to accept it's only temporary. I don't want anyone to get hurt."

"Me neither. I'm not good for anyone long term right now. I like being back on the farm, taking things slow, figuring stuff out. And I know your life is in the city, where I no longer belong. But I can't get you out of my head. Your scent and taste and voice. I want more of you."

Pure longing crashed over her. She looked deep into his eyes, searching for the lie, and found just the raw, gleaming, naked truth.

He meant every word.

The sexual chemistry took hold and twisted sharp between them, all that seething male hunger demanding she surrender. Her eyes half closed, and she took a deep breath. His head lowered. Their lips stopped an inch apart, and her entire body shuddered with longing. *Yes.* She'd do it. She'd say yes. She'd—

"Think about it."

Before she could process, he'd already stepped back, hands tucked in his pocket, rocking back on his heels like nothing had happened. Her skin flushed. How dare he proposition her and then calmly step away like her answer wasn't a big deal?

She narrowed her gaze. "I need some time." Thank goodness, her voice was steady with a touch of chill. Like she'd never even been tempted to jump into his arms and have him take her to bed.

"Of course." Even with the space between them, his leashed sexual energy whipped out at her in waves, trying to pull her back in. "I won't push, but you should know I'm used to getting what I want."

His arrogance stole her breath. She stuck her chin in the air. "So am I. You won't be able to push for anything I haven't decided to give."

He laughed, shaking his head. "Damn, you're hot. You're safe for now, princess. I'll check in with you later. Come on, Hei Hei."

The chicken gazed at his master, let out a screech, and inched his way back toward Mia. For some strange reason, satisfaction curled through her. "Just leave him with me," she said. "If he pisses me off, we'll have a nice barbeque."

Hei Hei bobbed his crazy head and practically cooed.

Ethan studied her for a moment, then slowly nodded. "Have fun." He sauntered away, that magnificent rear framed perfectly in his tight jeans, the slightest limp evident only when she paid close attention.

She let out a sigh. "He wants a summer affair," she said aloud. "And I'm not sure I can say no."

Hei Hei cocked his head and regarded her thoughtfully.

"Forget it. I cannot believe I'm talking to a chicken." She started walking, and Hei Hei followed. She glanced back. "Don't peck any of Ophelia's flowers, or you'll be sent back to the bungalow and Wheezy."

Damned if the fowl didn't nod.

This was certainly becoming a strange type of summer.

Chapter Fifteen

"We got a new horse."

Ethan kept his focus on rebuilding the portion of fence that kept collapsing. Harper stood to the side, hands tucked in the back pockets of her jeans, an intent look on her face. Flower, a sweet little gray filly, trotted over to push her nose to the back of Ethan's neck, insisting on attention. When he refused to give either female what she wanted, they both let out an irritated snort.

"Are you going to answer me?" the human one demanded.

"Good for you. A potential sale or racing investment?" His sister had been dabbling with various horses for the racing industry, but she was set on finding the proper trainer and horse to match. So far, nothing had given her what she needed.

"Not sure. He's a Thoroughbred. Saved him from the slaughterhouse."

"Must be a bad one."

"He is. A real pain in the ass. Black as midnight, with lighthearted hooves meant for running and eyes like fire. But he's messed up inside. Too many ghosts to flush out before we see the potential." She paused delicately. "He needs some help."

Ethan picked up the hammer and began resecuring the posts and wood. *No way.* He refused to engage in his sister's plot. Once, a long time ago, he'd had a gift but decided to pursue saving humans instead of horses. He'd failed spectacularly and wasn't about to take on a new project. Not in his current state.

The nightmares still came. His leg still throbbed. He'd gotten off the phone last night with Billy—an old teammate—and had been plagued by *what-ifs* and a pool of regrets. Being responsible for a broken horse would not be good for him right now.

Being responsible for anyone would be a huge mistake.

Seems his sister disagreed.

"Ethan, I need help."

He dropped the hammer in frustration and swiped at his brow. "Harp, I can't help you with a fucked-up horse. I'm not the kid who once believed he could change things."

"Bullshit. You're just scared to try. Just meet him. Please. Give him an assessment. An idea of what to do that may help. That's all I'm asking."

They glowered at each other in a pissed-off sibling contest they were masters of. "Fine, but I'm not promising anything. Don't put me in some screwed-up role as horse whisperer. I'm no fucking Redford."

She made a face. "Never said you were. Mia's right. You do have an ego."

He shook his head. "Had no idea you both have gotten so chummy."

Harper shot him a cheeky grin. "Just a chat here and there. You like her."

"Are we in kindergarten?"

"I caught the way you looked at her. It was cute."

He gave her a dirty look and walked past. Flower reached out to nip at his hair, dancing around him for attention. He gave her a quick rub. "I refuse to discuss this further. I once parachuted into enemy territory, broke my arm landing wrong in a tree, ran eight miles, and still managed to extract the target to safety. I'm not cute."

"Sure you are. And why did you land wrong in the tree? Didn't they give you training in Special Forces?"

"You're a real ballbuster, Harp. I pity the guy you fall for."

She laughed, her long legs matching his stride as they headed toward the barn. "I'm more interested in the four-legged kind who will love and adore me without playing dumb games."

"Not all guys are like the assholes in school. There are good ones out there."

"Not related to me?"

He knew she made a joke, but he worried about Harper the most. She was so focused on the horses and rescue operation, she'd isolated herself, preferring her own company along with the animals. At least Ophelia was surrounded by guests from the inn. Not that he was one to judge the level of normalcy or happiness. He'd been stranded on an island of one for a while and was just starting to poke his head out of the sand.

Mia had helped.

The thought of her brought a rush of excitement. She'd pushed him to engage, not even knowing what she was doing. She lit his body up and made him feel alive again. She heard his story and didn't give a crap or treat him differently.

He wondered if she'd take him up on his offer of a hot summer affair.

He intended to tempt her in any way he could.

They reached the barn, and he said hello to each of the horses. Some butted their heads out of the stalls to greet him, some kept their attention on munching hay or leftover carrots but pricked their ears up in acknowledgment. He'd forgotten what it was like to gain a horse's affection. They were so unlike dogs—testing their owners to prove their love and competence and loyalty before committing their hearts. Ethan respected the mighty breed, who could mimic the wind and allow humans to feel like gods for a short time while riding on their backs.

"I kept him in Barn Five in the paddock, but I isolated him for now. Not sure how he'll react with the other horses yet." She tapped the door and gave a low whistle, her habit whenever she greeted a horse in its space. It gave them a sense of routine and respect for approach. "Hey, buddy," she cooed. "I'm back. I want you to meet Ethan. He's my brother, and he'd like to take a look at you, if you'll let him."

The horse backed up and snorted in warning. His whole body quivered with pent-up nervous energy, and the choppy aura of fear and adrenaline pumped out in waves. Ethan rested his hands on the door and regulated his breathing, channeling a calmness for both of them.

"Aren't you a pretty one?" he said in a deep, soothing voice. "Understandable to be skittish, especially after an escape from slaughter. I'd be pissed off, too."

The horse pawed at the ground, walking in tight circles as if trying to gain his bearings. The paddock was pretty large, with enough space for the horse to run in brief bursts of speed, but it was also safe until they figured out what he needed. Ethan's gaze took in his lean body and dancing hooves. A real beauty. Definitely undernourished and scared shitless. But this one didn't seem like he was broken—his aura was too bright. Ethan kept talking in the same tone for a while, and suddenly, the horse tossed his head and met his gaze head-on.

Ethan caught his breath. Those dark, knowing wide eyes burned with a fierceness and fire that pegged him as a fighter. A survivor. Oh yeah, there was abuse and broken trust. But this one hadn't given up.

He reared up in one magnificent *fuck you*, then tossed his head again to stomp away.

"Told ya," Harper said.

"Triggers?"

"Loud noises. Impossible to get into the trailer. Quick motions. Not sure how he was used or the history, which makes it more difficult."

"Biter? Kicker?"

"If you approach from the side. I took my time from the front and was finally able to get him in. He needs a name."

He turned back to the horse, studying the matted mane and too-skinny body and hellfire eyes that had seen too much pain.

Phoenix.

He must've said it aloud because Harp nodded. "A good name. Can you help me?"

It'd be a long road, but he had an instinct about this horse. There were never guarantees, but he deserved a chance. Something deep inside reared up, demanding to be seen, and Ethan gripped the edge of the door in a rush of raw emotion. There was something about that horse that affected him. The horse needed help.

The pain slammed into him, buckling his knee as Aresh's lifeless eyes flashed before him. He reached down to rub it away, forcing the image aside.

Ethan stepped back from the horse, turning away. "I can't, Harp. I'm sorry."

She got in his face, dark eyes desperate. "I know you can reach him. Why won't you try?"

The pain throbbed in his leg and his heart, making him empty. "Because I have nothing left to give," he said simply.

He walked away, ignoring the disappointed look on his sister's face, reminding himself it was for the best.

"The entourage has arrived," Chloe said. Her voice dripped with sarcasm, but it was the flare of hurt in her blue eyes that made Mia worry. She peeked out the window. Jonathan unfolded his long legs from the sleek black Mercedes, dressed in a sharp charcoal suit and red tie. His sidekick, Bob, flanked his right side, a towering beast. His shaven head gleamed, and he wore dark sunglasses to hide his eyes. Mia shivered. That man was scary but good.

A younger man flanked Jonathan's left. He sported the hot-nerd look with thick, wavy hair and thick black-framed glasses. Probably his assistant. Nothing like a cozy family visit accompanied by your pit bulls to make an impression. Mia held back a breath of disappointment but pushed away her judgment. She knew how badly Lake was fumbling lately, but he was in a tight race to be elected mayor, still grieved for his wife, and was trying to juggle a daughter mandated to community service.

He was probably doing the best he could.

Chloe, it seemed, disagreed. Screwing her face into a tight expression, she regarded Mia with pure resentment. "Guess we should go down and get the meet and greet over with. I'm sure he brought a photographer to capture the tender moments that will get leaked to the press."

"Chloe, he's not like that," she said softly, but the girl just *humph*ed, and Mia followed her out. Ethel and her crew were absent, thank goodness, and Lake's sidekicks stepped away when they caught sight of Chloe, giving them privacy. Jonathan's face lit up when he gazed at his daughter, and in moments, he'd closed the distance and wrapped her up in a tight hug. Mia's throat tightened. God, how the girl needed such affection, even though she fought it. Without her mom, her father had now become the most important part of her life and her last safe place to fall.

"I've missed you so much," he said, allowing the embrace to linger. "I'm sorry I couldn't come sooner. How are you doing here?"

Chloe shrugged, but she didn't fight the hug. "Not bad. I like working with the horses."

"Becoming a country girl, huh?" he teased, tugging at her purple hair. "Since when did you decide to go goth? I almost had a heart attack when Mia told me you looked nothing like your pictures. And I told you no piercings. They'll ruin your skin."

"It's not goth. It's just my new style. And everyone has piercings."

"I thought the country was supposed to be pigtails and overalls. You look worse than the punks in the city I try to put away."

Chloe rolled her eyes. *"Dad,"* she half wailed. "Lame."

"Sorry." Lake pressed a kiss to the top of her head and let her free. "Mia, thank you for taking care of her. Looks like you're blooming here. Must be the country air."

Was she? Sure, her skin had turned a nice golden brown even with consistently slathering on sunscreen, and she'd gained a few pounds now that Ethan tempted her with homemade treats he insisted she have a few bites of, and she didn't obsess over her phone 24-7 since there was no place to run out to, but were they good changes or not? Hmm, something to ponder later on . . .

"Thank you, Jonathan. Chloe's doing really well. I'm sure you'll meet Ethan, who's in charge of her work schedule. Ophelia owns the inn, and she's already invited us to have dinner with her family tonight."

"Sounds good. I need to rest up a bit, do some work, and then I'm looking forward to spending some time with both of you." Already he was gaining that distracted look Mia knew all too well. He patted Chloe on the shoulder and motioned his team over. "You both know Bob, and this is Owen, my new assistant."

"Umm, Jonathan, why don't you and Chloe take a walk around the property while we get you set up?" Mia suggested.

He waved an elegant hand in the air, his watch flashing in the sunlight. "Definitely, but later, okay? I want to see everything, but I need your input on some new additions to my schedule, Mia. Did you see the article in the *New York Times*? It concerns me, and I want an analysis of it immediately. I'll need a work space cleared. Let's move."

His daughter forgotten, he motioned to his team and marched up the stairs like it was the White House. Computers and phones were whipped out, and Mia watched her most important client bark orders and fall back into the mode she knew intimately.

Work.

Chloe watched her father's retreat. "Nice chatting with you, Dad."

Mia clenched her fists. "He just needs to settle. I know he's looking forward to getting time with you."

"Don't lie for him, Mia," she said furiously, turning on her combat-boot heel. "I'm outta here."

"Where are you going?"

"To the stables to help Ethan. You can tell my father I'll see him at dinner."

"But—"

The girl stalked off, shoulders back, and Mia groaned. *Ah, crap.* This hadn't gone as she'd hoped, and now Jonathan would need to work harder to break down the girl's barriers. She had to get him to listen before Chloe slipped further away.

She glanced around at the empty porch. In a few minutes, she'd be elbow deep in computer reports, phone calls, and all-important poll stats. Social media charts would be pulled up and analyzed. She'd be lucky to make dinner on time.

She waited for the hit of adrenaline to buzz through her body, but she felt oddly flat. She never cared before what sacrifices had to be made to win an election. Chloe had been a distant figure in her mind, another piece of the puzzle to be moved accordingly to get Jonathan the votes he needed. Now, she wished the girl's father had just pushed work aside for once and given his daughter the time she craved. And why did her job suddenly seem shallow, like Ethan always accused it of being?

Irritated with her spinning thoughts, Mia tried to refocus. But she began to wonder when Chloe's feelings had become just as important as winning an election.

Chapter Sixteen

Ethan watched dinner unfold and tried to smother his anger.

He'd decided to join his sisters tonight in order to see Mia. Since his proposition, she'd been cautious and kept her distance the past two days. He appreciated the fine art of patience, but he figured tonight was a perfect opportunity to remind her he was ready if she changed his mind. He was also curious about Chloe's dad and Mia's special client.

Lake was everything he should be as a politician. Smooth, charming, and a gifted speaker. He seemed to care about people and not be an asshole. Ethan watched him help Ophelia set things on the table and chat with Harper about the horses. He had a laugh that actually seemed genuine and not fake. Even more important, the man seemed intelligent, especially when he engaged in a thoughtful discussion about the disappearance of the middle class and actual ideas to change the future of a city he seemed to passionately love.

Ethan liked him. He could see why Mia had focused her energies into getting him elected over the selfish pricks currently involved in politics now.

But what pissed him off was the way he treated Chloe.

Hadn't he come up specifically to see his daughter? Sure, everyone believed Mia was the girl's aunt, but Ethan knew the truth. The past few weeks had shown him something important that had switched up the game plan for him.

Chloe was a good kid.

He couldn't picture her vandalizing a damn car. Even cheating on a test was a reach for her, but he figured she'd been acting out for attention or panicking over her grade. Ethan realized running for mayor was a big fucking deal, but Chloe needed the politician's focus, not an affectionate, distracted pat on the head like a pet he noticed now and then. Ethan also had a gut instinct she was nearing trouble again. He figured her father would be the one to pull her out, but it didn't seem like it was going to happen.

By the end of the meal, Chloe had dropped her head to stare at her plate, completely disengaged with the discussion at the table. Ethan raised his voice and interrupted Lake's speech on trying to deal with the city's homeless problem. "Your daughter seems to have a gift with the horses. Since you're staying till Sunday, maybe you'd like to go horseback riding together. We can show you the trails."

"That sounds like fun. Seems Chloe has taken to being away from the city." He studied his daughter with a slight frown. "Still, I've been thinking about it, honey. You really don't have any family up here, and there aren't as many opportunities for a psychology degree. I've contacted NYU to see if you can transfer."

Chloe dropped her fork. Her blue eyes widened in shock. "No! No, Dad, I never wanted to go to NYU. I like it here."

Lake gave a sympathetic nod. "I understand, but I think it would be best. If I get elected in November, my workload will double. It will be easier for you to stay in the city so we can work out our schedules together."

"I don't care about your schedule," she said through gritted teeth. "I care about being at a school that fits me. I have friends here."

"Not proper ones, from what I've heard," he clipped out. "But now's not a good time for this discussion. Why don't we have a chat after dinner?" He shot an apologetic glance around the table. "Ophelia, the meatloaf is incredible. I've never had anything like it."

"I'm so happy you enjoyed it."

Chloe jumped up from the table, her form bristling with raw emotion. "You don't get to come here and put on your act and pretend you know what's best for me," she burst out. "You don't get to care about who I see or what I do on an occasional weekend when it fits into your schedule. And I'm not getting trapped in the city while you follow your own dreams!"

"Chloe—"

"No, I can't take this anymore. I'm outta here."

"Chloe!"

With a low sob, she tore out of the room, slamming the front door and leaving a stunned silence behind.

Yeah. Ethan had seen that coming a mile away.

Lake rubbed his temples and placed his utensils carefully down on the plate. "I apologize," he said. "Chloe and I have some issues to work out. Will you excuse me?"

Ophelia and Harper traded sympathetic glances. "Of course. It's so hard growing up," Ophelia said. "I still remember screaming at my mother that I hated her, and I can't even remember why."

"We lost her mother a while ago," Lake said quietly. "I think we're both relearning how to live."

He scraped his chair back and left the room.

Mia sighed. "I better go try to find Chloe."

"No, let me. She probably went to the stables. That's where all of us used to run when we needed some time," Ethan said. "Why don't you go talk to Lake?"

She hesitated. "Are you sure? I'm not sure if she'll talk to you."

Her beautiful features were twisted with worry and a care that made him stare deeper into her gleaming amber eyes. It was hard to feel things in a world of PR, where demands for surface perfection dominated. He was beginning to learn her heart was a lot softer than he'd originally given her credit for. He also sensed she wasn't thinking about the election or Lake's image or worried about Chloe causing a public outburst. She was invested on a deeper scale.

That was the part of Mia Thrush that intrigued him.

He leaned over and ran a finger down her soft cheek. "I doubt she's talking to anyone lately. I'll bring her back. She needs her father."

Mia nodded, reaching up to grasp his hand. They stared at one another for a few minutes before a loud cough interrupted.

"I'll help clean up," Harper announced. "Just let us know she's okay."

"We'll bring out some coffee to you and Jonathan on the front porch," Ophelia added.

Ethan thanked them, dropping Mia's hand with reluctance. He headed out the back door to take the shortcut to the barn. The woods closed around him, twilight squeezing the last drop of sunlight and letting the night rush in. The clouds thickened, warning of rain. Though he'd refused to work with Phoenix, he'd been stopping in daily to check on him, trying to get the horse used to his presence. Yesterday, Phoenix had even allowed him to approach briefly, but the animal would be skittish around thunder or lightning. Ethan would need to check on him again tonight.

His feet followed the familiar path, but Chloe wasn't in the stalls. He took a while to check the other barns, then finally spotted the girl perched on a rock with Wheezy at her feet. She stroked the old Lab's head, staring at the jagged rocks of mountain frozen in the glorious dying sun.

"Permission to approach."

She glanced back. He'd expected sharp jabs and defensiveness, but she surprised him by sliding over on the rock, making room for him. Not one to waste a gift, he plopped down next to her and stretched out his jean-clad legs.

They sat in silence. Watching the sky. Absorbing the calm presence of Wheezy's canine energy. Letting their thoughts wander without forcing words. He wasn't sure how long he waited before she finally spoke, but he knew he would've waited easily another hour to hear her voice.

"I hate my dad sometimes." He didn't answer, and eventually she continued. "I don't want to. I get all twisted up and feel guilty for it, but I still do. I hate the way he cares about his job more than anything else. I hate feeling like I'm a thing to help him get elected. I hate that he doesn't listen to me and that he doesn't seem to miss my mother like I do. And sometimes, I just want to close my eyes and not wake up in the morning. Sometimes, I'm just so fucking tired of it all, and I wonder if this is it. If this is the best it's gonna get." She gave a frustrated sigh. "But it's okay. I don't need the suicide hotline or anything. I'm just . . . pissed."

Her words punched through and shattered over him with the truth. Damn, he liked her. "Yeah. That's about as real as you can get, right there. I know you feel alone right now, but you're not. We've all been there."

"When?"

"When I was twenty-five, I lost my mom to cancer, too."

She narrowed her gaze, studying his face intently, searching for lies. "Really?"

"Yeah. I had joined the military, so I wasn't around when she got sick. My sisters took care of her, but I missed most of it until the end. Afterward, I was messed up for a while. I missed her more than anything. My mother was the best."

A faint smile curved her face. Her nose and brow piercings winked. "Mine too. She had a cold that wouldn't go away. No one could figure it out. When they diagnosed her, she died in three months. I thought I'd have a lot more time."

"We always do."

"What about your dad?" she asked.

"He had a heart attack when I was young, so I lost him, too."

"I'm sorry."

"Me too." She pet Wheezy. Her profile was sharp in the shadow, giving him a glimpse of her strength. The question popped out of his mouth before he could stop it. "Why'd you cheat on the test, Chloe?"

She stiffened. It took her a while before she seemed to decide to answer. "I was afraid of failing. I panicked and made a mistake."

"Makes sense. I did a lot more screwed-up things when I was your age. Did you vandalize the car to get attention from your dad?"

"No." Her denial rang with truth. "I don't want to talk about that now."

"Fair enough."

They sat for a while in more silence. She picked at her thumbnail. He shifted his weight on the rock. "I just want him to listen to me, you know? I'm not going to NYU, and I'm sick of him treating me like a baby."

"But you did screw up," he pointed out. "Community service is no joke. He has a right to not trust you for a while."

That seemed to throw her off course, but she gave a grudging nod. "I guess. But none of it matters. He'll get elected, and he won't need me anymore, except to play the part of his perfect daughter. It's all bullshit."

He chose his words carefully, knowing what came next was important. "Chloe, you know what adults do when they're missing someone they love? They throw themselves into work. They concentrate on things they can control—things that don't hurt. Your dad probably realizes you're starting your own life, and he's going to be alone. Want to know my opinion? If your dad wins this election, he's going to need you more than ever. You will be his only soft place. His only truth. You, Chloe Lake, are probably his whole world. And though he acts like an ass sometimes, I can pretty much guarantee that man knows no election or work will ever be worth losing you."

Slowly, he got off the rock, absently rubbing his aching knee. "I think you should head back and try to talk to him. I think you both deserve a break. But if you ever need to talk to someone, I'm here. So is Mia—I know she cares about you."

"Ethan?"

"Yeah?"

"Why didn't you want to help that horse?"

He stiffened. The pit in his gut lay like a stone, weighing him down. "Some stuff happened in my past. I don't want everyone to depend on me to help him when I can't."

"Because it'll make you feel bad if you fail?"

A half laugh strangled from his lips. Damn, she was observant. "Yeah."

"But didn't your mom say every soul deserves a chance—both animal and human?"

He closed his eyes and wondered when the conversation had tipped. When she began to help him see more clearly. "Yeah, she did."

"Okay. Just wondered."

He began walking away again when her faint voice hit his ears and lingered on the evening summer breeze. "Thank you, Ethan."

"Welcome."

Mia sat down in the white wicker rocker while Jonathan paced like a caged animal. "What the hell is going on up here?" he growled in demand, hands stuffed in pockets. "First, you tell me she's parading around with a bunch of hooligans; now she's talking back to me at dinner and running off? I thought I was past this stage! Fifteen was a nightmare. She's supposed to be okay now!"

"And she will be. But she's a young nineteen, and the first year at college is rough. She still misses her mother."

Jonathan stopped, turning his head away from her. "So do I," he muttered, a touch of anguish threading through his voice. "But we can't live in the past. She needs to concentrate on her future, and I cannot have another of her screwups. It's not good for her here. I need to keep a closer watch."

"Well, you can tell her not to hang out with them anymore, but with a rebellious teen, that may backfire."

"Then I'll yank her out of here as soon as she finishes her community service."

"And if she fights you?"

"She has no money! She has to do what I say."

Mia rubbed her temples, searching for a way to explain to the man what Chloe needed. "She needs to know she's more important to you than the election."

He spun around, his mouth falling open. "Are you kidding me? She's my daughter. She's the most important thing in the world to me, and she knows it. She's using it to manipulate me. Acting out to punish me for being here when her mother isn't."

She winced at the visible pain in his face. "I don't think so. Just talk to her, Jonathan. Spend some time with her outside of politics and surveys and numbers. Tell her exactly what you told me, and listen to her. I know it's hard."

"No, you don't," he said. "I asked you to keep her out of trouble, not try to crawl into her psyche and tell me what she needs. You're in charge of my PR campaign. Maybe it's time to remember that."

Her temper flickered. "I'm not the one who asked to put my life on hold to be with *your* daughter," she shot back. "I'm the one running around making sure we both get through this summer without any scandal."

"Good. Keep your focus, and leave being a parent to me."

"And what am I supposed to do when her so-called friends stop by or she wants to go out?"

"Nothing. For the rest of the summer, there's one rule: she's not to leave the inn unless you accompany her. No visitors. There's not much time before she's done with community service, and I'll bring her back home."

Frustration pumped through her body. He was missing the whole point again. "You can't ground her! She'll think it has to do with the election, don't you see? Just talk to her."

"This topic is closed. Unless you want me to switch over to Bennett & Associates PR? They've been begging me to jump and promising much better results."

She stiffened, struggling to remind herself he was a father scrambling for answers and didn't mean to act like an asshole. "That insults both of us at this point," she said quietly. "And if you mean that, you should've never asked me to watch Mia as a friend."

Regret flashed in his blue eyes. He muttered a curse and raked his fingers through his hair. "Shit. I'm sorry. I didn't mean that."

She nodded. "Okay. I know you're her father and trying to make the hard decisions. But I'm trying to explain I've been with her every day, and she's changing. She loves working with the horses and feeling responsible for something. She's looking for a connection with you, and ordering her to transfer to NYU isn't the answer. Please. I have a feeling there's something she hasn't told you about the vandalism."

"You think she did something else?"

"No, I can't explain it. Just a gut instinct I'm missing something. I'm asking for you to listen and hear her out before making a rash decision."

He regarded her in weary silence for a while, then nodded. "Fair enough. I'll try."

"Good. I'm sure Ethan is bringing her back, so I'll be in my room." Mia stood up from the chair and walked off the front porch. Why was Jonathan being so damn stubborn? What a mess. She hated getting involved with family matters, but spending time with Chloe had affected her. She cared what happened to the girl, and she had no one fighting for her. It would be so much easier if there were a bad guy and good guy in the scenario, but she felt bad for both of them and only wanted to help.

She prayed Jonathan would give her what she so desperately needed. She'd done her best.

Now it was time to hope they could find a way back to each other before it was too late.

Chapter Seventeen

The crack of lightning streaked through the sky. The ground rumbled with fury as thunder followed, but the air remained bone dry and humid, barely stirring. Ethan shrugged on a T-shirt and shorts, thrusting his feet into old sneakers, and closed the door behind him. Another night of no sleep was the norm. He might as well head out to the barn and check on the horses. Storms spooked even the steadiest, and they may need the company.

He had to pause a few times to rub his knee. Weather seemed to affect the muscles, along with memory. The ache seeped into bone and sinew, but he kept walking, embracing the pain, and remembering.

"You're not going to die. I promise you."

Bullets . . . agony . . . life bleeding away while he did nothing but watch.

If he'd been faster. Just ten seconds faster. Five. Would things be different?
Ah, fuck.

Sweat pricked his skin. Nausea swirled in his gut. Ethan leaned against a tree and concentrated on his breathing, forcing air in and out of his starved lungs until he managed to calm. Then he kept moving, sensing the rain would come shortly.

He reached the barn and checked on the horses. Most slept or rested, barely stirring even when they caught his presence. He made his rounds and opened the door to the final paddock, wincing as another boom of thunder split through the quiet.

Phoenix paced his stall in nervous fury. Ethan studied the shiny sheen of sweat on his coat, the pricked-back ears, and the desperate sounds coming from his mouth. Catching his scent, the horse whirled and stared at Ethan.

The ghosts had come.

Inky eyes rolled back, filled with desperation and rebellion. Heads raised, they assessed one another. Something rose up inside Ethan, driving him forward. The horse needed touch. Needed grounding. Needed to know there was comfort here. Love. Trust. All the things a human had taken and twisted needed to be relearned in the horse's mind and heart.

"Hey, Phoenix. Crappy night, huh? What is it about loud noises and rain that brings the bad stuff? But I think both of us need to be reminded it's a memory. A part of who we are now, but it shouldn't be enough to take away the right to live a life. A good life. Maybe right now, this could be the start of something good. But you have to take a leap one more time and trust me."

Nostrils flared. Recognition and wariness flickered in the horse's gaze. Thick humidity clogged and blocked fresh air, so Ethan peeled off his shirt and tossed it in the corner of the stall. With deliberate, careful motions, he unlatched the door and stepped into the stall. The horse's lips curled back in warning.

Ethan raised his hands slowly, a stream of soothing words falling from his mouth. "I'm going to find the sweet spot. Every horse has one—the place that reminds them of comfort and being safe. You're a beauty. Did someone try to race you and not like who you are? Try to beat you into submission? No one deserves that."

Phoenix backed up, his ass hitting the back of the stall. Ethan kept moving and talking, finally able to reach out and slowly rub his nose. Firm, but light. He deepened his voice, hypnotizing both of them away from the demons that raged outside and in. "That's a good boy. I'm not going to hurt you. No one will again. I made a vow not to break a promise. I did once, but I won't again. I swear it."

He murmured nonstop, stroking Phoenix's skin, watching every move and expression to sense what he liked or didn't like. Down the neck, over the left flank, to the side of the belly and back up, Ethan kept up the light massage until a tiny softening of muscle told him Phoenix liked touch right under his chin.

"Right there, huh? Figured you'd like your ass scratched, but I'm happy with this place. Good boy. Beautiful boy."

Another roar of thunder. Breath hissed out, and Phoenix jerked back. Ethan rubbed the spot under his chin, murmuring compliments, and the horse began to steady and relax once again.

Peace curled within. A small smile rested on his lips. He gave himself to the moment, to this one specific horse who deserved a second chance, and wondered if maybe he did, too.

A storm was coming.

Mia watched the sky from the front porch. A faint prickle of warning shot down her spine. Another night of insomnia had driven her outside, but a restless need for movement drove her forward.

She left the sanctuary of the porch and began to walk. The trees stirred with the same type of edginess, and the scent of ripe earth and pungent florals rose to her nostrils. Storms meant cuddling up under thick blankets to watch as an onlooker. Rain meant fancy umbrellas and designer boots not meant for splashing in puddles. She'd never walked in the rain without proper cover. Never craved the feel of water on her skin or the violent, naked sky above her.

Tonight, she did.

The memory of that heartfelt dialogue between Jonathan and Chloe hours ago haunted her. The shouted words vibrating through the walls, dragging her into such an intimate encounter.

"I will not have my daughter ruin both of our futures because of a few bad choices guised in teen rebellion!" Jonathan had hissed, frustration and temper mingling in a poisonous cocktail. "You've proven I can't trust you. At NYU, you'll have a fresh start and people who care about you."

Chloe's shout shook with her own mixture of pain and fury. "Like who, Dad? Who's in the city who really cares about me? Bernard? Your new assistants? Your secretary? It's not like you have time to see me. You barely got here and were already engaged in one of your new marketing plans to show the world what a great guy you are. You had no interest in seeing what I've been doing these past weeks!"

Mia imagined Jonathan's confused look. He must not have realized how selfish he looked by choosing to ignore his daughter in the first hour of his arrival. "You're doing community service—this isn't a paid vacation I sent you on. Do you think I like burying myself in work night and day? Don't you think I'd rather spend more time with you? I have no choice, unless you're telling me to drop out of the race. Is that what you want?"

"Why would I bother to ask? If you didn't do it for Mom, you wouldn't do it for me. All those nights spent at work. All those trips you missed because of your cases. Don't you know how much she hated it like I did?"

The silence was more shattering than a scream. Mia shuddered, pressing her hand against her lips. She almost headed out the door to stop them from hurting one another, but his next words stopped her cold.

"Your mother was the love of my life, Chloe. If she'd asked me to give it all up, I would've done it. But she wanted me to serve the public just as much as I did. To try and make a difference out there. She believed in action over intentions. Kindness over duplicity. Every single decision I make, I think about your mother and what she would've wanted me to do."

"Dad—"

"No, I'm not doing this with you any longer. I love you, but I'm not going to let you manipulate me by using your mother's memory. You cheated and vandalized. You're not the person I thought you were, and if I have to force you home in order to protect you, don't think I won't do it."

"Dad!"

The door slammed, echoing in the air, and then there was just silence.

Mia had checked on Chloe a bit later, but the girl refused to answer. The stillness inside had finally forced her outside for some peace.

Her path took her toward Ethan's bungalow, silent and dark. She ignored the flare of disappointment when she saw his light wasn't on. She'd fantasized he'd be waiting for her, waiting to take advantage of this strange mood and make good on all his promises of dirty, orgasmic, wonderful sex.

God, she didn't want to be alone tonight.

Mia hesitated and considered knocking on his door, but she didn't have the guts. So she kept going and went to the barns. A jagged arc of light exploded in the dark sky. Drops of cool water hit her overheated skin, offering some relief from the heavy heat. She tilted her head up, embracing the rain while trying to count the endless stars, and jerked only a little when the crack of thunder vibrated the ground beneath her.

In the silence that followed the explosion, she heard a low voice. She frowned, straining her ears, but it was snatched up in the wind. The rain picked up, slowly gaining force, and soon her cotton shirt and matching shorts were soaked. She should get back before she got caught in the storm. But something kept her in place, a gut instinct she'd miss something if she returned to the inn now. Not wanting to disturb the horses, she edged forward, closer to the large isolated pen in the back, where Harper kept her new rescues. Had Harper come out to check on the horses?

Wiping dripping rivulets of rain from her forehead, she moved farther into the last barn. The familiar rumble of a rich masculine tone echoed. Quietly, she slipped through the space of the half-open paddock and stopped short.

Ethan stood in the stall with a beautiful black horse. She watched while he murmured in the animal's pricked ear, his hand stroking under the horse's massive head. Man and animal seemed caught in the moment, completely connected. Transfixed by the scene, her hungry gaze roved over the man.

Shirtless, those lithe, sleek muscles stretched under damp golden skin. Back turned toward her, jeans slung low on his lean hips, thick thighs were braced apart, giving her the perfect view of his tight ass. Two nasty scars crisscrossed down his meaty biceps. A simple black tat scrawled across his upper back, but she couldn't read the words. God, he was a work of art. His ginger hair brushed the back of his neck. She practically salivated at the thought of walking over and dragging her tongue down the length of his spine, testing the solidness of those muscles with her teeth and nails.

Suddenly, the air charged, and he stilled. Slowly, he pivoted his body and slammed her with his burning gaze.

Electricity crackled through the barn, echoing in the scream of thunder that shook the walls around them. The horse jerked slightly, but stayed put, still under the spell of the man who had his hands on him.

This was a man who'd faced war, who ran toward all the things people ran away from. Hardness and strength shimmered in waves, along with a raw sexuality in the curl of his lush lips, the gentleness of his fingers on the horse, the promise gleaming in his pale-blue eyes. His gaze raked over her body, lingering over the stiff thrust of her nipples under her wet shirt, the squeeze of her thighs as she fought to contain her arousal.

And Mia craved something she'd never had before. Not only to be claimed by him—to be marked, taken, and ravished tonight.

No. It was the promise beneath that called to her, urging her to close the distance between them. The need to feel treasured. Cherished. Adored.

Just for a little while . . .

"Insomnia?" His voice stroked like gravel wrapped in velvet. He didn't move, just regarded her under heavy-lidded eyes. His fingers danced over the horse's side in a hypnotic rhythm. She imagined them trailing down her naked skin, between her legs, over her throbbing clit . . .

She nodded. "Nightmares?"

"Yes."

Rain pelted the windows, sounding like stones. She tried to clear her throat. Anticipation stretched between them, thrumming under every movement and word spoken, but Mia didn't know if she was ready to unleash what was inside. It may scare him.

Because it terrified her.

"Is this a new horse?"

She waited to see if he'd allow her the safety of conversation. Her muscles sagged with relief when he decided to answer. "One of Harper's rescues. Definitely been abused—just not sure of the extent. His name is Phoenix."

Sadness clung to her as she gazed at the magnificent creature. "I can't understand anyone who could hurt an animal. How do you help him heal?"

"Didn't think I could, at first. Changed my mind. Gonna spend the next few nights sleeping in the barn. Constant attention. Care. He needs to learn trust again, but touch is a faster way to get there. It grounds them. You can tell I found the sweet spot."

"Sweet spot?"

His lopsided grin sent shivers over her body. "Horses like certain places rubbed. Think of a dog who kicks his leg. A kitten who purrs." Wicked heat blasted from his gaze. "A woman in the throes of orgasm."

A strangled noise escaped her lips. She tried again. "Good to know."

"Thunderstorms sometimes set off bad memories. Figured I'd bunk here tonight. Keep him company." He paused. "Did Lake leave?"

"Yes. He had a talk with Chloe, but it ended up being another epic fight. He got a call about a last-minute fund-raiser appearance and decided to take it. I guess he wanted to give Chloe some space."

"Wanted the easy way out. And you're supposed to pick up the pieces?"

She sighed. "He's struggling. I tried to tell him more about Chloe, but he got upset and threatened to fire me. I think I hit a nerve."

His jaw clenched. He uttered a vicious curse. "I'll kill the son of a bitch myself if he gives you a hard time over trying to help his daughter."

His anger soothed the raw spot inside. She quirked a brow. "I can take care of myself, you know. He was just blowing off steam. He apologized and backed off right away."

"I know you can handle yourself, Mia. But there's nothing wrong with beating a guy up to help clear his head as a reminder. In fact, it's fun."

She laughed. "I don't think Jonathan would agree." She paused. "You talked to Chloe earlier?"

"Yeah."

"I overheard some of your conversation. You were sharing a story about your mom. I'm glad you were able to give her some comfort."

She waited for him to laugh it off or make light of the heavy emotions in that moment. Instead, he pondered her words and nodded. "I just told her the truth. I've been in therapy for my . . . incident. Spoke with a ton of guys on my team who all had different upbringings and crap to deal with. I wanted to give her a different perspective because when you're young and confused and screwed up, it's hard finding your way."

"Were you ever like that when you were young?"

"My mother centered me. She allowed me to go off and do the things I craved, even if it was different from her dreams. She wanted me to be a vet, you know. Run the horse-rescue operation. I seemed to have a gift with the horses."

"Harper called you a horse whisperer."

"She overromanticized things from the damn movie. I can just sense what they need, that's all. But I didn't want to stay stuck in this town as the local vet. Mom was disappointed but never tried to stop me."

"I didn't realize you also lost your dad when you were young."

"Again, those were the cards I was dealt. Some are much worse, but I have good family memories. Many people don't."

"I think you helped Chloe. Even if the talk didn't go well with Jonathan, you gave her something to think about."

A sad smile flickered on his lips. "Moms love you unconditionally. I know the pain Chloe is going through. If she leans on her dad and he helps her, they'll get through it together."

Mia stared at him as the words wound their way through her head and heart, tangling up into one big knot. She'd met hundreds of men. Dated dozens. Fallen in love or lust twice.

But not once had she wanted a man as badly as she wanted Ethan Bishop.

The way Ethan saw the world, the way he looked into Chloe's soul and saw what she needed, the way he gave of himself without thought to a broken horse—this was the type of man that could be everything.

The air charged. As if he'd caught her actual thought, he dropped his hands and walked away from the horse. She watched his lithe animal movements, every motion slow and deliberate, as he closed the stall door and moved forward, standing a few inches away. "You didn't come here just because you couldn't sleep, did you, Mia?"

She didn't answer. Couldn't. He eased closer and pushed her still-dripping hair away from her face. Caressed her cheek. Leaned forward and breathed out the words against her ear. "You came looking for me."

Heat blasted through her veins. Barely able to gulp air, she stood helpless under his spell, relishing the uncivilized look of masculine hunger and raw promise of those stinging blue eyes.

"You're wet."

Oh. God.

She shuddered. Slowly, his hand dropped, and his index finger traveled down her jaw, the side of her neck, and stopped at her breast. He traced the outline of her tight nipple, watching her breast swell beneath the damp white cotton and beg for his attention. The eroticism of the gesture made a moan escape her lips. "Yes."

"Definitely on the outside. But what about the inside?"

Her heart stopped, then rocketed into a crazed rhythm. The world slowed down to that one finger as it dropped from her nipple and coasted down her stomach to pause at the waistband of her shorts. Oh God, how badly she willed that hand to slip underneath and give her some relief. Her clit throbbed, and her panties were already soaked. His nostrils flared and satisfaction curled his lips. "Will you tell me? Or shall I find out myself?"

Her teeth sank into her bottom lip. Her knees began to give way, so he backed her up the last step toward the wall. An arc of light shot through the dirty window and illuminated the room. The scent of man and horse and hay swamped her senses, and she clutched at his shoulders, dizzy with the choppy waves of need surfacing inside her.

"Mia?"

She blinked up at him, way past caution or embarrassment or doubts. Arching her hips with invitation, she grasped his hand and guided those graceful fingers to the burning heat between her legs. "Touch me," she hissed. "Please."

He uttered a vicious curse. Bent his head and stamped his mouth over hers. And plunged his fingers under her shorts, under her panties, to dive deep into her dripping core.

There was no seduction or finesse or tentativeness—just the carnal pump of his fingers and the swipe of his thumb over the screaming bundle of nerves that had become her focus. His tongue ravaged her mouth, and his hand rubbed and worked her with a ruthless precision that rocketed her straight to the edge of climax and pushed her over in moments.

Mia convulsed and gave herself over to the delicious, pleasure-inducing orgasm that seized every muscle of her body.

Holy fuck.

She was on fire.

Ethan watched her come apart under his fingers with just a few strokes and drank in every gorgeous expression on her face. Those whiskey-colored eyes were drugged with bliss, skin flushed a rosy pink. Swollen lips uttered his name in a beautiful symphony of sound. Her pussy squeezed his fingers without mercy, wet and sleek and hot. His dick wept against the barrier of his jeans, and it took all his military training not to come right there like an inexperienced teen.

The moment he caught her in his stables, she'd mesmerized him. Honey-colored hair tangled and messy, white shorts and shirt plastered to her skin, emphasizing the lush curves of her breasts and the shadowed delta between her thighs; Ethan swore she wouldn't escape him tonight. She practically buzzed with the ripeness of a juicy peach ready to be picked, savored, licked, eaten. His plan included a bit of flirting, some seductive kisses, and a trip back to his bungalow, where he could enjoy her in his bed for hours.

Instead, he'd made her come against the wall in the barn, and it had been the hottest thing he'd ever experienced.

A bit of the savage danced in his veins, the carnal hunger to take her right here, right now, pounding through his body. He'd never experienced a woman so honest and real in her passion. No games or false intentions—just a beautiful surrender to the pleasure he could give her.

And he needed more. So much more.

"Oh, baby, you have to do that again," he murmured, his lips gentling on hers to tease and play.

"I'm sorry. I came so quick."

Her confused tone filled him with fierce satisfaction. He nipped, sucking on her lower lip while his hand stayed buried between her legs. "It was fucking beautiful. Better than my fantasies, and I've been quite creative with ways to make you come."

She moaned and opened her mouth, and the kiss quickly turned, catching fire and gripping them again in violent need. She arched against the wall, her hands greedily running over his chest and back, scraping her nails over his skin, causing him to shake.

"What's happening to me?" she whispered, sliding both palms underneath the back waist of his jeans to cup his ass and drag him closer. "I feel mad . . . crazed . . . on fire . . ."

"Me too. I planned to go slow. Be more civilized. Seduce you." He yanked her shirt down over her shoulder, baring her breast. He sucked on her nipple, flicking the hard tip, testing with his teeth. She shook in his arms, and he hurriedly dragged her shorts and lace panties down her hips, kicking them away on the muddy floor.

She ripped at the buckle of his jeans and plunged her hands down the front. "Don't want civilized. Want this." Hot, soft hands gripped his erection, squeezing softly, ripping a curse from his lips.

"Baby, we're in the barn. Let me take you back to my house."

"No time."

A half laugh fell from his lips. He fought for sanity under her stroking, talented hands, one last attempt to control the situation. "I don't want to get you dirty."

Her eyes darkened to a fall amber, half-crazed with lust. Breasts bared to his view, lips swollen and red, naked from the waist down, she embodied the symbol of Eve, bare in the garden of temptation. She stroked the tip of his cock, and he jerked in her hands. "I want dirty. Filthy. Everything." She licked at his nipple, sinking her teeth into his biceps in feminine demand. "I want what you promised me."

He lost control.

His vision blurred. In seconds, he divested himself of his jeans, grabbing a condom from the back pocket, and hitched her high up in his arms. "Put your legs around my waist and don't let go," he commanded.

She did, and he swung her from the wall, walking a few steps toward a pile of fresh hay in the corner. Slowly, he lowered himself to his knees and pressed her back down. Another bolt of thunder shook the barn, and he practically roared with Mother Nature in victory as he took in her naked body, trembling and open and shaking for him. Her pussy was swollen and ripe, and he dragged her legs farther apart, his shoulders pressed against her thighs as he lowered his head.

She gasped, wriggling in his grasp. "Ethan, please, I can't, I'll—"

"I want you to. Again."

His tongue swept over her slit, and he settled in to feast. The musky essence of her made him drunk within seconds. Once again, he surrendered finesse in the pumping need to possess this woman completely, in every way possible. His lips closed over her throbbing nub and sucked while his thumbs held her open so his tongue could dive deep, enjoying the minijerks of her body as she writhed in her pleasure, and then—

She came hard against his mouth. He extended her orgasm by giving her light licks, massaging her core, and then he reared back up and fit himself with the condom.

He slipped his hands under her knees and pushed forward. Her thighs trembled in his grip, her body still in aftershocks, as he slowly pressed home. Her pussy clenched around his dick, squeezing tight, and his eyes practically rolled back in his head at the exquisite sensation of being buried deep inside her.

"Mia? Look at me."

Her eyes opened. She clutched his shoulders, her body wet and welcoming.

"We're not done yet."

He began to move. His hands cupped her cheeks, forcing her to keep his gaze as he rocked his hips against her, sliding all the way out, then thrusting deep. Arousal flickered in those whiskey eyes as her body woke up again. Her hard nipples pressed against his chest, and she lifted herself higher to meet every stroke. When he pulled out, he dragged the tip of his cock over her clit, slamming back in her tight channel, and in seconds, she was caught back on the edge, tiny sobs emitting from her throat, her pussy pounding around him in a vise of heat and demand.

"Ethan? Oh God, feels so good, I can't take it. Oh, Ethan, please."

"Yes, that's it, you're so fucking tight. Come for me, Mia. Again. Now."

He pounded into her in a few short, hard strokes, and she screamed, shattering around him.

He savored every last pulse of her orgasm, and then his balls drew back, and he was coming, jerking his hips in ecstasy as he spilled his seed and roared her name.

The rain pounded and the lighting flashed. Phoenix gave a low nicker, his hooves a dull echo. And Ethan collapsed with Mia in his arms and wondered why nothing had ever felt so right as this very moment.

Chapter Eighteen

It had finally happened.

She'd had the best sex of her life.

Mia hummed as she skipped down the stairs and tried desperately to tame her goofy grin. Unfortunately, the damn thing kept popping up, curving her mouth in delight at the delicious memories. They'd stayed in the barn all night, literally rolling around in the hay. When they both managed to disentangle from one another as dawn threatened, he walked her back to the inn, gave her another toe-curling kiss, and sauntered away without another word. Her muscles ached pleasantly, and her thighs were sore. Her entire body felt like it had woken up after a long Rip Van Winkle sleep.

Damn. Her man had stamina.

The words rolled deliciously in her mind while she stopped at the breakfast cart to pour herself a cup of coffee. The antique floral pot delivered a stream of perfect hot brew she'd become addicted to. And to think, she'd believed she would never get a decent cup of coffee out of the city. Ophelia had officially spoiled her.

Lemon scones sat on a matching platter. Freshly frosted, they looked buttery and moist.

The image of Ethan's appreciative gaze raking over her naked body slammed into her. She'd gained five pounds since she'd come to the inn by allowing herself to indulge in special treats.

Odd. She'd waited for panic when she stepped on the scale, but when she gazed in the mirror, she liked what she saw. Her skin glowed, and her hips had a nice flare that didn't look bad. Sure, she'd need to dump the Gucci, but right now, she wanted that scone more than she wanted the dress.

Decision made, she scooped the pastry onto her plate and carried her treasures to the front porch. Ethel and Priscilla spotted her first. "Mia, we were waiting to meet Chloe's father. Did he leave already?"

She dropped into the rocker and nodded. "Sorry, but yes, you missed him. Where were you out so late last night?"

The ladies grinned. "We got drunk at P&G's after our skydive," Ethel said, sipping her tea. "It was wild. We played beer pong."

"You did not."

Priscilla waved her hand in the air. "Of course we did. Had to celebrate surviving the jump and living to see another day. Plus, there was a young man there who looked exactly like Captain America. I was hoping he'd be drunk enough to take his shirt off."

Mia laughed. "You are so bad, Priscilla. It's a good thing your husband puts up with you."

"There are other reasons," the woman said proudly. "We let them sleep in a bit this morning. They can't keep up with us sometimes."

"I doubt I could. What's on the agenda today?"

Ethel sighed. "We're leaving, sweetheart. This is our last day. Checking out at noon."

Mia stared at them in shock. "No, I thought you were staying a few more days."

"We can't. Our next scheduled stop is the Jersey shore, and Ed signed up for the poker tournament in Atlantic City. We've had the most fun here, though. Priscilla and I were hoping you'd come and visit us in Florida over the winter. Those damn senior homes are boring as hell, and we'd love the company. We reverse snowbirds have to keep ourselves engaged, or old age hits."

Mia blinked as emotion clogged her throat. *Ridiculous.* She'd gone from desperately avoiding the crazy crew to seeking out their company. She genuinely cared about them and hoped she could own half the delight for life they did. "Definitely. I'm going to miss you. It won't be the same around here."

"But you'll have Ethan," Priscilla said. "The two of you were practically holding hands at *Mama Mia.* And you should've seen the way he looked at you when you danced on the stripper pole."

"Has he made a move yet?" Ethel asked.

"Umm, well, we kind of had a date again last night, and—"

"She slept with him!" Priscilla crowed. "I knew you looked different this morning, but at first I thought it was the scone!"

Oh God, she was blushing. How did they manage to make her squirm with embarrassment? "Well, we had a good talk and then—"

"He ripped your clothes off, and you had sex!" Ethel finished.

"How many orgasms did he give you?" Priscilla demanded.

Mia shoved the scone into her mouth to avoid talking and then almost had another orgasm. Holy crap, Ophelia's sweets were deadly. Tart lemon, vanilla frosting, and sweet-cream buttermilk danced on her tongue. "A lot," she finally muttered, giving up. She couldn't fight this dynamic duo. Might as well surrender now.

The women squealed. "Then our work is truly done here," Ethel announced. "Just don't go thinking about it too much and ruin the fun. You strike me as the type to get into her head."

"I do. But we agreed to take the rest of the summer and see what happens. Nothing serious. A summer affair."

Priscilla frowned. Tapped her finger against her orange-colored lips. "Both of you agreed to these terms?" she asked.

Mia cocked her head. She'd never seen the woman look so grave. "Yes. It works for both of us."

"What if you fall in love?"

Ethel laughed and waved her hand in the air. "Pris, what are you talking about? She just said they agreed to keep it light. That's what we wanted for her."

"Yes," Mia said. "There will be no talk of love or commitment or the future. I'm finally going to just go for it."

Priscilla stared at her through her thick-rimmed glasses. Her watery green eyes held an array of emotion. "Mia, it's too late," she said seriously. Her wrinkled hand trembled slightly as she reached out to squeeze her arm. "The sex is too good. The man is too exceptional. The connection is too strong. You're going to fall in love with each other."

"What?" Ethel cried.

"What?" Mia screeched. "No, that's not going to happen. You said I could handle it!"

Priscilla gave a long sigh. "I know. I got caught up in the heat of your romance. I didn't think it through. The same thing happened with Pete. We fell into bed with each other, and I stayed with him for the sex. Then, of course, it turned to love."

Mia buried her face in her hands, trying to wipe that image from her brain. All of her unicorn dreams of great, commitment-free, no-guilt sex drifted away in the breeze. Hadn't her gut warned her Ethan Bishop was too much for her? What if he broke her heart?

Ethel patted her knee. "It's okay, Mia. Just follow this one rule: concentrate on the physical. If he charms you with conversation or makes your belly do that funny dropping thing, jump him. Keep the focus on the sex. No friendship. No respect. No love. Got it?"

Pris shook her head sadly. "Great sex always leads to love. She's doomed."

She was saved from answering when the husbands came out. They wore matching plaid shorts and golf shirts, socks pulled up to the knee, and fancy leather loafers. They fumbled with canes and false teeth and glasses, grumpily complaining about the noise of the roosters waking them up too early, and Mia couldn't help it. A wave of affection crashed over her. She got up from the rocker, stretched out her arms, and hugged them both. "I'm going to miss you," she said.

The men *humph*ed but hugged her back. Ethel and Priscilla jumped up and joined in the group hug, and Dolly spotted them from inside and came running out to wriggle in the middle.

Mia's stomach got warm and mushy. She wondered what was beginning to happen to her.

Even worse, she was beginning not to care.

Hours later, she got up from her laptop and decided to take Chloe to dinner. The girl had spent all day at the stables, squeezing in another horse riding lesson, and deserved some downtime. Jonathan had called earlier because Chloe refused to pick up her cell phone to talk to him. Mia advised him to keep trying. Maybe a conversation tonight would help soften the girl's anger toward her father.

She arrived at the stables and took in the organized chaos. Groups of riders were getting ready to go out on the trails, and she spotted Harper saddling up a pretty brown horse, who stood patiently as she cinched the belt tighter under his belly. Other horses were being washed down by various helpers, and a red tractor pulled bales of hay up to one of the open doors. Wheezy trotted over to greet her, followed by a flock of chickens and, *oh no*—

Hei Hei spotted her and immediately began bobbing his head up and down in a mad frenzy. White feathers shook with his excitement. His red jowls jiggled. He let out a squawk and raced toward her as if she were the long-lost mother he'd finally discovered.

A laugh escaped her lips as the crazed fowl pecked at her leg with affection and rubbed his feathers over her bare skin. "Okay, let's not get overemotional," she said. "We spent lunch together yesterday, remember? And I refused to get the chicken or turkey sandwich since it was too close for comfort."

He clucked, scratched the ground, and stepped on her toe with his clawed foot. "Dude, these are Gucci sandals. Have some respect." She let out a sigh, but she didn't mind as much anymore. In fact, she'd begun looking for Hei Hei when he wasn't around. He gave her a weird type of comfort.

"Please don't tell me I'm jealous of a chicken."

She turned, shading her eyes in the sun, and met Ethan's twinkling blue eyes. Immediately, she realized something had shifted between them. Before, there'd been banter and possibility and caution. Now, he'd been buried deep inside her, and the knowledge that she knew him on a whole new level was something she couldn't ignore. Her fingers curled, aching to touch him. Brush his hair from his brow. Run her fingers over his lips and jaw. Kiss those firm, lush lips until he whispered her name in that intimate tone and dragged her closer.

The emotions swirled in her gut, but she was in front of an audience and didn't know how to handle him. Did he want to keep their affair a secret? And if he did, how much would it bother her? She focused on their conversation. "You have a desire to peck at my feet?"

His gaze dropped, lingering over every curve that had experienced his mouth and tongue and teeth. "I'd hate to say I neglected any part of you."

She blushed. Actually blushed. "You didn't."

A delighted grin curved his lips. "Good to know."

She shifted her weight and stepped back for distance. Oh God, did he think she was at the barn to see him? To catch a glimpse like a love-struck teen? "Umm, I'm here to see if Chloe wants to go to dinner when she wraps up."

"Hmm, just to see Chloe?"

"Well, yes. I mean, I'm not here to bother you or stalk you or anything."

His grin widened. "You're shy," he said.

Her mouth dropped open. She blushed deeper. "No! Of course I'm not shy. I'm fine. I'm cool. With . . . whatever."

He threw back his head and laughed out loud, startling her. She tried to take a step back, but Hei Hei blocked her way. "God, you're adorable. Hot. Sexy. And I missed you."

He did? His open affection warmed her, and she relaxed, smiling back. "Me too."

"Then get over here and greet me properly." He snagged her around the waist, pulled her in, and kissed her. The sweetness of his lips moving over hers stole her breath and shattered her defenses. She kissed him back, basking in the sun on her shoulders; the delicious taste of coffee, mint, and man; the rough scratch of his jaw rubbing against her chin. Slowly, he released her, but his gaze kept her pinned in place. "Better," he murmured.

A few loud whistles cut through the air. She peeked over his shoulder and saw some of the workers giving them the thumbs-up. Mia groaned at the boys' juvenile fun. "I guess this is okay with the rules? People seeing us?"

His brow creased in a frown. "There are no rules, Mia. It's whatever we both feel comfortable with, but I have nothing to hide. There's no need to sneak around like teenagers. I want to be with you. Spend as much time as possible with you this summer. Don't you?"

The silly grin was back. "Yeah, I do. Would you like to join us for dinner?"

"I'd love it."

"Hey, Mia, what's up?" Chloe came toward them. Dust clung to her jeans and black tank, and her boots were encrusted with mud. Her purple hair was pulled back in a ponytail. Her skin had turned a warm brown under the sun's rays, even though Mia kept reminding her to reapply sunscreen every three hours. Her face was free of makeup. She looked tired, but her blue eyes were bright and clear. Mia had been afraid she'd find the girl depressed or angry, but it seemed that work agreed with her. She wondered if Ethan had talked to her again.

"Wanna go to the diner?" Mia asked.

A shadow fell over her face. "No. I'm not crazy about it there. Can we go to the Market? Fran says she's running dinner specials now."

"Sounds great. Is it okay if Ethan joins us?"

Chloe glanced back and forth between them. A knowing smile curved her lips. "Of course. I was wondering when you two would hook up. Ethel and Priscilla had a bet going, you know?"

Mia groaned. "I'm not surprised. Unfortunately, they had to head out this morning, but Ophelia said a girl your age will be staying for the week with her parents. Maybe she'll be cool."

"Maybe. I'll go get washed up—unless you need me, Ethan?"

"No, you're good. Thanks, Chloe. I don't think I could've managed today without you."

Her face flushed with pleasure. "Thanks. I'm getting better at riding now, so I can help out more with the guests. If you want me to."

"Good idea. Let's talk more over dinner."

She disappeared with a light step, her purple hair a beacon. She'd come a long way since their first meeting. Mia wished Jonathan had stayed to watch her horseback riding. It was as if her worries lifted, and she could just be happy being herself. Mia had a feeling the girl's father regretted that decision.

"She'll be okay, Mia."

She looked up at him and smiled. "I know. I'm hoping she doesn't mention her friends again. She's got orders not to see them."

"If they come around, I'll talk to them."

"Think I can't handle trouble?"

"Mia, I think you court trouble. I'll be trying to keep you out of it."

She laughed, and he grabbed her hand to pull her in for another quick kiss. "Let me shower, and I'll come pick you up."

She watched him retreat, appreciating the stretch of denim cupping his magnificent ass. Now she knew what it was like to dig her nails into the hard muscles while he buried himself deep inside her. He had a tendency to unleash something dark and sensual and free. It was the first time sex had become an experience of exquisite pleasure rather than a race to orgasm and a faint guilt she wasn't enough.

She firmly pushed the thought away. It was just great sex. No more, no less. Stick to the rules and no one gets hurt.

Right?

Hei Hei stomped his claws over both of her feet in demand for her attention and shrieked. Wheezy heard and bounded over, licking Mia's leg and the chicken's feathers. Who would've thought a dog and a chicken could be so close?

"I'm right here, guys, take a chill pill. Let's walk back while Chloe and Ethan get cleaned up. I found this organic chicken feed at the pet store that's supposed to be the new hot thing. Figured you'd want to give it a try. If you like it, Tara said she'd run a special promotion on it."

Hei Hei bobbed his head in agreement.

"And I found some bones that are really good for senior dogs, especially for their teeth."

Wheezy barked.

"Good. Let's go."

The chicken and the dog followed her while she continued to chat.

Two hours later, Mia, Ethan, and Chloe were seated at the Market, eating a shrimp ceviche that was so fresh and delicious, Mia insisted Fran put it on the weekend special and create an entire menu around it. The crowd was now doubled, and a line formed at the deli and fish counters. A new seating area now boasted comfortable padded chairs and sleek tables surrounded by vases of brightly colored fresh flowers. "How did you manage to get this reinvigorated?" Ethan asked, forking up a chunk of rosemary potatoes. The side dish looked so damn good, but Mia still struggled with her love/hate relationship with carbs.

"Once I pulled apart the target crowd, I redesigned the advertising campaign for her. Many times, the real problem is brand recognition and what you originally believe will be the basis of the business. For instance, Fran created the Market to compete with Whole Foods and other gourmet supermarkets. The town wasn't interested in that as much as her unique ability to offer fresh prepared foods and meal entrées. Instead of just selling fish now, we incorporated specials so people can run in for lunch or stop and get a meal to go. No one wants fast food all the time, and Italian places have their niche with pizza and heroes. The diner has their burgers and fries and milkshakes. Fran now offers fish entrées, vegetable frittatas, grilled paninis, and organic health options. It was just a matter of figuring out what the Market truly is."

Ethan and Chloe stared at her.

She blinked. "What? Am I boring you?"

Ethan shook his head. "Hell no. I'm just amazed at the way your brain works with this stuff. Is this another part of what you do at your company?"

"Yes. But that's for small businesses looking to break out and succeed. My current clients are much bigger, so I'm mostly fielding and spinning press stories, scheduling appearances, and making sure there are no surprises."

"You do that for my dad?" Chloe asked. "I thought you just helped with his social media pages."

"I do, but I work closely with his campaign manager so your dad is protected from people trying to misalign his reputation."

The girl's face turned serious. She fiddled with her straw. "You mean, people can say bad stuff about my dad just because they don't want him to win the election?"

"Exactly. I help make sure that doesn't happen."

Her voice was so quiet, Mia had to strain to hear. "So you made sure the press didn't hear about my community service thing?"

"Yes. With the election so close, if the world found out you'd gotten in trouble, it would affect your father's rankings. Unfortunately, you're not just a normal kid right now. Your dad is running for mayor, and that's a big deal."

Chloe kept her gaze down, not answering. Mia shared a glance with Ethan, but he just nodded, so she let the girl ponder her words in silence. In all their conversations, Chloe never brought up what she did, choosing to treat working at the horse farm like a summer job rather than probation. Mia never pushed. Denial was a lovely place to live, but she knew from experience that eventually it shattered. Maybe that was beginning to happen to Chloe.

"I screwed up." The raw words seemed torn from her. "I could've cost my father his dream. And even though I'm pissed at him and I think he's wrong to try and tell me what to do all the time, I want him to win. I want him to get what he wants and what my mom always wanted for him."

Emotion choked Mia's throat. She ached to reach over and hold the girl's hand, tell her she understood and was forgiven, but nothing seemed to come out. A short, awkward silence fell.

"You did," Ethan said. "All kids do, especially if they're being real. But you paid for it. You've shown up at the barn every day to work. You don't complain. You work hard. I've seen more guts in you than I have for a lot of nineteen-year-olds, Chloe. The slate is clean. Which is another thing I wanted to talk to you about."

Mia and Chloe waited.

"You've almost completed your time. Hell, you worked so many extra hours, when I logged in your schedule for the judge, I realized you only have a week left to fulfill your obligations."

"You mean I'm done?" Chloe breathed out in surprise. "I thought I had to work till August."

"Not anymore. You've doubled your hours at the barn, and I never counted them for free. So you can make a decision, and I'll respect it either way. I'd like you to continue to work for me. For pay. I'll give you ten bucks an hour and free horseback riding lessons. You continue to stay at the inn until the college semester starts, just like we originally planned. I'll let Judge Bennett know you paid your dues."

"What's the other option?" Chloe asked.

"You go back home with your dad. Of course, you can stay here if Mia agrees, but there's no reason if you're not working. Personally, I'm hoping you help me out, because you've shown a real talent with the horses. But I respect your decision either way."

Mia caught the mingle of emotions flicker over Chloe's face, but she was focused on Ethan.

Chloe could go home.

Which meant so could she.

Her breath caught in her lungs. Thoughts rioted like mad in her head. She should be happy about the opportunity to get back to her real life. November was too close for comfort, and she could focus the next few months on Jonathan's campaign. Pavement under her feet, Starbucks coffee in her hand, designer clothes back on her body. The crazed chaos and excitement of being back in the game. Her trendy loft apartment with its endless space and fabulous cocktail parties every night.

Why wasn't she excited? Why did the thought of returning home rip her apart with regret?

She wasn't ready. She didn't want to leave Ethan before she could soak up every last moment of his company. She wanted a bit more time to dig deeper and learn more. She wanted to finish up the summer on Ophelia's front porch and meet the new guests arriving tomorrow. She had to finish the marketing plan for Brian's comic book shop and get Bea up to speed on boosting her social media.

She couldn't go home. Not yet.

"I want to stay," Chloe said.

Mia almost sagged in relief. It was Chloe's decision, not hers. It should be Jonathan's, but if the girl wanted to work and finish up her commitment for the next few weeks, she knew it was the right thing to do. They'd already booked the inn, and everyone expected them to be here till August.

And then the words popped out of her mouth before she could stop them. "I do, too."

Ethan nailed her with his gaze. Pale-blue eyes glimmered with heat and promise and a hunger that exploded fire in her belly. Satisfaction coated his voice. "Good. Because I didn't want either of you to leave."

Chloe smiled. "Just one more thing."

"What's that?" Ethan asked.

"How about twelve dollars an hour?"

He grinned and Mia laughed, and Chloe let out something that was suspiciously close to a giggle.

Chapter Nineteen

The bedroom was cast in shadow. The full moon hung suspended over the edge of the mountains, glowing so brightly, she bet werewolves were running rampant. It was a crazy moon, big and round and ripe, tempting the world to shed inhibitions and go wild.

Since they'd already made love twice, Mia had no problem following Mother Nature's instructions.

"Tell me about Hollywood."

He regarded her lazily. "Wanna hear about the stars?"

She laughed. "No, I want to hear about your job. You were a bodyguard. Who did you protect?"

"A few different people—no big celebrities, at first. Then I was assigned to Delilah Devlin."

"The actress from that popular HBO series?"

"That's the one."

She lifted her head with a frown. "Wait, I think I remember reading something about her. Yes, she was with a Special Forces guy and got engaged and—" She broke off, stunned. "Ethan, were you engaged to her?"

"Yes."

A rush of jealousy gripped her. The idea of him sleeping with a famous actress and actually proposing shook her foundation. She tried to pull back to gather some space, but he seemed to sense her discomfort and tugged her back against his hard chest. He tipped her chin up to look at him.

"Mia, it's not what you think. We were engaged for three weeks before I left on a mission." His face hardened, but he met her gaze head-on and continued. "When I got back, I was fucked up—both my brain and my leg. She came to see me in the hospital, and we realized immediately everything had changed. She wanted things to go back to the way they were. Hollywood parties and red carpets and fun. She wanted me to be her bodyguard again and leave the military behind, along with my memories. She couldn't understand I was too damaged. I had changed. I could never go back to the man I was. To what we were."

Something shifted inside, opening her up to the faint regret in his voice as he spoke. She waited, sensing there was more. "Did you try to fix it?" she asked softly.

"There was nothing to fix. She was concerned about how a breakup would look—not about losing me. I told her it was okay to spin the story so I took the blame and seemed like a cold-hearted bastard. We didn't care about each other enough to fight for the relationship."

She caressed his rough cheek. "Do you miss her? Wish it could have ended differently?"

He tucked her hand in his. "No. The only regret I had is thinking I knew what love was. I thought love was fun and frothy, like some cocktail you get on a remote beach. I thought it was easy and neat and tidy. When she walked away, I barely even missed her. I'm ashamed I allowed myself to believe in that type of world, when I was fighting so hard for real stuff in the other."

His words rocked her to the core. She kissed him, needing the touch, and he kissed her back. Something had changed between them, but she didn't know what it was yet.

"Thank you for telling me."

He smiled, and she lingered in the following silence, stroking his body. Her fingers ran over the bare skin of his back, tracing the beautiful scrawl of ink that declared the motto he lived and breathed: *So Others May Live.* His muscles jumped under her touch, and satisfaction curled deep within. It was nice to know she had the same power over his body that he commanded over hers. "When did you get your tattoo?" she asked.

"After I joined. I worked with a pretty tight team, so we all went out one night and got matching tats."

"How sweet. Male bonding at its essence."

"Hey, it was hardcore. We'd just gotten off a mission in Mosul, and they joined me for a few days in LA. We got drunk, stumbled to a hole in the wall, and demanded to get matching tats. I was the lucky one."

"What do you mean?"

"Let's just say Wingbat's tat says, '*So Others May Lie.*'"

She laughed. "No way."

"Way. What a fuckup."

"Is his name really Wingbat?"

"No, it's Kevin. But when he jumps from a plane, he tends to look like a crazed bat, so the name stuck."

"Ted says he'll give me a free tattoo for helping him with his marketing campaign."

He quirked a ginger brow. "You gonna take him up on it?"

"Maybe." She took in his grin and pursed her lips. "You don't think I would?"

"I think you never considered it a possibility before. Maybe it's time to indulge in a little rebellion you missed in your youth. What would you want?"

She cocked her head, considering. "A rose?"

He groaned. "Lame. Everyone gets a flower or peace sign. You need to think of something that will mean something to you, even when you're old. It needs to be a symbol that remains timeless."

"Damn, you take this stuff seriously. Oh, wait, I know!"

"What?"

"A pair of Christian Louboutin shoes. I can never have enough, and they're timeless."

"You're such a brat."

Mia giggled and went back to her playground. His body was magnificent, and too much of it had missed her attention. She scored her nails down the line of his spine, stopping to press a kiss in the center of his back. "So we have 'Wingbat.' What's your nickname?"

"Ethan."

"What about these?" Her hands coasted toward his left biceps, where three deep gouges formed a jagged oval. "How did this happen?"

"Someone tried to give me a nickname."

She laughed, pinching his ass for his punishment and her pleasure. "Stop, for real. What happened?"

"Stray bullets. Had to dig them out in a warzone, so it got a bit messy. They're kinda ugly, huh?"

"They're beautiful." She dropped an open mouth to kiss the scars with tenderness. "What about your other arm? This crisscross scar?"

"Bullets got me in the leg and right there on my last mission. Another messy surgery."

"I think they're manly and sexy." His snort turned into a groan when she worked her way down his naked body for more investigation. The sheets tangled around his ankles, and she savored his musky, male scent. She pushed him onto his back and straddled his thighs so she had full access. Even after two rounds, he was hard again, his massive erection throbbing for attention. She ignored it, choosing to bestow her attention on his broad chest, generously sprinkled with hair, her thumbs flicking his tight, flat nipples. He jerked in a breath, reaching out to grasp her shoulders, but she lifted her head and wagged a finger.

"No touching."

"Ah, are we playing now? 'Cause I do enjoy a good game."

A shiver shot down her spine at his dark, almost threatening tone. That dominant voice he used like a flick of the whip got her instantly wet, but it was her turn tonight. She'd never embarked on bedroom adventures before, never comfortable enough in her own skin. Sure, she'd donned lingerie, lit candles, and tried to play the role of seductress, but something had always fallen short. Looking back, she realized it was her own insecurity in her sexuality. But Ethan made her feel not only secure but also sexually wanton, the open approval and hunger in his eyes soothing her nerves, tempting her to take what she wanted, how she wanted. Mia liked this new part of her.

A slow smile curved her lips. "Maybe. If you're really good, I'll give you what you want, horse man."

"Princess, you have no idea what you just promised me." He propped up both arms behind his head, giving her free rein. "Go play."

Her gaze dropped to caress his stiff cock. She licked her lips, enjoying the buzz of challenge between them, and lowered her head with slow, deliberate movements. "This should be fun."

His smug smile faltered.

When she dragged her tongue down the line of hair on his chest, he stiffened.

When her teeth nipped at his hip, he muttered a curse.

Mia reveled in every tremble and growl as she steeped herself in the beauty of pleasing him. His battered body was rock solid, with a lean strength and powerful muscle demanded of his job and his dedication. She slid down lower to stroke his damaged knee, where the skin was raw and puckered, a reminder of the bullets that had shredded flesh and muscle and bone with an intent to kill. She left no inch untouched by her lips and tongue and fingers, showing him with each stroke how she worshipped him.

By the time she worked her way up, a faint sheen of sweat gleamed on his skin. His fists clenched behind his head, and his pale-blue gaze met hers with a desperation and need she couldn't deny. "Mia."

She grasped his hard cock by the root and took him fully inside her mouth in one long, slow movement.

He gave a vicious jerk. Burying his hands in her hair, he held the back of her head and arched his hips for more. Crazed by his response, she took him deeper, moving back and forth to lick the tip, then slide him toward the back of her throat. His balls tightened, and he grit out her name, but she kept up the pace, not slowing down, using her hands to squeeze and stroke every last inch, sucking harder, and then with a mighty roar, he let himself go.

Before she had time to gentle her grip and take him back down, he'd grabbed her by the hips and flipped her over on the bed. Sliding his palms under her ass, he lifted her up to his descending mouth and devoured her.

He sucked and licked and teased, and in moments, she edged near orgasm. Digging her heels into the mattress, she reached for more of that wicked tongue dancing over her clit. "Ethan, I need you."

"I'm playing. Don't bother me."

She moaned in torturous agony as his tongue circled the hard nub, and his fingers thrust deep into her pussy, curling just right to hit the sweet spot. Again. And again. She begged and cried his name until finally, he pulled back and donned a condom. Almost sobbing with relief, she tried to drag him toward her, but in one swift motion, he tossed her onto her knees. "Head down, baby. Hips back. This is my reward."

He pressed his way inside her inch by slow inch. His fingers dug into her hips, holding her still until he was fully seated. The raw intimacy of the moment, along with her vulnerability, shattered the last of her control. She shuddered and moaned into the pillow, wiggling to get closer and force him to move.

"You feel so fucking good," he groaned. He reached out and fisted her hair, turning her face toward him. "Eyes on me."

He moved. With each slap of their bodies, the tension twisted tighter as his cock buried deep, filling every empty space inside her, shoving her closer to release. And with each thrust, his gaze locked on hers, until Mia was helpless to deny him. She shattered with a cry, and his mouth took hers in a rough, intimate kiss, and she let herself go.

Later on, she realized she was already lying to herself.

"Hey, Ethan, we got a problem over here."

The sun had just broken over the horizon, but he'd been getting used to being up by dawn and already on the farm. He headed over to the barn on the far side of the property. It was the smallest of the bunch, holding mostly equipment and a handful of horses who were more senior and had been with the farm for a while. Harper and John stood aside, examining something with matching looks of worry. He stopped beside them and studied the wall of the barn.

Spray paint in blood red scrolled the word **BITCH**.

Underneath, in inky black, the word **PRICK** was in fat block letters.

Two of the barn windows were smashed in. Broken glass scattered on the sill and littered the ground.

"Horses okay?" he asked, his mind working quickly to piece together the strange vandalism.

"Yep," Harper said. "Nothing's been touched inside the barn. Anyone hear something last night?"

John shook his head. "Did my nightly check and found no trouble."

Ethan regarded the crude words on the side of the barn. "Hey, Harp, any pissed-off boyfriends we don't know about?"

She snorted. "Hell no. How about you? Piss off Mia last night?"

"Ha ha. Seems like our criminal isn't gender specific. Did you call it in?"

Harper shrugged. "Not yet. I will so there's a report on file. Sometimes the college kids drift off on a drinking spree and get mean. I've been thinking about installing cameras for extra security, but we haven't had any problems in a long time."

"Let's get them installed this week," he said. "Just in case it's not a fluke. What about you, John? Gambling debts? Cheating on the wife?"

John cracked out a laugh. "I wish my life was that interesting. I'll ask around to see if any of the other workers saw anything."

"Okay. I'll check with Chloe when she gets here, too. Also Ophelia. Probably nothing to worry about, but I'll have the cameras up by this afternoon."

"Thanks."

Harper and John started the cleanup, and Ethan grabbed his phone to look up Gary from Beltran's Alarms. The bashed-in windows were more common than the profanity. It was just a bunch of horses and farm workers here. Who'd want to send a clear message of hate?

A few hours later, he'd lined up Gary to come out and had spoken with all the other workers. No one had heard or seen anything, and no one seemed to think it was a specific grudge. Must be kids.

He was heading over to work with Phoenix when Chloe entered the barn. "Hi, Ethan. I freshened up the hay in Barn Two. Can I help John with Missy's bath?"

"Sure. Hey, I want to show you something. We had an incident last night, and I wanted to check if you heard anything."

She frowned. "What incident?"

He led her over to the damage. Her skin turned sheet white, and she gasped in horror. "Oh my God."

"Not the most welcoming message." He studied her face, noting her shocked expression, and relaxed. He didn't think she had anything to do with it, but with the past vandalism, he needed to consider it. "Any idea if someone was targeting the farm? Anyone mad at you? Or me and Harper?"

She paled further. Her hands trembled slightly, but the girl shook her head, hard. "No. No one." Her voice sounded faint. Ethan watched her, noting the hesitation in her voice, the tone of someone covering up the truth. "Did you see who did it?"

"Nope, but we're getting cameras installed so it doesn't happen again." He paused and drilled her with his gaze. "Did you do this, Chloe?"

Her features turned fierce. Her blue eyes blazed. "I didn't do it, Ethan. I'd never do anything to hurt the farm or the horses. Please believe me."

He studied her for a moment, then nodded his head. "I know, sweetheart. I believe you." And he did. Working with Chloe the last few weeks had bonded him to her in a way he hadn't expected. He was protective over the girl and proud of the way she'd grown under his watchful eye. Seemed like his intention to stay unattached to any person or animal who needed him was slowly fading away. Mia was in his bed every night. Phoenix had intrigued him. And Chloe allowed him a flash of what it felt like to mentor someone in his field—so different from the military.

What was happening to him? When had his temporary retreat begun to turn permanent?

He refocused on Chloe. "I don't want you to worry about this; we have it under control. I have to work with Phoenix, so John could use your help with the baths."

"Okay." She walked off, her shoulders a bit slumped. Maybe he should talk to Mia about her reaction. He didn't want the girl to be scared of intruders when she was his responsibility while working here.

He caught sight of Gary coming out of his truck and walked over to meet him. He'd feel better with the cameras. Maybe he'd dig a bit in town later on in the week and see if anyone had been causing trouble.

Chapter Twenty

Ethan regarded the horse grazing in the open field. Another week had passed, and now Phoenix allowed him near. His regular visits helped the horse get used to his presence. The horse now allowed him to stroke and comfort. And he took his treats—he had a terrible sweet tooth and a weakness for iced oatmeal cookies—with a trust that built a bit more each day. It had taken longer for Ethan to finally get a decent bridle on him and lead him outside, but he got there. Even the horse's sensitivity to noise was getting a bit better. Ethan banged an old tin can against his door a few times per day. When the horse spooked, Ethan was right there to soothe, until Phoenix began to realize noises weren't associated with pain. It was all good, but now the real challenge began.

To get him to accept a rider.

"He's bonded to you," Harper commented, watching Phoenix munch his way through the field. "Must be all those hours in the barn and Ophelia's cookies. He's a pig, too. They must've been starving him."

"Probably."

"Do you think he was raced?"

Ethan kept staring at Phoenix, running the rope through his hands as he pondered his approach. "Yeah. I'll know more once I ride him, but that may be a while. Gonna need to find his hotspots and have him reconditioned. You know, there's no guarantees."

"Just need a chance. He deserves it. There's something about him. Something—"

"Special." The word popped out before his brain made sense of it. He'd bonded with horses before, especially since he was young. Ethan figured this one had dug under his skin because it had been so long since he'd tried to heal a horse, but it was more than that. His gut screamed there was a fire in the horse's soul that burned bright. It had been smothered, and Phoenix had forgotten it was there.

Ethan intended to show him it was still there, ready to ignite.

"You're coming for dinner tonight, right?" Harper asked.

"Yep." A knowing grin tugged at her lips. He smothered a groan, realizing it was teasing time. "What?"

"You and Mia. You make each other happy. I like seeing you both together."

He quirked a brow. "Do you know you're channeling Mom right now?"

"Nah, that's Ophelia, not me. I just like torturing you. So is this a summer fling or more?"

"None of your business."

She laughed again. "Sure it is. I have to look out for my big brother. Make sure she's not some hussy looking to manipulate and steal all your money."

"She probably has more than I do," he muttered. "And I happen to like hussies."

"Come on, just give me a little something so I'll leave you alone."

"We're just having fun this summer. She has to go back in August when Chloe goes back to school."

"No talk of the future?" she asked.

"The moment we do, I'll be sure to call."

He pushed away from the fence and headed toward Phoenix. Unease trickled through him at her sister's words. *Ridiculous.* Things were going great with Mia, and there was no need to analyze further.

They'd fallen into an easy routine—working separately during the day, then eating dinner with Ophelia and Harper and Chloe. After sitting on the porch, chatting with various guests, they'd retire to his bungalow and spend the night together. Hei Hei was delighted at his new nightly companion and took pride in waking them both up before dawn with his enthusiastic clucking. Only Mia's appearance made him stop. It was getting to be quite a love story.

Each night, another layer seemed to be stripped away, both physically and emotionally. He craved her body like a drug addict, but it was her brain that kept him long engaged after his stamina gave out. She combined a shy sweetness with a sassy spice that kept him mesmerized. She was smarter than him in too many ways and had a delicious sense of humor.

She was the whole package.

And she'd be leaving in three weeks.

Shoving the disturbing thought out of his mind, he concentrated on the horse who had stilled and was waiting for him to approach. Ethan swung the rope back and forth in his hand, registered the slight tremble of nervousness shaking through his body. Yeah, it must've been bad. The horse had gained weight, and his coat was now a healthy, shiny black that gleamed in the sunlight. But Ethan knew it wasn't the outside that mattered. It was the scars on the inside that needed to be addressed.

"Hey, Phoenix, how are you doing, boy?" He kept talking in a low voice, reaching out to stroke and coddle, enjoying the way Phoenix ate it up like he was starving for kindness. "See this rope I got? We're going to try to do some work with it, okay? I'd never hurt you, which you still don't know now. But in order to get to the other side of this mess, you need to go one way, which sometimes isn't pleasant." He rubbed under the horse's chin with one hand, lifting the rope overhead to throw over his back.

The horse reared back, snorting madly.

Ethan remained still, the rope still swinging in his hand. "Bad memory, huh? Yeah, this may suck. But eventually, you're going to realize what it feels like to carry someone on your back. To become one with a rider. To be free, the way you need to."

Phoenix rolled his eyes back and pawed at the ground in a pure temper tantrum.

Ethan grinned. "Yeah, that's what I thought. I never said it wasn't going to take a while. Let's calm you down and do it again."

And he did.

For the next few hours, he swung the rope. Phoenix retreated and gave him shit. Ethan soothed. The routine went on and on under the hot sun, until they were both sweating and tired. Until, finally, the rope swung over his back and he didn't move. Just panted madly, gaze fixed on Ethan, as if letting him know he'd try this only once, and if he got screwed, he was done.

Damn, this horse was magnificent.

He tied the rope around the horse just so he could get the feel of it, and then pulled the oatmeal cookie out of his pocket. It was smooshed, but Phoenix pricked his ears in delight and gobbled it up, slobbering all over Ethan's palm. He talked and stroked and patted all the horse's favorite places, then pulled the rope off his back.

As he headed back to the stable, Harper and Chloe began clapping. "That was amazing," Chloe said.

"Thanks, but it's only the first step in a long process. Patience is the number one item needed when working with horses. Consistency is another."

"Well, you're on the right track," Harper said. "Three people told me this horse was a lost cause."

"No such thing. I'm gonna shower and head into town for a few. Meet you for dinner at six?"

"Sounds good."

He took his time changing into fresh jeans and a blue button-down shirt, then drove his pickup into town to stop at Bea's Diner. He had a plan for seducing Mia tonight, and it all started with one thing.

Pastries.

Damn, how he loved to feed her. Loved to watch her eyes roll back in ecstasy as the sugar hit her tongue. Loved the little sounds she made at the back of her throat—the same exact sounds right before she came. He had become officially obsessed with surprising her with various treats that were as high quality as he could get.

Mia wasn't cheap. She didn't eat carbs or sugar unless it was extraordinary. And that was a challenge he relished.

The cheery bell rang as he entered. A few of the townspeople waved him over, and soon he had been roped into having coffee, sharing the normal gossip and news. Mia seemed to be the hottest topic of conversation—and quite popular. Seems all the local shops were clamoring for her advice and wanted to put her on payroll. He dodged the most private questions and eventually got back to the pastry counter. "Hey, Bea. Ready to hook me up?"

"Of course, sweets. I have something special I just made today for Mia."

He frowned. "How'd you know it was for her?"

Bea gave a tinkly laugh. "Sweets, I see it all over your face. You're smitten. Fran told me all about the cupcake festival and how you went to dinner there and insisted she try an apple cider doughnut. Said you both practically combusted when you looked at each other."

Ah, shit. Was he blushing? Ex–Special Forces did not blush. "Just a summer thing," he mumbled.

"Sure. Lacey Black got all pissy because you said you didn't want to take her friend out. That true?"

Why was he surprised? There was never any privacy in this town. "Yeah."

"Well, there you go. It's serious. Is she getting a tat from Tony? It's free."

He shook his head. "How the hell does word get around so fast here?"

"Nothing else to do but gossip and look out for our own—especially in the summer. Soon the college will be open, and those adorable teens will be filling my booths. I tell you, they may talk a good game about eating organic and vegetarian, but my burger-and-fries supply triples when they come back. Most of them are good for business."

A shadow crossed her face, and he frowned. "Some giving you trouble?"

She let out a frustrated sigh. "Just a group of four who ran out on a check a while ago. Then they came back and caused quite a scene in here. I told Ronnie at the station, and he wrote it up as an incident, but so far they haven't been back. Reminded me of the vandalism you had over at your place. They're not welcome here any longer."

"Did Ronnie open up a police report?"

"Yes, plus I have people looking out for me."

"What do they look like?"

"Two girls, two boys. The boys make me shudder, and not in a good way. Short brown hair, dark eyes, piercings, and a crappy attitude. Curse a lot. One of the girls has hot-pink hair. She's short and curvy. The last one has purple hair, with nose and brow piercings. Tall, willowy. Gorgeous blue eyes. She's the one that seemed the most anxious about the incident."

He stiffened. Tingles of warning shot down his spine and crawled into his gut. "The one with the purple hair. Anything else you remember about her?"

"Not really. The only things that stood out were her combat boots and short shorts. I mean, who wears boots in ninety-degree heat?"

Ah, shit. Chloe. He remembered the way her face paled when they mentioned eating at the diner. Her strange fear over the vandalism.

Had she gotten wrapped up with the wrong crowd again? Did this group have anything to do with her community service or marking up his barn?

Prick.

Bitch.

It could've been a message to him and Harper. But damned if he just couldn't believe the girl was involved. Something was off.

"Anyway, keep an eye out for me, will you? Now, let's get to the good stuff. Magic dream bars just out of the oven. Coconut, chocolate, graham cracker crust—everything you need to seduce a woman right, sweets."

"I'll take it."

"Bet you will."

They both laughed, and he left Bea's with two very different plans in mind. One for the seduction of Mia.

The other to unearth the truth about Chloe.

Chapter Twenty-One

Mia gave a drowsy sigh and lay her head on his shoulder. After dinner, they'd spent some time going for a walk with Chloe and ended up back at his house on the front porch. He'd surprised her by showing off his new lounger that comfortably held the both of them. The bright-red cushions and dark-brown wicker were visually pleasing. She'd been noticing a few new items showing up in his bungalow in the past few weeks: A large, tropical pitcher he filled with water and fresh cucumbers and mint because he knew it was her favorite. Carved wood wind chimes that danced in the breeze, the beautiful sound drifting to his open bedroom during the night. An extra large bamboo pillow that mysteriously showed up when she'd confessed they were her favorite type to help her sleep.

She remembered the first time she entered the bungalow and found everything Spartan. Oh yes, there was basic furniture and appliances and a large bed, but nothing adorned the walls, and there was no sense of the person living there. It was as if Ethan were just a visitor.

Now, she loved the framed photos of his family that were propped up on the coffee tables, the canvas painting of horses running on the wall, and the floral wreath Ophelia had bought him for the front door. There was now a sense of home and permanency that hadn't been there before.

And little by little, she was becoming a part of that scene. Belonging to him and his home more and more each day.

Mia tried not to analyze it too deeply, but it was getting harder. Because as each day slowly unfurled with him, her feelings were growing deeper.

If only she knew it was the same for him.

"I wanted to talk to you about something that happened at the diner today," he said, his fingers lazily stroking her hair.

She gripped her wine glass and twisted slightly to look up at him. "Is Bea questioning our new marketing plan?"

"No, she's enamored of you, just like the rest of the town. This is about Chloe. Seems Bea mentioned there was a group of four teens that ran out on the check and was causing trouble at her place. She described one of the girls as having purple hair and blue eyes."

Dread pooled in her gut. "Wait—you said there were four? The friends I saw her with had two guys and a girl. The girl had hot-pink hair. The boys had buzzed-cut hair, dark eyes, kind of looked alike. Definitely older. Both looked a bit smarmy to me."

"Ah, crap. Yeah, that's exactly who Bea described. It must be Chloe and her friends. Unfortunately, it's looking like they may have vandalized the barn, too."

Mia groaned, half closing her eyes with anguish. "No, it can't be! She'd never do anything to hurt the farm; she loves it here. What is going on? I think these kids are forcing her to do things she's not comfortable with."

"Me too. I've spent most of the summer with her. I can't reconcile her acting out like that."

"It makes more sense now. I remember when I suggested eating at the diner, she freaked out. And at the cupcake festival, when I mentioned Bea's name. I wonder how long this has been going on. But graffiti and broken windows? Ethan, I just don't know."

"You gonna call Lake?"

She bit her lip. God knows, she had no right to keep this knowledge from Chloe's father. He was owed the truth. But she wanted to talk to Chloe first. Just so she could hear her direct response. "I will. But first I want to tell her what we found out."

"Good plan. Let me know if you need any help. I can talk to her, too."

"Thanks." She leaned into his warm strength, breathing in the comforting scent of cotton and man. "You're different from what I expected, horse man."

"Yeah? How so?"

"Besides my original assumption that you were an asshole?"

He laughed, tickling her slightly under the ribs. "Yeah, beyond that. Is it my expert prowess in bed you doubted?"

"I plead the Fifth."

"I'll make you talk about my abilities later." His lips lifted in a half smirk. "Loudly."

A shiver of excitement shot down her spine. She tried to refocus. "I thought you were cold. I never expected you'd care about Chloe or help broken horses or own such a big heart."

His features softened, and those blue eyes warmed as his gaze delved deep. The familiar connection between them tightened, buzzed, sang. "You're gonna get rewarded for that comment."

She smiled, snuggling closer. "Oh goody."

"You're not the only who got surprised. The moment you walked up to my place, I figured you were a rich, snobby, stuck-up city girl who looked down on anyone who dared to live in a small town."

"Oh." She ducked her head so he couldn't spot her emotions. Why did the words sting? Of course, she knew he'd made his own silly conjectures from their first meeting. Still, Mia never meant to put out such an aura. Her insecurities flared up. Did he still believe that? Was he just enjoying the physical pleasure of a female warming his bed for the summer with no respect for who she was?

"Mia." His dark, commanding voice washed over her. His thumb tipped her chin up, forcing her to meet his gaze. "Let me finish. After one additional conversation with you, I was already reeling from my asshole assumptions. Besides being drop-dead gorgeous, you were funny, wicked smart, and didn't take any crap from me. I've never felt challenged before." The truth shimmered from his being, from his words and his gaze and his touch. "I've never felt this damn happy being with a woman before. Understand?"

Giddy feminine pleasure flooded her body. "Thank you," she whispered. "Sometimes I get caught up in the past, and it's hard for me to trust my gut. I've learned to doubt and question myself. When someone says they love you, cheats, and then looks you in the eye and lies, you start to get a little shaky."

He muttered a curse. "If I could beat the shit out of those men, I would. Cheating is bad enough. Making you doubt who you are and what's real is a fucking crime."

A thrill curled in her belly at his primitive protectiveness. This was a man who would never hide behind lies or half truths. In a way, he was beginning to heal that cracked part of her that had never seemed to truly mend.

"Time for your reward." He unfolded himself from the lounger, sliding her to the side, and disappeared in the house. Wheezy lifted his head in sleepy curiosity, then flopped back down with a long canine sigh. Hei Hei had retired to the chicken coop for the night, but Mia knew he'd be clucking away at five a.m., waiting for her. Who would've thought she'd be living in a real-life Disney movie? She had to see one soon. Chloe was always begging her to rent *Moana*.

Ethan returned and retook his seat, sliding her legs over his strong thighs. "Close your eyes."

She regarded the wrapped treat, guilt and excitement warring for dominance. "Baby, I already gained seven pounds. I don't know if I should eat sugar tonight."

"You had a fruit shake for breakfast, a salad for lunch, and a tiny piece of salmon and broccoli for dinner."

Her mouth fell open. "How did you know that?"

He shrugged. "I'm spying on you."

A half laugh escaped her lips. She knew he'd respect her wishes if she said no. The man seemed to get as much pleasure with these feeding sessions, and the extra pounds around her hips actually looked good on her. Who would've thought indulging would be a good thing?

"Okay, but just a few bites. Not the whole thing."

"Deal. Close your eyes."

She obeyed. The crinkle of a wrapper hit her ears. The scent of rich chocolate and buttery goodness drifted to her nostrils. A fine tremor began to shake through her in anticipation.

"Open your mouth."

She did, and the treat was placed on her tongue. The intense flavor of dark chocolate, sweet chewy coconut flakes, and buttery graham crust exploded in her mouth. *Oh my God, there are also walnuts!* She moaned, curling her fingers into his forearms, licking her lips with a mad glee she couldn't contain. "Magic bars," she whispered in ecstasy.

"More?"

"Yes, please."

He fed her slowly and deliberately. She kept her eyes shut so she could focus on the full experience of the flavors. Her muscles loosened, and she slumped against him, caught in a hazy fog of heaven. "Ethan, that was so—"

His mouth covered hers, taking the kiss deep. His tongue stroked her, catching the last essence of sweetness left, and she opened up to allow him full access. She drowned in the kiss, relishing his dark male taste and the undercurrent of tenderness that shook her to the core. When he pulled away, his thumb pressed against her swollen, damp lips. "Mia?"

"Yeah?"

"You're enough. Never doubt you're more than enough for a man. Because if you belonged to me, I'd get on my knees in gratitude every damn night and make sure you never doubted it."

Emotion stung her eyes, her heart. She ran her fingers over his smooth, chiseled jaw and stared into those beautiful, haunted eyes. "It's already too late," she whispered back, a smile curving her lips.

"What is?"

"I already belong to you."

Mia gave him the words without pause or edits. She didn't add the phrase *for the summer*. She didn't laugh it off or try to make a breezy joke. The past few days had already told her what she'd known since the moment he'd made love to her in the stables.

She was falling in love with him.

Every moment in his presence drove the knowledge deeper into her soul. Yes, she was scared. Yes, she was wary. Yes, she was afraid he'd break her heart and ruin her for any other man. But it didn't matter any longer. Mia had nowhere else to hide, and she was sick and tired of being cautious.

Those stinging blue eyes pierced deep and stayed. A vicious curse escaped his lips. He didn't respond, just dragged her to him and covered his mouth with hers. But his kiss was sweet—a complete contradiction—and told her more than he could ever say.

Then they didn't talk anymore for a long time.

"Chloe, we need to talk."

She'd found her at the stables, mucking out the stalls. A frisky tan horse kept leaning his head in between the vats to try and bump her from behind. Her open, laughing face told Mia there was a healing going on with each day that passed. But as much as Mia would love to avoid the whole topic and hope nothing would happen again, it wouldn't be fair to anyone to let the girl get away with a crime.

"Sure. I'm almost finished. Did my dad call again?"

"No, but he'll want to talk to you tonight. Want to go for a walk?"

"Sounds good." Mia waited while the girl finished cleaning the stall and grabbed a towel and a water bottle. She wiped the sweat off her brow and called out to John that she was taking a break. "Ethan showed me a really cool trail off the horse path. Beautiful view of the mountain."

"Lead on."

They started off in companionable silence, soon entering the shaded woods that hid them from the stinging sun. Chloe's combat boots snapped over twigs and leaves. The sound of rushing water echoed in the air, and they began moving down a massive hill.

"There's no bears around here, right?" Mia asked.

Chloe laughed. "No, that was the first thing I asked Ethan."

"Great minds think alike."

"Agreed. What did you want to talk about? Is everything okay with you and Ethan?"

Mia stared in surprise. "No, we're fine. It doesn't make you uncomfortable, does it, Chloe? Because I never meant for that to happen."

"Oh no! I'm glad to see you both happy. Wish I could meet someone that makes me feel like that. The boys at college are a bit rough. Really immature. I haven't really made a lot of friends my first semester."

"Boys take forever to mature. You seem to be getting along with Kristen really well."

"She's really nice. I'm glad she's staying for an extra week."

Kristen had come to the inn with her parents for a two-week getaway from Michigan. The girls were the same age and seemed to hit it off immediately. Mia really liked the parents and was grateful they let Kristen spend some time with Chloe.

"Well, I actually wanted to talk to you about friends. Specifically, the ones I met a while ago. I haven't seen them in a while."

Chloe stumbled, then righted herself. Her whole body was stiff. "Umm, yeah, they've been busy."

"You mentioned they didn't actually attend your college, right? What do they do?"

"They work. No big deal. Why all these questions? My friends are none of your business. I don't know why you had to get my father all freaked out over them."

The return of her hostility told Mia everything she wanted to know. "Because your father had a right to know about the people you hang out with."

"For his stupid campaign! That's his main priority. He just wants me to be friends with people who fit his expectations, and I hate it."

Mia stopped walking. "Chloe, it's more than that. I know about the diner. I know you ran out on a bill, caused a scene in the place, and scared Bea."

Mia waited to see if the girl would lie or try to deflect, but it was the shocked guilt on her face that told her the truth. The girl's lower lip trembled, and she spun on her heel to look away, probably humiliated she was about to burst into tears. Mia waited, letting her take her time.

"Who told you?"

"Ethan and I figured it out from Bea's description of the kids."

"Oh my God, Ethan knows? He won't want me to work for him anymore!"

"You told Ethan you had nothing to do with vandalizing his barn. But do you know how this looks now? Chloe, listen to me, please. I know I'm not your mom or your real aunt, but I feel like we've become friends this summer. I'm asking you to talk to me. Trust me. Maybe I can help. What happened?"

Mia watched the girl's shoulders shake and fought the urge to go and comfort. Something needed to break loose, and Mia needed to allow it to happen. Finally, the girl turned and faced her. Anguish filled her blue eyes. "I'm so tired of the lies and trying to convince myself it was okay. It's not okay. It's never been okay."

Mia nodded. "Tell me everything."

"This semester was hard. I pressured myself to get straight *As* so I can prove to my dad that I picked the right college, and then that professor was brutal. I just couldn't seem to grasp the section on molecular, and he wouldn't give extra credit, and I freaked out. I knew if I didn't ace the final, I'd flunk and then I'd be a failure. Then one weekend, I went to this off-campus party, and I met Theresa, Anthony, and Ben. They were talking about how easy it was to cheat, and I told them about bio, and they showed me how to make sure I get an *A*."

Misery etched her features. She dragged in a breath and continued. "I got caught. The professor put me on academic probation, and I realized what an idiot I'd been. I saw them again, and when they asked me how I did, I told them. They freaked out and said they'd help me get revenge because the professor was a dick. It felt so good to have someone back me up, you know? It was like they understood how hard things were. But I told them no because I was scared."

"You told them no because you knew it was wrong," Mia said quietly.

"Maybe. I don't know anything anymore."

"What happened then?"

"I got called out of class, and I was questioned by the dean, and I was told the professor's car was vandalized. I told the dean I didn't do it, but I knew he didn't believe me. He asked for witnesses, but I was alone in my room that night and didn't go out, so I had no one to vouch for me, and I didn't want to get Theresa or Ben or Anthony in trouble, so I didn't say anything. I was hoping it'd go away."

"But it didn't?"

Chloe shook her head. "The professor decided to press charges, and I knew I was going to court. I figured I'd fight it, and Dad would help me, but then Theresa came to see me and begged me to fess up to the vandalism. She said Anthony was on probation, and she'd just gotten a decent job trying to get away from her abusive father, and if they found out what really happened, it would ruin all of them. She was crying, telling me shit about how Anthony and Ben helped her, and they were a family, and if I took the fall they'd be grateful and help me with whatever I needed. They said with my clean record, I'd get a slap on the wrist and nothing would happen. I felt bad for her, Mia. And she seemed to really need a friend."

Finally, things made sense. "So you told her you'd confess."

"Yeah. I went back to the dean and told him I did it, and suddenly everything went out of control. I went to court right away, and Dad said he'd handle it, but the judge didn't care about Dad and sentenced me to community service. And now everyone thinks I'm not only a cheat but a criminal and a liar, too."

Mia sighed. "Oh, sweetheart, what a mess. You never told your dad you didn't vandalize the car?"

"No, I was afraid if I told him the truth, he'd force me to tell the dean who really did it."

"What happened with these kids you thought were your friends?"

Chloe swiped at her eyes. "They were so grateful for what I did. We began hanging out, and I really liked them at first. They were fun and always treated me so nice, but then they started doing things that bothered me. Stupid stuff like picking fights with people they thought were judging them. Or stealing from stores they said had too much money. The guys smoked a lot of pot, and that's never been my thing. I started realizing maybe I had made a big mistake, so I began telling them I was busy."

Oh, Mia knew that feeling well. How many times had she not trusted her gut because she wanted something to work out so badly?

Chloe craved a group of tight friends that made her feel safe. "What happened when they picked you up at the inn?"

"At first, it was fun. We hung out and hiked, but then later they said they wanted to go to the diner. They started acting all crazy there, making a scene, and Bea came over to say something, so they got pissed and ditched the check. It happened so fast, I didn't know what to do. I told them I didn't want to do that shit, but they just laughed at me. Called me a pussy." She shook her head hard. "That's when I said I was done. I told them I didn't want to hang out anymore, but they kept calling, and when I finally asked them to just leave me alone, they threatened me. Said if I told anyone about the truth of the vandalism, they'd make sure I regretted it. They ended up going back to Bea's Diner to cause more trouble, then sent me a picture with a nasty text. And a few days later, Ethan found the barn messed up. I freaked out and was afraid to tell you or Ethan the truth. I know it was them trying to scare me." Her lower lip trembled. "I haven't seen them, but they keep calling. I'm so screwed up, Mia. I hate myself. What am I going to do?"

Mia couldn't hold back anymore. She reached out and took Chloe in her arms for a long hug. There were so many pitfalls growing up. Yes, the girl had made serious mistakes, but Mia also knew in her gut no one could punish her more than herself. Chloe hugged her back, and it was a while before she finally pulled away.

"They're users, Chloe. They feel crappy inside, and the more so-called friends they pull in, it helps divert attention from their real problems. Does that make sense?"

Chloe nodded.

"Ethan's right about one thing: you paid your dues with community service, and you weren't even the one who did the vandalism. That's a clean slate. As for Bea, I think the best thing to do would be to march into that diner with your head held high and apologize."

"Do you think she'll press charges?" she asked. Her skin looked pale with fear. "I'd be in more trouble."

"I don't know," she said honestly. "But if you're straight with her, she may give you a break."

"Okay. I can do that."

Mia squeezed her arm. "Good. The barn wasn't your fault, but we need to let Ethan know so he can protect the property. I think you should tell him the truth, too. All of it. And if I know him at all, that will square things with him, too."

"What about my dad? He'll force me to leave, I know he will."

"Do you want to stay here? Even with all the trouble that happened?" Mia asked.

"I do. I love the town and the horse farm and the college. I don't want them to chase me away. Dad would tell me that's the way you let the bad guys win."

Mia smiled. "Well said. We have to tell your dad. But I can try and help convince him that you're owed a second chance to make things right."

"Mia, can you just wait to tell him? Please? Just a few more days. There's only three weeks left here, and I have a feeling he may just yank me back. I want to finish what I started. That's it. I swear, I'll tell him everything."

It was the determination and truth in her blue eyes that helped Mia make the decision. "I'll give you until Friday. I can't wait any longer, Chloe, it just wouldn't be fair to him."

"Okay, I can work with that."

"Let's finish our hike, and you can talk to Ethan. Then I'll drive you to the diner."

"I feel like I'm going to throw up."

Mia laughed. "I know, sweetie. Life really sucks sometimes, especially when you're trying to do the right thing."

The girl turned to her, eyes filled with emotion. "Thank you, Mia. Even when I gave you a hard time, you had my back. It means a lot to me."

Mia smiled at the girl and squeezed her hand. The birds chirped and the creek gushed and the trees bent in the breeze. Mia savored the moment with this young girl who was finding her way and giving her a trust that meant the world to her. She didn't know how things would end, but one thing was for sure: Mia was going to fight for the girl.

Chapter Twenty-Two

"Steady, boy. I have a feeling this is gonna be the day."

Phoenix stared back, gaze fixed on the saddle held in front of him. But the horse's head was high up, and no nervousness emanated from his form. As usual, Ethan greeted him by stroking his sweet spot, and the horse bumped his pocket, looking for the oatmeal cookie he expected from these regular sessions. This time, Ethan didn't offer it right away. Keeping up his chatter, he presented the saddle to him, stroking his left flank, and began to slowly move toward his body. The horse stood and allowed the saddle pad to be adjusted, waiting with patience as Ethan buckled the straps and adjusted the stirrups. Good. They'd moved ahead, but now it was time for the true test. It was time for Ethan to ride him.

Grasping the reins, Ethan put a leg in the stirrup and began to haul himself up.

The horse backed up in stubborn refusal.

Ethan regarded him. Phoenix held his gaze, the battle of wills finally to its breaking point. After hours of getting him comfortable with his presence and the saddle, it was time to test the trust issue. The sessions had indicated Phoenix had been whipped, probably forced to race under duress, and what he'd once loved in his Thoroughbred heart had been warped. But Ethan sensed if he could get him to run again with pleasure, they'd finally reach a turning point.

Ethan grinned, stroking his pocket. "Gonna make you work for this treat today, boy. You let me ride, and you get your cookie. I think it's a fair deal. Especially since Ophelia made this batch especially for you."

Phoenix snorted and moved a few inches closer. Ethan stroked his head. "I'm asking one more time for trust. I won't let you down if you give me a chance."

Ethan stared into those beautiful brown eyes that had seen way too much but still held a tiny glimmer of hope. Opening himself up to the animal, he let his emotion flow through his stroking fingertips and in his gaze. Then he lifted his leg to mount.

And swung himself into the saddle.

Phoenix remained still. Pride filled Ethan's veins, along with a fierce burst of adrenaline and power that sitting on top of a racehorse gave. It was a gift that went both ways, and it never failed to humble him. He held the reins in a firm yet light grip and gave a whistle.

"Let's go, boy. Nice and easy."

His heels nudged the horse's flanks with just a gentle touch, and Phoenix took off. He stretched his legs in a leisurely walk, as if rediscovering the feel of carrying a rider again. Ethan let him set the pace, eventually moving to a nice steady gait, keeping up a stream of encouragement. They left the fenced-in area behind and took off into the open meadow. Horses grazed freely, chickens flocked around, and the two hound dogs howled in pleasure as they chased squirrels. The mountains sprawled before them in majestic glory and a reminder of how small their presence was, how fleeting their time, how precious their moments.

Phoenix began to trot, seeming to catch the energy in the air, and broke into a canter. Ethan guided him toward the flat space where earth met sky and the meadow spread out in endless acres of green. "When you're ready, Phoenix. When you're ready, go for it."

The horse caught his words on the breeze. Ears pricked, his strong, graceful body kicked up a few notches, and then they were racing across the meadow.

Time stopped. The horse ran with a freedom that took Ethan with him for the ride. The world blurred as power unleashed from the animal, and he raced harder, hooves pounding, mane flying in the wind, the wicked speed unfurling at a rapid pace Ethan had never experienced.

He let Phoenix run it out for a little while, all the demons and memories left behind in the dust, freeing them both. In those precious moments, Ethan was able to let go and realize the past didn't have to dictate his future. And when Phoenix finally slowed down, Ethan guided him back toward the stables, slightly stunned from the experience.

He slid off the Thoroughbred, sliding his hand over the sheen of sweat gleaming on his coat, and took out the cookie. Phoenix munched on the treat with the same ecstasy Mia exhibited when she allowed herself to indulge, making a grin curve his lips.

"Good boy. You are magnificent, just like I always thought. Thank you."

His name echoed in the air. He turned and found Harper walking toward him, her face alight with joy. "You rode him," she breathed out in respect. "I saw you racing in the meadow. Dear God, Ethan, he was amazing. He's like lightning. How did he do?"

Ethan faced his sister. A lump lodged in his throat. It took him a few times to clear it before he was able to speak. "He's special, Harp. A racehorse through and through. He just lost the way." He paused, a bigger realization looming before him that he couldn't ignore. "We both did."

Harper reached out and took his hand, squeezing hard. "We all do, big brother. But you found it again, and so did he. And this one's going to accomplish amazing things. I think I finally found my winner."

"I think you did, too."

They both watched Phoenix dig out another cookie, happily munching without realizing something extraordinary had just occurred. The inner lockbox inside Ethan shook and released a series of truths he'd only been trying to hide from himself.

And just like that, he realized he'd fallen in love with Mia Thrush. Now what the hell was he going to do about that?

Mia watched from a distance as Ethan dismounted Phoenix and began speaking with Harper.

A fierce shaking thrummed through her body, moving from her limbs to her belly to her heart. The melding of horse and man she'd witnessed was almost holy. It was as if both of them had freed a piece of themselves within that ride. The devotion and pride etched on Ethan's face—glimpsed from the shadows of the barn—humbled her.

What was she going to do?

Precious days were left. Jonathan had already emailed her with a loaded schedule for when she returned. Her assistant had officially declared herself overrun and said she was marking down the days of her return. Mia had just managed to sign a new client who was in the running for the new face of Cover Girl but was fighting a murky past that unfortunately included a sex video. *Damn ex-boyfriends.* Mia had already warned Chloe about taking her clothes off on her iPhone for anyone, and the girl had laughed and swore she wouldn't. At least Mia had a firm plan of attack and defense sketched out, but she needed to be back in the city.

Away from Ethan.

She watched him walk toward her with Phoenix in tow, then noticed his slightly exaggerated limp. She'd suspected he was in pain last night, but when she tried to fuss, he distracted her by getting naked. His body was like sugar to her—a sweet addiction she had no control over. And damned if she hadn't savored every last taste.

Hei Hei walked over her foot and rubbed his head feathers against her leg. She looked down with a laugh. "It's not about you, right now. It's about Phoenix and his incredible ride."

The chicken squawked.

Chloe ran over, squealing with excitement. "Mia, did you see? He rode Phoenix! He was so fast. Is that normal, Ethan? Are horses usually that fast?"

Ethan grinned, sweat dripping from his brow, but as usual, he was more concerned with the horse. "Haven't seen one this fast other than at the track. Let's get him washed down and some fresh water. Chloe, do you want to help John do it? I've noticed you've been visiting Phoenix a lot, and he's getting comfortable with you."

The girl beamed. "Yeah, I've been sneaking in some extra time with him. I'd love to help. Thanks."

Mia watched their easy interactions, relieved their relationship had grown stronger after Chloe told him the truth about the vandalism and the diner. He'd actually accompanied them to see Bea, and the united front, along with Chloe's honesty and raw apology, helped heal the breaks. Chloe had given Bea the first week of her pay, and Bea had taken it. With that exchange, they'd reached an understanding.

"Welcome." He helped set it up and let John take over once the horse was settled. Then he turned and pinned her with that bright-blue gaze. "Spying again?"

She didn't hesitate. Just walked into his arms, lifted herself up on tiptoes, and kissed him. He growled deep in his throat and kissed her back, his arms grasping her hips to keep her in place. He withdrew slowly, nipping at her bottom lip, and regarded her with suspicious eyes. "What brought this on?"

"That was hot."

He laughed. "Saw the whole thing, huh?"

"It was amazing, Ethan. It was so . . . beautiful."

His gaze softened, and he stroked her cheek. "Still a long way to go. He's got amazing potential, but we don't know how far we can push."

"You gave him back something precious that he'd lost."

A mixture of raw emotion hit her like a fist through her solar plexus. He hesitated, as if struggling to tell her something, then dropped his hand and stepped back. "All in a day's work," he said lightly.

Disappointment crashed through her. She noticed him shift his weight again. "Your knee is bothering you."

He glanced down. "I skipped doing PT this week. Doctors said sometimes the scars can cause phantom pain. I better finish up here. Catch you later?"

She forced a smile. Why did he suddenly seem so distant? "Sure."

She turned, took a few steps, and his arm shot out to stop her. "Mia."

"Yeah?"

"Dinner at the inn, right?"

His gaze held a heat and need he allowed her to see. This time, the smile bubbled up from inside. "Definitely."

She headed back with Hei Hei at her heels.

Later that night, she looked around the dinner table and wondered how this family had managed to make her feel so at home so quickly. Ophelia had finally let her help with the dishes. When had it become so important to be treated like she belonged rather than a mere guest?

Chloe's voice cut through her thoughts. "Ophelia, Mia has never seen a Disney movie."

Ethan's sister froze. Distress flickered over her graceful features. "Please tell me that's not true."

Mia sighed and shot Chloe a look. "It's true. We're more of a History channel family than Disney. In fact, my father warned me it would give me false expectations about the real world."

"Bull," Ophelia shot out. Her blue eyes flashed fire. "Watching Disney movies is the only thing that can prepare you for the real world," she said passionately. "They help kids deal with the tough stuff—losing parents at a young age, getting lost, growing up, being bullied, etc."

Mia glanced over at Ethan for help, but he was shaking his head. "Don't get me involved in this discussion," he said, grabbing another ear of fresh corn. "Why do you think every animal we ever owned is named after a Disney character?"

"I think that's so amazing," Chloe sighed. "It's like each of them has an identity and a force that lives inside."

Mia's mouth fell open. "Did you just wax poetic over cartoons?"

"You don't know the power until you've experienced it," Harper warned. "Mom was a huge advocate, and every time a DVD was released from the vault, we'd make a celebration out of it."

"Popcorn, and pillows, and staying up past bedtime," Ophelia added. "And we all have a favorite movie that comes out in our personalities."

"Fascinating," Mia murmured. "Which one is yours?"

"*Peter Pan,*" Ophelia answered. "Ethan's been calling me Tink since I was young. Says I look like a fairy."

Ethan reached over and pulled on one of her red curls. "You do. Plus, when things don't go your way, you get mad and sulk. You're a bit of a control freak."

"I don't sulk! And I just like things organized. How is that a bad thing?"

Mia jumped to her defense. "It's not," she told Ophelia, throwing a stern look in Ethan's direction. "You couldn't be successful running this inn if you weren't organized."

Ophelia grinned. "Thanks."

Ethan groaned. "Why am I always surrounded by women who never take my side?"

Harper stuck out her tongue. "'Cause your side is always the wrong one."

"What's yours, Harper?" Mia asked, getting into the swing of the game.

"*Dumbo*," Harper answered, rolling her eyes. "A fascinating study in being bullied, abused by higher-ups to perform on command, and the eventual growth into power once you find your unique talent."

"Impressive, Harp," Ethan said with a grin. "At least you finally reached your goal of ridding all the circuses of show elephants."

Satisfaction curled in her voice. "Took a damn long time, but we got there."

Chloe spoke up. "Wanna guess mine?"

Everyone at the table studied her in silence, trying to make up their mind. Mia had heard of a few, of course, but had never personally watched them, so she waited for the consensus. "I can't decide if you like princesses or not," Ophelia murmured, tapping her finger against her lip. "Maybe. Is it *Brave*?"

"Nope. But you're kind of close."

"*Sleeping Beauty*?" Harper tried.

"No. Give up?"

"Elsa from *Frozen*." Everyone swiveled their gaze to stare. Ethan shifted in his seat, looking as if he already regretted speaking up. "Elsa isn't your normal princess. She's a bit of a badass, trying to find her way and carve out her own path."

"Yes," Chloe whispered. Her face flushed in pleasure. "That's it."

"Which leaves Ethan," Mia said. "Now I'm dying of curiosity."

Ophelia and Harper shared a pointed look. Seemed like they were enjoying torturing their older brother. "It's time to admit it," Ophelia prodded. "Don't be embarrassed."

"What?" Mia asked. "Tell me!"

"It's *Cinderella*!"

His mouth dropped open. "It is not!" he roared, practically shooting out sparks of masculine irritation. "You're lying!"

The girls burst into giggles at the joke. Ethan still looked pissed off, shooting them a deadly glare, but Chloe was laughing too hard, and eventually Ethan shook his head. "Unbelievable," he muttered. "And I actually fell for it."

"It's *The Lion King*," Harper managed to say between giggles.

"What type of movie is it?" Mia asked curiously.

Ophelia swiped at her eyes. "It screams leadership. See, Simba loses his father early on in the movie and believes it's his fault. He spends the rest of his life trying to run from his guilt until he's faced with the truth—he had nothing to do with his father's death. He has to return home and save his home by becoming king."

Tingles crept down her spine. She made a mental note to rent the movie ASAP. It was the perfect fit for the proud, strong man beside her, who took the world on his shoulders and didn't give himself a break.

"Hey, can we show Mia her first Disney movie this week?" Chloe asked. "Since Hei Hei adores her, I thought she'd love *Moana*."

Ophelia clapped her hands. "Such a perfect choice! Yes, how about tomorrow night?"

Harper nodded with a grin. "I'm in. Been a long time. Mia?"

"I'm game."

"Ethan?" Ophelia asked.

He let out a long-suffering-male sigh. "Fine. But you need to make that special cheddar-cheese popcorn I like, or I'm out."

"Deal."

They helped clean up, and Chloe went to her room early to read and listen to music. Mia went upstairs to get her small overnight bag, trying not to blush when they said good night to Ethan's sisters and began walking toward the bungalow. "I feel like a teenager sneaking out with her boyfriend," she confessed, swinging his entwined hand.

"Me too. I catch a glimpse of you, and I'm ready to tumble you in the back seat of my car."

She snorted. "As if I'd let you mess up my hair."

He gave her a wicked look. "Already gave you a roll in the hay, princess."

"Be quiet, horse man."

He laughed and walked inside the house. Shifting his weight back and forth, she caught the faintest flicker of discomfort cross his features. She dropped her bag on the couch and turned to face him. "Okay, I've had enough. Pants off."

"Damn, you're insatiable, woman."

She cocked her head and glared. "You're in pain. I want to massage your leg and relieve some of the pressure."

"You don't have to." His voice flicked out hard and unyielding. She tamped down a sigh at the pride in this impossible male and how he hated to admit he was hurting. How he hated to show weakness.

"I want to, Ethan. Please let me."

He studied her face, then kicked off his boots. Keeping his gaze on her, he slowly pulled the belt from the loops and unbuckled it. A snap of the wrist released the button. The tab lowered tooth by tooth to reveal the line of bare skin that told her he was going commando. Then he shucked his jeans off, ripped the T-shirt off his chest, and faced her.

Holy hotness, Batman.

Her entire body was seeped in heat. Nipples straining against her blouse, she practically salivated over the gorgeous sexiness of the man before her. Golden-brown skin dusted with dark-red hair. Lean, solid muscle rippling with power. Legs braced apart, his heavy cock aroused, arrogance shimmered from his aura as he faced her, comfortable in his nakedness. Barely able to swallow, Mia fought to chop through the sudden fog of need that devoured her whole. Then those lips lifted in a hint of a smug grin, and she knew that he knew that she was helpless to resist him.

"Where do you want me?"

She tried to speak but let out a squeak. Then tried again. "On the bed."

His brow lifted, but he followed her instructions. He stretched out on his navy-blue comforter, bracing his head up with a few pillows. Arms propped behind his head, he regarded her under heavily lidded eyes.

Why did she suddenly feel like his prey?

She kicked off her heels and approached the bed. Sliding tentatively next to him, she extended his leg over her thighs, so his knee rested in her lap and she had access to his full limb. Dragging in a breath to relax her mind, she placed her fingers over his hot skin. His muscles jumped under her touch. Slowly, she began to guide her way downward, learning where his muscles were tight and knotted and where skin had been scraped so raw, there were no longer any nerve endings. "How often does it ache like this?" she asked.

"Depends on the weather and my activity. I've been pushing myself a bit, so that's why it flared up."

Mia studied the puckered skin and gouges where pins and screws had held bone together so he could walk. She worked her way down, massaging around and under the knee, taking her time. He sprawled back on the bed, eyes half-closed, and she made sure to watch his face for the slightest reaction to her various strokes. "I have to call Jonathan tomorrow and tell him about Chloe."

"A fair deal. You haven't seen that ragtag crew around anymore, right?"

"No, maybe they've decided to finally leave her alone. Chloe said she hasn't texted them back."

"Good. Do you think Lake will force her to go home?"

She frowned, her hands gaining strength as she pressed deeper into the massage. "I don't know. I'm going to do my best to help Chloe be heard, but the decision is his." Mia caught the tiniest wince around his eyes. *There.* She'd found the problematic spot. Her fingers danced around the sore muscle, taking her time. "How many operations did you have?" she asked curiously.

"Change of subject?"

"Yes."

He stirred. At least he seemed to be enjoying the massage. "Three."

"You mentioned you were lucky to be able to walk."

"Almost lost the leg. Shrapnel damaged blood vessels and nerves, so they did an IM surgery. Basically put a bunch of plates and screws in there. Then did it twice more."

"How many months were you in the hospital?"

"About a month, but then I was moved to rehab, so that was another few weeks. Damn, that feels good."

Pleasure skated over her—both from his praise and the amazing view of his naked body sprawled out for her enjoyment. "Are you happy you came home?"

"Not at first. I felt as if I returned home a loser."

Shock hit hard. She paused, staring at him. "How in any possibility imagined could you be a loser?"

He gave a half shrug. "It's a guilt thing. All mental. An important man died on my watch, and I'd looked him in the eye and promised I'd save him. Felt like a liar. Then my leg was so busted up, I'll never be able to work again in Special Forces. It was part of my identity—who I was. I had to find a new life for myself, so being back home under those circumstances was hard."

"And now?"

"Now, I'm glad. I forgot what it's like being around my sisters again and my childhood home. I forgot what it's like to live with people who care about important things and not designer dresses and movie premiers and who said what on Page Six."

"There's nothing wrong with designer dresses," she pointed out.

He grinned. "Agreed."

"You plan to stay here, then?"

"Yes. This is where I belong now. I can concentrate on the simple things in life again. Find some peace."

The way he spoke held no sympathy for himself, just a basic truth he'd accepted. Her heart slowly broke into pieces because he didn't seem to know how extraordinary he was.

"Did you ever see the movie *Pretty Woman*?" she suddenly asked.

He snorted. "Every man is forced to watch it eventually. Do you know how many dates I had who expected me to send her a red evening gown and diamonds and to take her to the fucking opera?"

She laughed. "Fine, I get it. Do you remember the part where she says it's easier to remember all the bad stuff than the good?"

"Yeah."

"Ethan, how many people did you save when you served?"

He stiffened. Opened his eyes and caught her with his gaze. She remained steady, refusing to buckle. This was important. She sensed the pain within him. Saw when his eyes got that distant look and sadness emanated from his figure. Even though he was human, he blamed himself for that one loss. It was a part of him she knew words couldn't change, but God how she wanted to soothe some of the ache.

"Why?"

"Because it matters. Every person that has a life because of you matters. Don't brush them off or forget because you lost one."

"I think I could've run faster."

The words bled out of him, and her heart clenched. Raw pain clawed at her insides, but she remained calm. Gently, she moved his leg from her lap and crawled up the bed until she knelt right next to him. She stroked his smooth cheek, traced the line of his lips, and rested her forehead against his. "I know, baby. But maybe you couldn't. Just don't cheapen what you *did* accomplish in the pursuit of perfection that isn't possible."

Shock filled his eyes. He jerked back, staring into her face with a desperation that had her leaning forward to kiss him. Sensing he was on the edge, she took the kiss deeper, her tongue ravaging his mouth in the role of aggressor, her nails digging sharply into his shoulders. With a low growl, he answered the call and slammed her back into the mattress, rolling over to pin her thighs wide open. He ripped her clothes from her body and fitted himself with a condom. She sank her teeth into his lower lip with pure greed and thrust up, wrapping her ankles around his hips at the same time she slammed her palms on his ass to force him down.

He drove into her in one violent plunge.

She gasped. His dick filled her, hot and hard and throbbing with demand, taking up all the empty spaces inside.

"Fuck me," she growled in his ear.

With a low roar, he grasped her hips, slid out, and rammed deeper, ripping a cry from her throat. There was nowhere to hide, and a flicker of fear rose up—the fear he'd swallow her whole—but when she tried to retreat, it was too late.

His naked body loomed over her like an ancient sex god bent on dominance. His fingers thrummed her pulsing clit while his gaze locked on hers, drinking in every one of her moans and gasps as if they belonged to him. And still he hammered inside her, over and over, never letting up the pace while he teased and flicked and stroked the hard nub. Shoved to the edge of climax, he held her there ruthlessly, every slam of his hips and his dick taking her further. She fought wildly, for climax, for retreat, for safety, but he wouldn't allow her.

"All of it," he commanded, his thumb pressing down while he angled his hips to thrust deeper, hitting that shimmering, magical spot that drove her mad. "You took us here. Now I'm going to fuck you until you scream my name and give me everything you have."

"Ethan, please."

"More. Yes, like that, you're so wet and hot, take all of me. Now, Mia."

She gave up, gave in, and gave it all to him.

With one last plunge, he hurled her over the edge and she came. His shout of satisfaction echoed dimly in her ears. Her body released as wave after wave of pleasure broke through her. She sobbed and called his name, clinging to him as her vision faded and she was helpless to do anything but ride out the brutal ecstasy of her unending climax.

They collapsed on the bed, panting, skin damp with sweat. He was still inside her as he rolled to the side, pinning her against him. Arms wrapped around his shoulders, Mia looked into his face.

"I love you."

He stroked her tangled hair back. "I love you, too."

She searched his face, found the truth, and snuggled deeper into his embrace. Then slept.

Chapter Twenty-Three

Mia clicked off her phone and groaned at the stack of notes in front of her.

One week left.

How had she managed to fall in love in just a few weeks?

Of course, Ethan Bishop was no ordinary man. She remembered Priscilla's words and fought the urge to text her with an "SOS" sign. Since the night they'd confessed their feelings, they hadn't talked about it. It was as if both of them were afraid to bring in reality and the obstacles between them.

She lived in the city. He belonged here.

Yes, they could do long distance, but would it eventually break them? With her demanding schedule, could they make it work? And more important, Ethan might not be thinking of a future between them. Saying you loved someone didn't guarantee anything.

She had learned that hard lesson a while ago.

Tonight, she'd insist they have a long talk about their expectations and if there was something more for them past the summer. And of course, Jonathan would arrive tomorrow. After he heard about Chloe's problems with her so-called friends, the vandalism, and running out on the check, he'd flipped. He'd informed his daughter he'd enrolled her at NYU and would be picking her up to come home.

She had refused.

Mia was stuck in the middle. She wasn't part of the family, but her gut drove her to back up Chloe and help get her a second chance. Once her father got elected, her world was going to change yet again. She didn't think it would be fair to the girl to start new again when she'd just begun to blossom.

Well, it was no good brooding about it until Jonathan arrived. She left the comfort of air-conditioning, deciding to head to the stables. Time was running out, and she wanted to enjoy every moment with both Chloe and Ethan. She had just reached the front porch when a familiar black sports car careened into the parking lot, spitting out gravel in its wake.

Ah, crap.

She watched them approach. Practically vibrating with hostility, they stopped a few feet from her. "Chloe here?" the pink-haired girl asked.

"No. She's working."

The kids shared a glance. One of the boys sneered. "You been keeping her locked up for slave labor?" he challenged, puffing up his scrawny chest. His tank proclaimed FUCK OFF.

Real nice.

"Actually, Chloe doesn't want to hang out with you any longer. You probably knew that since she hasn't been texting you back."

"You're lying. We're her friends. We protect her from bullshit, like adults who don't know a thing."

"Friends, huh? Must be nice to have someone in your group who takes the blame when you screw up. I know about the vandalism of the professor's car. I know about the diner. And I know you had the gall to deface this property. My advice to you is take off, don't look back, and leave Chloe alone."

The taller guy—she thought it was Anthony—smirked and shook his head. His gaze dragged over her body, setting off creepy vibes. "You can't tell us what to do, bitch. Mind your own business, and let Chloe make her own decisions."

Holy hell, they were only around twenty-one, twenty-two years old. If no one intervened, who knows what they'd be doing next? The girl with the pink hair looked back and forth, a touch of nervousness emanating from her figure. Mia tried to direct her next words at the young girl, who still had a shot to break from the assholes. What was her name? Yes. *Theresa.*

"Why are you with them, Theresa?" she asked softly. The girl's dark eyes flickered with a mix of emotions. "They're using you, too, and they won't think twice about throwing you up for bait when shit goes down."

"No, they wouldn't," she said shakily. "You don't know them."

"Yes, I do. Because at one point, we've all been vulnerable, looking for acceptance or someone who makes you feel decent about yourself. But these guys are a mirage. You're stronger than that."

"Bitch, you got a mouth on you!" the other guy growled, moving forward. "I think you need to be taught a lesson. Easy enough to shut you up."

She kept talking. "You committed a crime. We haven't pressed charges yet, but that will come next if you show your face around here or bother Chloe again. Understand?"

"The only thing you're gonna understand is how loud you're gonna beg for mercy."

"Not as loud as you are, asshole."

Ethan stepped behind him, his phone casually held in his hand. Chloe was behind him, face pale and sickly.

"Chloe! About time, girl, now tell them you're with us," Anthony yelled.

Chloe shook her head and stayed by Ethan's side. "Not anymore," she managed to say in a firm tone. "I don't want to hang out with you. I told you by text and on the phone, I don't want you bothering me anymore."

"After all we done for you?" the pink-haired girl asked. "You ditching us?"

"Theresa, you vandalized my professor's car and let me take the blame! You threatened me at Bea's Diner and trashed the barn where I work. I'm done. You've never been my friends, and I want you out of here."

Ethan closed the distance until he loomed over the group. They tried to stand their ground, but it was obvious from the flicker of fear on their faces they knew they'd gone too far.

"Here's how it's gonna be," Ethan said in a soft, menacing whisper. "I don't beat the shit out of you today, and you do me a few favors: One, you never try to speak to or see Chloe again. Two, you stay out of my town and the local businesses here, or I'll know about it. I just got your threats on video, and we have you on camera for destruction of property. I'll keep both of these gems handy if I hear of you making any further trouble. Now, nod if you understand me."

Eyes wide, bravado temporarily forgotten under the leashed rage of the man before them, all three nodded.

"And don't think after a few beers and bruised egos you can come back to my place and try to wreak revenge. 'Cause I will bury you, and you'll spend the next few years making real intimate friends with your prison mates. Now get the hell off my land."

Without a word, they shot off into the car and disappeared. Ethan turned toward Chloe and gripped her arms. The girl's body shook. "Sweetheart, are you okay?"

Chloe nodded. "Yes. Thank you. I've never seen anyone stand up for me like that."

Mia walked toward the girl and gave her a hug. "That's what real friends do for each other," she said. "I think they wet their pants once Ethan threatened them."

Chloe laughed. "Yeah, that was pretty badass. And I heard you, too, Mia. Thanks for believing in me. Thanks for everything this summer."

The words were sweet to her ears, and she shared a smile with Ethan over the girl's head. "You're welcome."

"Why don't you head inside and take a break, Chloe?"

"Okay." With a last squeeze, she disappeared into the house.

"Think they'll be back?" Mia asked.

"Doubt it. They're true bullies. Once someone stands up to them, they go away looking for another victim. I don't think they'll bother Chloe again."

"Good. I must say on a personal note, all that male assertiveness was quite sexy."

His blue eyes darkened with intention. In seconds, his mouth was inches from hers, that delicious smirk resting on his full lips. "Sexy enough to get naked with me tonight?"

"Maybe." She licked her lips with anticipation.

"How do I up my odds to one hundred percent?"

She whispered the words against his mouth. "Bring a cupcake with you and feed it to me. Naked."

He growled, lowered his head, and kissed her.

And everything was suddenly perfect.

Mia leaned forward, pressing the blanket against her mouth in a feeble attempt to smother her cry of anguish. Her gaze was trained on the television. Her fingers gripped Ethan's as she silently prayed it wouldn't happen. It couldn't. It would be too horrible to witness. After all, this was a children's movie.

That's when Mufasa—the lion father—tumbled down the cliffs to his violent death.

"No!" she cried out, jumping up from the couch. Ophelia fumbled for the remote and hit the "Pause" button. Mia gazed at her in furious betrayal, even as she noted the woman's tears. "This is wrong on too many levels. Tell me he didn't die. Tell me he's hiding and will appear later in the movie, or I refuse to watch another second."

Chloe giggled. How could she possibly have such a casual attitude after such a tragedy? "He's dead, Mia. But you have to watch the rest. Simba gets revenge and justice is served and it's all about the circle of life."

"I don't like the circle of life, and I hate this movie. *Moana* was so much better! No one died except the grandmother, and that's totally acceptable due to her age!"

Ethan's lips twitched, but he squeezed her hand in sympathy. "I know, sweetheart. I warned you, but you were insistent you wanted to see *The Lion King*. Will more popcorn help? Another glass of wine?"

"I can't do it. I'm never going to sleep tonight after that scene. How is this a fun family night?"

Harper laughed, unfolding her lean length from her position on the floor. "Ah, the poetry of pain and pleasure, life and death, good and bad. It's epic, ain't it?"

"Stop making fun of her," Ophelia said. "Maybe you forgot how you bawled so hard over *Bambi*, Mom had to call the doctor to see if she could give you half a sedative?"

Harper stuck out her tongue and disappeared into the kitchen.

"I can turn it off," Ethan offered. "Just say the word, and we'll be watching *Miss Sloane* or *Our Brand Is Crisis*."

Her heart melted a bit. Two movies about strong women in the PR and political environment fighting for their clients. He really did get her.

"No, I can do this." Mia blinked, trying to get herself back in control. If they could watch Disney movies without losing it, she'd rise to the challenge. Besides, she really did have to see Scar brought to justice. "I want that damn lion to pay for what he did."

"There's my girl." Ethan tucked her back into his shoulder, his arm around her in an almost protective gesture.

"You'll like how Simba gets revenge," Chloe said. Jumping up from her post next to Harper, she resettled next to Mia on her other side. The scent of watermelon Sour Patch Gummies drifted around her in odd comfort. The girl stretched out, crossed her ankles, and pressed against her shoulder. "But I think you'll still get upset at this particular scene later. I can get more tissues if you need it."

A lump settled in her throat. A rush of fierce emotions shook through her at the innate care the girl showed her. Snuggled between Ethan and Chloe, she realized how important they had both become to her—how treasured she felt in their presence.

God, how she loved them.

She squeezed both of their hands. "I'm ready now. Hit the 'Play' button, Ophelia."

The movie began to play again, but this time she knew it would all be okay.

Chapter Twenty-Four

"Mia, I need you back in the city with me ASAP."

Jonathan regarded her with a serious intensity and a nervousness she hadn't glimpsed before. He'd arrived just a few hours ago, and though he shared a warm hug with his daughter, their conversation hadn't delved into any of the uncomfortable subjects yet. He'd only brought Bob this time, and he greeted Ophelia and Harper with genuine warmth, thanking them for what they'd done for Chloe this summer.

Ethan hadn't shown up yet.

"Has something happened?" she asked with concern. She'd been keeping a tight rein on his social media, and her assistant was in constant contact. Bob gave her regular detailed reports. Things have been going smoothly, and the polls showed Jonathan as the clear front-runner with a comfortable margin.

"No, but we're in the home stretch, and this is commonly when disaster can strike. I want Chloe where I can keep an eye on her, and I need you back in your office, where I have constant access. I'd like you there for the governor's charity ball this week. He's a supporter, and it's a great opportunity for press. I want to leave in the morning."

She'd expected it, and though Jonathan couldn't tell her what to do—he was only one of her clients—he was the most important and needed her full attention. She'd never forgive herself if she extended her time with Ethan only to screw up the election.

Ethan.

His name brought a series of shivers. Last night, they'd made love for hours and talked about the future. They'd decided they wanted to be together, but the problem always came down to geography. Her life was in the city, and his was here. He craved a quieter setting, and she was consistently thrust into the limelight with her clients and chaotic work life. Nothing was solved except how they felt about each other.

Mia nodded, ignoring the pang of loss in her gut. "I agree. I'll make arrangements to leave tomorrow and attend the ball. But Jonathan, you have to talk to Chloe. She's made some decisions of her own, and I think you should listen."

His brow arched. "We'll have time to sort it out after the election. NYU is a good choice for her."

"I've watched her grow and change this summer. She needs a chance to do things on her own, and she desperately needs your support. She's so happy here. If you rip her away and put her in a school she doesn't choose because of your own personal reasons, I'm afraid something will break between you. She needs to feel like *she's* your primary concern, not the election."

He frowned. "She's my daughter, Mia. She always comes first, but sometimes the right decision isn't the most popular." He tunneled his fingers through his hair and regarded her with frustration. "You think this is easy on me? I hate playing the bad guy. I know you've said she's changed this summer, but all I see is a young girl who fell into the wrong crowd and had no one to rely on. If she's close by, I can help."

"Did you ever consider that she needs to be on her own to figure things out? To find herself and who she wants to be in this world?"

Regret flashed in his eyes. "She lost her mother and made bad choices in an attempt to stop the pain. I'm worried about her. I want to be a bigger part of my daughter's life—but I just have to get through this damn election. Then we can figure things out together. Does that make sense?"

Her heart softened at the evident love for his daughter warring with his political aspirations. "I understand. Just promise me you'll let her say her piece and really consider it. Working on the farm has changed her." She paused, pinning him with her gaze. "It's changed all of us."

He nodded. "I will. I can't thank you enough for taking care of her, Mia. I know I haven't told you, but there's no other person in the world I would've trusted with my daughter." His eyes held a touch of regret. "I know I can act like an asshole. I know you may think I only care about winning, and sometimes, I wonder if you're right. I wonder if I'm making a huge mistake by putting everything I have into helping a city—or eventually, a world—that may not care. I just want you to know I question myself more than you know. If this whole thing really is worth it."

It was the lost look on his face that made the memory strike. A memory she knew it was time to share. "Do you ever wonder why I took you on as a client?"

His laugh held a touch of arrogance. "Because I could make your career?"

She grinned. "Actually, no. I was intent on never taking on a political client I couldn't believe in. To be honest, I'd looked at some other potential clients before, but I was always disappointed. I found lies and greed. I found things that I couldn't be a part of, not after what happened to my father."

He waited for her to finish with a patience that she'd always admired. He'd never been one to rush over someone else in the need to talk louder or make his opinion count more.

"I kind of stalked you for a few days. Wanted to get an idea of the person you were outside of the office, when no one was looking. I needed to be sure I wanted to represent you. One night you were coming home from court. You were heading toward Times Square, dressed in your suit and tie and some nice cashmere coat. I remember it was cold and rainy—one of those typical New York winter evenings that cuts through your bones and makes you wish you could book a ticket to a Caribbean island."

She watched him frown, as if searching for the memory she remembered so clearly. "You passed a homeless person with a dog. Nothing unusual, we pass them every day. There's so many of them; sometimes you feel as if you've helped enough, then sometimes you feel sick that you passed one and could've made a small difference. I didn't think anything of it, but you suddenly stopped, backed up, and knelt down in front of that man."

She saw the scene unfolding in her mind. The small cardboard sign drawn in slanted black marker. **HOMELESS. PLEASE HELP FEED MY DOG.** The way human and canine hunched together to battle the cold. The way Jonathan had laid a hand on the dog, on the man's shoulder, and had seemed to talk to him.

"You got up and went to the hot dog vendor and bought five of them. You gave three to the man and two to the dog. And then you took off your coat and wrapped it around them."

Jonathan nodded slowly. "I remember now. There are so many who need help. They won't go to the shelter because it's safer on the streets."

"Another one of your platform promises you want to change. But you did something right then and there, Jonathan. You gave him what you had, and there were no cameras or people watching. No Facebook live feed or viral news for that evening. It was just you and the person you were. And after that, I called your office and said I'd take you on as a client. Because I knew, for sure, that you would make a difference."

They stared at one another for a while, emotion crackling in the air. Then he smiled, nodding his head. "I'll talk to Chloe. I can't promise anything, but I'll try to listen."

"Thank you, Jonathan."

"No, Mia. Thank you. For everything." He disappeared and Mia dragged in a breath. She could only hope he heeded her advice. But now she needed to have her own heart-to-heart with the man she loved.

And explain why she had to leave.

Ethan knew immediately Mia was leaving him.

Her beautiful face looked haunted; those whiskey eyes were filled with an anguish he intended to soothe. She'd spent the night in his arms, and there was only one truth that mattered: they loved each other. But right now, she had to focus on her career and needed to be in the city, giving her all. God knows, he understood that type of passion—and he had no right to ask her to stay on an isolated horse farm in a small town and run local Facebook pages. She was meant for so much more than that.

How many times had he asked himself if he could live in Manhattan to be with her? But now that he'd begun working with Phoenix, he realized part of his soul belonged here. He wanted to start a riding group with the local vets in the area, and he had just begun research. He was excited about Phoenix and had dedicated himself to working with him long term. With his PTSD, the idea of being surrounded by tall buildings, chaos, loud noises, and boots on pavement rather than fresh earth, crippled a piece inside him.

He wasn't ready to make that leap, and neither was she.

So he had to let her go.

He stepped out of his bungalow to meet her. They stared at each other for a few moments, acknowledging what was about to happen, and then he opened his arms and she stepped into his embrace.

He breathed in the fresh coconut scent of her hair, relished the sleek, sun-warmed length of her body fit perfectly to his. His hands traveled every curve he'd memorized with his lips and tongue and touch. And he realized this woman had healed him, with her fiery passion and kind heart and stubbornness.

Her voice drifted to his ears like a wisp of smoke. "I have to leave."

"I know."

"I don't want to."

He pressed a kiss to her temple. "I know."

She tipped her head back, a smile curving her lips. "Who are you, Han Solo?"

He laughed. And though his heart ripped apart at the idea of her gone from his bed and his daily routine, he recognized what a gift she'd given him this summer. "No. Because I have no problem saying *I love you*, Mia. But right now, you have an election to win."

She blinked furiously, a damp sheen evident in her eyes. "Damn you. Why do you have to be so reasonable?"

"I won't be tonight."

She caught the intention, and the fierce sexual energy crackled between them. He lifted her up and kissed her, taking his time savoring the taste of rich wine and sweet honey, diving deep and demanding everything.

And she gave it.

"I want to talk to Lake," he murmured against her mouth. "Then I want you in my bed."

She trembled but her smile was full of her usual sass. "You better be ready to keep me there a long time, horse man."

"Princess, you better be ready to beg for mercy."

She nipped at his bottom lip, turned on her heel, and winked. "Then get your ass in gear. 'Less talking, more action,' I've always said."

He laughed and followed her to the inn.

An hour later, Ethan found Lake on the porch holding a beveled glass filled with whiskey. The man stared into the darkness, his features shadowed with melancholy. Usually Ethan wouldn't interrupt, but it was important to say his piece. When they'd arrived at the inn, shouts could already be heard echoing from the window, and Mia decided to take a walk with him to give Lake the privacy they needed.

Ethan guessed the talk hadn't gone so well.

"Mind if I join you for a quick drink?"

Lake looked up, obviously shaken from his thoughts. His face smoothed out to a politician's expression, giving nothing away. "Of course. Ophelia was generous enough to share the good stuff. I love a good aged bourbon."

"Me too." He poured a glass for himself and settled into the wicker chair next to Lake. "You and Chloe leaving tomorrow?"

His voice came out hard. "Yes. It's for the best. I know she loved working here for the summer, but it was forced community service. I gave her a chance to try things on her own, and now she has to come back where I can keep an eye on her."

"You know she didn't vandalize the car, right?"

Lake nodded, pondering his drink. "Yes, she finally told me. Explained her motives. I should've known it didn't make sense and prodded more. That's not the daughter I know."

"You can't know what she doesn't tell you. I think she's learned to be more open, though. I know for a fact she's made up for her mistakes. She really pulled her weight around here."

Lake looked up, curious. "She really liked working with the horses, huh? Funny, her mom was a huge animal lover. Not me. Always preferred the city, but her mother was a country girl at heart. She moved from Kentucky when she was young. She also loved horses, but we never introduced Chloe to riding."

"She has a gift," Ethan said simply. "I've watched her work with some of the skittish horses, and she's brought them around. It's not an easy task, and most don't have the skills to communicate on that level with a horse. In fact, I wanted to let you know she always has a job here. A real paying job, not volunteer work. She proved her worth. My sisters also liked having her around. She was good company."

"Yes, they said. Chloe expressed how badly she wanted to stay here for another semester. Finish out the year to show me how she can turn things around. But I think NYU is the right answer for both of us. I don't want her around those kids if they decide to give her trouble. And I'll be able to regularly check on her and assign a team to watch her in the city. She'll be safe."

"And so will the election."

Lake shot him a look. "Judging me for my parenting skills, Bishop?"

Ethan sat back in the chair and took a sip of his drink. "No. I'm not a father. I've never been faced with decisions that affect not only the country but also my daughter. I've never had to watch my wife leave this world and know I need to be two parents."

Anguish gleamed in the man's sharp blue eyes. Slowly, he nodded. "Yeah. You never know how life is going to turn out."

They drank and sat in silence for a while, both pondering their own thoughts. "Mia and Chloe really bonded, didn't they?" Lake asked.

"Yes. They care about each other."

"And so do you."

Lake didn't phrase it as a question, so Ethan didn't answer it like one. "Mia has a job to do, and we both understand it. I just came to ask you to think about giving Chloe a chance to stay."

Lake shook his head, but a small smile rested on his lips. "You too, huh? I did. I was prepared for screaming and sulking and running off. It was a bit rough at first, but then I watched my daughter conduct herself like an adult and accept my decision." A faint gleam of regret glinted in his eyes. "I can also tell she pulled back from me. I can only hope I'm doing the right thing, but there are no fucking guarantees in anything.

I have to do what's best. But I'll keep your offer in mind, Bishop. I appreciate you taking care of both of them this summer."

Ethan drained his drink and stood up. "It was the other way around."

"Huh?"

"They were the ones who took care of me. Good talking to you, Lake. I really hope you win the election."

"So do I."

They nodded and Ethan left him alone, sipping his whiskey in the dark.

Chapter Twenty-Five

Mia poked her head into the kitchen. "Ophelia, I'm all set. It's time for me to check out."

The woman wiped her hands on a daffodil-yellow dishtowel and walked over. "Can I say you're my very first guest that I actually don't want to leave?"

Mia laughed. "I don't believe you. I overheard you telling every guest they were your favorite."

"All lies and propaganda. But you? My brother's not the only one here who feels like he's lost someone special."

Emotion clouded her eyes. "Now, don't start. I'm going to be visiting regularly. I'm going to be in detox for your scones."

"No, you're not! I have a present for you!" Ophelia glided over to the freezer and withdrew a large package of perfectly wrapped scones. "They're already cut. Just pop them in the oven for fifteen minutes to warm, and you're all set. There's lemon and blueberry."

"You are amazing."

"Nah, all part of the job."

Mia shook her head. "No, it's not. I hope you know how special you are. How much you're really worth."

Ophelia jerked in surprise, color flooding her cheeks. Ophelia was the perfect hostess, and she ran the inn with both a firm and loving hand. Guests always felt special and pampered, and she worked tirelessly behind the scenes to give that effect. With her elegant grace, easy smile, and Irish beauty, she seemed like a woman who had everything.

But Mia sensed something deeper that seethed beneath the surface. Sometimes, when she caught Ophelia out of the spotlight of the guests, a sadness clung to her figure. Maybe it was the boy she once spoke of. Ophelia Bishop was simply a mystery she wished she had more time to explore.

"Back atcha, Mia Thrush." The women hugged one last time. "Safe trip. Did you see Harper?"

"Yep, said goodbye at the barn. Did Chloe and Jonathan come down yet?"

"They're putting their stuff in the car."

"Thanks."

Mia walked outside and found Chloe and Ethan waiting for her. Jonathan was talking on his cell by the car. Mia smiled at the girl, her heart aching. Though Chloe and Jonathan had fought over her father's insistence she come back to New York, Chloe eventually surrendered with an adult grace and dignity that had shocked her father. She promised to give NYU one semester and wait for the election results. Then they'd agreed to renegotiate depending on how the future steered. Though the girl was obviously disheartened, a new steely strength shone from her blue eyes. The proud tilt of her chin showed a woman, not a girl, and one who had confidence. Mia cleared her throat as Chloe came over and gave her a big hug.

"I'm going to miss you," the girl whispered.

"Me too. Do you absolutely swear to stop in and see me at the office? Or text me? Or Snapchat me? Or Instagram or Twitter or Facebook?"

Chloe laughed and drew back. "Yes, I swear."

"Good."

With one last squeeze, Chloe let her go. Then she turned to Ethan.

Mia watched them stare at each other, as if words were too little for what they were feeling. Like Phoenix, Ethan seemed to communicate with her on a whole other level. And when he opened his arms, Chloe stepped in and hugged him with a pure affection that brought tears to her eyes.

"Do good at NYU," he whispered roughly. "I may not be on Snapchat, but I text."

The girl laughed against his chest. "Will you send me pics of the newest horses? And Phoenix?"

"Yes. Maybe you can come up on break and spend some time here."

The girl pulled back and nodded eagerly. "I'd love that."

Jonathan motioned Chloe over and mouthed *We gotta go.*

Ethan regarded her with serious blue eyes. "You always have another home here, Chloe. Remember that." With a small smile, he gently pushed her away toward her father. "Bye, sweetheart."

"Bye, Mia. Ethan. Thanks. I had the best summer of my life."

Mia leaned against Ethan and watched them drive away. "Why do goodbyes have to suck so bad?" she asked.

"It means you care." He stroked her cheek, blue eyes filled with intimacy. They'd been starving for each other last night, making love over and over, trying to desperately delay the coming of dawn. His touch and scent were imprinted on every inch of her body. "I packed your car. Gave you some extra water bottles for the trip."

"And Ophelia gave me scones."

"Good. If I find out you're not eating at least one baked good per week, I'll be pissed."

"Magnolia Bakery is close by. I'll just stop putting blinders on when I pass it."

"Good girl."

They smiled at each other. A loud squawk filled the air, and Mia glanced over to see Hei Hei scrambling toward them, head feathers bobbing with excitement. Wheezy shot out after him, tongue lolling, and Mia met the animals halfway, crouching to her knees. The crazed chicken flew into her embrace, rubbing his feathers over her and pecking at her feet. Wheezy gave her a tongue bath, pushing his furry head against her. She laughed, blinded by the sheen of tears. Damn this chicken for making her love him. Damn this dog for making her crave such loyal companionship. Who would've thought they'd all become so close?

"Hei Hei, Wheezy, I just might miss you the most," she murmured, stroking his beautiful feathers and patting the dog's back. "Ethan promised to give you the special organic food I ordered and those treats you like. You have to stop eating the rocks like your namesake from *Moana*. It's not good for you."

Hei Hei screeched.

"Okay, I love you. I promise I'm coming back to visit. I promise."

The chicken cocked his head, as if considering her words. Wheezy seemed to understand and slowly, bones creaking, lowered himself to the ground. She unfolded herself from the ground and walked toward the car, where Ethan waited.

"I'll call you when I get home. I'll check my calendar and let you know when I can drive back up."

"Sounds good."

"Guess this is it." She bit down on her lower lip to keep it from trembling. "I love you."

"Love you, too. There's just one thing you have to promise me before you go."

"Anything."

He kissed her hard, with a fierce intensity that shook her to the core. Then he lifted his head with that sexy half smile curving his lips. "Win."

She nodded, stepping back, gaze glued to his. "We will."

"See you later, baby."

She got into her car, drinking in his presence: Thighs braced apart. Fisted hands on hips. Head tilted up in a proud arrogance that was all male. Ginger hair blowing in the wind. Leashed power emanating in waves around him. And those beautiful pale-blue eyes locked on her through the window.

Hei Hei was right beside him. As if the chicken knew something terrible was happening, those crazy feathers fell limply to the side of his head instead of sticking straight up. He kept still and silent, his entire demeanor sad. A choked sob rose up from her throat. Dear God, it hurt so much. It was as if she was losing a piece of herself she'd just found.

With one last heart-wrenching smile, Mia reversed in the lot and drove away.

This time, she couldn't look back.

She knew if she did, she'd never leave.

Chapter Twenty-Six

"Girl, you got it bad."

Mia shook herself out of her trance and looked at her assistant. Gabby stood framed in her office, a huge stack of folders in her hands. Impatience radiated from her in waves. "I'm sorry? What do you need?"

Gabby sighed, walking in to drop in the chair opposite her desk. "I've called your name three times. I need the approval on the new media campaign for the mommy blogger. Plus, Tanya's scheduling a press release about the sex tape, and you need to be by her side with the Cover Girl people. Did you get a dress from Rent the Runway for the gala this Saturday?"

"What?" Dammit, she'd been planning to try and sneak upstate for the night. "Which one is that?"

"Jonathan's being honored for his work with Saint Jude's Hospital, remember?"

No, but she'd pretend. "Right. I'm on it."

"No, you're not. I'm worried. It's like you're only half here, with your head in the clouds back on that horse farm you were supposed to hate. Tell me again how hot he is."

Mia laughed, lowering her face into her hands with defeat. "Really, really hot."

"How many times did you do it in one night?"

"Five. But I had even more orgasms."

"I am so signing up for a horse farm on my next vacation," Gabby said with a sigh.

Mia shook her head, trying desperately to stop thinking about her time with Ethan. One full month had already passed, and she was so busy she barely had time to breathe, yet every spare second, his face drifted in her mind. With the election only a month away, every free moment was spent on Jonathan's social media campaigns, appearances, spinning solid press, and keeping him in the spotlight so voters were consistently reminded to vote. She'd managed to sneak in a visit with Ethan one brief weekend and a short lunch when they both drove half-way to save on time.

They'd spent the two hours holding hands, talking nonstop, and trying to pretend things were fine apart. On the drive back, she got stuck in horrific city traffic and was late for her next meeting. It had almost affected her ability to sign a new client, but she'd rallied and now safely held the career of a long-term basketball athlete who'd been arrested for drunken behavior in her hands. As a mentor to young kids, the incident had killed him in the press. Mia needed to piece it back together again. Normally, it was a challenge she thrived on, reminding herself once again of the importance of her job and giving people a valuable second chance.

Except lately, she just wasn't that happy.

She missed dinner with Ophelia and Harper and Chloe. She missed the smell of the barn and Wheezy's howls and Hei Hei's crazed affection. She missed the stark beauty of the mountains and the quiet of the woods and the scents of musk and earth and sunshine. She missed the way the air reached deep into her lungs when she breathed and how she'd finally begun sleeping through the night. Her damn insomnia was back with a vengeance now that Ethan wasn't in her bed. And she missed him so much, it was like a physical ache throbbing in her gut.

Usually, her job gave her a thrill like nothing else. She lived on adrenaline and hunting new clients. She adored social engagements and being in the spotlight. But lately, there was an emptiness inside her she couldn't seem to fill with work, no matter how much she tried.

"I'm sorry, Gabby," she said quietly. "I'm trying. It's just hard getting readjusted."

Her friend gazed at her with sympathy. "I get it. I'm on your side, and I'll help as much as I can. Maybe once the election is over, you'll have more time to see each other. Why can't he come down here more often?"

"It won't help if I'm running from event to event and can't give him any time. He's not really comfortable in the city, either."

"What are you guys going to do?"

Mia shrugged. "Nothing for now. Work it out. Take time when we can."

"Phone sex?"

Mia shooed her out of the office. "I am not discussing it, Gabby. I already gave you way too much info."

Gabby laughed, dropping a fat folder on her desk. "Fine. If you don't want to share the dirt, you can contact Reese Donovan, who's been trying to hire you to clean up his reputation."

"Ugh, no way, I only take on clients who deserve a fair break. He's scum."

"Exactly. I'm not up to another round with him."

Mia assessed her assistant, then sighed in surrender. "Fine. Yes to phone sex."

Gabby lifted a brow. "Webcam?"

"Once."

"Orgasms?"

"Three. In half an hour."

Gabby shuddered. "That's just too delicious. Fine, I'll deal with Reese the pond scum." She grabbed the file back and flounced out of her office.

Mia laughed and got back to work.

Ethan dragged in a lungful of air and knocked on the door. He'd only been in Manhattan a few hours, and already his nerves were wrangling. From the clogged city streets and beeping cars, to the confines of his monkey suit and tight, shiny shoes, he realized how far from this world he'd strayed. A year ago, he'd been king of the cocktail party and Hollywood scene. Now, he was counting the hours till he was back in his jeans and working with Phoenix.

He heard a few low mutters before he spotted her eye behind the peephole. The screech of delight and scramble to unlock the door affirmed he'd made the right choice to surprise her by accompanying her to the gala.

"Oh my God, Ethan!" She jumped into his arms without pause, and he caught her tight against him. The tension in his muscles relaxed, and the warmth of her body reminded him the evening would all be worth it to please her. "What are you doing here?"

"Every princess needs a date to the ball," he teased.

She blinked furiously, pure emotion filling her gorgeous whiskey eyes. "Thank you," she whispered. "But you didn't have to do this."

He tipped her chin up and smiled. "Yes, I did." He kissed her long and slow and deep, until his head spun like one of those old cartoons when a character got slugged and saw little birdies. He lifted his head and pushed her gently away from him. "Let me look at you."

She was gorgeous, dressed in a clingy gold gown that showed off just enough cleavage and hugged every curve—his dick was hard in an instant. That thick, honey-blonde hair was pinned up, emphasizing the graceful curve of her neck. Her shoes were wicked stilettos clustered with gold sparkles. He imagined her naked except for those shoes and smothered a groan. "Sweetheart, you're killing me. How am I supposed to keep my hands off you?"

"You don't." Her gaze swept his black tuxedo, and pure lust shot at him in waves. "Because I'm not keeping my hands off you, horse man."

At that moment, the discomfort of his clothes was completely worth it. The sheer pleasure in her gaze as she took him in made him want to roar and beat his chest like an ape. "Keep looking at me like that, and we're going to be real late," he warned.

Her wicked smile knocked him to his knees. "We can't be late, but we can leave early," she drawled.

"Done. The limo's outside. Let's get this over with."

Her laughter warmed him as she grabbed her sparkly gold purse and wrap. He escorted her into the sleek vanilla limousine, where a bouquet of red-and-ivory roses waited for her, along with champagne. She quirked a brow and sipped the bubbly brew. "Oh, you're smooth. Was there ever a woman who could resist you?"

He drank his champagne and tried to keep his gaze off the lean length of naked leg the slit in her dress revealed. "Yes. You."

"Yet here I am."

He snagged her hand and entwined his fingers with hers. "And every damn day I'm going to make sure you don't regret giving in."

Her features softened. "Ethan."

"Yeah?"

"We're going to leave really, really early."

He grinned. "I know. Now drink your champagne."

The ride to the New York Public Library was way too short. Ethan would've been happy spending the evening riding around in the limo with her, drinking champagne, stretching her out on the cool leather seats, and bringing her to orgasm with his mouth.

Instead, they pulled up to the red carpet, and the driver opened the door.

Flashbulbs exploded in his face. The roar of the crowd surrounded him, and microphones were shoved close, a mingling of voices peppering endless questions. Ethan concentrated on Mia, tucking her arm under his elbow and guiding her up the steps. She smiled and nodded, laughed and answered questions with a witty air that told him she was comfortable in front of cameras and enjoyed being in the public eye.

Ethan managed to keep a grim smile on his face and focused on getting one foot in front of the other. Sweat coated his skin. The fabric of his expensive tuxedo squeezed him like a vise. The noise came in a huge rush of waves, at first dim, then growing to massive proportions of sound that wrung his ears and rattled his foundation.

Ah, shit.

It was happening.

They stopped midway to the entrance to stand in line. He dimly recognized a few celebrities and politicians, impeccably dressed and chatting nonstop in an effort to get a handle on who was most important, and who they should get their pictures taken with. A siren screamed and flashed past them; another flashbulb went off, and suddenly Ethan froze, held in the throes of a massive panic attack that drove him to drop halfway to his knees.

Mia's face faded in and out, but it was her voice he clung to as she repeated his name and angled her body to block his, guiding him firmly away from the crowd. He leaned against the giant column and fought the crippling fear chopping away at his sanity.

He looked up, frantic, and gazed straight into amber eyes.

"Breathe, baby. I'm not going anywhere."

He ripped at his tie and fought for air. Dragged in a breath. Again. Then again. Her hands clasped his, her gaze calm and controlled as she breathed with him, encouraging him to slowly take in more air.

It took a while for his lungs to accept the air and his heart to stop thundering and the sweat to dry on his skin. As he gathered more control, straightening up and coming back to reality, she smiled at him. A beautiful, loving, sweet smile that punched through his chest and squeezed his heart.

"Better?"

He managed a nod. Shame filled him. She deserved so much better than this. Than him. Than all his fucking issues.

"Don't you dare," she whispered fiercely, poking at his chest. "Don't you even think it, Ethan Bishop, or I'll . . . I'll . . . beat the crap out of you!"

That brought a grin to his face. God, she was magnificent. How had he ever managed without her? "Then I won't."

"Good. I have an idea. How about we blow this lame party and go back home, where you can show me all the dirty, filthy things you want to do to me?"

And right then and there, Ethan fell in love with her all over again.

Shoving back the fear, he shook his head. "Not a chance. I want to see you in action here. Plus, the crab cakes at these functions are really good."

A frown creased her brow. "They suck and you know it. I'd rather get naked."

He reached out and cupped her cheeks. Careful not to mess up her lipstick, he drifted a whisper-soft kiss over her lips. "Thank you, but I want to go in. I'm okay now."

She seemed to sense the need for him to prove he could conquer his fear and slowly nodded. "We're only staying an hour. Tops."

"Sounds like a plan."

She squeezed his hand, and they rejoined the line, which was now moving through the elaborate doors. The charity fund-raiser and gala was for Saint Jude's Hospital and boasted the crème de la crème of New York. The inside of the library had been transformed into a dream ball. Candles and white lights highlighted the gorgeous gleaming floors, and fat bouquets of flowers were held in Roman vases. Linen-covered tables supported a massive array of foods, and tuxedoed service staff brought around platters of appetizers. Dazzling gowns in blinding colors filled the space as tightly knit groups chattered away while a full string quartet filled the high ceilings with soaring melodies.

They grabbed cocktails and found Jonathan immediately. Ethan noted the man lit up when he gazed at Mia and seemed genuinely happy to see him again. He pumped his hand with enthusiasm. "Mia, you look stunning. Ethan, so nice of you to join us. Chloe's missed you."

"I miss her. How is she doing at NYU?"

The man lifted his hands. "She's been giving it a fair shot, but I can tell she's unhappy. I've noticed a difference in her since she's been back. A new maturity. I think it was the summer she spent with you."

Ethan smiled. "Good to know. As I've said, I'd welcome her back anytime."

Lake's eyes took on a mischievous look as he glanced at Mia. "Ah, why do I feel like you'll be leaving the farm quite soon?"

A trickle of unease spilled through him. "What do you mean?"

"Well, I field more and more calls about my PR representative, so I think Mia's client base will soon explode. The two of you will do well here in Manhattan. Let me know if you need help finding an apartment; I have a few priceless contacts. Mia, can I just steal you away for a few moments?"

She looked over, and Ethan smiled. "Go ahead. I'll mingle."

He watched Mia drift into the dazzling crowd and headed toward the bar to find a quiet corner. As he sipped his second scotch, he surveyed the room, taking in the scene before him.

Already his nerves were tingling in warning. The heat pressed down on him, and he grit his teeth and held on. He could do this for the woman he loved. It was just an hour—maybe two, tops. This was her world, and she deserved to enjoy her time in the spotlight. When Lake got elected, everything would change for her. She'd be the hottest PR company in the city, and Lake was right. There was no way she could run a thriving business on an upstate horse farm. Eventually, something would break.

When she rejoined him, they worked the room. He hated every second of surface conversation and glossy images and the nonstop cycle of meet, greet, and move on. He despised the fake laughs, the roving gazes of certain men when they looked at Mia, and the assessing stares that tried to figure out if he was worth conversing with. When they finally left and headed back to her apartment, his fingers shook slightly, and he had to shove them in his pockets to hide it from her. And when he made love to her, over and over, a desperation leaked into every touch and kiss bestowed on her skin. Eventually a decision had to be made—a decision he didn't know if he could handle.

Mia's world no longer belonged to him. But the bigger question remained. Could he live in it? Could he force himself to move to the city and learn to function in a world he no longer fit in? And if he couldn't, would he be able to handle the possibility of losing her?

She stirred in his arms, interrupting his thoughts. "You're troubled."

He pressed a kiss to her forehead. "I just came three times. I'm too stupidly happy to be troubled."

"Lie." Her fingers drifted over the crease in his brow. "I know it's been hard having a relationship long distance. But once Jonathan is elected, I can clear my schedule more. Spend time at the farm. We can trade weekends."

The niggling worry in his gut grew to a dull, spreading ache. It sounded logical, but the truth of what was going to happen needed to be faced. "Sweetheart, once Lake is elected, your client list is going to double. This is everything you've worked for. You may end up being even busier."

"So I'll hire more people." She propped herself on her elbow and tilted her chin up in that familiar stubborn way he loved so damn much. "I'll work at the farm and be careful about what type of clients I choose. This can work."

He smiled with a touch of sadness. "Your life is here, baby. And I'm so proud of you and what you've built. You shouldn't have to back off for anyone, especially me. But I can't help but keep wondering if I can be in this world any longer." He forced himself to say the words. "Something broke inside me, and being in the city brings it all back. I'm afraid I may not be able to give you what you need."

"All I need is you," she said fiercely. "Are you trying to tell me something, Ethan? Do you want to break up?"

He rolled over, pressing her deep into the mattress, pinning her wrists beside her head. "I love you, and I'm not giving up on us. But I need to face the truth with my limitations. I'm not going to be the man who holds you back and makes you regret what you could've done."

"The only thing I'd regret is not having you by my side."

He cursed under his breath. "You're so damn pigheaded."

"Then shut up and kiss me."

And he did. He pushed them both to the edge and over, her sweet cries echoing in the air as she shattered around him. Afterward, she slept in his arms. Ethan spent the night staring into the darkness until the sun broke free, wondering what the hell he was going to do.

Eventually, he'd have to make a choice.

And he didn't know if love would be enough for either of them.

Chapter Twenty-Seven

Mia kept her gaze fixed to the giant television installed on the wall. The crowd shimmered with tension and mounting excitement.

The newscaster came on, and the tallies flashed on the screen.

Jonathan Lake had won the election.

With that final confirmation, a roar rose from the crowd, and all hell broke loose. Mia stood frozen in place, filled with a mixture of relief, joy, and fierce pride. They'd done it. Jonathan would now be the new mayor, and he was one of the good ones. A man who believed in the people rather than money, a man who'd fight for right and finally buck the system that leaked greed and avarice through its very foundation. It was the start of something good. Something she believed in and had fought for.

Finally, Mia had achieved justice for her father.

Her cell rang. She clicked the button, tucking it against her ear, and melted back away from the crowd. His gravelly, husky voice poured over the receiver.

"You won."

"We won."

"I'm so proud of you, baby. Not that I ever thought you wouldn't win."

Pleasure shivered over her body. Even with a simple phone call, every exchange was filled with intimacy and care that only grew stronger.

Unfortunately, so was the frustration within her that wanted more. "I wish you were here. Chloe would love to see you."

"Me too. She already texted me a picture of the television screen showing her father as the winner."

She laughed. "You're kidding me. You were her first text?"

"One of them. I'm hoping she can squeeze a weekend to come see me and the horses during winter break."

"I'm already working on it." The phone hummed, but it was so much more than silence. It was a connection, a beautiful pause filled with emotion and intention that needed no words. Mia breathed it in, savoring every precious second. "Love you."

"Love you, too. Now, go enjoy what you worked so hard for."

She clicked off and smiled. Yes. It was time to enjoy the victory and let it be an evening to remember. She turned around, and Chloe parted from the crowd, moving forward, stopping right in front of her.

The girl looked beautiful in her simple black dress and heels. Her hair was still purple, but it was swept away from her face in a graceful upsweep. Her long neck and willowy body gave off an elegance she'd begun to grow into. The diamond winked in her nose, but she'd removed her other various piercings.

"He won," Chloe said, shaking her head. "My dad is the mayor of New York."

"Congratulations, sweetheart," Mia said, giving her a hug. "You supported him through this whole thing. I know it's been hard at NYU, but you did it, and now he won the election."

Chloe smiled with just a touch of sadness. "I'm proud of him. And I know right now Mom is throwing him the biggest political victory party in heaven."

Emotion squeezed Mia's throat. "Agreed. I just spoke with Ethan. He loved your text. Said he never doubted it a moment."

"Phoenix keeps getting stronger, and his race times are only decreasing. Oh, and Harper got a brand-new horse, and guess what she named her?"

"What?"

"Chloe's Pride. She said she's a white filly who'll be perfect for me to ride when I visit."

"Oh, I can't wait to meet her. Did you hear Hei Hei has been officially grounded indoors? I didn't realize Polish chickens needed to be kept warm because of all those feathers. Ethan says he's pissed off all the time and pecks at anything he can get to."

"'Cause he misses you," Chloe said.

Their gazes met, and the memories of the farm they both loved settled over them.

"Just the women I was looking for!" Jonathan came up behind them, bringing them all into a fierce group hug. "My most valuable team in the world. You're the reason this happened."

Chloe hugged him back. "You did all the hard work. Congrats, Dad. I was just saying that Mom is probably throwing you a huge party in heaven."

Jonathan's face flickered with a sad longing. "It would've been the party of a lifetime, honey." His hand stroked his daughter's face. "Thank you. I know it's been hard these past few months, and work isn't going to get easier, but I love you. Without you, this means nothing."

"Thanks, Dad."

"Mia, you're a rock star. Get ready to be busier than you can imagine."

She tilted her head. "You think so?"

"You just helped me become the mayor. I already fielded three requests to sign up with your company. Your name is the hottest one in town as one of the best PR agencies in the business." He winked, linking his arm through his daughter's. "Better hire a few more people. You're gonna need it."

He walked away with Chloe. Mia stared after them, waiting for the rush of adrenaline and excitement to hit. Her dream of being a company celebrities and political clients sought out had finally come true. She'd accomplished everything she wanted in one perfect night.

If that's true, why did she feel so empty? Mia wondered.

Ethan.

He was pulling away. Oh, they still spoke every night and managed to squeeze in some brief visits, but ever since the night of the gala, something had changed. The last time he'd spent the weekend in her apartment, he'd been edgy, his limp more pronounced as he walked. Shadows danced in the eyes that had been so clear and bright on the farm. She'd done everything possible to craft the perfect weekend, but with the bumper-to-bumper traffic, massive crowds in Rockefeller Center, and packed lines at the trendy restaurants, he seemed to drift further away with each hour.

Panic curled in her gut. She couldn't lose him. She'd just have to try harder to get upstate more often and convince him it could work.

Her name was called from across the room. She pushed away her disturbing thoughts and concentrated on the party, determined to do anything possible to make them both happy.

Ethan stared at the phone. Her voice still echoed in his ear, the throaty, feminine drawl that brought instant heat to his body and hardened his dick in seconds. The ghost of her scent hung in the air from her last visit. He was so fucking proud of her. She'd followed her dream and gotten it. *Score one for the good guys.* He thought of her at the victory party, surrounded by crowds and champagne and excitement, the beginning of a successful career that demanded a big city, important clients, and endless work. But God, did she deserve this? The problem wasn't about her. It was about him.

Because he wasn't sure he could give her what she needed.

Ethan studied the phone in his hand for a long time, worried about the answer. The last weekend spent in the city had ripped him apart. By the time he drove back, his nerves were shredded, and his head thrummed painfully. It seemed to get worse every time he stepped into one of the greatest cities in the world—a city he loved and thrived in for many years before moving to Hollywood. Now, it was everything in his past. His future was right here, the place he'd fled so many years ago.

Fucking irony.

A knock sounded on the door. Wheezy stirred from his place at the fire, and Hei Hei gave an annoying shriek. "Come in," he called out.

Harper stepped in. Her blue T-shirts had been replaced with long sleeves, but the rest of the ensemble remained the same. She shook snow out of her hair and stomped her boots on the mat. "She won."

Ethan grinned with pride. "Hell yeah, she won. I never doubted it."

Harp moved into the kitchen, grabbed a beer from the refrigerator, and got comfortable in the battered leather armchair. "How come you're not partying with her?"

As usual, her directness hit its target. "Figured it'd be best to stay back. This is Lake's night and hers."

"Bullshit." She tipped her bottle back and took a slug. "You're having trouble being in the city. You're dealing with panic attacks and don't know if you can keep seeing Mia."

"Guess you know all the answers. So why don't you solve my problem?" he asked, irritation coursing through him. "I've realized we can't go on like this. I hate the fucking city. I hate that type of life. But it's Mia's life, and I love her, and I don't know if I can live without her, Harp. So solve that one for me, will you?"

His sister's green eyes flashed with empathy and an understanding that came from growing up side by side. "I wish I could," she said softly. "Can she move here?"

"Maybe. But I had my career and my time in the spotlight. She hasn't. How do I live with myself if she leaves a flourishing career behind and regrets it? I won't be that guy."

"Yep. You're fucked."

He stared at her. "Really? That's all you got?"

She shrugged. "I'm trying, okay? Ophelia is much better at this stuff. Look, she makes you happy, Ethan. But I think you need to reach deep and figure out if you can make this compromise. Can you find a way to not only function but also *live* in the city? Will it destroy you, or will being with her make the pain worth it?"

He shook his head and groaned. "I don't know. All I know is, when I'm with her I finally sleep. I laugh. I feel like I'm seen for the first time, all of it, all the messy shit you get used to hiding, but she doesn't care. In a way, I'm whole again. She makes everything . . . better."

His sister smiled and tipped her bottle in the air. "There you go. So you choose her."

He blinked. "It's not that easy. You need me here."

"I love having you here, but I can hire someone."

"I can't live in the city. You just said it—I have panic attacks around crowds, and I feel like I'm jumping out of my skin. I don't feel at home there."

"Do you feel home with Mia?"

He considered the question. "Yeah."

She smiled again. "There you go, dummy. There's the answer: Mia's your home. Oh, sure, it may suck for a while and be a huge challenge. You may need to go back into regular therapy to help with the attacks. Maybe compromise on a place to live where you get some space and limit your big social events. Come up here on regular weekends. Look into opportunities where you can help animals—you certainly have the background and education with Special Forces to do anything you want. There are endless possibilities. You can make it work, Ethan."

Emotion choked his throat. "How do you know?"

"Because, even though you don't believe it, you're extraordinary. Sometimes a real pain in the ass, but whatever you focus on, you conquer. Mom taught us that. It's in our blood, that love for home and all that shit. Mia's home for you. Get it?"

Yeah. He got it. His sister may not be as poetic as Ophelia, but she shot straight and true, which was exactly what he needed.

"Yeah. I get it."

"Good."

They drank their beer and watched the fire. Ethan took the time to accept his decision and plan. And finally, he realized his breath was clear, and that awful tightness in his chest was gone because his decision was right.

He was going after Mia.

Chapter Twenty-Eight

Mia stared out the window. The snow dusted the pavement and covered cars. People rushed down the muddy street, huddled in coats, grumpy from the weather. With Christmas only a few weeks away, the city took a deep, collective, irritated breath and just held on. Constant crowds, traffic, bad tempers, and unrelenting social schedules overruled heart and stomped all over the Christmas spirit.

She placed her palm flat against the cool pane and wondered what Ethan was doing.

Thanksgiving loomed, and she was trying to carve out a few days to spend at the farm. She hadn't been able to see Ethan since election night over two weeks ago. They'd signed three big-name clients, and she'd spent the past weekend in crisis mode, trying to handle some big social appearances for a new boy band. She'd been to the hottest underground nightclub and hung out with some of the hottest boy bands in the business, then met with a potential up-and-coming senator who was as passionate as Jonathan about helping the working class. Gabby was working around the clock as they interviewed for additional staff. The company was growing so fast, her phone rang off the hook with clients begging for representation. She'd finally made the big time. Her dream had finally come true.

And Mia realized she wasn't happy.

She went through the motions of work, but her heart wasn't in it. The thrill she once had was gone. Instead, she had more fun on the phone with Fran and Brian and Tattoo Ted regarding their new marketing and social media strategies. They'd recommended her to a few more businesses, and though she had no time, she squeezed them in because they were her people. Who would've thought she'd spend more effort on recruiting crowds for a local comic convention than on the new client who wanted to play the role of Spider-Man in the brand-new television series?

Yeah. She was screwed up.

She just didn't know what to do about it.

Her entire life had revolved around building a company and securing justice for her father. Now, she was on the brink of greatness, and suddenly she was doubting her whole path. When had things so drastically changed? And could she give up everything she'd worked so hard for?

What worried her the most was Ethan. She was terrified he was beginning to pull away. The morning after the gala, she'd caught him staring at her with a sadness in his eyes she'd never glimpsed before. Sure, he denied it and covered it up with a smile, but his goodbye shook something inside her. What if he wasn't happy with a long-distance relationship anymore? What if he was beginning to wonder if the effort and frustration were worth it? What if each time he visited her, he was losing a piece of himself by being back in the city—in his old life? She couldn't forgive herself if he sacrificed his happiness for hers. But more important, this life she thought she wanted so badly wasn't what she expected. It didn't fulfill her the way being on the farm with Ethan had. All she did lately was lie in bed, not sleeping, trying to figure out the right answer.

Her speaker buzzed. "Mia, Jonathan Lake is here to see you."

Surprised, she clicked on. "Send him in."

She greeted him with a smile when he walked in. He looked polished in a charcoal suit with a conservative tie. But his face showed evidence of tiredness, lines bracketing his eyes and mouth. He took a seat across from her desk. "I didn't expect to see you this week," she said, slipping into her chair. "Is everything okay? Problems? Anything I need to solve?"

"Work is good. Busy, but good. Prepping my successor and trying to figure out a million other details, but I'm solid, Mia. Thank you."

"Of course, you know I'm always here for you."

"I know. You've always proven that, which is why I needed to see you." He paused, as if collecting his thoughts. "It's Chloe."

She leaned forward with concern. "What's happening? School? Friends? She hasn't gotten into any trouble, has she?"

He raised a hand in the air. "No, nothing like that. In fact, she's been perfect. She's getting all *A*s this semester. She's home in the evenings and hasn't been spotted at any crazy parties or social functions that could cause problems. She meets me for lunch on a regular basis and takes all my calls."

"Then what's the issue?"

He stared at her, blue eyes glinting with regret. "She's not . . . happy."

Mia let out a breath. "How do you know?"

He smiled grimly. "I'm her father. I may not notice everything, but my daughter has lost a zest for life that made her who she was. Like my wife. God, she's even lost her hostility and sometimes smart-ass demeanor, and I miss that. I think I made a big mistake, Mia. Forcing her to come back and attend NYU. She's done everything I've asked to get me elected, and she put her own life on hold."

Mia blinked back the sting of tears. "She loves you."

"And I love her. I'm starting to realize I've been selfish. I was so focused on helping the people of New York, I forgot about my own daughter. You know who she constantly talks about nonstop? The farm.

Ethan. You. Phoenix. Something happened this summer I've never seen before. It was like she found a second family, but I never saw it. Didn't want to see it. I was blinded by wanting to win this election."

"It's understandable, Jonathan. It was important, and Chloe understands. But I think you're right. I think she'd rather go back to SUNY New Paltz. Work for Ethan. Find her happiness, on her terms."

He nodded. "I think so, too. It's going to be hard losing both of you in one swoop. I've come to rely on you, Mia. But it's time for me to move on, too."

"I understand but—wait, what are you talking about? I'm not moving on."

He blinked in confusion. "Oh. I figured you'd be moving upstate with Ethan."

"I thought you assumed he'd move here with me. You're the one who got me all those extra clients."

He cocked his head and regarded her. "Well, that's what I originally thought, but you're miserable. You've been miserable since you left the farm, just like Chloe."

"How do you know that?"

"It's obvious every time I see you. Oh, sure, you go through the motions and do your job perfectly, but there's a lack of zest, like Chloe. You used to be so excited and focused and energized. You lived for challenges. That's why I thought you'd be thrilled when your business exploded, but now I realize it backfired. Because I don't think you want to do this anymore. At least, not like this." He got up from his seat, straightened his jacket, and headed toward the door. "I'm going to talk to Chloe and give her the news. It'll be nice to know she has you and Ethan to look out for her."

He shut the door behind him.

Jonathan's words dove deep and unearthed the truth she'd been struggling with since the moment she came back to the city.

She didn't want this any longer.

Jonathan saw what she had been trying to deny. She was living in a fog, only half-involved in her life because her heart was with Ethan. She didn't want to live in the city and work nonstop and go to glossy, famous parties and solve celebrity problems. She didn't want Ethan to travel to the city and lose a piece of himself just so she could add another client to her roster.

She wanted Ethan and Hei Hei and the inn and the farm.

She wanted *that* home.

Shaking slightly, her mind flashed through the endless tasks that needed to be accomplished to get her to the goal.

To get her back to Ethan.

She hit the "Speaker" button. "Gabby, get in here. And bring a bottle of wine. You're going to need it."

"Ah, fuck." Gabby groaned over the speaker.

Mia smiled with anticipation.

Chapter Twenty-Nine

Ethan rubbed under Phoenix's chin. Each time he tried to stop, the horse butted his head hard against his chest, then regarded him with a haughtiness that hinted at royalty genes. Every day, some of his broken pieces healed, and he regained not only his confidence and dignity but his love of racing, too. It was bred into his bones and that big pure heart of his. Watching him rediscover it reminded Ethan of how much he loved his job.

This time, he stepped back when the horse tried to butt him. "Nope, I have other horses to attend to, buddy. But I think you'll be happy with this." He took out the iced oatmeal cookie and fed it to him. "We're gonna get a snowstorm today, so this coat should work well." He adjusted the cover over Phoenix's body and closed the gate, heading down the line. When each horse had been coddled, fed, and wrapped warm and tight, he leaned against the barn door and stared out at the mountains.

God, it was beautiful here.

The peaks were coated in frosty white, and the snow blanketed acres of land in a nonending blinding silvery sheet. The sky was a cranky gray, and clouds hung low to give off a thick mist. He would miss it, but already, being away from Mia was a constant ache he didn't want to suffer any longer. He'd planned to tell her this weekend, but they'd canceled due to the storm. Ethan figured he'd finish up for the day and head out in his truck to surprise her tonight. He'd already been working with Harper to hire an additional hand, and he figured he'd plan biweekly weekend visits to the farm to keep an eye on Phoenix and the rest of the horses.

"Ethan!"

His name rippled through the air. Half turning, thinking it was his imagination hearing her voice, he watched in shock as Mia raced forward, furry designer boots pounding over the ground, snowflakes sparkling in her golden hair, face alight with an urgency that gripped him temporarily in panic.

"Are you okay?" he demanded, running to meet her.

"Yes." She threw back her head and laughed, her red-mittened hands thrown out to her side to catch the flakes. "Yes, I'm more than okay. I love you."

"And I love you, but dammit, Mia, I told you not to drive! Don't you ever listen to me?"

"No. Maybe, sometimes. Ethan, I have to tell you something."

"No. There's no need to do this any longer. I'm moving in with you, Mia. I can't take this separation anymore, and you deserve to be able to run your business and make a mark on this world. You were meant for greatness, baby. I'll come up some weekends, and we can make this work. Say yes."

She blinked. Snowflakes clung to her lashes. Those beautiful whiskey-colored eyes gazed into his with a swirling mixture of raw emotion. "You'd move to the city for me?" she whispered.

"Yes. I love you, of course I'd move to the city."

The smile broke open her face, filled with pure joy. "Thank you for that. But I've already made my own decision. I'm moving up here."

He shook his head. "No, there's no need, baby. I will not let you walk away from your business."

"Too late," she sang. "I already did. Well, kind of."

He froze, staring at her. "What do you mean?"

"Ethan, listen to me. I've been unhappy for a long time, and when Jonathan came to visit me, he made me see how I've changed. Yes, I love my business, but not at this breakneck speed and level where I'm required to live in Manhattan and work around the clock. I don't want that anymore. I want this. I want you. I want it all."

His heart stopped, then pounded in a crazy, uneven rhythm. "What do you want to do?"

"I'm making Gabby full partner. I'm hiring additional people. I'm assigning certain clients to representatives, and I'm going to work from here and oversee the whole production. I have clients clamoring for our services, so now I can pick and choose carefully and not overwhelm any of us."

"You won't be bored living in this small town? You won't miss the glamorous city life you're used to?"

She placed her cold mitten-clad hands on both sides of his face and smiled up at him. "No, silly. I can go into the city whenever I want. But what I really want is to take on clients right here, in this town. I have big plans for these local businesses, and I think I can be a huge help. Plus, Ted owes me that tattoo."

His hands shook and words failed him, so he did the only thing left to do.

He kissed her.

His tongue dove deep, claiming her for him. Her cold lips were slippery and delicious, and they stayed together locked in an embrace for endless, perfect moments.

"Oh, and Chloe's coming back to New Paltz for the upcoming semester. Jonathan agreed she was better off being where she was happy."

"I'm glad. Now, let's get you inside before you freeze. I know someone else who is dying to see you."

"Ophelia? Harper?"

"Hei Hei. He's been a beast lately, locked up and squawking for you nonstop. You stole his heart and everyone else's around here."

"As long as I have yours."

He stopped to gaze down at her. His heart broke open, and for the first time, all the pieces fit together in a perfect puzzle. For the first time, everything made perfect sense. Because he'd learned early on you needed to take the bad with the good and embrace it all. They'd started with something good, but they'd ended up with the best thing of all.

Love.

"Let's go home," he said, voice hoarse with emotion.

"Yes. Let's go home."

Epilogue

"Ophelia, you've officially outdone yourself."

The woman stood at the head of the table, pride glowing in her sky-blue eyes. The turkey was fat and roasted to a golden perfection. Each side dish boasted vibrant color and delicious scents of garlic, rosemary, and onions. Sparkling crystal glasses and matching dishes gleamed under the chandelier. A bottle of champagne chilled in the ice bucket. The table was set with the rustic fall colors of burgundy, rust, and forest green. Mia sighed with pleasure as she gazed at the beauty laid out before her.

"Thanksgiving is my favorite holiday," Ophelia said, waving off the compliment with her usual humbleness. "I enjoy it."

Ethan shook his head. "Tink, I watched you slave all week to make sure we all had our favorite dishes at the table. Just like—"

"Mom used to," Harper interrupted.

They all raised their gazes up, as if acknowledging another presence at the table. Mia squeezed Ethan's hand, and when he squeezed back, a rush of warmth and gratitude washed over her. Right here, at this table, she'd found everything she'd always wanted.

It had just been packaged differently than what she had expected.

"Let's eat," Ophelia announced, clasping her hands together. "Ethan, will you carve?"

They feasted and chatted and laughed and teased. The upcoming months were going to be full of change, but Mia had never felt more at peace with herself. They planned to renovate the bungalow, expanding it to a fuller house so they could stay on the property, and had already sketched out an office space. Gabby was thrilled to dive headfirst into the business as full partner and had hired a savvy associate to help with the overflow. They'd begun turning down more clients and had trimmed down their roster until they had a core group they were proud to represent.

"Has Chloe called yet?" Harper asked.

"We're FaceTiming after dinner. She'll be spending winter break here, though, so I can't wait to see her."

"Chloe's Pride is doing well," Ethan commented. "I'm going to surprise her. The filly is hers to take care of and be responsible for."

"She's going to be so lit," Mia said.

Ophelia laughed. "I'm glad she'll be coming back to New Paltz. I made a big mistake not hiring her at the inn. We have a nice crowd here for the holiday."

"Oh, I forgot to tell you," Ethan said. "I spoke with Kyle, and he's going to be staying here for a while. I told him it wasn't a problem, but you should block a room for a few months. He's writing some new screenplay and needs some solitude."

"That's your best friend, right?" Mia asked. "The one you grew up with and got into all that trouble?"

"Yeah, haven't seen him in years but—Tink? Are you okay?"

The woman stared back at him with eyes full of shock and a touch of fear. Her fingers gripped the edge of the table in a deathlike vise, and her throat seemed to work to emit words that wouldn't be uttered. The usual calm, cool competence she radiated was now replaced with an edgy panic Mia had never seen before. "I-I-don't understand." Her voice came out ragged. "He . . . he can't stay here."

Ethan stared at her. "What are you talking about? We used to be the three musketeers. I know it's been a while since he's been here, but he's like family."

Her gaze snapped to him. Blue eyes flashed with fire. "We don't have the room. I'm sure he'll be happier somewhere else that's better suited to him."

Ethan shook his head, as if trying to clear it. "Did something happen I'm missing, Tink? I know you had a fight out in California and stopped speaking, but we all grew apart and went our separate ways. Never figured there was bad blood between you."

A barrier slammed down over her face. Ophelia focused on refilling her dish. When she finally spoke, her voice was back to her normal calm focus. "I'm sorry, I didn't mean to snap like that. I'd prefer if Kyle stayed elsewhere. His father has plenty of space, and he'd be more comfortable there."

"Kyle's father is an asshole," Ethan said.

"Maybe it's time they deal with their issues, then," she shot back.

Mia cleared her throat, not wanting to bring tension to the holiday table. She sensed Ophelia needed to process the news that her childhood friend may be back in town. Her reaction was telling, though. There was much more going on than Ophelia's busy schedule. It was quite obvious she had no desire to see Kyle again.

Had something happened between them Ethan didn't know about?

Mia pushed the thought to the back of her mind and concentrated on lightening the mood. "Hey, did I tell you the big news? I'm getting a tattoo!"

Ethan frowned. "Princess, just because it's free doesn't mean you have to get ink."

"I want to."

"Whatcha gonna get?" Harper asked.

"A name. A very important name, of someone who I couldn't stand at first, but who eventually won my heart."

Ophelia shook her head. "Oh, no, Mia, don't do it. As much as we adore our brother, having his name permanently inked on your body may not be a good idea."

Ethan straightened in his chair. The pleasure in his eyes contradicted his statement. "That's sweet, but not necessary. I don't need a tat to know you're mine forever."

"Aww, you're so sweet." She leaned over and kissed him. "But it's not yours."

"Huh?"

She grinned with delight. "I'm getting the name *Hei Hei*!"

For a few seconds, everyone stared in shock. Then burst into laughter.

God, it was good to be home.

ACKNOWLEDGMENTS

Special thanks to the Montlake team, my fabulous editors, and especially Maria Gomez, for helping me bring this book to my readers. I love being part of the family! Special thanks to Kristi Yanta, who whipped this book into shape early on. Thanks to my agent, Kevan Lyon, for her support; my special Probst Posse reader team (I'm always looking for new members!); and my assistant, Lisa Hamel-Soldano, for all her help.

But most of all, thank you to Alana Payne at Payne Farms II. She's an extraordinary person who taught me about rescue horses and allowed me to step out of my writing cave for an hour per week to ride a horse and enjoy the world in all its haunting beauty. Any mistakes I made are my own. I used her farm as inspiration for this story and loved watching Ethan and Mia come alive week by week, ride by ride, story by story.

ABOUT THE AUTHOR

Jennifer Probst is the *New York Times* bestselling author of The Billionaire Builders series, The Searching for . . . series, The Marriage series, and The Steele Brothers series, among others. *The Start of Something Good* is the first book in her new Stay series. Like some of her characters, Probst, along with her husband and two sons, calls New York's Hudson Valley home. There, she enjoys reading, watching "shameful reality television," and visiting an animal shelter, when she isn't traveling to meet readers. Follow her at www.jenniferprobst.com, on Facebook at www.facebook.com/jenniferprobst.authorpage, or on Twitter at https://twitter.com/jenniferprobst.